THE INCUBUS

THE INCUBUS

DAVID PENNY

River Tree Print

River Tree Print

Publisher's Note: This is a work of fiction. Names, characters, places, and incidents are a product of the author's imagination. Locales and public names are sometimes used for atmospheric purposes. Any resemblance to actual people, living or dead, or to businesses, companies, events, institutions, or locales is completely coincidental.

The Incubus/David Penny – 1st ed.

ISBN: 978-0993076169

CHAPTER 1

Thomas Berrington saw the first body at the foot of the ravine, though in that moment he had no idea it would be the first, nor how many others would follow. He didn't even recognise it as a body. It was a splash of red, nothing more.

The body lay on the stony banks of a narrow river that had cut the gorge. Thomas would have missed it altogether if he hadn't been keeping his eyes on the rough ground for fear of tumbling over the edge. He knew on his return he would have to tell the others to take a different route. This way might be passable for a single man, even a dozen, but not by the numbers spread across the plain, nor the carts that accompanied them.

To his left white limestone cliffs drew the sun, a shattering of light and shadow rising to a barren plateau. He drew his horse to a halt and sat, staring at the tumbled shape, wondering how it had ended up there; wishing he hadn't seen it.

Thomas dismounted and led the borrowed horse to a stunted tree. He tied the reins to a branch and approached the drop. Small rocks tumbled from the edge, rattling away into the gorge. The sound of their falling echoed and re-echoed from the far wall.

Whatever lay at the foot of the ravine might have been mistaken for a bundle of rags, and Thomas had almost done so. He went to his knees and shuffled closer to the edge, leaning as far out as he dared to see what lay below and to search for a means of descent.

A bright silk robe, red, draped around the broken body. One arm was extended, the fingers buried among stones. Thomas's attention moved from the figure, knowing he needed to get closer before deciding what fate had dashed it onto the rocks. Knowing too he could not leave it where it was as others might have done.

To the right he saw a place where it might be possible to descend. Not easy, but possible. The question he had to ask himself was, did he want to take the risk? He returned his gaze to the body, knowing the decision had already been made. He rose and returned to his horse, took the water sac and drank. He wiped his chin, considering options.

The sun was high, heat trapped between the walls of the ravine. Thomas removed his robe and draped it over the saddle. He patted the horse's flank and said meaningless words. The horse continued to tug at a patch of dry grass, unwilling to partake in conversation. Thomas removed his boots and walked the short distance to where a dip in the path might mark the start of a way down, if he was skilled enough. Which, it turned out to his surprise, he was. The sound of running water grew louder and the heat increased the further he descended.

When his foot touched firm ground he stretched, easing the kinks from his back, the strain from his arms. The body lay forty feet away. Thomas more than half expected to be assaulted by the smell of corruption, but none came to him on the breeze. As he approached flies rose in a buzzing swarm, their senses more attuned to death.

He knelt and drew the robe aside – discovering it was indeed silk, and silk of high quality – to reveal the face of a woman that might once have been beautiful. Now one cheek was shattered, the forehead split open by the fall. She had been alive for a time after reaching this position. One foot had moved, making a depression beneath her toes. And the extended arm had buried her fingers into the surface.

Her skin was smooth, pale, as yet unmarked by putrefaction. There would have been blood, a great deal of blood, but most had run away between the rounded stones.

Thomas sat on his heels and looked at the far wall of the ravine. It rose sheer. Had she fallen from all the way up there? It was possible, but more likely she had come from the path he had been following. It was only forty feet above where she lay, and under other circumstances she would still be alive, broken-boned but alive. Here the nature of the ground, covered in stones large and small, had worked against survival.

Her face was too broken to provide much help with recognition, but Thomas didn't believe she was one of their party. He had heard of no-one going missing. Not that he listened to the gossip that flowed and swayed like the tides, but Jorge did. Jorge relished the chatter, however minor, and took great pleasure in relaying its minutia each evening when he joined them to eat. Jorge had passed on nothing that might indicate who the woman was, and based on the quality of her robe she would be someone known to him.

Her presence here was a mystery Thomas knew might never be solved, but his nature would not allow him to ignore her fate. Had she been with companions, or was she alone when she fell? Was the fall accidental or deliberate? And if deliberate, self-inflicted or the result of someone pushing her?

Thomas glanced at the route he had taken on his way down and made a decision. It would be impossible to make the climb back carrying her. She would have to remain where she was, except he couldn't leave her this way, broken and discarded. The flies had already found her, but so far no wildlife. He knew that wouldn't last.

Thomas walked downstream along the shattered bank of the river until he found what he was looking for. On a bend floodwater had scooped a dip in the ground, a little water still in its base. There were enough loose rocks scattered around for his purpose.

Thomas returned to the body, leaned over and placed his hands beneath the woman and lifted, cradling her like a child. She weighed little, and it was an easy matter to carry her to the water smoothed depression. He laid her in the crevice and was about to fold her arms across her chest when it occurred to him he should see if she carried anything that might identify her. He patted the robe, lifted it and ran his fingertips along the seams, but nothing. There were no pockets and beneath the robe she was naked. Thomas placed her feet together even though one of them was barely attached. A sense of guilt, of abandonment of duty filled him as he began to lift rocks and cover her body. What he was doing didn't seem enough, not nearly enough, but he knew there was little else could be done.

Thomas laid a hand across the woman's brow and spoke the *dua* for the dead, Islamic prayers he knew the words of even though he held no faith of his own, neither that of his homeland or this, al-Andalus, his adopted one. Then he began to cover the body with flat stones until nothing showed.

She would be safe from predators now, at least for a while. Thomas stripped from his clothing and strode into the blood-warm river, desperate to wash away the taint of death. Afterward he stood at the water's edge, allowing the hot air to dry his body before dressing. He returned along the foot of the ravine to stare at the place the woman had first lain.

He was about to leave, duty done, when something drew his attention. A spot where the stones were disturbed, and he recalled the way the woman's hand had burrowed between them. He went to his knees and dug into the stones, tossing small pebbles aside. The package wasn't buried deep, barely beneath the surface, wrapped in waxed cloth to repel water. Thomas drew it out, dusted it down. It weighed little, but contained something she had valued enough to attempt to hide. He unwrapped the cloth to reveal three letters, each sealed with wax. He glanced along the ravine to where the woman's makeshift grave lay.

Why had her final act been to conceal the package? Was it the reason she had died? Were the contents so important she had lost her life for them? Thomas was aware the answers might lie in the letters, but was reluctant to break the seals. Each was addressed to the leader of those he had left on the plain, the leader of al-Andalus even if he lacked the title. Al-Zagal's party spread across the valley below, a host of over four hundred travelling from Gharnatah, where there were too many Sultans, to Ronda, where there was none until they arrived. Thomas tapped the letters against his nails, reluctant to do what almost any other man would and open them. He didn't

want the knowledge, the responsibility of what lay inside.
Let someone else take it.

CHAPTER 2

Thomas continued along the rising path, knowing hours remained before he had to turn back. He had been enjoying the isolation, the harshness of the land, but the day had been spoiled by his discovery. Despite the afternoon being not yet half gone the sun had slipped behind the high clifftops, casting him into shade but bringing no lessening of the heat. As he rode he began to re-evaluate his opinion of the route. Where the woman had fallen was the narrowest point of the track. Farther on it widened, and he gave some thought to how they might bring carts and people through the narrow section, not entirely convinced it was feasible.

The path steepened and veered away from the gorge, opened into a dusty clearing fringed by gnarled trees. On the far side sat a small cart, its shafts empty. Thomas dismounted and allowed his horse to wander in search of whatever it could find. He pulled himself onto the empty bed of the cart. When he leaned forward to examine the front he saw a bloodstain on the seat. There was a great deal of blood. More than could be sustained by one person and still allow them to live. Could this be where the woman had been attacked? Or did the blood belong to someone else? He doubted anyone would carry the woman so far before discarding the body. There was a surfeit of places closer, places where she would never be found.

Thomas dropped to the ground and walked around the cart. At the front the ground was disturbed and he knelt to examine the marks. A mule he reckoned by the tracks. He rose and dusted himself down, began to circle the cart, working his way out in search of other signs. He saw where the mule had been led away along rising ground. He found a second patch of blood, the ground disturbed around it. Thomas looked back to see his own horse had come to stand patiently beside the cart.

That death had come to this place was clear, but how many, other than the woman? It was unlikely she would have travelled alone. Her robe hinted at wealth, or if not wealth then influence. She would have had companions. Companions who were now also dead?

Thomas walked to one side and climbed a small tumble of rocks so he could see farther, but it was no help. He stood, listening, but there was only a soft breeze rattling dry branches. Even the sound of water from the gorge had faded away. He clapped his hands together, the sound echoing from the cliffs. He was rewarded by sight of a swarm of flies rising into the air from a depression a hundred feet away. Thomas started toward it.

He found the body of a soldier discarded there, a clear trail showing where he had been dragged, and Thomas berated himself for not seeing it earlier. He went to the body and examined it. The man had been killed with a crossbow, the bolt still in his chest. The man was a Moor, but it was impossible to tell whether the weapon used on him was Spanish or not. This man would need to be covered too before the wildlife found him. Thomas considered tying his own horse into the shafts of the cart and taking him back to camp, but doubted anyone would care, and he didn't like the idea of trying to tease it through the narrow section where he had found the woman's body.

He returned to his horse and drank again, feeling the sweat running across his belly beneath his robe. Thomas wondered if the small group had been seeking out al-Zagal's protection. Almost from the moment they set out from Gharnatah people had begun to join their number, seeing safety in the size of the group, and its leader. The farther they had gone the more had come, sometimes as many as a dozen a day fleeing a perceived threat from Spain.

Thomas patted the neck of his horse and ran his palm along its chin, the movement rewarded with a snicker. He stood, listening, but there was only the wind. He had left the other scouts soon after setting out and had seen no-one all day. But someone had been here, that was clear. The woman and her companion had been dead less than half a day. Nobody had passed him, which meant whoever had killed these two had gone on, upslope and over the head of the pass.

Thomas glanced at the sky and shook his head. There was another body to cover, so he rose and walked across the dry clearing.

An hour later he mounted his horse and tugged on the reins to start back down the gorge. The sound of his passage came back from the cliffs, lulling him into a trance. His mind drifted, tired, weary of death. There were times he wondered if it sought him out deliberately, but he knew death was a constant presence in this land, one that would grow only more frequent. Then, with a start, he realised there was a noise, and that it had been there for some time. He reigned in and dismounted, heart beating faster. Two horses at least, coming at speed from behind. Thomas dragged his own horse to the side, searching for some place he could conceal himself and finding none.

He mounted again and drew his sword, turned back and prepared to fight, afraid whoever was coming were those who had killed the woman and her companion. If it was two men, even three, he was confident enough in his own abilities. He only hoped they were not the outliers of a larger force.

The sound of hooves grew louder, filling the confined gorge. Thomas moved sideways and placed a large rock behind him, the best he could do. He breathed deep, trying to calm himself in the moments remaining before the men appeared.

"Thomas!" Yusuf reigned his horse hard, its feet skidding on the rough ground. Behind him Faris al-Rashid brought his own mount to a more elegant stop. To Farris elegance outweighed almost everything else.

Thomas dismounted and moved away from the rock, sheathing his sword, but he kept his hand on the hilt. Yusuf he trusted. The youngest son of Abu al-Hasan Ali, the current ruler in Gharnatah, he had changed much over the last year. While his older brother Mohammed had been a captive of the Spanish there had been talk of Yusuf becoming the next Sultan. Now Mohammed had returned to live in his mother's house on the Albayzin such talk had faded, but such were the tangled politics of al-Andalus they would never fade completely. The presence of Faris with Yusuf gave evidence to that. Faris al-Rashid's presence with someone was never accidental.

Yusuf dismounted and put an arm around Thomas's shoulder, some of the excitable boy still remaining. Faris remained in the saddle.

"Have you seen anyone on the path?" Thomas asked.

"Only you," said Yusuf. "Faris has something to show you."

Thomas considered whether to tell them of his own discoveries. He could feel the weight of the letters addressed to al-Zagal in the pocket of his robe as if they were made of lead not paper. If it had only been Yusuf he might have spoken of what he had found, but the presence of Faris complicated matters. Besides, they would know soon enough once he delivered the letters.

"It will be dark in a few hours," Thomas said.

"What I have to show you won't take long," said Faris. He tugged at the reins to turn his horse the way they had come.

Thomas and Yusuf mounted their own steeds and followed as Faris moved away.

"I'm glad it's you we found," said Yusuf. "People trust your word."

Thomas was aware of the message Yusuf sent without him needing to state it. "They trust you too," he said.

"My uncle still considers me a child," said Yusuf. "I could help more if he allowed it. I'm not a fool, and I know how power works. I've been around it long enough to learn that much."

Ahead of them Faris took a side track that led up the steep hillside, twisting back and forth on itself as it climbed. The man was close enough to hear their conversation but appeared to be uninterested.

"Be careful what you wish for," Thomas said. "Power might look attractive, but it's like a beautiful woman with a black heart."

Yusuf made no reply, which was unusual in itself,

perhaps an indication of other changes in him. Stones rattled down from where Faris was already above them on the switchback. As they climbed they moved back into sunlight, softer now, painting the hillside with a flattering brush.

Yusuf started to say something but Faris held up his hand to silence him. They were almost at the crest of the ridge. Faris stopped and dismounted, waiting for them to reach him.

"We go quietly from here," he said. "And don't show yourself at the top."

At the ridge line Thomas saw the reason for his instructions. No more than a half mile away in the wide valley beyond the ridge, the ground was dark with soldiers. Spanish soldiers, their pennants hanging limp in the faint breeze.

"How many, Thomas?" asked Yusuf.

Thomas studied the army. It was impossible to count, easier just to estimate. "More than our force," he said. "Eight hundred to a thousand, I'd say."

Faris nodded. "That's what I reckoned too. A thousand."

"Are they looking for us?" Thomas said.

"More likely than not, don't you think?" said Faris.

Thomas agreed. Beside him Yusuf's shoulder pressed against his arm and he could feel the youth trembling. He suspected from excitement more than fear.

Thomas surveyed the geography of the valley, tracing the route the soldiers had taken, trying to judge where they were headed.

"They are a day away at least," he said. "But only if they come through this pass. If they take the easier way at least another day."

"Except they are moving fast, and in the same direction we are," said Faris. "By the time we close half the distance to Ronda they will have done so too. Our paths will converge."

"Not now we know they're there," Thomas said.

"Will there be a battle?" asked Yusuf, excitement in his voice, still young enough, protected enough, to consider men fighting to be romantic. This despite him suffering an injury several years before that still left his right arm weak.

"Hopefully not," said Faris, and Thomas was pleased to hear him state it. He slid down to where the horses waited.

"Someone needs to watch them," Thomas said. "To find out where they are headed."

"We know where they are headed." said Faris. "Word of our journey has spread. When we skirted Antequera most likely, and that's where they've come from. They want to capture another Sultan."

"We need to send someone to observe them," Thomas said. "It will give us some warning, at least." He lifted himself into the saddle and urged his horse on with his heels, allowing it to pick its own way down the narrow track, all thought of the dead woman and her companion pushed aside.

Chapter 3

Thomas watched Faris al-Rashid guide his horse through the crowd of people preparing for the coming of night. For the last half-hour as they neared camp Thomas had struggled with a decision. He knew Faris enjoyed al-Zagal's confidence, but didn't know if he could trust him with the letters. His presence in the mountain pass seemed too much of a coincidence, but however he worked the problem he could see no way Faris might benefit from the woman's death. And Faris never did anything if it offered no benefit.

Thomas glanced at Yusuf, who remained at his side. "Aren't you going back to your uncle's tent?"

Yusuf shrugged. "I'd rather stay here." His eyes flickered to meet Thomas's, shy. "And eat with you and Lubna. If that's all right?"

"You're welcome, of course, but your uncle has better food."

"More than likely true. But worse company."

Thomas smiled, pleased Yusuf had not completely grown-up yet. He turned his horse away from the disappearing figure and guided it around the outskirts of the camp. Yusuf followed.

A little light remained in the sky but the sun had disappeared beyond distant hills. Al-Zagal, or more likely the Imam, had chosen this spot to camp. A narrow stream ran nearby where people filled water sacks and jugs. In the centre, where it would be best protected by those surrounding it, al-Zagal's tent was being erected. It was a large structure with space for twenty people, although tonight it would hold only a quarter of that number. The Sultan himself, two concubines and a personal servant. Guards would be posted at the entrance but expected to remain outside. A dozen concubines accompanied them, including Helena, who had once shared Thomas's bed, and whose life he had saved the year before.

Thomas drew his horse to a halt and from his elevated position scanned the crowd, looking for Lubna. It was Yusuf who found her first, raising a hand to point. "There, Thomas."

Thomas urged his horse forward, still outside the crowd, making his way to an area set apart where other horses waited. He and Yusuf removed the saddles, bridles and reins, and passed each horse on to the small group of men tasked with their care. Thomas had no horse of his own and knew in the morning it was unlikely he would be given the same one he had ridden today. He would ask for it again, for it had served him well today on the difficult terrain, steady rather than fast, which had been exactly what was needed. Yusuf's mount on the other hand was a fine Arabian which would be kept apart with the horses al-Zagal owned.

When they finally managed to pick their way through the throng Thomas leaned down and touched Lubna on the shoulder. She glanced up, smiling. "It took you long enough to find me. I saw you and Yusuf ride in together an age since." She rose and embraced Thomas, kissing him on the mouth, holding him tight. Then she hugged Yusuf, his kiss on the cheek, and Thomas saw him blush and had to hide a smile.

He sat cross-legged on the blanket Lubna had laid on the ground to mark their personal space for the night. Other blankets and other people stretched across the plain. In the centre of a circle of a score of people a fire had been lit, now burned to embers. Iron pots containing evening meals simmered around the edges, the scent of cooking drifting through the air to mingle with the conversation.

"There is enough food if you want to stay," Lubna said, leaning around Thomas so Yusuf could see her. "You are staying, aren't you?"

"If I can. We saw the Spanish army today, Lubna."

"Keep your voice down," Thomas said. "We don't want rumours spreading."

"What rumours are these?"

Thomas turned to find Jorge directly behind him and knew he would have heard Yusuf's words.

"Will there still be enough?" Yusuf asked, moving aside to make space for Jorge between him and Thomas.

"I assume Faris will tell your uncle about the Spanish," Thomas said.

"How far away are they?" asked Jorge before Yusuf could make any reply.

"Beyond the mountains," said Yusuf, raising his arm to point at the peaks they had recently ridden from. Thomas reached across and lowered the youth's arm before anyone else saw. "They are a thousand strong, possibly more." This time Yusuf kept his voice low so he wouldn't be overheard.

"Who's hungry?" asked Lubna, rising to make her way to the fire. Others – mostly women – were following suit. Thomas's eyes tracked Lubna, her slim figure familiar to him now, as she used two sticks to lift a clay pot. She carried it to them and tipped the contents into a large bowl before handing out flatbreads she had baked earlier.

Thomas saw there wasn't really enough food for four. He allowed Jorge and Yusuf to start dipping their bread into the stew before wrapping it around nuggets of meat. He noticed Lubna also refrained and smiled. They had brought limited provisions with them for the journey, which was already taking longer than expected. It was no surprise to Thomas – the only surprise was they had managed to come as far as they had. Too many voices offered advice, all of it conflicting.

They would be better traveling farther north – except the Spanish owned the lands to the north.

They should have set out earlier in the year. Or later.

Through it all al-Zagal showed himself a true leader, listening to sage advice, dismissing the idiots, before making his own decision. The route was one Thomas would have chosen, a compromise between speed and safety, except when they left Gharnatah the Spanish hadn't known of their presence and now it appeared they did. Unless the presence of the Spanish army was a coincidence.

Thomas didn't believe in coincidence.

Lubna leaned closer, her shoulder pressing against his. "Are the Spanish really so close?"

He nodded, staring into the fire, then beyond to where other fires and other groups were scattered across the plain. Their own companions had grown familiar during the journey, the same faces gathered each evening. Thomas even knew some of their names, had spoken with a few.

All light had left the sky, the only illumination coming

from cooking fires. Orange points of light scattered across the plain, the edge of each group delineated with the onset of darkness. Now was when they were at their most vulnerable, but now was also when they were least likely to be attacked.

Voices sounded, laughter, an occasional argument flaring before others shouted it down. Thomas glanced toward the mountains, visible only because they obscured the bright stars to the north. He scanned their peaks, looking for a light there, but if the Spanish were watching they gave no sign of their presence.

"I saw them," he replied at last, his voice only loud enough for Lubna to hear. Beside them Jorge was amusing Yusuf with a tale of the harem, no doubt embellishing his own role. "The question is whether they know we are here, or are on some other mission that is nothing to do with us."

"Which do you think?"

"North is Spanish land, which is where they were, so it may be nothing more than normal troop movements. Except they were travelling west, and the closest town west of here is Ronda. Which is not Spanish land."

"They might be making for Ixbilya or Qurtuba," said Lubna.

"Both a long way off."

"You think they are planning to cut us off from Ronda?"

Thomas smiled, reminded that Lubna was Olaf Torvaldsson's daughter. Her father being the Sultan's general meant she always understood such matters.

Yusuf belched and wiped his mouth with a hand before stuffing the last piece of flatbread in. Thomas took it as a sign and picked at what remained with his own bread. After a moment he reached inside his robe and drew out the wrapped bundle of papers the dead woman had concealed. He didn't know why he had kept them. He should have given them to Faris al-Rashid, but there was still time to correct the mistake.

He held them toward Yusuf, who was staring at something on the far side of the fire. A handsome man Thomas had not seen before was making overtures to a merchant's wife right in front of the man, his hand fondling her breast while the merchant carried on a conversation. There might be trouble, might not, and there were many people in their party Thomas had never seen before.

He nudged Yusuf to distract his attention. "Take these to your uncle. Make sure he gets them."

"What are they?"

"Letters – addressed to him."

"From whom?"

Thomas shook his head. "I don't know, but he might."

After Jorge led Yusuf away to his uncle's tent, after the fires were allowed to die to coals, Thomas lay beneath a rough blanket with Lubna's skin silk against his own. He listened to the sounds of other couples drifting across the camp. The first night after leaving Gharnatah everyone had been as near silent as four hundred souls could be. Then as the days passed inhibitions faded. Thomas had seen it before. The journey, distance, all conspired to loosen restraint. It was how that man beyond the fire was able to seduce a woman who normally would never consider infidelity. All their lives had been changed by journey.

Even Thomas felt the power of it, of the darkness. So too, it seemed, did Lubna. Her hand came across and ran along his flat belly. Thomas gasped when her fingers found the target they sought.

"People will hear us," he said, whispering into her ear, a whisper that turned into a kiss.

Lubna giggled and crooked her neck so his lips could explore further. "I think people are too busy to be listening to us. And I promise to be quiet as a mouse."

And it was true. The sounds and glimpsed sights which added to Thomas's arousal affected Lubna too. She was demanding, greedy for his touch, and when the blanket fell away to expose their naked coupling neither made a move to draw it back until both were sated.

With dawn no more than a grey promise Thomas slipped from her side and dressed. Around him most people continued to sleep. Only one or two figures stirred. The handsome man had gone, as had the merchant's wife, and Thomas smiled. They had no doubt found some secret spot beyond the circle of bodies. Their infidelity did not concern him, it was their own business. He only hoped they didn't cause trouble.

Thomas crept away on bare feet before pulling on his boots. He made his way to where the horses were kept and found the same steed he had used the day before. The stable hands had drifted away to their own dreams and Thomas saddled the horse himself. He led it away before mounting, let it walk slowly away from camp while he raised his eyes to the jagged peaks already caught by the approaching sun.

Was that movement he could make out? He narrowed his eyes, wishing there was some means of seeing better. He considered the arrangement of lenses he used in his workshop to enlarge small objects and wondered if the same could be used to enhance a man's vision over distance. Perhaps he would experiment when he returned home. For now he had to make do with the eyes he had been given, and they were too feeble for the task. There might be movement, or nothing more than shadows creeping over shattered rock. If it was soldiers they would be able to see the camp clearly, able to judge their number, to know how few they were.

Thomas urged his mount into a canter, guiding it toward the foot of the pass. The closer he got the more certain he was men were moving along the high peaks. He was about to urge his horse into a gallop when he heard the sound of other hoofs behind. He twisted in the saddle without slowing, then pulled on the reins. Three men were coming fast, their robes flying behind as the sun finally broached the eastern hills and struck the plain. Faris al-Rashid was the lead rider and he kept his breakneck pace until almost too late, his horse's hooves skidding and scattering stones when he finally reined in.

"I don't need company," Thomas said.

"Don't flatter yourself, that's not why I'm here. The Sultan wants you."

"I think the Spanish are watching us," Thomas said.

"Almost certainly, but getting yourself captured isn't going to change that." Faris spun his horse around and started away. The two soldiers who accompanied him waited, staring at Thomas with blank expressions.

CHAPTER 4

"Where did you find these?" Al-Zagal, no Sultan but that didn't stop everyone present calling him one, flicked his hand toward a low table where three letters, opened now, were scattered across its surface. The seals were broken, flakes of blood red wax beside the paper.

"A woman in a silk robe," Thomas said. He stood because he had not been invited to sit, but he preferred to stand rather than sit on cushions. The air within the tent was thick with the smoke of burning incense. As he had waited beyond the inner sanctum women of aching beauty had come and gone. At one point Thomas caught sight of Helena, now returned to al-Zagal's harem.

"Did she tell you her name?"

"No, Malik. She was dead."

"My brother tells me you have a strange attraction for the dead. He claims they seek you out. I didn't believe him, but now..." Al-Zagal didn't appear surprised, nor upset there had been a murder. "Where did you find this dead woman?"

"In the gorge to the north, Malik. I was scouting in search of a faster route."

Al-Zagal turned to Yusuf and Faris al-Rashid who stood patiently to one side. Yusuf a little closer as fitted a member of the Nasrid dynasty, despite the fact Faris could buy and sell them both ten times over. "Did you see this body?"

Yusuf shook his head. Faris said, "We did not even know of it." A smile, quickly suppressed, flitted across his lips as he glanced at Thomas. This was another opportunity for Faris, something to hold over him.

"Why did you say nothing? You trust my nephew and Faris, don't you?"

"I considered the presence of the Spanish more important, Malik. A dead woman would have been a distraction."

"That is not your decision to make," said al-Zagal. "You should have told Faris of this woman, he might have recognised her."

No mention of Yusuf, Thomas noted. His uncle still regarded him as the innocent youth he had been until recently, but the boy had grown, matured, become watchful and careful around his family. No doubt aware he was a valid contender for the position of Sultan in place of his father now his brother, Muhammed, had been banished from the palace in Gharnatah.

"She was not recognisable," Thomas said. "The fall had crushed her face."

"Her body, then. Faris knows many women by their bodies. Is that not true?"

Once again the smile, a flash of white almost hidden by the oiled curls of Faris's beard.

"Are the letters important?" Thomas asked, confused at the conversation. The Spanish were observing them from the hillside and they were talking of a dead woman. He was sure none of these men shared his curiosity over her fate.

Al-Zagal waved a hand. "Day to day correspondence relating to our arrival in Ronda. There is only one of interest." He leaned forward, his arms resting across his knees. "It claims a killer is at work in the town." This time it was al-Zagal's turn to smile. "That is your kind of work, I understand."

"What, killing or the pursuit of killers?"

"Both, I expect. Death is your trade after all, is it not, *qassab*?" Al-Zagal deliberately used Thomas's nickname among the soldiers: *butcher*.

"I prefer to prevent death when possible."

"And yet I hear you are also the cause of much when you finally track down those who have killed. One of my concubines, for instance."

Al-Zagal's voice was cold, and Thomas knew the man had not yet forgiven him for the death of the concubine Eva the year before. Not that he'd had much choice in the matter. Eva had thrown herself from the palace walls to take her own life on the rocks below. Similar to the woman yesterday, except her fate had not been of her own choosing.

"I would prefer to capture rather than kill, Malik, but there are times it is not always possible. What does the letter say?"

"Did you not read it? The seals were broken when they were handed to me."

Thomas glanced toward Yusuf, but he only looked bored. More likely Faris had intercepted the letters, or Jorge persuaded the boy he would deliver them and opened them himself. There were times the eunuch's curiosity got the better of him. Except Thomas knew Jorge possessed skills nobody else was aware of. If it had been he who read the letters the seals would have been re-applied perfectly.

"The seals were intact when I handed them across,

Malik. Did the letters not identify who the woman was?"

"I do not even know if they are from her, but without knowing who she is how can I tell?" Al-Zagal glanced toward Faris. "Did you see nothing at all?"

"An abandoned cart when we encountered Thomas, nothing else."

"The cart was hers," Thomas said. "When I found it there was a dead soldier nearby."

Al-Zagal turned back to him. "Where is the body?"

"I buried it as best I could, the same as I did for the woman."

"Why?"

"For humanity's sake – to stop them being violated by vermin."

Al-Zagal snorted, his feelings on the matter clear. Thomas knew a leader of men might have made a different judgement to the one he had. He wondered did all generals share the same lack of humanity, and suspected they must. How else could they lead a thousand men into battle knowing half would die?

"I want you to go back and bring the cart here. Someone might recognise it."

Thomas couldn't see the point, didn't understand why al-Zagal was so insistent. They would be in Ronda in four days, five at most. It would be clear then who the woman was.

"And if the Spanish have already started down the hillside?"

"The Spanish aren't coming. They are not fools. If they're watching us they know our number."

Thomas glanced at Faris. Obviously he had not passed on the information about how many men they had seen in the far valley. The party accompanying al-Zagal might be four hundred, but only three hundred of those were fighting men. There were considerably more soldiers in Ronda, but men in Ronda were no good to them here.

Al-Zagal picked up one of the letters and began to read, his lips moving slowly as he did so.

"You want me to ride into the gorge and bring the cart back," Thomas said.

Al-Zagal looked up. "I thought you had gone." He turned back to the letter, Thomas dismissed.

Yusuf caught up with him outside the entrance to the tent as Thomas took deep breaths, clearing the taste of incense from his mouth and anger from his heart.

"Can I come with you? There's nothing for me to do here. Faris and my uncle are already deep in conversation."

"About me?"

Yusuf glanced at Thomas. "Not everything is about you."

Thomas returned the smile. "I'm glad to hear it. Yes, come if you want. But if we see the Spanish we turn and run. I don't want you captured like your brother was. Understand?"

Yusuf nodded.

"And you do as I say."

"Of course." Yusuf tried to suppress a grin and almost succeeded. Thomas flicked his ear and the youth laughed. "Like I always do, Thomas."

"Yes, like you always do." Thomas hoped his own son William would grow up as sweet natured as Yusuf. He wondered how the boy was. The journey to Ronda was no place for a fourteen month old so Thomas had left him in the care of Lubna's parents. There was no safer place than living with Olaf Torvaldsson, a man feared by all who had never seen him bouncing William on his knee and making him laugh. Already the child had a few words, two of them Swedish: *far* and *mormor* – grandfather and grandmother – and Olaf was teaching him to fight with a wooden sword he had fashioned himself. Thomas wasn't so sure about this last, but supposed it was better to know how to fight and not have to use it than be caught wanting. His own skill had saved his life several times when he was barely thirteen, suddenly orphaned and cast adrift in the south of France after the Battle of Castillon.

"Are you going to tell Lubna where we're going? I'll come with you."

"Yes, I suppose we better had." Thomas hid a smile. He knew Yusuf carried what was meant to be a secret torch for Lubna. The boy fell in love far too easily for someone in his position, still too innocent for a prince.

CHAPTER 5

It was gone noon by the time they reached the cart, which stood where Thomas had left it, forlorn, baking in the midday heat. There had been no sign of the Spanish, not even as they approached close enough to see the top of the ridge clearly.

"Did you and Faris not see the cart yesterday, before I found it?" Thomas asked as he dismounted. He drank from his water bottle and wiped his mouth.

"It wasn't here when we rode up."

"Strange that," Thomas said. "It would have had to pass you on the way down to end up here."

"We climbed to the ridge, remember," said Yusuf. "When we first saw the Spanish. It might have come down while we were there."

"I'd have thought you might hear it in that case."

Yusuf looked at Thomas, frowning. "You don't think we had anything to do with the woman's death, or her companion, do you? Faris was with me almost the entire day."

It *was* what Thomas had considered. He wanted to push Yusuf, to test him, sure he was incapable of murder, not sure he believed the same about Faris.

They ascended the pass so Thomas could show Yusuf where the body had been. At least he thought it was the place. It was difficult to be sure. The gorge looked the same along its length, and the track showed no sign of a struggle anymore, no scrap of clothing or other clue to mark where she had been tossed over the edge.

Yusuf was satisfied, incurious, as he had been about the cart. It was the way he had been raised, Thomas knew. Trained in poetry, literature and music. Yusuf could wield a lute better than a sword, unlike his older brother. He had never been expected to rule so had not been raised to do so. Except now there was talk of making him Sultan in Gharnatah, the old one too debilitated to be effective. Thomas wondered what Yusuf's uncle thought of the idea.

Back at the cart again Yusuf dismounted and sat on the narrow seat up front, pretending to hold reins which were missing.

"Did you bring anything to eat?"

Thomas reached into his saddle bag and pulled out a linen wrapped parcel, urged his horse forward with his knees, and laid it on the seat beside Yusuf.

"A little meat, fruit, nuts, and bread left over from last night."

"Lubna's a good cook, isn't she?" Yusuf helped himself to the largest slice of lamb.

"Unlike her sisters."

"Her sisters have other skills." Then Yusuf blushed and mumbled, "I'm sure Lubna has such skills, too, it's just…" His voice trailed off as he looked away. "At least there are no Spanish."

"They might be keeping out of sight. They could be watching us even now, lining up a crossbow bolt."

Yusuf smiled. "You're teasing me. Are you trying to get back at me for what I said?"

"I don't know. What did you say?"

Yusuf flicked a stone at Thomas. "Before we take the cart back we should go to the ridge again and look for them so we can report back to my uncle." Yusuf picked up a fig and turned it around in his fingers before replacing it and choosing another. "I don't think he likes you much."

"Who, your uncle? You're right, I don't think he does. But I'm not losing sleep over it. Not many in your family like me. Besides, I don't think he likes many people."

"I like you, Thomas."

"Yes, I know you do, but you're not typical, are you."

Yusuf frowned. "Is that a compliment or not?"

"I'll let you work it out." He bit into a hunk of meat wrapped inside flatbread. The bread was stale but the meat, heavily spiced, filled his mouth with heat. "And you're right, we should ride to the ridge."

The far valley stretched flat bottomed for several miles before rising into a tumble of low hills dotted with scrub oak. It was devoid of any sign of man, even that man had ever been there. No towns, no villages, not even an isolated farmhouse. This was a valley without water, a place unsuited for living. Except the day before over a thousand Spanish soldiers had filled it.

Thomas turned to sit with his back against a rock as his eyes tracked the barren pass to the valley they had climbed from. The camp had broken long since and now its people moved slowly across the ground.

"I see something," said Yusuf, from where he remained looking beyond the ridge.

Thomas climbed up and lay beside him. "Show me."

"There. A moment ago, people." Yusuf pointed to a

place no more than four hundred paces distant. Nothing showed now, but as Thomas peered more intently he made out a narrow track similar to the one they had used to ascend to the ridge.

"How many?"

"Eight men, possibly more. They came from behind that outcrop," Yusuf pointed again, "And disappeared behind that one. Is it the Spanish, do you think?"

"A scouting party, maybe. Or someone trying to escape the Spanish." Thomas remained where he was, body relaxed because he knew tension was pointless and would only sap his strength.

High above an eagle hovered, its cry drifting on the wind. As the sound faded Thomas heard the rattle of dislodged stones. He shifted his gaze, trying to judge where the noise had come from, but the jagged peaks echoed and re-echoed every sound.

And then men appeared. Seven of them. They came into a narrow depression and halted. One of them turned back and made a gesture, and a moment later two others joined them. Words were exchanged but the sound was lost, too distant to travel.

"Those are no soldiers," said Yusuf.

"Not dressed as soldiers, certainly." Thomas kept his voice as soft as Yusuf's. "But look, each wears a sword." An uneasy memory surfaced within him, one he suppressed as impossible. The men were dressed as monks, armed monks, their pale robes stained dark from travel.

"Should we kill them?" said Yusuf.

Thomas glanced at him and saw he was serious. "Nine of them and two of us?"

"But one of us is Thomas Berrington," said Yusuf. "And I am skilled with a sword, too."

Thomas shook his head at Yusuf's naive view of the world, not to mention his unrealistic expectation of him. "We stay here and see where they go." As he spoke a tenth figure appeared, moving more slowly, showing signs of age or infirmity. Like the others he wore a robe that might once have been white but was now stained to a mottled grey. His hood was raised, face turned away to look toward where one of the others pointed. It seemed they were trying to decide whether to continue their ascent or look for an easier way to cross the ridge. Two of them turned and stared directly at where Yusuf and Thomas lay, and he ducked down quickly. When next he looked the tenth man was facing toward him but his hood continued to hide his features. All that showed was a long grey beard and the tangled ends of his hair. Even that was enough to make Thomas uneasy. If he had not found the severed hand of Abbott Mandana above a gorge far to the north two years before he might have believed that was who stood below him now. He knew it was an impossibility. Whoever this was reminded him of the man, nothing more. And when the group began to work their way sideways in their direction Thomas slid backward, dragging Yusuf with him.

"We can fight them," said Yusuf.

"No, we can make the sensible choice and flee," Thomas said.

Thomas saw the expression that flitted across Yusuf's face, both pleased and disappointed. It was time he learned that Thomas wasn't some kind of superman. He turned away and scrambled to the clearing where their horses waited. One had already been tied into the harness of the cart and Thomas climbed to the seat and urged it into a trot. The sound of its hooves echoed from the far cliff face and he knew the men beyond the ridge would hear them, but there was nothing he could do about it. At least they hadn't appeared to have horses of their own and would be unable to catch them. Yusuf remained behind the cart, still hoping for a fight. Thomas twisted on the seat and saw him stopped in the middle of the track, facing toward the ridge. Thomas raised his eyes to see men appear there, standing upright, unafraid of being seen.

"Yusuf!" he yelled, but the youth remained stubbornly where he was and Thomas turned away, needing to control the horse along the narrow path. The next time he turned he was relieved to find Yusuf had abandoned his pointless show of bravado and was trotting to catch up with the cart.

As they cleared the trickiest part of the gorge and came onto the wider path that would lead them to the valley floor, Thomas saw al-Zagal's caravan had split into two. A large group raced away on horseback, another had come to a halt. It was too far to see what was happening until Yusuf called out.

Thomas turned, half expecting the men from the ridge to be coming. Instead, from the north-west a horde of Spanish soldiers spread out from a second pass, riders in the vanguard, carts and cannon dragged behind to spread them over almost a mile.

"What's happening?" said Yusuf. "Why have our band split up?"

"Your uncle has abandoned those too slow and who cannot fight," Thomas said. "He has taken his soldiers and is racing for safety."

Dust rose in a great cloud behind the galloping horses. No banners snapped above them. These men were intent on only one thing – flight.

Thomas climbed down and unshackled his horse, led it to the rear and pulled his saddle from where he had tossed it on the bed of the cart.

"The Spanish will block us before we reach them," said Yusuf.

"We're not going to your uncle," Thomas said, jerking the leather bindings tight. "There are others who need us more." He glanced at the approaching forces. A smaller group of Spanish had split away to make their way in the direction of the abandoned group, which had started to move toward a group of hills to the south. Thomas mounted and dug his heels into the horse's flanks, clinging on as it launched itself down the slope with Yusuf in pursuit.

CHAPTER 6

Thomas and Yusuf were within half a mile of the abandoned group of men and women, a mile ahead of the smaller Spanish band, when three horsemen raced toward them. As they drew near the lead rider held a hand up, palm out, making it obvious he wanted them to halt. Thomas recognised him as one of Faris al-Rashid's personal guard and slowed.

"I was told you'd most likely to come this way," said the rider. "I have orders to take you to al-Zagal. Both of you."

"We're not running," Thomas said. "Join your master and leave us to our task."

The man glanced at Yusuf. "You at least, Prince, must accompany me to your uncle."

Yusuf straightened in the saddle, his shoulders going back. "I stay with Thomas."

The man glanced to left and right, gave an almost imperceptible nod and drew his sword. "We were told to bring you both, but if there was trouble the prince was more important." The other two riders shuffled their mounts sideways and forward, forming a loose barrier.

Thomas sighed and shook his head. "I have no wish to do you any harm. Let us pass and you can return to your master and tell him you failed to find us." He glanced to one side. "We have a quarter hour, no more, before the

Spanish reach our position."

"More than enough time to kill you, *qassab*, and I will admit the notion gives me pleasure."

"You will have to fight us both." Yusuf drew his own sword.

Thomas looked beyond the men. The fleeing women and others considered disposable had almost reached the low hills. A narrow defile cut into them and the leaders started to stream through. Thomas heard the sound of the Spanish approaching as he drew his sword and urged his horse at the lead man. He raised an arm as the man's blade descended, flicking his wrist, catching the blade with his own and tossing it aside. The man stared at his empty fist in disbelief. Thomas took the opportunity to move closer, his leg pressing into the flank of the soldier's horse.

"This doesn't have to go any farther. Ride away while you can."

The soldier pushed back at him, face dark with anger. He reached to his waist and drew a dagger, its blade honed to a razor edge.

Thomas lifted his sword in a sudden rush and placed the tip beneath the man's chin, drawing a bead of blood. He risked a quick glance to one side. Yusuf was relaxed, his sword hanging loose. Thomas wondered how skilled he really was, and whether his arm had healed as well as he claimed. He hadn't seen him train for over a year, and then he had been unengaged with the process.

"The prince will come with you, but I remain here."

"They told me to bring you both." The man spoke through gritted teeth, his head tilted back as Thomas applied more pressure.

"No, I'm sure they said I could be disposed of if I

proved difficult." Thomas smiled, no warmth in the expression. "Well, is this difficult enough?"

"I stay with you," said Yusuf.

"No," Thomas said without taking his eyes off the soldier, "you go with these three and ride like the wind. The Spanish must not capture you. If you stay that is what will happen." Thomas flicked his blade away from the soldier. "Now all of you, go. Go as fast as you can. I suggest you skirt those hills the others are trying to hide amongst and work your way around the edge of the valley."

The soldier wiped at his chin, examined the smear of blood on his fingers. Thomas knew if they were to meet again in some quiet place, unobserved, he might have to kill the man to protect himself. But that was in the future, another world altogether, and nothing to be concerned with at the moment.

Yusuf urged his horse forward until he stood beside Thomas, who leaned over and took the sword from his hand. He slid it back into its scabbard. Then he reached out and pulled Yusuf against him and kissed his cheek.

"Do this for me, my prince. Save yourself. I will see you again soon. Don't worry about me, you know how difficult I am to kill."

Yusuf nodded and wiped at his face, pretending to clear the dust from it. "Make sure you look after Lubna, won't you."

"I will."

Thomas turned away and began to ride. The three men let him go. When he heard their horses start away Thomas didn't turn his head, knowing Yusuf would be with them, because he had asked it.

* * *

The group of a hundred women, the elderly and the young, and all others considered expendable were fortunate. They had found a good place to defend, even though they had done so by accident. Sometimes you needed a little luck.

Thomas rode into the defile and through it into a circular bowl, soft hills rising all around other than where the entrance lay. He saw a ragged band gathered, mostly women, but a scattering of old men, traders and their wives. All the children present were under the age of fourteen. They had brought the carts with them, abandoned by al-Zagal in his rush to flee. He saw Lubna on the far side, organising the meagre cache of weapons. Thomas dismounted and left his horse where it stood, pushing his way through. There were some complaints until people saw who it was and then they parted to let him pass.

He touched Lubna's shoulder and she spun around, a hand raised. She stopped, a smile replacing the worry on her face.

"I thought you weren't coming. There were men here who'd been told to take you with them."

"They were satisfied with Yusuf." He glanced at the weapons. "How many crossbows?"

"Two dozen."

"And how many can use them?"

"I was trying to find out."

Thomas nodded. "Carry on. Pass me one, and a quiver of bolts." He glanced around, judging, before pointing at two boys and an old man. "You three – you know how to shoot a bow, don't you?"

They nodded, and Thomas wondered if they would have nodded regardless of their skill, but he knew they were the best he had.

"Follow me." He took the crossbow and ran across the clearing, began to climb the dusty bank. At the top he shaded his eyes and looked out on the approaching Spanish soldiers. They were no more than a quarter mile away, slowing as they came closer. Less men than he had thought at first. More than a hundred, but not many more. And they would not be the best, those were reserved for the chase after al-Zagal.

Thomas wound the bow and inserted a bolt.

"Draw your weapons. When I say, I want you to loose, but aim ahead of the horses, I don't want anybody injured. Not yet."

The three men followed his example. Thomas walked to the edge of the narrow defile and stood in clear view, the bow hanging loose in his hand. He waited as the soldiers approached. Two hundred yards. One hundred. Then he raised the bow and loosed a bolt. It thudded into the ground twenty feet ahead of the lead rider, who pulled up sharply as three other bolts followed, landing farther away than his own.

"There's nobody you want here," Thomas shouted. "Women and children. Old men and the infirm."

"You're not old," someone yelled back. "And I don't think you're a woman, even if you are wearing a dress." Around him his companions laughed. Rough looking men in leather jerkins and knee-high boots, their mounts hung with weapons. Thomas cocked his bow again, trusting the others to do the same. He saw some of the soldiers reach for their own bows and he raised his aim higher, making it clear the next bolt would find flesh rather than dirt.

The leader of the group was a sturdy man dressed in

fine clothes, his mount a spirited Arabian most likely stolen from a dead Moor on some battlefield. He shifted in the saddle as though seeking greater comfort, preparing for a long conversation. He looked to one side, the other, then shaded his eyes and checked the position of the sun. It was late afternoon, the hottest part of the day only now starting to fade, the position of his soldiers pitiless without any shade.

Thomas heard the noise of others joining him and glanced back, pleased to see a score of them, each with a crossbow. Twenty against a hundred. Not good odds, but he had faced worse in the past and triumphed, although none of those here would know of it. That other man was a stranger now, someone he no longer recognised.

"I see you've gotten yourself into another situation."

Thomas grinned as Jorge stopped beside him.

"The Sultan didn't want you at his side? Does he not recognise your superior fighting skills?"

"He sees the eunuch, not the man beneath the silks."

Thomas nodded. "More fool him. I'm glad you're here."

"So am I. I'd forgotten what it was like to feel scared. I can't say I want to get used to it, but it does make a man feel alive, doesn't it?"

"Just so you know, if they plan to make anything of this fight, I'm going to kill their leader. Either they'll think again or, more likely, simply charge us. How many can you take before they reach us?"

Jorge looked around. "They'll have to slow through the entrance, or climb to our position if they come straight at us. Five. Ten maybe." He glanced at his quiver. "Of course, I only have ten bolts, so I might be optimistic thinking I'll hit a man with every one."

"The rest of our people won't be accurate," Thomas said. "But those men don't know that." He was pleased everyone had lined up along the crest of the low rise. From below he hoped they looked threatening. It was a shame at least half of them were women, who the soldiers would carry little respect for, but they might respect the weapons.

"Do you think they want to surrender?" asked Jorge.

Thomas snorted a laugh, pleased to have his friend beside him. He felt no fear, only concern for those in his care. His laughter died away as he saw the Spanish captain dismount and start a slow walk in his direction.

"Well, I'm damned."

"More than likely," said Jorge. "Should I go down and negotiate? Of the two of us you know I am the better talker."

"But the less dangerous looking. I'll go." He handed Jorge his crossbow and moved to the edge of the rise. The slope was steep. Thomas knew he could scramble down, but also knew once down he would be vulnerable. He glanced back. More people were arriving, most of them carrying a weapon of some kind, holding them like they were more afraid of the weapon than the Spanish arrayed across the plain. He saw a flash of almost white hair, surprised to discover Helena with their company. The handsome man from the evening before stood beside her, as impressive as ever in fine clothes, his hair perfect. Jorge had told him his name last night but Thomas had forgotten it. Something Italian. The presence of both told him all he needed to know of al-Zagal's panic.

He breathed a sigh and began to slide down the loose stone, knowing he presented a less than elegant figure but unable to do much about it. At the base he dusted himself off and walked to meet the Spanish captain. They halted with ten feet between them. Thomas examined the man's features, unsurprised not to recognise him. Despite riding with King Fernando and a troop of soldiers when they pursued Abbot Mandana after Prince Juan had been kidnapped, Thomas knew there were tens of thousands of men under arms in Spain. However, it seemed the man knew him.

"You are Don Berrington, are you not? There could be no other." The man spoke in Spanish.

Thomas wondered how he was so recognisable, but when he replied in the same language he knew it offered a clue to his identity.

"You have the advantage of me, sir."

"So it is true, you are him. I am Coronel Hernandez, and these are my men. My task is to accompany you and your party to a place of safety."

"My thanks, Coronel, but we feel safe where we are. Is the King with you? If so, send him my regards when you return empty handed. He will not be surprised."

"His Grace has better things to do than chase down a rogue band of heathens."

"No doubt. I would suggest to return to your companions and tell them we escaped and you were unable to find us." Thomas leaned sideways, making a show of examining the soldiers. "It would be a shame to lose so many of your men on such a pointless expedition."

"We outnumber you, and we are trained soldiers. You are nothing more than women and children." Hernandez grinned. "My men will enjoy both, I am sure."

"I have no doubt. Rapists and child killers, like all the Spanish."

Hernandez's grin snapped shut and he stepped

forward, trying to get his face close to Thomas's, the effect spoiled because he stood six inches shorter and had to look up at him. Thomas smelt the rankness of him beneath his clothes, unwashed for months, possibly years. He saw the dirt in the pores of his cheeks, the accumulated detritus gathered in moustache and beard.

"I can say you were slain by your own people when you refused to surrender. Fighting broke out between you, and the women were killed by their own."

Thomas reached down and grabbed Hernandez's wrist as the man reached for a knife at his belt. In turn he used his left hand to reach across and draw his own blade. An intense calm settled through him, as it always did when danger threatened. It had been something Thomas believed he must have been born with. He had never known fear for himself, only others. The tougher the odds the cooler his mind became, and the sharper his reflexes. He revelled in the moment even as he despised himself for it, constantly wishing he could move beyond such base emotion. It did not stop him pressing the point of his knife into Hernadez's leather jerkin until he felt it give in the same way skin does when pierced. He saw Hernandez wince and knew he had pricked him beneath the leather.

"We both know I could kill you in this instant. And I know if I was to do so your men would tear me limb from limb. But that would not make you any less dead." Thomas smiled as though they were the best of friends discussing which game of dice they should play. "So what is it to be, Coronel, your life and mine, or should we both walk away to fight another day?"

Hernandez's gaze tried to bore into Thomas, as best he could, but there was more fear in it than threat.

Eventually he nodded.

Thomas jerked his knife free, saw a bead of blood on the tip. Good.

Hernandez turned away without another word. He walked to his horse and mounted.

This was the moment, Thomas knew, when his gamble would pay off or not. He had angered Hernandez, but he hoped not so much the anger would get the better of him.

It seemed he had judged right when Hernandez raised a hand and rode along the front of his men before turning them back the way they had come. Thomas watched, some looking at him, puzzled, while others turned to follow their master without any curiosity whatsoever.

Thomas heard stones rattle and expected Jorge to join him, but instead a fist punched him hard in the back. Lubna appeared in front of him, her face wild.

"You could have gotten yourself killed. And then they would have killed us all!"

Thomas breathed deep, breathed again, letting the air wash the coldness from his heart. The presence of Lubna helped. Helped a lot. He put his arms on her shoulders but she shrugged him off.

"But they're riding away, see? I knew exactly what I was doing."

Lubna snorted, not believing him, and he knew she was right not to. He felt he was getting too old for such shows of bravado. Too old, and with too many responsibilities. This woman was one. William another. He glanced beyond her, making sure the Spanish were still moving away.

"We should marry," he said when he looked back, the words taking him as much by surprise as they did Lubna.

She grunted. "If we live long enough." She punched him again, but the blow was softer this time, and Thomas took it as a good sign.

CHAPTER 7

"Stop this! What do you think you're doing? You should choose your own leader, not follow the first man who starts giving orders." It was Helena, of course, who started the rebellion.

Thomas stopped issuing instructions and turned to her. She stood to one side, her back straight, perfect body clearly delineated beneath a silk robe that fell to the ground.

He held his arms out to his sides. "I agree. But someone has to do something now, not tomorrow, not in an hour, now."

"Thomas is best suited—" Jorge began but was cut off.

"Why is it always a man has to be in charge? Why not me? Don't I know as much as him? Am I not capable of leading us?" She raised a hand and pointed at Thomas. "He claims to have sent the Spanish away, but how do we know they will stay away? We should have thrown ourselves on their mercy. They're not animals but civilised men."

"She thinks she can persuade them," Jorge whispered into Thomas's ear. "She doesn't care about the rest, only herself."

Thomas shrugged, fighting impatience. He knew he couldn't simply override Helena, that would only play into her hands. But time was passing. Already the shadows were starting to lengthen, and in his heart he knew the Spanish wouldn't ride away. The problem he had was the majority of the group were women, and they might back Helena.

He leaned close to Jorge. "Say something. I can't or I'll be accused of taking over again. Get them to vote or something. A show of hands."

"And if they don't back you?"

Thomas looked at Jorge. "Make them back me."

Jorge shook his head and moved away. He climbed a little way up the slope and turned back, held his arms wide.

"You all know me. I don't have the balls for an argument." He smiled as a few in the crowd laughed and others clapped. "Thomas is right – we need to make a decision quickly. And Helena is also right – he was wrong to start issuing orders. Nobody is in charge here. Not yet. But a simple show of hands can decide the matter. Raise your arm if you support Hel—"

"Wait. There are three candidates." A man at the rear of the crowd pushed his way forward. "My name is Giovanni del Caccia. Some of you know me, but most do not. I am a mariner and soldier. As qualified as anyone here to know what must be done." He climbed the slope to stand beside Jorge.

Thomas moved away, walking around the edge of the crowd, which seemed to be enjoying the entertainment. He began to unpack the goods from a cart, tossing them to the ground. A woman ran to him.

"What are you doing? Those are my things."

Beyond them Giovanni del Caccia and Helena were arguing.

"We need to block the entrance," Thomas said. "For

when the Spanish return."

"If they return. And when they don't I will have to put everything back."

"Believe what you will, I still need to block the entrance. Don't worry, it won't be just your cart I use." He continued emptying the cart, began to push it toward the narrow rock cleft which offered easy entrance to their place of safety. The defile was only just wide enough for the cart, which is what he had hoped. He strained, trying to lift it off its wheels and balance it on its back, but it was too heavy for him and he cursed. Another man shouldered him aside and took the other shaft. Between them they heaved, rocking the cart until it tipped, hanging on to prevent it turning over completely.

Thomas clapped the man on the shoulder and thanked him. When he turned back to bring another cart he saw the crowd breaking up.

Jorge came toward him, grinning.

"So, what are her orders?" Thomas asked, trying not to scowl.

"They voted for you."

Thomas frowned. "Why? She has a point. And that Giovanni man sounds like he can manage as well as me, probably better."

"They were talking while you were doing. These people know that right now action is more important than words. Now – go tell them what to do."

Most people tried to sleep, tension exhausting bodies and minds. Thomas sat on the crest of the low hill and stared across the plain. The sky was clear, stars pricking a velvet blackness, their glimmer matched by the glow from a

48

score of fires a half mile distant. The small Spanish force had not left, but Thomas hadn't expected them to. He was wondering what to do when they returned. And return they would, he knew.

A second figure stood at a distance, standing not sitting, arms wrapped around himself. It was the man Giovanni del Caccia who had put himself forward as leader. When Thomas had been chosen the man had appeared content, but he had come out here a half hour after Thomas. He made no approach but kept his distance, staring out across the Spanish. He had stood like a statue for close to an hour. Thomas had observed him as the entire group worked to complete the barrier of carts, rolling larger rocks down from above. It would make leaving difficult but would offer some protection.

Giovanni was handsome. Exceptionally so. Not like Jorge, whose masculinity was closer to female beauty, whether because he was not an entire man or, as Thomas suspected, because he was simply made that way – and more than likely the reason he had been chosen to be a eunuch in the first place. Giovanni possessed high cheekbones and dark eyes, his hair luxuriant, longer than Thomas's and far better cared for, as was his entire being.

Giovanni looked and acted more like a member of royalty than what he claimed to be, a mariner. His Arabic was good, but tinted with an accent, not the distant English underpinnings Thomas showed, rather the softer cadence of Italy. Giovanni had an effect on women. Even Thomas, who rarely noticed such things, was aware of it. He recalled watching his attempted seduction of the merchant's wife and wondered if the act had reached its natural conclusion or not.

Thomas decided he should walk to him, attempt

to engage in conversation. Giovanni was someone he would need when the Spanish came. But as he turned to go he heard the sound of scrambling behind and saw Jorge come into sight, little more than a silhouette, but unmistakable. Nobody moved with the elegance of Jorge, not even Giovanni.

Jorge sat, lithe, crossed his legs and arranged his robe. Satisfied, he turned to Thomas. "They're still there, then."

"Where would they go? And why?"

"Then perhaps we should. Go."

Thomas nodded. "I've been thinking the same thing. How many are we?"

"A little over a hundred."

"So al-Zagal took all the soldiers and more."

"He took all those he considered essential." Jorge had no need to complete the logic of the statement. He glanced sideways. "How long has he been standing there?"

"An hour, a little longer."

"You need to befriend him. The women like him, they'll do as he asks."

"So why was I chosen?" said Thomas. "There is a majority of women."

"You are known and he is not," said Jorge.

"Where does he come from?"

"Naples, he claims."

"Not then. Now. What is he doing in al-Andalus, and why?"

"What are we all doing here? You more than most."

"I belong here," Thomas said, then smiled. "Not exactly here." He patted the smooth rock beneath him. "I admit I would rather be somewhere else at this moment, but al-Andalus is my land now. Yours too, I suspect. You could have stayed in Qurtuba after I healed the prince but you didn't."

"I have no place there anymore. I love my women too much and prefer them bathed."

On the plain some of the Spanish began to chant, a deep, guttural cry, clashing their shields as they did so. The sound caught against the far cliffs and echoed, filling the valley. Thomas hoped the noise didn't wake too many.

"Silly boys' games," he said. "All they're doing is keeping themselves awake."

"When will they come?"

"At the first glimmer of daylight. As soon as they can see without stumbling. We'll be gone by then."

"We will?"

"Of course." Thomas glanced toward Giovanni, a statue against the night sky. "Go talk to him, Jorge. Make him your friend and bring him to me. If you think we need him then we do, and you're good at making people like you. I don't seem to have ever acquired the skill."

"I'll tell him you need his help. Everyone likes flattery."

"I do need his help."

Jorge stood without a sound. "Then I won't be telling any lies. That always helps." He wandered off as though on an evening stroll. Thomas watched him go before turning back to the Spanish. Another hour and it would be time to wake everyone. He sat, listening as Jorge and Giovanni's voices drifted to him. From the plain there came a sharp crack and a flare. Someone had fired a musket, trying to scare them. Thomas knew the Spanish had invested heavily in modern weapons. He had seen and heard them, smelled the gunpowder, treated the wounds inflicted. And now they had brought in cannon, heavy iron monsters big enough to shatter walls. The Moors continued to believe in speed and agility, in sword and bow. It was why they were going to lose the battle for this land.

Thomas rose to his feet with a grunt, aware he used to laugh at his father when he did the same. He hoped he was not turning into him, because he had hated the man.

He turned away and made his way into the dip, stepped between sleeping bodies and on up the far side, seeking a way of escape for them all.

CHAPTER 8

In the first hint of pre-dawn, barely a light at all, the three of them, Thomas, Jorge, and now Giovanni, moved through the sleeping figures, bending to shake a shoulder, passing a whispered message.

Bring only yourself. Leave your goods. Leave everything but water and food. Follow Thomas Berrington. He knows a way.

They grumbled and moaned, but they rose and picked through their meagre belongings, packing what little food they had managed to save. There wasn't enough water, but they would find more on the way. Thomas had assured them. He hoped he was right.

Far to the north-east the sky turned from black to violet, stars fading out one by one. Sound came from beyond the low hills as the Spanish began to form themselves into an attacking force. They would come hard and fast, and they would come soon.

Thomas had walked into the hills to the south looking for a way through. He still wasn't convinced he had found one, but knew he could lead the group deeper into the safety of their folds. If there was no way through they might find a better place to defend than where they were. The defile blocked with carts was a statement of resistance, little more. Without men with bows on the ridge the Spanish would simply climb over them. And there would be no men on the ridge.

Thomas untangled his weapons from where they were still tied to his saddle. He would have to leave the horse, all of the animals would be abandoned. He freed it and slapped it on the rump so it ran off before stopping, looking back, confused. It would end up as the property of some Spanish soldier, no doubt; or dinner for their number. There was nothing he could do about it.

As Thomas strapped the sword to his waist and tucked a knife into his belt a woman approached. He recognised her face but didn't know a name, the same as many others in their company, familiar but unknown.

"You have to come," she said, her eyes catching his then skittering away.

"We're about to leave."

"There's something you have to see first."

"Tell Jorge," Thomas said. There were only three of them young and fit enough to offer meaningful resistance if it came to a fight, and Thomas was determined Jorge should be considered his lieutenant.

"It needs to be you."

"I don't have the time," Thomas snapped, making the woman take a step back, but she was determined and he saw her draw on reserves of courage to approach again.

"You must see this. It's important. It was Jorge sent me to find you."

Thomas pushed a hand through his hair, clearing it from his face. "All right, show me, but make it quick."

She turned aside. "I want this even less than you."

The woman picked her way through the throng, each of them making preparations as Thomas had been doing, but in most cases without the weaponry. He felt the weight of steel hanging from his waist, even more felt the weight of responsibility he carried for these people. Taking charge didn't worry him because he barely recognised he had done so, too used to being in command to question it. He knew he was poor at taking orders and good at issuing them, but it had been many years since he had led a band of ragged outlaws through the southern wilderness of France, and he felt out of practice.

Whatever she wanted to show him lay at the base of the rise to the protecting hill, near the opening of the narrow defile now filled with discarded carts and tents and cooking pots. A poor protection but all they could offer.

A bundle lay on the ground, dark against darkness, only visible because the sky continued its relentless lightening that would soon bring the Spanish down on them.

Thomas knelt and drew back the edge of a robe to reveal a pretty face. The woman had been young, probably five years younger than Lubna's twenty-three years. Her eyes were open, staring at the last of the stars, only the brightest showing now. Open but seeing nothing. Thomas pushed a hand beneath the blanket, sliding it under her clothing. He placed his palm against her belly. She was cool but not cold, a last vestige of warmth clinging to her. She had been dead no more than four hours, more likely three.

Thomas wished for more light. They had lamps and candles but he didn't want to use them. He leaned close and to one side, trying not to mask what little illumination there was. He ran his fingers along her hairline, drew her robe down in search of a wound, but there was nothing. He checked her neck and jaw, moving it and finding it still pliable. There was no sign of violence. She was young, but he had seen the young die for no apparent reason. It happened – the world did not reward youth with eternal life in the same way it did not reward age with wisdom.

"Who found her?"

"Her husband. He is over there with his other wives."

Thomas looked to where the woman pointed. Saw an older man about his own age, somewhere in his forties, well dressed. He wasn't sure why but he had half expected to see the cuckolded merchant, but this was another stranger. Three women stood beside him, eyes downcast, their ages between sixteen and twenty.

"He is wealthy, I take it?"

"I do not know the man," said the woman. "My only involvement in this is as a messenger, and the message has been delivered. I should be preparing for my own departure."

Thomas nodded. "Go then, get ready, we leave soon." He rose and went to the man, saw him straighten his shoulders. "When did you find your wife this way?"

"When we were woken to prepare ourselves."

So not long. "Were all five of you sleeping together?"

The man scowled. "Of course not, do you think us immodest? I take my responsibilities as a husband seriously."

"But she would have been close, wouldn't she?"

"We all of us made our beds, such as they were, in this corner of the clearing."

Thomas imagined the man was more used to feather mattresses and fine linen sheets. He disliked him instantly, but knew that was no reason to suspect foul play, and there was no sign of such. It was something that happened. Rarely, but happened all the same.

"I'm sorry," he said. "We have no time to give her a funeral or bury her. You'll have to hope the Spanish offer her the rights, but they'll likely be Christian."

The man was unworried, and Thomas saw he wasn't particularly upset at the loss of a wife. No doubt there were many other young women in the world willing to sell their bodies for a fine roof over their heads and little to do other than sleep with her husband on occasion. Thomas was tempted to question him more harshly, but knew it was only his dislike of the man making him want it, and he had better things to do with his time.

"Say your goodbyes if you wish, we're leaving now."

Thomas turned and strode across the clearing, allowing thoughts of the dead woman to fade from the front of his mind, too much else crowding through in its place. He knew his ability to let go easily made many consider him cold, but he preferred to give his attention to the living not the dead.

He caught sight of the shadowed figure of Giovanni clambering from the slope above the clearing and went to him.

"It is done?"

The man nodded. "As best we can. I'm still not convinced they'll fall for it."

Thomas glanced at the sky, saw it had lightened further, but the light was mainly to the east and his plan might offer a little extra time. Earlier he had sent Giovanni with a group of women, together with spare clothing and wood stripped from the carts. They had erected scarecrows, hoping their presence on the skyline might make the Spanish cautious and slow them a little.

"It will be what it will," Thomas said, slapping

Giovanni on the shoulder. "You did well, but we have to leave. Gather everyone you can and follow me. We're out of time."

As Giovanni moved away Thomas continued to the far side of the clearing where Jorge and Lubna waited. Thomas had wanted Lubna to lead one of the groups but she had pointed out people were unlikely to follow a woman, which is why Giovanni del Caccia had taken her place.

Thomas had split them into three groups. The first would leave immediately, led by Jorge. Lubna would be in the second with Giovanni. Thomas would bring up the rear. His group would contain the few men of fighting age, together with the older ones, and a few women who had expressed a willingness to fight. They had bows and some swords, though how effective they would be against a determined Spanish army was questionable. At worst they might slow them a little. Enough to give the others a chance of escape.

And then they were ready. There was nothing left to keep them in this place and Thomas waved an arm to Jorge, who in turn gestured to the forty women standing around him. They started into the shallow valley that cut into the low hill to the south.

Thomas waited until they had gone from sight, then waited a little longer before gesturing to Giovanni. Only when he too had disappeared did Thomas turn and run up the northern slope. He was pleased to see as he reached the top that the scarecrows might work from a distance. Some even had wooden swords tied to wooden arms and Thomas smiled, pleased at the deceit.

His smile faded as he looked across the plain. The Spanish had gathered faster than he had hoped. Fires still burned, shelters remained, but mounted men were already starting out, banners snapping in a growing wind as the day shouldered the night aside. There was a dryness to the air that smelled of earth and woodsmoke. Nothing more could be done, and Thomas turned away. He needed to lead the final band of refugees to safety.

As they climbed the shallow rise between low hills a sound reached them, like heavy rain, the sound of many hooves growing louder, caught between slopes and magnified. They pushed on faster, losing sight of their temporary camp. Thomas urged them on, touching shoulders, offering a word of encouragement as each passed. He remained as the last man, pressed against a rock, and stared back.

Shouts came, the clash of weapons, though against what enemy he could not imagine. Then the breaking of wood as the Spanish started the task of demolishing the barrier. Thomas had hoped it might hold for an hour, but in less than a quarter of that the first men emerged into the clearing. Others swarmed over the slope of the hill. Thomas waited a moment until he saw them begin to search the goods they had left. It had been hard to persuade many to leave their riches behind, jewels and coin and fine silks, but he was pleased to see that, as he had hoped, greed slowed the soldiers more than the barrier. He was about to turn away when a small group of men caught his attention because they were not acting like the others. Eight of them stood to one side. One of them pointed, but fortunately not in Thomas's direction.

He leaned against the rock at his back, hoping the growing light would not reveal him, but unable to follow the others until he was sure.

One of the men walked to the side, examining the

ground as he went. Thomas knew it would do little good. The dirt was scuffed by the hundred who had camped there overnight. Except this man was persistent. He walked far enough to move beyond the disturbance, then began to follow the edge of the depression. As he approached the point the group had left from Thomas tensed. The man walked on and Thomas relaxed, but the soldier stopped and turned back. He called to his companions, who trotted to join him. They were too far for Thomas to overhear the conversation, but it was clear these men wanted more than plunder.

Thomas slipped away. Once he was out of sight he started to run. He caught up with the tail of his group after a quarter hour and called them to a halt. It took him a moment to catch his breath before he could speak.

"Soldiers. Coming." He stopped, leaning on his knees, cursing his lack of fitness. "They may not come this far, but if they do we need to make sure they go no farther. How many of you are accurate with a bow?"

Two raised their hands, one old, one barely old enough to grow a beard.

"Crossbow or bow?" Thomas asked.

"Bow," the old man said.

Thomas nodded, realising the pair were related. Father and son or, more likely, grandfather and grandson, both of an age for al-Zagal to have abandoned them to their fate.

Another man lifted an uncertain hand. "I fired a crossbow once."

"Did you hit anything?" Thomas waved a hand. "No, don't answer, it doesn't matter. You two, one each side. Hide among the rocks." He turned to the third man. "You, over there." Thomas pointed to the far slope. Only a few boulders dotted it, but they would provide some cover. As the man picked up a crossbow and started away Thomas called him back and handed him a quiver of arrows.

"The rest of you who can wield a blade stay with me." Thomas turned a full circle, judging the location. It could have been better, but it could have been worse. A little way down the slope a tumble of boulders had fallen from a steeper slope and would offer cover to a dozen men. Except they weren't a dozen men. Only three came forward, the others hung back, shuffling their feet as they moved away upslope.

Three archers and four with swords. Would it be enough against eight trained soldiers? Thomas doubted it, but it was all he had to work with. They could try to run, but the soldiers would only pursue them, and it wouldn't take long to send for reinforcements. At least whatever time they bought would give the rest a better chance of escape.

The stand would be made here.

CHAPTER 9

As the others took up their positions Thomas walked downslope to where the narrow valley turned. He knew from there a long straight run led back two hundred paces. He peered around a corner of rock but saw nothing.

Thomas looked back, pleased to see no hint of his people. When he turned again he saw the tracker come into sight, his companions appearing close behind. They weren't running but walked fast, eating up the ground the way only trained soldiers can. The lead man, obviously used to following a trail, came with his head down. He barely needed to look at the ground, the passage of a hundred feet had left enough sign for even a one-eyed man to follow. Thomas waited until he was sure they were not going to stop then ducked back and ran to the others. He secreted himself behind a rock and put a finger to his lips.

The minutes passed and nobody appeared. One of Thomas's men started to say something. He reached across and slapped the back of his head to silence him.

The lead man came around the turn, head down as before. Thomas waited as he approached their position. His companions came into the narrow valley behind. They were talking, laughing, and as they passed Thomas heard them speaking of loot. So they were like the others, only greedier.

Thomas allowed all eight to pass. He could sense the fear in his companions and ignored it. If the archers did their job the odds would improve. He shifted position, trying to keep the rear man in sight, trying to judge the moment. Glancing upward he caught sight of the youth as he moved from behind cover and cursed. Before one of the Spaniards also sighted him Thomas stepped from cover and yelled, "Now!"

The youth already had his bow part drawn. At Thomas's cry he pulled until the string touched his lip and almost immediately released. Whether from skill or luck his arrow flew true to strike the man behind the tracker full in the chest. By then the grandfather had also released his own shaft but missed a target. The youth re-nocked and loosed, over and over, excitement affecting his aim so his arrows flew wild. The wielder of the crossbow failed to show. Only one of the Spaniards had been downed and the odds shifted even further against Thomas's untrained band.

The hardened troops ignored their fallen comrade. One of them grinned at the sight of Thomas, then the grin faded as an arrow whistled past his ear. Thomas saw the youth dancing on his toes, seeking a target.

Thomas called his own men to him as he slashed at a man on his left. The soldier moved close, swinging his blade in a savage overhead blow. Without thinking, reacting only, Thomas ducked beneath the sword and stepped nearer still, breathing the rank odour of the man as he thrust a knife between his ribs. Blood gushed from the soldier's mouth and he went to his knees. Thomas kicked his blade aside and spun as a second man came at him. Three others started from the far side and Thomas, so long confident in his own abilities, knew the odds were against him. The old men and boys he had brought stood back, watching, seeing the blood and unwilling to get involved.

The next soldier came more slowly, having seen how his companion had fared, more cautious but still sure of his own skill. What he saw was a tall man in ragged clothes, no soldier, with nothing more than luck on his side. He smiled.

An arrow skidded off the leather jerkin of one of the others, who cursed and turned, seeking the archer.

Thomas nodded at the man coming toward him, as though greeting an old friend.

"Give my regards to your God," he said in Spanish, and for a moment the man's surety flickered. Then he came fast, sword in one hand, wicked knife in the other. His uninjured companions spread out, widening the threat.

An arrow thudded into the dry dirt between two of the men, who ignored the shaft. It had missed. The next one might not, but they already had an enemy facing them. These were skilled soldiers, hard men with hard faces, and Thomas wondered how much longer the fight could go on. He thought of all the people these men had killed, how they would kill him too without a second thought. He spun around, his sword flashing, meaning to take the man across the throat. But instead his opponent darted back fast and Thomas's blade whistled through the space he had occupied.

Thomas stepped closer, his knife rising, but it met empty air as the man twisted aside again, then came back almost instantly, using his shoulder to batter Thomas's face.

Thomas staggered, flailing with his blade as the other

soldiers swung at him, seeing an enemy weakened. Metal clashed against metal. The second man moved in, drawing an arm back ready to inflict a fatal thrust. Beyond him Thomas saw the young archer dancing about, looking for a safe shot but unable to find one, fearful of hitting Thomas instead.

A faint swishing sound alerted Thomas and he leaped backward as a sword flashed through the space he had occupied a moment before. The man's swing carried him around. Thomas steadied himself and stepped close. He readied to thrust his knife when out of nowhere he was thrown to the ground. He had forgotten the man behind. He rolled fast to avoid the first man's blade. Now both stood over him, far enough back he couldn't reach, close enough to stick him with a lunge. Thomas scrabbled, trying to get to his feet, but the soldiers advanced as fast as he moved backward, giving him no space. He jarred against a rock, almost stunning himself, aware he had been too confident.

As he prepared to mount a final show of defiance a figure came into sight. At first Thomas thought it one of his companions, but he was too fast for any of them, and too tall. The uninjured soldier heard him and turned, but too late.

Giovanni del Caccia rushed forward, swinging wildly with a sword. He was unskilled but fast, and a lucky blow caught the soldier on the side of his helmet. He shook his head, anger on his face. As he stepped away from Thomas, Giovanni swung again. The soldier deflected the blade easily, grinning now.

The respite allowed Thomas to regain his feet. He feinted at the closest man, who moved back so fast he tripped and fell. Thomas lunged, striking his arm, making it useless. The sword dropped from his grip.

Instead of finishing him Thomas moved past to help Giovanni as another tall figure rushed to join the fray. Jorge, better with a sword now, better than Giovanni, attacked fast. In an instant the odds turned. Three against six rather than one against seven. They were still outnumbered, but Thomas saw uncertainty in the Spanish soldiers' eyes. The tracker and another turned and sprinted back the way they had come. The man Thomas had injured staggered to his feet and followed. Now only four against three.

Thomas moved fast, lunging at the man to his left. Too late the soldier sensed him. Thomas's blade took him through the side, emerging from his belly. The man clutched at it with his left hand, his right continuing to swing. Thomas jerked his blade half clear, angled it and thrust again, seeking the heart. The man dropped like a felled tree, and Thomas turned to the other three, but already they were backing away before turning to follow their companions.

"Damn it, they'll bring the others," Thomas said.

"Thank you for your help, Jorge and Giovanni," said Jorge.

"Yes, yes, thank you, of course. It would have been interesting if you hadn't turned up."

"It's him you need to thank," said Jorge, indicating Giovanni, who had gone to talk with the others. Thomas scowled, disgusted at their cowardice. Only the youth had been of any use. "He came to find me and said you might need assistance."

"I was getting the upper hand," Thomas said.

"Yes, I noticed you were."

"Where are the others?"

"Lubna found a cave," said Jorge. "Not large enough for everyone to hide in, but it leads to a rock ledge where they can wait until the Spanish get tired of searching for them. The entrance is masked by bushes. I've no idea how she found it."

"Lubna sees things others don't," Thomas said.

He looked around. Two dead Spaniards. He knelt and relieved them of their weapons, knowing they might come in useful later, but made no attempt to hide the bodies. When he rose he saw Giovanni leading the others away at a brisk pace.

"He's not much of a swordsman, is he," Thomas said.

"But brave," said Jorge.

Thomas nodded in agreement. "How far is this cave?"

"A half mile. Come on, we need to move fast before those bastards come back."

The cave was dry and clean. Light spilled in from the rear where it sloped upward to a hidden valley. There were old bones in one corner, all the flesh gone from them. Judging by the marks on them a bear had once made this place home, but if so it had been long ago. Thomas crouched near the doorway, staring out through thick bushes which guarded the entrance. Lubna had wanted to stay with him but he had sent her away to join the others.

A score of Spaniards had gone past half an hour earlier, their voices loud. Another dozen had come a little later, moving slower, looking around, but Lubna had done well to find this place and they too had moved on. As well as the thick bushes guarding the entrance the cave was angled to one side, not easy to find even if you knew it was there.

A scrabbling noise caused Thomas to turn and he frowned at the figure that came running toward him. Helena, her face grim. He stood and caught her around the waist before she could run outside.

"What do you think you're doing!"

Helena struggled. "Let me go. We have to throw ourselves on their mercy before they find us."

Thomas pushed her away. She stumbled, fell.

"We've had this discussion and the subject is closed. They have no mercy, not for the likes of us. And if you think your looks will save you you're mistaken. Your fate will only be the worse. They'll use you, all of them, before they kill you."

Helena came to her feet slowly, eyes narrowing. Thomas saw her judging whether she could get past him. Then, in the moment before she sprang, Giovanni appeared behind her. He put his arms around her and pulled her against him. Helena squirmed like a caught fish but Giovanni only held her the tighter.

The sound of voices from beyond the cave caused Thomas to turn. The Spanish were returning, all of them, a band of over thirty. He heard someone say they must have taken a different route, another remark that he knew how to follow a trail and they'd come this way.

It was then Helena called out.

Thomas span around, but Giovanni had already judged the danger and his hand was clasped across Helena's mouth, his other over her breast. Helena continued to struggle but Giovanni was strong.

Thomas trusted him to keep her quiet and went back to his position at the entrance. It seemed nobody had heard her single cry, and as he waited the last of the soldiers passed, the sound of their feet, their chatter, fading. Only when there had been silence for several minutes did he rise.

"You can let her go now."

Giovanni nodded and withdrew his hand from Helena's mouth, but kept the other holding her tight against him, taking obvious pleasure from the contact.

Helena twisted from his embrace, strode to Thomas and slapped him hard across the face. "You have killed us all."

CHAPTER 10

Thomas and Jorge sat on the crest of a low hill that barely deserved the name. They stared through a gathering dusk at the towering cliffs protecting Ronda. They had left the safety of the cave three days ago to make their way through unknown hills to this point. The ground between them and the cliff was stained dark by the Spanish army. Four thousand, possibly more. Smoke from fires rose into the sky hundreds of feet before encountering some vagary of the wind and smearing northward.

"So what now?" asked Jorge. He sat with knees raised, arms draped across them. His beard was starting to show, a matching shadow darkening his skull. His eyes had lost the softness they showed in Gharnatah. "Do we consult the others, find out what they want to do?"

"They'll want to go back to Gharnatah or flee south to Malaka," Thomas said. "Those are the only options if we can't gain entry to the town. But it's pointless to ask – they'll want to retreat."

"And you don't?"

"It's at least a week back to Gharnatah, and the land between is thick with the Spanish. Malaka is the more rational choice, it's closer to start with, but we don't know what dangers lie between us and the city."

"So we try to get inside?" said Jorge.

Thomas nodded.

"Do you have any idea how?"

"Have you ever been here before?"

Jorge shook his head.

Below them, a half mile away, a group of soldiers started to argue and there came a clash of steel before one of their commanders bellowed them into submission.

"Do you think he's down there?" said Jorge, having no need to state who.

"Fernando? Possibly. But this is not the entire Spanish army – I hear they have over twenty thousand men under arms."

"He might still be here."

"Indeed." Thomas glanced at Jorge, his face shadowed as light drained from the sky. "What do you propose, I go in and plead with him to let us pass?"

"We're no threat. A hundred women and old men. But you're right, he's not stupid. So, what is it to be?"

"I need to talk to someone who knows the town. There will be a way in if we can only find it."

Jorge was silent for several minutes. Fires sparked the darkness. The lights of Ronda spread across the skyline. When he did speak it wasn't anything Thomas wanted to hear.

"Helena has spent time in the harem here."

"She's not observant," Thomas said. "If it doesn't have a cock and balls she's usually not interested." He saw Jorge's teeth flash in the dark. "All right then – if it hasn't got a cock. Didn't I hear you and Giovanni talking? I'm sure he said he'd been to Ronda before."

"I haven't seen him since noon," said Jorge. "He's making himself scarce."

"The man has courage," Thomas said, "but he's led too easily by what hangs between his legs."

"True, but he's not the only man to be that way. He'll have gone off with one of his women. They worship him, you know." Jorge's voice sounded wistful. "There's something about him. Some inner quality I've never encountered before. Damn it, I could fall in love with the man myself."

Thomas smiled. "You fall in love with everybody, except for me. I've seen you and Lubna together."

"My love for Lubna is chaste and you know it. And who says I don't love you?'

Thomas laughed, covering his mouth so the sound wouldn't travel. He doubted anyone in the Spanish camp would hear, but he preferred to be careful.

He stood. "Let's go talk to Helena, if we must."

They found Helena sitting with a group of women, all of them destined to join al-Zagal's harem. Beautiful women, skilled, but obviously disposable because their master had abandoned them to the Spanish.

As Thomas approached Helena looked up, firelight dancing across her features, the beauty of her face now fully restored. He was relieved to see no scowl. Since bearing him a son and his saving her life a year before she had warmed to him, at least a little.

Jorge folded himself to the ground without effort, more used to it than Thomas, who took several lurching attempts before he could cross his legs.

None of the women spoke to them, although they continued their own conversation. Helena was their leader and they would leave it to her to talk with the intruder. Jorge was accepted of course, and Thomas believed he should be too. He had attended these women in his role as physician over many years, knew their bodies almost as well as their master, but still he was kept at arm's length, an outsider.

"Is there a way in?" Helena asked. She knew it was down to Thomas to make the decision. Everyone else waited on him.

"I came to ask you the same question."

"Me? I know nothing of warfare."

"It's not warfare." Thomas leaned forward, staring into Helena's eyes. Even now, knowing what she was like, the attraction was palpable. It was the reason he had weakened and lain with her despite it being her sister he wanted. The firelight caught the silver of her hair, reflected it against her pale cheek. Thomas caught a hint of perfume and straightened, unwilling to be drawn in. Despite her dislike of him it was in Helena's nature to seduce. It was what she had been born to do. "There are four thousand Spanish between us and Ronda. What I seek is a means of entry without encountering them."

"Then you should ask someone else."

"You have spent time in Ronda."

"It was long ago, and I took no interest in matters outside the harem."

"You must have spent some time outside its walls," Thomas said. His only reward was a flat stare, and he knew Helena had likely never set foot in the town. "Rumour then. Women talk. Did you hear anything that might help us?"

Instead of answering Helena turned away and spoke to the dozen women around her. "Thomas wants to know if there is some secret entrance to the town."

One of the concubines laughed. "I have a secret entrance he is more than welcome to use."

Helena scowled. "If we can't find a way in it means another week on the road. Don't any of you know of something?"

The women looked blank. A few returned to their conversation, but one he didn't recognise spoke up.

"There is an iron gate at the foot of the cliff, at the end of a narrow roadway that leads down so townsfolk can visit the baths. And the bridge across the gorge, of course, but the Spanish will know of that and be defending it. I heard there is some entrance where water is carried from the river, but I know nothing of it."

"The gate to the baths will be locked," Thomas said. "And the Spanish will be watching both it and the bridge."

"Of course," said the woman. "There are other gates beyond it before you can gain entry to the main streets. Everyone knows Ronda is impregnable."

"I am sorry, Thomas," Helena said, and for once her regret sounded genuine. "I will keep trying. If I discover anything I will come and find you. Where are you and Lubna camped?"

"On the north side, close to the base of the hill. So I can see what the Spanish are doing."

"Of course." Helena looked down, an oddly demure gesture Thomas barely recognised from her.

He rose awkwardly and moved away. He had expected Jorge to accompany him, but his friend stayed, his job to look after the women of the harem. Thomas had noticed several of the concubines showing an interest in Giovanni del Caccia as they travelled. The man was popular with everyone, but had a habit of disappearing for hours at a time. Liaisons, Thomas suspected. Despite his unreliability Thomas liked the man – it was almost impossible not to, he was amusing, knowledgeable and, when present, willing to involve himself in any task demanded of him.

Thomas found Lubna setting out their meagre belongings. There was no fire, not this close to the ridge, but she had laid out dried meat and saved some flatbread from the day before. She was sitting with her legs tucked beneath her, staring into the darkness that began beyond their campsite. She turned at his approach.

"You've been gone a long time." She stood and put her arms around him, laid her head against his chest. Thomas held her, comforted, some of the tension he carried fading beneath her embrace.

"I thought Helena might know of some way into Ronda," he said into her hair, unwilling to let go yet.

"And did she?"

Thomas was constantly amazed at Lubna's lack of jealousy. He had, after all, spent the night with Helena before leaving for Qurtuba two years ago. Had planted a seed in her belly that grew into his son, William. At least that was his belief. Helena claimed the boy was not his. But it didn't matter because Thomas loved him regardless, as did Lubna. She had wanted to bring him with them, but a journey through dangerous territory was no place for a child of fourteen months.

"She claims she never left the harem."

Lubna laughed into his robe. "That sounds like my sister. She lacks curiosity more than anyone I have ever known."

"It doesn't help us. She says she'll ask the others, but I don't expect them to be any more observant. One woman claimed to know something, but not enough to be of use. I think concubines are chosen as much for their passivity as their beauty."

Lubna finally released him and knelt to place meat on the flatbread. She handed some to him. Thomas took it and knelt on the dry ground.

"Of course they are," said Lubna. "They don't want strong women in the harem."

"Helena is strong."

"She is, but only in some ways. In others she is weak. She might be my sister, but there are times I cannot believe she is the daughter of my father."

Thomas knew what Lubna meant. Olaf Torvaldsson was no weakling, either physically or morally. He was the Sultan's general, a giant of a man who had come from his native Sweden as a mercenary and through skill and guile worked himself to his current position. Thomas had once tried to ask him if he regretted choosing to fight for the Moors, whose end was now inevitable and with it, more than likely, Olaf's own life. A general was expected to fight until the last blow was struck. Olaf hadn't replied. Instead he had told him of the beauty of his children and the love for his wives, both the first and the current one.

Lubna brushed stray hair behind her shoulder, loose now she considered them alone, despite the hundred other souls close by. "He brought me here with him once. Not mother, only me. I think he wanted to see if I could find a man, but I was only thirteen."

"Thirteen year old girls marry," Thomas said. "But I'm glad you didn't."

"Did you mean what you said the other day?"

"What did I say?" Thomas knew perfectly well.

"About wanting us to marry?" She took a delicate bite of her bread. "You know I don't expect it. I love you whether we are linked in the eye of Allah or not. But if you ask again I will say yes. You know I will say yes."

Thomas looked at her and knew he wanted no-one else. Lubna lacked the beauty of her sisters, all of them by Olaf's first wife who must have been a great beauty herself, but she possessed something none of the others did. An enquiring mind and sharp intelligence. She was his companion in more ways than just sharing his bed. She shared his life too, in a way nobody else could.

"So what did you do when you came to Ronda at thirteen?"

"When I wasn't seeking a husband, you mean? I played. I explored the streets and alleys. I learned where all the important people lived. I went everywhere."

"Was it safe?"

"People knew who my father was. Nobody would be fool enough to accost Olaf Torvaldsson's daughter. Not if they wanted to live." Lubna laughed. "There was one boy I liked but he was afraid of father. He would have nothing to do with me, even though I knew he liked me too."

Thomas smiled, imagining the young girl and how sharp she must have been, the world opening up to her.

"So I know of a way into the town," she said.

Thomas looked up from his food. Beyond the ridge someone blew a trumpet and he tensed, but it fell silent almost at once, a voice shouting in Spanish telling the bugler to shut up.

"Tell me."

"You will have heard about a gate next to the baths," said Lubna.

Thomas nodded. "Also another gate, but the woman who told me knew nothing about the second one."

"Few do, or wish to. Before the aqueduct was built the only source of water for the town was the river, and that flows at the bottom of the cliff. More years ago than anyone remembers a tunnel was carved through the rock. It leads from the town to the river bank. They use it now to bring water for washing and bathing."

There was something about Lubna's telling that hid more.

"What else?" Thomas asked.

Lubna stared out to the pale cliffs, the town perched atop them. Some called it the eagles' eyrie. It was certainly high enough.

"There are prisoners locked in cages within the tunnel," she said at last, continuing to stare out as if she could see them. "Captured soldiers, slaves. They carry water in leather buckets on their shoulders, and when one dies there are always more to replace them."

Thomas saw her shiver and reached out to place a hand on her shoulder. Lubna leaned her cheek against his touch.

"Is it a way in?" he asked, voice soft.

"Not the way you mean," she said. "Hammering on the gate would not be heard at the top, and would alert the Spanish besides. Someone will have to descend and unlock the gates before we can enter. You need to get into the town first and find someone to do that."

"And the other gate, next to the baths, is that no good? Won't there be guards there?"

Lubna glanced at him. "Almost certainly. But it's too obvious. The Spanish will have men there, too." She smiled, teeth white in the dark. "I used to pass through that gate almost every day. It was my escape route to freedom. I fished in the river and ran through the woods." She glanced down, shy. "I even asked that boy I mentioned to come with me, but he would not."

"Lucky for me he didn't," Thomas said, "or you might be married now with half a dozen little Lubna's hanging off your skirts."

"Perhaps." She stared into space, and Thomas knew she was thinking of those days with fond memories. Sometimes those years were the sharpest in peoples' memories. Thomas knew his own were but for a different reason. Lubna would have been in a privileged position because of who her father was. At thirteen Thomas had faced a different kind of life. His own father dead, he an orphan abandoned in a foreign land. He should have been dead too but even then he knew how to wield a sword. How to hide from French soldiers searching the field after the battle of Castillon, killing any wounded Englishmen they came across.

"So how do we enter the town and get this gate opened?" Thomas asked.

"There is a way, possibly. For a single man."

"For two men. Thomas is going nowhere without me."

Thomas turned to find Jorge standing behind him.

"How long have you been there?"

"A few minutes, no more."

Thomas was more upset he hadn't heard his approach than by his presence. He knew he had no secrets from Jorge. There were times he believed the man knew him better than he knew himself.

"Did you come for a reason, or just to annoy me?"

"Both, obviously. The one would be no fun without the other. Helena was going to come, but I thought you might prefer if it was me who brought her message."

"Possibly."

Jorge sat on the ground, leaned across to pick up a piece of bread and meat. "You didn't want this, did you? She says one of the women recalls a door, but it seems Lubna has already told you of it. Does she also know of a means of entry to the town?"

"There is only one way," said Lubna. "Can you climb?" She looked at Jorge when she asked the question, but it was Thomas who replied.

"Jorge claims to be the best climber there is. It's me you should be worried about." He recalled the descent to the woman's body in the gorge, surprised to have done as well as he had. "Is it a difficult climb?"

"Not in daylight."

"It's not daylight," Thomas said.

"There is a good moon," said Jorge.

Thomas glanced at the sky. It was true – the moon hung almost full. It had risen an hour ago and would give good light for several more hours yet.

"Where is this climb?"

"In the gorge where the water drops into a deep pool and the gate to the tunnel lies. It is possible to climb the side of the waterfall. Once at the top there's another pool. To the side there is a way, but it is another two hundred feet from there."

Thomas examined the ground at his feet. "Did you ever climb it?"

He lifted his eyes in time to see Lubna suppress a grin. "I was a thirteen year old wildcat. Of course I climbed it. Many times."

"You could have fallen, been killed."

Lubna tilted her head to one side, not needing to say the words: *look at me, here I am*, and Thomas laughed because it was exactly what he would have done.

His amusement faded as he came to the realisation of what he needed to ask. He lifted his eyes to Lubna's and took a breath.

"Of course I will show you the way," she said before he could frame the question.

Chapter 11

They waited on a soft ridge line as midnight came and went and still Thomas didn't move. Beside him he heard Jorge shift position but knew the sound wouldn't carry. Ahead, spread across the plain, the Spanish army slumbered. Thomas was waiting for it to fall quieter still, for the guards patrolling the perimeter to grow bored and lose sharpness. He was also waiting for the moonlight.

A near-full moon hung to the east. Thomas was waiting for it to move across the sky so its light would cast into the deep gorge that cut through Ronda's eastern side. They would need to enter the foot of the gorge just before light fell into it so they had illumination for the difficult climb.

Eventually he tugged at Lubna's sleeve, at Jorge's, and rose to a crouch. They descended the gentle slope, moving in a wide circle around the Spanish camp. After a time they came to the foot of the cliff and stopped. Thomas looked back. Fires burned across the plain, banners flapped in a warm wind that came from the south, dry with the scent of the desert. The sound of water was loud between the confining walls, louder still as they ascended a rough track beside the river. Lubna led them onto a level area, the thunder of a waterfall blocking out everything else. Mist hung in the air, drenching Thomas's clothes in an instant. At the tail of the pool the water roiled, at its head was a maelstrom.

Thomas pulled Lubna close, shouted into her ear, "Is this where they carry the water up? I see no gate."

Lubna pointed rather than attempt a reply. Thomas stared, eventually making out a stout wooden door set into a recess in the cliff face. In daylight it might be easy to find, but in the darkness he would not have noticed it.

He turned to look across the plain. With the extra height they had gained the extent of the Spanish army was even clearer, its organisation laid out like a map. Heavy cannon had been pulled to the front, barely four hundred feet from the towering cliff and city walls. In the moon's light he saw how the front of each had been chocked up with wood to raise the barrels higher. He expected come morning the guns would begin to fire.

When he turned back Jorge was removing his clothes. Lubna had moved away, not that it would have worried Jorge if he had an audience of a dozen. When he was naked Jorge pulled on a pair of white linen pants but left his chest bare. He stuffed his clothes into a sack. A length of rope was tied to the neck and Jorge coiled it around the sack for the moment.

Thomas moved beyond Lubna, offering her a sense of propriety, and did the same. When he was done he walked to her and tapped her shoulder. She turned, stared at them both and laughed, the sound plucked away among the roaring water. She waved a hand and started along the edge of the pool until she came to a tumble of rocks on one side and began to work her way upward. Thomas allowed Jorge to go ahead before following. As they climbed over rock and scree sometimes the waterfall was close enough to reach out and touch. The sound increased, then faded as they moved higher.

They reached the lip of the waterfall, which proved the trickiest section. There was little space, streaming water taking up almost the entire width where the gorge constricted the flow. Lubna showed them how to negotiate a narrow ledge until she disappeared over the lip. Thomas waited, watching Jorge, knowing he was a skilled climber. Finally he went himself.

It was quieter at the top. Water still sounded, but muted here, and they could talk using no more than raised voices.

"So where is this route?" Thomas said. He stood at the edge of the river and stared up at the towering cliff. They had ascended a third of the way but two hundred feet of what appeared to be sheer rock remained.

"This way." Lubna walked along the edge of the water. The gorge widened a little, offering a flat platform pitted here and there by round water-filled depressions. Thomas had seen them before, knew they were formed when stones tumbled and turned in a hole, gradually boring into the rock. In some of the holes stones still remained, a reminder of the power of the water that had used them.

Lubna stopped and pointed, and at first Thomas saw nothing.

"There," she said "See the fissure in the rock face?" She lifted her arm, pointing higher. "The first section is the hardest, then you come to a ledge. Beyond that you'll find more holds."

"How often did you climb this?" Thomas asked.

Lubna's teeth flashed. "A lot. Too many to count. There are different routes. Some are dead ends, others easier."

"How do we know which to take?" said Jorge. He stared

at the wall of rock. Behind them an equally fearsome cliff face rose from the far bank, except there the water ran hard against the rock, offering nowhere to stand.

"I think I can remember the best ways," said Lubna. "When you come to a place you're uncertain of stop and wave. I'll try to point you the right way."

"Point us the right way?" said Jorge, his face expressionless.

"You can take your chances on your own if you prefer," said Lubna.

"How long since you last climbed the cliff?" Thomas asked.

"Eight years, closer to nine now."

"And you still remember the way?"

"I told you, I played here all the time." She shook her head. "It's not difficult once you start, and the sooner you start the sooner you'll be able to open the gate."

"How long will it take?"

"An hour." She looked him up and down. "Possibly two."

Thomas glanced at the sky. The moon had almost reached a position where it would shine into the gorge, and they needed to start soon. An hour would be better than two. Once at the top they still had to find someone to open the gate and lead the group of women and children through. Helena was preparing them. Once he and Jorge reached the easier upper section – easier according to Lubna – she would return to help her sister. It would be a close thing, daylight chasing night the entire time. They had perhaps four hours in total, no more.

"There's someone up there," said Jorge, pointing.

Thomas stepped back and examined the lip of the cliff. The upper walls of a house showed where it was set back from the edge, but a narrow walkway ran along the top.

"I see nothing."

"There," said Jorge. "Look for the upper window in the middle. Now look directly beneath it."

"I still see—"

"And then go left twenty paces," said Jorge. "I think it's a woman."

Thomas saw it now. A shrouded figure slight enough to be a woman was pressed against the wall of the house that rose from the walkway. Her hands were raised to her throat as if she was trying to release some constriction.

"What's she doing, hiding?"

"You need to go," said Lubna, ignoring their interest. The first rays of moonlight had flooded the gorge.

"She'll be gone by the time we get there," said Jorge, reaching up to test a hand hold.

"Wait!" Thomas held up a hand. Above them a second figure appeared, a man. Taller, wider shouldered. He stopped and Thomas knew he was searching for the woman. Was she a wife run from home, or something else?

As Jorge stepped back from the cliff the woman began to run. The man saw her at once, closing the gap quickly. As he reached her a third figure came onto the narrow path. Slighter even than the first, a wind catching her robes and wrapping them around a slim figure.

"What—" Jorge's question was cut short as the man clutched the woman. He tore at whatever was wrapped at her throat, then grasped her around the waist, lifted and tossed her into empty space. For a moment it seemed as if the laws of nature had frozen as she hung there. Then she fell, her clothing fluttering, and a cry sounded.

"Back!" Thomas yelled, grabbing Lubna and dragging her into the water, which foamed around their thighs, deeper than expected.

The woman fell, plummeting to earth to land with a sickening wet sound. Lubna covered her face. Jorge was closest and he turned to one side, bringing up what food his stomach contained.

Thomas climbed from the water and approached the figure, but not before glancing up. The man continued to stand at the top, looking down on them. He would see the woman, would see Thomas, Jorge and Lubna too, but their presence appeared not to disturb him. Despite being caught in moonlight the man was too distant to recognise. A shape against stone, dark hair and beard, but that could be almost anyone, Spaniard or Moor.

The other woman who had appeared was gone. Had she seen what was happening and fled? The man turned away and Thomas wondered if he knew he had been observed and was now in pursuit of another victim. If so there was nothing could be done about it from the base of the cliff.

He knelt beside the woman and turned the body over. Blood pooled beneath, soaking away between rocks to taint the river. Both arms were shattered, legs and hips too. Her face was unmarked on one side, unrecognisable on the other.

Could the same man have killed both this woman and the other in the gorge, tossing them both from a height? If so, why? Thomas knew, because he was there himself, it was possible to be in the gorge only a few days before and inside Ronda's walls now. Probabilities danced through his mind. Faris al-Rashid and Yusuf were there that day. Both would have entered Ronda in the company of al-Zagal. Thomas found it difficult to suspect Yusuf, but knew Faris more than capable of murder if it suited him. Except it would be unlike Faris to do the deed himself.

Lubna pulled at his shoulder. "Thomas, you have to go. Leave her, there's nothing you can do. You have other responsibilities now."

She was right, but he felt it an abandonment of both duty and profession to leave her where she lay.

"We can report her murder in the morning," said Lubna, tugging at him once more. Thomas rose, steeling himself to ignore the shattered body lying at his feet. Seconds only, that was all that separated her from a living, breathing woman.

As he moved away he took in what Lubna had said. Murder. It had been no accident, no suicide. The man had tossed her away like a used rag. He pushed the thought aside. She was one life and he had a hundred to concern him.

"Here?" Thomas said, reaching into the crevice.

"Push your hand inside and make a fist," Lubna said. "It will hurt but it's the only way."

Thomas started to reach up but Jorge pushed him aside. "I'll go first. I don't want you falling on me."

Under normal circumstances Thomas would have said something, but these were not normal circumstances, and the woman's death played on his mind. With an effort he pushed it aside and closed himself down. He needed all of his concentration for the task ahead.

While he waited for Jorge to climb ten feet he hugged Lubna, then followed.

She had been right – it hurt.

CHAPTER 12

Thomas grew acutely aware of the passage of time. The climb seemed to have gone on for hours, but he knew his mind played tricks. When he found a position that allowed he turned to look east to see the sky remained dark. The moon had shifted so now he climbed through shadow. When he glanced up it was to see the top of the cliff taunting him with its closeness. His limbs ached and his hands were an agony. The linen sack holding his clothes hung from his waist on a length of rope, twisting in the breeze, tugging at him with an insidious pull. A little to his right and thirty feet higher Jorge had found a narrow ledge, sitting there as if it was the widest, most comfortable seat he had ever encountered. His legs dangled, the toes of one foot bloodied. The climb had been hard on both of them, but harder on Thomas.

"Lubna has gone," said Jorge. "An hour ago. The others will be making their way to the base of the cliff now. We need to finish this climb and get the gate open."

Thomas nodded, a tremble starting up in his calves to tell him he had clung on too long. He reached up, found a hold with his fingers and pulled himself higher. He ignored Jorge, but Jorge chose not to ignore him.

"Reach right as far as you can. There's a good hold there, and then swing across and your foot will find another."

Thomas stretched. Jorge was taller than him, but he found a small depression. He reached with his right foot, searching.

"You have to swing. The foothold is there but you've got to support yourself with your hands. Trust me."

Thomas wanted to ask how Jorge had known to do such a dangerous thing but didn't think he had words to spare. Instead he gripped the rock harder and swung out. His right foot kicked against something. He jammed his toes in and hung on, pressing himself against the smooth rock face.

"You're done now," said Jorge. "It's easy from there. Either hand has a good hold and there are places for your feet all the way up. I'll go ahead and wait for you at the top."

When Thomas reached up, fingertips searching, a hand grasped his wrist and pulled. For a moment he hung in space, safe only because Jorge's strength held him. Then he swung sideways and up. He tripped as his feet landed on solid ground, stumbling to his knees.

"That was fun," said Jorge.

Thomas looked at him through hair that had fallen across his face. "You have a strange sense of fun."

He crawled to the foot of the building and leaned against it while his breath continued to catch in his lungs.

"You should climb more often, it would do you good."

"I don't need to climb at all," Thomas said. "Not until tonight, in any case." It was not the truth, but the truth was long in the past and another life altogether. "Do you see any sign of what happened here?"

"What happened?" Jorge's face was blank.

"The man and woman." Thomas used the wall to lean against as he climbed to his feet. He glanced at the lip of the cliff, its siren call pulling at him even now. He watched Jorge walk to the very edge and examine the ground.

"It's rock all the way to the edge," he said without looking back. "There'll be no sign."

"Nothing at all?"

Jorge shook his head, stepped away and untied the neck of his sack. He tipped the contents out and began to dress. They had to appear as men of influence if they were to persuade someone to open the gate.

Once dressed Thomas was tempted to toss the sack and linen trousers he had worn for the climb over the cliff until he remembered what lay at the base. He pushed it from his mind. There would be time to examine the death later. Now the night was fading.

On the edge of the small square where the head of the tunnel emerged, running water sounded and Thomas made his way to it. A pipe jutted from the wall, spilling clear water into a trough. He washed his face, gasping at the coldness, then drank directly from the pipe, the water clean in his mouth.

Lubna had provided directions to the palace so Thomas turned north, an unintuitive direction but she had assured him it was the quickest way. As the cramps from the climb eased he broke into a jog, soon after a run. He glanced to the east as he reached a wider street. Was the sky lightening? He ignored it and turned left, Jorge falling into place beside him. They passed dark windows. There was barely any sound other than their footfalls to disturb the night. At one point a dog leaped out at them, barking, pulled up short by a stout rope tied to a hook set in the wall.

The entrance to the palace was smaller than the one in Gharnatah, less even than the accommodation used by Isabel and Fernando in Qurtuba. A heavy oak door barred the way, Islamic script carved with the same phrase that ran through al-Hamra: *There is no victor but Allah*.

Thomas hammered on the door, waited.

Jorge put his ear to the wood.

"Anything?" Thomas asked.

"Can't tell. Too dense."

"You or the door?"

"Both, most likely."

Thomas hammered again, louder and longer.

Eventually Jorge said, "Someone's coming."

Thomas examined the sky. It had not changed since he last checked only minutes before, but already he could feel the heat of the sun dawn would bring burning between his shoulders. The day was coming, nothing could stop it.

From within, metal bolts were thrown and then there was silence for a while, broken eventually by the sound of a wooden bar being lifted away and set to one side. Finally a door set within the larger door opened a crack and a pale face peered out.

"It's the middle of the night. Go away."

"I am Thomas Berrington, surgeon to the Sultan. My companion is Jorge al-Andalus, eunuch to the harem. We are here on urgent business. The women the Sultan was forced to leave behind are waiting beyond the walls. Someone needs to take us to the gate at the foot of the cliff so they may enter."

The man looked from one to the other. Then he shook

his head and closed the door.

Thomas hammered again.

"I am opening it!" A shout from within. A moment later the small door swung wide. "Have patience."

"There is no time for patience," Thomas said. "Take me to al-Zagal."

"The Sultan sleeps and is not to be woken. Tell me what you want and I will try to find someone if I think it important. I know nothing of any women."

"By now they will be waiting beyond the gate where water is carried up from the river."

The man, dressed in a linen nightgown that showed signs it was overdue for laundering, stared at Thomas. Then he nodded and turned away, stopped. "Wait here. Go nowhere." He bustled away along the stone floored corridor, bare feet slapping.

They stood in a passage illuminated by flickering torches set in sconces, one either side of the doorway, two more forty feet away where a second door gave access to inner rooms. The air was cool, dry, the scent of burning oil in the air.

"Do you know him?" Thomas asked Jorge, who shook his head.

"You forget I have never visited Ronda. He isn't one of al-Zagal's people. Probably serves the palace here." Jorge looked around. "Such as it is. More like a fortress than a palace."

"I thought so too. Doesn't everyone consider Ronda impregnable? Why build a fortress rather than something more elegant?"

"We are in the far west of al-Andalus here," said Jorge. "Safe the town might be, but the land twenty miles away has been in Spanish hands for centuries. The rulers no doubt feel safer protected by strong walls."

Thomas tapped his foot on the floor, unable to stop his leg shaking. A thrum of tension ran through his body.

"Relax," said Jorge. "It will be whatever it is. Your impatience affects nothing and will only wear you out."

Thomas glanced at his friend. "How do you manage to do that?"

Jorge lifted a shoulder. "I have found over the years worrying at something does no more than inflame the itch rather than calm it. You and I, despite what you may think, are nothing in the scheme of things. I find acceptance a more rational approach than anger."

"I might agree if a hundred lives didn't depend on us. I notice you were happy for me to take on that burden."

"Acceptance," said Jorge.

For a moment anger flared in Thomas. He was about to say something but was saved by the return of the watchman, accompanied by an older man also called from bed.

"You are asking something about the water gate," said the older one, waving a hand to dismiss his companion.

"Do you know the general Olaf Torvaldsson?" Thomas said, deciding on an alternative approach.

The man required only a moment's thought before nodding. "He has visited Ronda on several occasions, but not for some time now."

"The last time he came, perhaps the time before that, he brought his daughter with him."

Thomas watched the man's eyes move to study a point on the wall. He tried to bank down the fires burning inside, tried to emulate Jorge's calm, but found it almost impossible.

Then the man smiled. "Yes, a bright little thing. Tiny.

Wiry. Fearless."

"Yes, you know her. It is Lubna who told me of the gate. Did your companion explain why we need it opened?"

The man waved a hand. "Something about abandoned women."

"We were a part of al-Zagal's party until four days ago. When the Spanish attacked our forces were split and we lost sight of him. We took it as our duty to guide them to Ronda."

The man stared at Thomas, who wondered what story he had been told, and if it was close enough to his own. He had no intention of telling the truth: that they had been abandoned to their fate.

"Have you come alone? Are you expecting my master to launch some kind of rescue party?" The man sneered. As the last traces of sleep left he was becoming himself. "Have you seen the forces that are arrayed on the plain beneath us?"

"The women and children are waiting at the foot of the cliff," Thomas said. "If you do not show us this doorway then they will be discovered when the sun rises. I have not led them across eighty miles of enemy territory to have them fall at the last step."

"One hundred women could not pass without being discovered." Once again the sneer. "Their chatter would give them away."

"Not these women. Not my women," Thomas said. "If you will not help then take me to your master and we'll see what he has to say."

"He is not to be woken."

"And when he *does* wake and discovers you have caused the capture of those he could not save, what then? Is your position such that you do not fear his anger?"

95

"I am Abraham al-Haquim, Governor of the city state of Ronda. I am charged fully with making decisions on behalf of the Sultan when he is not available."

Thomas breathed hard through his nose, fighting to stop his hands grasping the man around the throat, afraid if he did he might not be able to stop. There were no windows in the corridor or he would have been tempted to glance through them.

"What is the harm in it?" Jorge stepped between Thomas and the man, this Governor. There was little space but he seemed to place himself effortlessly. He took the man's elbow and led him a small distance away, ignoring Thomas, who tried to instil calm in himself. He knew if anyone could persuade the man it would be Jorge. He listened to their soft voices, and waited.

It took ten long minutes before Jorge turned and nodded. "Follow Abraham, he will show us the way. He knows of the gate we seek. He says it is a long way down and asks we wait while he dresses." Jorge stared at Thomas, daring him to object, and Thomas forced his shoulders to relax in an attempt to appear less threatening.

Abraham al-Haquim scurried away.

"How can we trust him not to lock the door and leave us imprisoned here?" Thomas said.

"Because instead of offering threats and reminding him of his master's treachery, I told him of the beauty of the women who have travelled so far, and what injustice it would be if such beauty and skill was to be wasted on the Spanish."

"And he believed you?"

Jorge smiled. "Not all men are as you, Thomas. Most are simple souls, led by their cocks, even an old Jew like al-Haquim. Did you not hear him? He is Governor of the city state of Ronda. An important man, with privileges."

"So you promised our concubines to him?"

"Not promised. He is fully aware that when they arrive it will be impossible for them to all service the Sultan, there are too many, and a man in his position expects certain rewards. And they're not *our* concubines."

"I'm sorry, that was wrong of me."

Jorge grinned. "They are *my* concubines. Don't ever forget that." He turned as al-Haquim returned, dressed in his official robes, head turbaned, fingers ringed. He held the inner door open and motioned for them to follow.

Chapter 13

"I want to ask you again about these letters," said Al-Zagal. "And why you refused to follow my orders and accompany my nephew to join me." He sat cross-legged on cushions arranged on a raised platform so his head was higher than Thomas's, who stood in front of him. A series of open arches framed a view across the plain, dark with the Spanish army. Al-Zagal's gaze was constantly drawn to it.

It had taken over an hour to lead the women, children and stranded men through the narrow tunnel carved in the rock. Giovanni had been one of the last to appear, smiling, his arm linked through that of a woman.

Close to the head of the passage other chambers had been cut. Iron bars enclosed those who were enslaved to carry water three hundred feet in almost complete darkness. Most were captured Spaniards, but there were others too. So filthy were they, each dressed in the same coarse cloth, it was impossible to tell if they were male or female other than the lack of beards on some.

Thomas's head spun with exhaustion but he knew he could not rest yet. Jorge had accompanied him to the Sultan's formal rooms but now hung back, as he usually did, seeming to be distracted by something else. The women, perhaps. There were three of them arranged on cushions. They ignored Thomas, but he caught them casting glances toward Jorge, who they would know of. Occasionally they talked among themselves but made sure their voices did not rise to distract their master.

"Had I followed orders the women would have been raped," Thomas said, "and a hundred killed." His legs ached, also his knuckles where he had taken the skin from them during the climb.

"The Spanish would not have killed them," said al-Zagal.

"They do not have a good record in such matters."

"I have studied these letters again," said al-Zagal, flicking them with the fingertips of his right hand. "One in particular. And I have asked questions. The woman bringing them to me is dead at the bottom of a gorge, you say."

"It appears she was present on the cart but fled and was caught. I believe whoever killed her was after the letters."

"She did not write them. She was a messenger, nothing more. These two warn me of the presence of Spanish forces close to Ronda. Hardly enough to kill for." Al-Zagal tossed them aside. "This one might offer some clue to the nature of her death." The Sultan leaned forward, holding the letter out. He shook it. "Here, take it."

Thomas closed the short distance and took the letter. He made no attempt to read it.

"May I keep it, Malik, to study?"

Al-Zagal nodded.

Taking it as a good sign Thomas continued. "Do you know the name of the woman who carried the letters?"

"Najma," said al-Zagal. "She has been a servant of the harem for over ten years. She was well liked."

"Who wrote the letters if it wasn't her?"

Al-Zagal shook his head, his eyes still on the Spanish army. "The first is from the Captain of my army, the second the Governor. The third, the one you hold, is written by the palace librarian, Khalil bin Ahmad Basri. He talks of some creature, an Incubus, but I do not believe spirits can kill. It looks more like the kind of business you would deal in."

At last al-Zagal turned from his obsessive study of the enemy army and his eyes locked on Thomas's. "My brother tells me he has used your services in the past. That you have been of assistance to the Spanish also." Al-Zagal's mouth turned down as he spoke of his enemies. "He told me you have an affinity for death and those who inflict it." He stared at Thomas, who made no attempt to reply. He had learned in the little time he had known the man how to interpret his ways. When he expected a reply he would glance away, as if uninterested in what the other had to say. "Is that true, Thomas Berrington?" Still no answer required, even though the question might hint at one. Thomas felt as if he stood on the lip of the cliff again, teetering. "Is this because you deal in death every day? A man who holds the life of others in his hands. A man willing to take life too, is what I hear. That is good. I do not like cowards or weaklings. But I do not altogether trust you."

Al-Zagal glanced aside to the view, an itch he could not stop scratching.

"Do you need to trust me, Malik? It is true I have gained somewhat of a reputation, but it is not something I have sought."

"It seems to me it is something that seeks you out. You draw death to you." Al-Zagal nodded, pleased with his own analysis. "Take the letter, Thomas Berrington, and do for me what you have done for others. Find the man who killed the woman. If what is written there is true others are at risk. I will have no more deaths in Ronda." The Sultan uncurled his legs and dropped to the floor. Thomas turned away, taking the move as a dismissal, but he was called back.

"Wait. I also hear you are a skilled fighter. Even Olaf Torvaldsson is said to respect you, and I believe he respects few men." Al-Zagal walked to one of the arches. He raised a hand, an invitation for Thomas to join him.

The Spanish forces were arrayed across the land. Trees had already been felled, their trunks split to supply firewood. Smoke from the fires rose into the air, tugged away to the east. Above the distant hills white cloud bubbled, but over the plain the air was a dust-hazed blue.

"Tell me – why don't they attack?" said al-Zagal.

"It is true I know how to fight, Malik, but only another man, not a battle."

Al-Zagal shook his head, not believing the words. "They have cannon, they have muskets, they have men in plenty. And yet they wait, and I would know what they wait for."

"Perhaps our surrender, Malik?"

Al-Zagal turned to Thomas. "Then they will wait a long time. Ronda is impregnable, they must know this. So why are they here?"

Thomas said nothing, believing he had already made his position clear.

"You are friend to the Spanish King and Queen, are you not?"

"Friend may be too strong a word, Malik."

"That is not my understanding." He turned back to

the view. "Do you think they are out there? The King? The Queen?"

"The Queen would not be on the battlefield," Thomas said.

"Perhaps. Fernando, then. That is his name, is it not? Is that what you call him when you and he are alone at dinner? When the three of you are sharing a supper? Do you call them Fernando and Isabel?"

Thomas shook his head. *Please, let me go find a bed and sleep.* He had sent Lubna into town in search of accommodation. She should have found something by now.

"They are waiting to talk," Thomas said. "Instead of attacking they would prefer to negotiate. They want you to surrender the city without a fight."

"Why would I do that when my position is so strong? If I sent you to them you would know if the King is there, wouldn't you? You can report back to me what their forces are, how the men act, if they are ready for a fight or not." Al-Zagal nodded. "Yes, perhaps I will send you out to talk."

"When?" Thomas asked. "Before or after I solve the murder?"

"My brother told me you can be insolent. He may have given you more allowance than he should. Be aware I am not him. Do not think you can treat me in the same way." Al-Zagal waved a hand. "Go, find me the killer. Let someone know where you are. When I am ready for you to talk with the Spanish I will send a message."

CHAPTER 14

Thomas believed the library empty until he heard a voice call from around a shelf of papers and a slim man appeared. He was dressed simply in a rough cotton shirt and felt trousers, his feet bare. A dark beard reached half way down his chest and his hair was hidden beneath a turban. He looked Thomas up and down, doubt on his face, but he was hardly one to judge.

"Can I help you?"

"Are you in charge here?" Thomas was aware of the letter al-Zagal had given him but did not want to reveal any information yet. He wanted to judge the man for himself first.

"I am." He glanced around at the shelves, the books and maps, an expression of satisfaction on his face. "This is my domain, such as it is." A familiar scent of paper filled the air and dust motes drifted through sunbeams that spilled through high windows.

Thomas gazed around the treasures assembled. "It's a fine library. How many documents do you have?"

The man smiled. "Over ten thousand." And when he saw the look of confusion on Thomas's face, added, "What you see here is merely the entrance. The main collection is farther in. You are a scholar?" There was no judgement in his gaze now.

"I am a physician," Thomas said.

"Ah, we have a fine copy of *al-Kitab al-Mansuri* containing many illustrations, if you would like to see it." The man warmed to his topic, keen to show the breadth and depth of learning within his reach.

"I have my own copy at home in Gharnatah, but the drawings are poor."

"Let me show you, sir." The librarian turned away. Thomas followed, slowing when he rounded a corner which revealed the extent of the entire library. It stretched two hundred feet, fine shelves holding books stacked to the ceiling. Only one space was clear, a low table set with papers. Thomas realised this must have been where the librarian had been working when he entered.

He allowed the man to bring a heavy book with leather bindings and lay it on the table. Thomas sat, crossing his legs. He made a show of studying the tome though he knew the content well. The librarian was correct – the illustrations were exquisite, and Thomas wished his copy was as fine as this. The detail shown for operating on the eye was the best he had ever seen.

"It is a fine example," he said, causing the librarian to look up from a book he had been studying. "You possess an impressive collection. You must have many visitors."

"Not as many as the books deserve. Is it true the libraries of Gharnatah possess over a million tomes?"

"Three million, I have heard."

"More than a man could read in a lifetime."

Thomas laughed. "More than a man could count in a lifetime." He was pleased to see the librarian smile. "Even so you have a wonderful collection. A friend told me I had to visit."

"We do not possess millions of books, certainly, but the ones we have are of fine quality, I believe. Who is your friend?"

"You probably do not know her."

"But she must know the library if she recommended it."

"Yes, I suppose she must." Thomas turned more pages of the al-Mansur, not concentrating, using his peripheral vision to study the librarian. "Her name is Najma." He took care to use the present tense. He slid a hand inside his shirt and withdrew the letter, laid it flat on the table so the librarian could see its contents. "I believe she carried this letter from you. Your name is Khalil, is it not? Khalil bin Ahmad Basri?"

Thomas watched as the man stared at the letter, trying to judge what he knew. Trying to judge if this man might be involved in some way but failing to see any link.

Khalil reached for the letter but stopped before his fingers touched it. He glanced up, meeting Thomas's eyes. "Yes, this is my writing. My signature, as I'm sure you already know. Where did you meet Najma?"

"A few days ride east. Is she a friend?"

Khalil raised a shoulder, his eyes returning to the letter. "Not a friend. But I know her. I heard she was taking messages to the Sultan and asked would she carry another." He lifted his gaze to meet Thomas's. "Did this reach him?"

"It was he who gave it to me," Thomas said. "I am curious about the contents. Do you state the truth here?" He reached out and tapped the paper.

Khalil's eyes flicked away and Thomas saw unease.

"I seek the person you write of," he said. "What did you say the town calls him, the Incubus? Why is that? Your note seems deliberately mysterious. How much more do you know, for this does not state everything, does it?"

"There is too much to put in a single letter," said Khalil, his eyes continuing to find something fascinating on one of the shelves.

"Then tell me," Thomas said. "The Sultan has tasked me with finding this man and stopping the deaths."

Khalil snuffled a laugh. "Stopping him? How is that possible when no-one has ever seen him? Why do you think they call him the Incubus? He comes in the night, darker than shadows, and steals the breath of his victims. People say a man – no, a creature – haunts Ronda. A wraith that can never be seen. It appears in the bedrooms of women, young, beautiful women, and makes love to them. Sweet, exquisite love such as they have never experienced before. And then, in the morning he is gone." Khalil's amusement faded as he spoke, his eyes turning distant.

"I take you for an intelligent man," Thomas said. "You cannot believe in a supernatural creature, can you?"

"No. But not all are as me. Many do." His gaze finally returned to Thomas. "The Sultan has truly asked you to search for the man?"

Thomas nodded.

"I went to the Governor with what I knew, but he dismissed my fears. I sent this to the Sultan in hope he would believe me."

"Could it not have waited until he arrived?"

"The deaths are coming more often. At first there was just one, and for a long time after no more. This was before they called him what they do now. And then, a little less than a year ago came a second death. Then a third." Khalil shook his head. "There have been over a dozen that I know of, and there may be others. Not all are recognised, some people prefer to say nothing for fear they might be chosen next."

"Do you know names?" Thomas asked.

Khalil nodded.

"Then make me a list, and where they lived."

"Where who lived?"

Thomas jerked upright, aware he and Khalil had been leaning closer together as they talked. He reached out and drew the letter toward himself before turning to see a slim woman standing with a hand against one of the shelves. She had long dark hair, ornately curled, her face beautiful other than for a strain around her eyes that detracted from the perfection.

"Nobody," Khalil said before Thomas could reply. "This man was looking at the *al-Mansuri*. He is a physician."

The woman turned her attention to Thomas and it was as if he had been captured in its intensity. He had known many women such as this, had lived with one such for half a year and mistakenly believed himself beyond their wiles. "You must be Thomas Berrington." She smiled, but the expression lacked warmth.

"You have the advantage of me."

"Oh, I think not. I am Francesca. A friend of Khalil's. Is that not so?"

Thomas saw Khalil nod, a look of infatuation on his face.

"You are a friend to our new eunuch, are you not?" Francesca said. She remained where she was, making no move to approach closer.

"If you mean Jorge, then yes." Thomas stood, wanting to assert himself. "Are you a member of the harem?"

A laugh. "Me? Oh, I am not worthy. I work there, that

is all. He is handsome, your friend, isn't he?"

"He thinks so," Thomas said. He was aware of Khalil also standing. The man came past him. He approached Francesca but a flash of her eyes stopped him in his tracks. "Are you here to visit Khalil or for some other purpose?"

The sharpness of her gaze met his, something of ice in hers, ice crazed with frost, something not quite right lying beneath the surface. "I like to visit all this knowledge." She stroked her fingers across the spine of a book. "And Khalil is a perfect guide to the wonders that lie within. Are you not, my sweet?" She smiled at the librarian, who nodded so hard it seemed he might be doing so for days. "But you are obviously discussing matters beyond the knowledge of a mere woman. I will leave you to your business."

As she began to turn away Thomas said, "No, stay. I have to go." He glanced at Khalil. "But you won't forget what I asked?" He didn't want to mention the names or the killer again, not in front of this woman. He left them to their pursuit of knowledge, or whatever else Francesca had truly come for. When he reached the end of the long room Thomas turned back. Francesca and Khalil stood together. She had placed a hand on his shoulder, having to reach up to do so. A strange couple, Thomas thought. Such a plain man with such a beautiful woman. Just like he and Helena had been.

As he turned away he smiled. Khalil's list would be the start of his investigation. Whatever was going on Thomas was sure he would have the puzzle solved before long. All it required was logic and determination. He believed he was starting to learn the way of such things.

Chapter 15

"Tell me what you saw on the clifftop," Thomas said, "in the moments before the man threw her over." He sat in the small room which was all Lubna had been able to find. The room was in the eaves of a house on the edge of town. She and Thomas sat side by side on a hard, narrow bed. Jorge had taken the only chair, more a stool really, his knees almost touching his chin. Jorge had accommodation within the palace and an expectation he was to manage the affairs of the harem alongside Helena.

"I saw little," said Jorge. "Enough to see what was happening, but not enough to identify the man even if he walked into this room now. It was all too far away and too dark."

Thomas looked toward Lubna who, he knew, had sharp eyesight, but she shook her head.

"As Jorge says, it was dark. It was almost as if he knew we were watching and didn't want to show his face."

"Whoever it was would have no idea we were below," Thomas said. "There was no reason for him to hide his identity."

Lubna smiled. "If a man is intent on murder then surely hiding his identity is part and parcel of what he does. And don't forget the woman we saw. Was she part of it, too?"

"I don't know. Could there be two working together?

It would be unusual."

"This librarian you spoke with, could he have done it? The letter might be nothing more than a pretence to hide his involvement."

"He was strange, I admit. Cold. But I didn't see him as a killer. Besides, he doesn't look strong enough to lift a woman and throw her the way we saw."

"How much strength does it take to kill someone if you take them by surprise, or push them over a cliff?" said Jorge. He leaned forward, intent. "You said the woman's dead companion was a soldier. Not such an easy victim."

Thomas shook his head. "I don't see the librarian capable of murder. I believe he wrote the letter with the best of intentions and passed it into Najma's care. I intend to visit the barracks to try and find out who was detailed to accompany her, whether there was a second companion."

"You said there was one horse drawing the cart, and assumed another. Doesn't that point to only one soldier accompanying her?."

"So where did the his horse go? I believe someone took it and fled. A second man. Perhaps another soldier."

"Or the horse wandered off, or was killed and you simply didn't find the body." Jorge shook his head. "What does this letter say?"

Thomas unfolded it, though he had studied it long enough and could have related the contents without reference. The words were few, written in neat Arabic.

There is someone hunting down men and women in the town. A dozen dead so far and, I fear, more to follow. Nobody knows how the killer strikes and nobody has ever seen him. The most recent death occurred within the harem itself –a place that is

*meant to be safe from strangers. I have spoken with
a woman I believe survived an attack. She told me
a man came to her over several nights, and on the
last night he tried to kill her by strangulation. She
cried out and the man fled when he heard others
coming.*

There was no signature.

"We need to know who these others are," said Jorge as
he took the letter and examined it. A pointless gesture.

"I asked Khalil to draw up a list of names and where
they lived. If one victim was from the harem then you
are the best placed to find out more about the death he
speaks of."

"We need to find out who last night's victim was first,"
said Lubna. "The letter doesn't say when the previous
killing occurred. It could have been months ago. Go back
and question your librarian. We need dates, details."

Thomas looked at her. She was right, of course. His
mind was still clouded by events of recent days, and he
wasn't thinking straight. He needed more sleep.

"I know what we need," he said. "But before we can
identify the woman her body has to be found."

"Can't we just tell someone what happened?"

"And that we failed to report the death immediately?"
Thomas shook his head. "It would look suspicious. We
might be suspected of throwing her over ourselves."

"They have no reason to suspect either of you," said
Lubna.

"Who is beyond suspicion?" Thomas said. "Who can
we ask to pass that way and notice her lying at the foot
of the cliff?"

"It has to be someone we trust," said Jorge.

"Helena?" said Lubna. "She was outside the city walls

at the time." Her eyes met Thomas's but he read nothing there.

"And she has been a little less hostile lately," he said. "She was helpful leading the others to the gate, even if she did want to betray us to the Spanish."

"We need someone else, too," said Jorge. "Someone of influence, like Faris or Yusuf. I don't suppose al-Zagal will venture out of his palace, even for Helena."

"He has other things on his mind."

"Yusuf will do it if you ask," said Lubna. "You could even tell him the reason."

Thomas thought it through. "We shouldn't tell him anything yet." He reached out and picked up the letter. "The deaths this tells of will not have gone back many months or it would have been written before. We need to know who was present in the town when the killings took place." He looked at Jorge. "Ask Helena to come here, tell her I want to talk to her."

"If she will come," said Jorge, standing. He had to bend over to avoid hitting his head on the ceiling.

"She will come," said Lubna. "She has changed this last year." She placed a hand on Thomas's leg, as if to say her sister might have changed, but he still belonged with the youngest of Olaf's daughters.

"Tell her the reason if you want," Thomas said, "but I agree with Lubna, she will come." Thomas indicated the chair. "Sit again first, I want to ask you something."

Jorge did as requested, his knees ungainly once more. The sun beat on the tiles directly over their heads and sweat beaded each of their faces. The single small window was thrown wide, the door too, but no breeze entered to alleviate the stifling atmosphere. The sound of other lodgers in the house came from below, many of them those Thomas had led through the hills.

"Ask away," said Jorge, "but if it's advice on women, remember I believe you a lost cause."

Thomas offered a sarcastic scowl, knowing it was lost on Jorge. "I need to know who can be trusted and who not," he said. "I already have a list of suspects but it is a short one, and there are almost certainly more."

"Start with your list," said Jorge. "I have given it some thought too, so let's see if any match." He wiped a hand across his face, clearing his eyes of sweat, but more popped up instantly across his brow.

Thomas held up a finger. "Faris is at the top."

"Because you dislike the man, or do you have some other reason?"

"It's true, I do dislike him, but he was present in the gorge, and we both know he wouldn't hesitate to kill."

"Usually he has others do the killing for him."

"This is more intimate, isn't it?" Thomas said. "All the victims we know of have been women, all beautiful. Though Khalil says men have died too. Faris wouldn't send someone else to kill a woman. He would relish performing the act himself."

"So Faris," said Jorge. "Agreed. We need to know if he was present in Ronda when the others were killed."

"You know he moves around on business. I suspect he deals with Moor and Spaniard alike. We know there are leading families in al-Andalus already talking with Spain to ensure their positions when the end comes, and there will be such in Ronda. I suspect Faris considers himself a go-between in such matters. He will take his cut, too."

Jorge nodded but said nothing.

"And if Faris is on the list there is someone else, reluctant as I am to put him there."

"Yusuf," said Jorge, his face uncharacteristically grim.

"No, not Yusuf," said Lubna. "He has eaten at our table. He is your friend, Thomas."

"He was. But he spends much time with Faris now. They were both in the gorge that day. Najma hadn't been dead long when I found her, a matter of hours. Either of them had the opportunity, or both together. Perhaps they lay in wait to ambush the cart, killed the guard and pursued the woman."

Jorge stared at the wooden floor, marked by worm holes. "If it is one of them you know we can do nothing."

"We have to do something. I have punished those close to the Sultan before."

"But not a Sultan's son," said Jorge. "And Faris is more powerful than a Sultan. Richer, certainly. Threads of influence link all these people, threads mere mortals such as us dare not interfere with."

"So we let them go on killing?"

"If it is them. You have made a case, although I cannot believe Yusuf is involved. Yes, he has changed, but not as much as this would indicate. I see him when he is with you. He still worships you, Thomas."

Thomas waved a hand, but Lubna said, "It is true. You don't see it because there is much you don't see about people. If he was capable of doing what you say I would have sensed something, and Jorge certainly would." She glanced at the eunuch. "You believe him incapable of killing, don't you?"

Jorge frowned. "Of killing, no, your father has made sure of that. Yusuf has been well trained, as the son of a Sultan should be, and we know he has fought. But there's a difference between killing a man in the heat of battle and killing a woman in cold blood. Yusuf likes women, he loves them. He has a sensual soul I approve of." Jorge shook his head. "No, not Yusuf." He looked up. "So, who else?"

"That man, Giovanni," Thomas said.

Jorge laughed. "You're jealous is all. Why him?"

"He was present in our camp."

"So was I," said Jorge. "If you start suspecting every male in our party where will it stop? There were three hundred soldiers with us, each of them capable of killing in cold blood. It's what they do. And you were there at the head of the tunnel when Giovanni came through. He couldn't be at the base of the cliff and the top at the same time."

"He said he had visited Ronda before," Thomas said, unwilling to give the man up as a suspect yet, despite knowing what Jorge said was true. The man annoyed him with his good looks and ease with people.

"Is there anyone you don't suspect?" asked Jorge.

"Only the three of us," Thomas said.

"I'm glad to hear it." When Jorge rose from the stool for the second time he banged his head on a beam and cursed loudly. "I will ask your questions and bring any answers I find. You need to get some sleep and then talk to this librarian again."

"I don't believe you can even consider Yusuf capable of such a thing," said Lubna.

Thomas lay on the narrow bed, a hand across his eyes. He had started to drift from the world but Lubna's words brought it crashing back. He dropped his arm and turned toward her.

She had taken the chair vacated by Jorge.

"There could be more than one. Faris and Yusuf, Yusuf and the librarian…" Thomas shook his head. It ached from a surfeit of thought.

"Not Yusuf," said Lubna.

Thomas sat up. "All right, not Yusuf." But he didn't mean it, not then. "I'm tired, and I'm not thinking straight."

"You are hopeless, Thomas Berrington. It would break his heart if he discovered you suspected him."

Thomas put bare feet on the floor. "Leave it now, Lubna. I was wrong. But am I wrong about the others?"

"Oh, how can you know so much and yet so little?" Lubna stood with no need to crouch. "I'm going out. Go to sleep, it might improve your mood."

Thomas lay on the bed. "Close the door when you leave."

After Lubna had gone he lay for a time listening to the sounds of the house, cries from the street. A wind picked up and made a moaning sound in the tiles above his head, finally bringing a little breeze.

He put his arm across his eyes once more and said to the empty room, "There's nothing wrong with my mood."

Then he pushed it all aside and let sleep take him.

CHAPTER 16

When Thomas opened his eyes the room was splintered by sunlight, the heat even worse. His shirt stuck to his chest, hair plastered across his cheek. He looked around for what had roused him, sleep still hovering on the edge of his mind.

At first he believed the figure sitting at the foot of the bed was Lubna, then his eyes began to work and his nose caught a different scent, one once familiar.

"I didn't expect you to come." He sat up, leaning against the bare plaster wall at his back.

"Jorge said you wanted to talk to me," said Helena, as if that was more than reason enough.

Thomas wondered how long she had been sitting there, how long she had watched him sleep. "I'm surprised you found me."

Helena scowled, the scar that once disfigured her face now almost invisible. "Jorge told me where you were, of course. I can go if your brain is still addled, but next time you'll have to come to me. I'm not at your beck and call anymore."

Thomas ran a hand across his face. "Give me a second." He rose and went to a small table beneath the window, poured himself a cup of warm water and drank.

He turned and leaned on the edge of the window, the faint breeze cooling the shirt that stuck to his back.

"You know Faris well, don't you?"

Helena nodded. "Of course. He is an important man."

"I meant as a woman knows a man."

Helena's eyes held his. "That too." Thomas didn't expect to see a show of modesty, not from her, but the guile he had grown accustomed to was absent.

"What is he like as a man to a woman? Is he…" He realised it was he who was reluctant, but knew he must ask. "Can he be demanding?"

The ghost of a smile flickered across Helena's lips. "Say what you mean, Thomas. Do you want to know if he's rough? Or demanding in other ways?"

"Rough, yes," Thomas said. "Does he take pleasure in hurting a woman?"

Helena shook her head. "Not with me, and not with anyone else. I'd have heard if he was. They would come to me if they had a complaint. Are you asking for a reason, or are you concerned for my wellbeing all of a sudden?" Once more there came the trace of a smile, and Thomas believed she was enjoying his discomfort. Petty victories.

"And Yusuf? You have shared a bed with him?"

"Not often, but yes, in the last year. Two or three times, and…" This time it was Helena's voice trailed away. Her eyes moved to examine the rumpled bedclothes. She smoothed a section with the flat of her hand.

"What," Thomas said. "Is Yusuf violent?"

Helena laughed, her mood broken. Her reluctance too. "Yusuf? We are talking of the same sweet boy, aren't we? No, too much the other way if anything. He needs to be more forceful, not less. I have tried to teach him, but he seems unwilling to learn." Helena's eyes returned to Thomas. "Do you know what he spoke of the first time I was with him? He asked about you. Even as we coupled he talked of you and I had to shut him up."

"You should have told him what we did together," Thomas said.

"Oh, I did, and he wanted to mimic everything we ever indulged in. Wanted to know how you made love, as if it was something to model himself on." Helena laughed, making her own view on the subject clear. "Was that why you wanted me? To ask about my sex life? Does it interest you all of a sudden?"

"I'm trying to find a killer," Thomas said.

Helena stared at him. The room was growing darker, but her intense blue eyes and almost white hair seemed to gather what light there was. "Again?"

"Yes, again."

"Why do you do it?"

"Because nobody else cares."

"Have you ever considered it may be you who does not allow anyone else to care?"

"You know better. When I was in Spain—" Thomas stopped, waved a hand in annoyance at himself. What he had learned in Spain had nothing to do with here and now. "Do you like the new man who was on the journey, Giovanni?"

Helena smiled. "He has a certain something about him, does he not?"

"Have you seduced him yet?"

"No."

Thomas sighed. He would have to find another way.

"It was he who seduced me," said Helena. "And extremely well, too. Perhaps I should have him teach Yusuf technique, because that is something any young man would do well to strive for. Do you want to know if he could be your killer? That is what these questions are about, isn't it?"

Thomas nodded.

"I would say not," said Helena. "He understands a woman's needs well. Almost too well – better than anyone I have ever known. Better even than you." Again the smile. Helena was incapable of ignoring the slightest opportunity for an insult. She rose, the top of her head almost touching the roof tiles. "Is there anything else, or have we finished discussing my sex life?"

"I want you to discover a body for me," Thomas said, pleased to see surprise on her face. He leaned forward to explain the plan, catching Helena's wrist and drawing her down to sit on the bed. Which is how Lubna found them a half hour later when she returned with food. It was too dark for the subterfuge to work now, so they arranged to meet early the following morning.

"Oh help, help! Someone is dead!"

Thomas watched with amusement, recalling the Mummers' plays that came to Leominster at Christmas time. Their performances had been truly awful, and Helena was worse. But she didn't need to be good.

Poor actress that she was, Helena's timing was perfect. As a guard rounded the corner she let loose a second scream. The man broke into a jog which brought him to her side. Beyond, Thomas came into view around the other corner, also at a run. He dared not allow Helena full rein for her theatrics, not based on current performance.

"There," she pointed. "There is something at the foot of the gorge."

The guard approached the lip with care. There was no barrier here, no wall or fence. One false step would send him tumbling after the woman already lying at the bottom of the cliff.

Sunlight streamed into the narrow gorge and the body lay in full view. Thomas was surprised no-one had discovered it already, but knew without Lubna's efforts it was likely it would never have been found. After he and Jorge began their ascent she had spent some time examining the body, but found nothing useful to them. What she had discovered, by looking up, was that the body lay too close to the bottom of the cliff and would be invisible from the top. So she had dragged the broken woman closer to the edge of the river until it lay in full view.

"Did you see her fall?" asked the guard.

Helena shook her head, a hand covering her mouth. "I was taking my usual walk when I saw her." She gasped a sound, as if heartbroken. "Down there."

Not a her, Thomas thought, we cannot tell that yet, not from this distance. But the guard barely noticed, if at all.

"This is a dangerous place to walk," he said. "You should find somewhere safer. There are some fine walks to the north of the town."

Thomas shook his head. This wasn't going to plan, not at all.

"It is obviously dangerous," said Helena, lowering her hand to reveal her beauty. "I can see that now." The guard swallowed, unable to look away. Helena cast her eyes down and shook her head, brilliant white hair shimmering in the sunlight.

"What is going on here?" Thomas asked, feeling the need to take control before the situation descended into absurdity.

"Who are you?"

Thomas wondered why guards always asked that, even in a situation such as this. "I am Thomas Berrington, charged by the Sultan to investigate a series of deaths in the town." He turned to look into the gorge. "I can see I came at the right time." Listening to himself he knew his own acting abilities were no better than Helena's.

"I've heard of you," said the guard. "You're friend to the eunuch."

"I am. Someone should go down to see if they're still alive. Is there a way?"

"There's an iron gate where they fetch water, but..." The man looked across the plain to where the Spanish army sat.

"I understand there is also a gate to the north," Thomas said. "The body has to be recovered. If I go with no more than two companions we will be no threat to the Spanish. They may not even see us. The Sultan will be pleased I am making progress." He felt more comfortable, aware he was no longer putting on a pretence.

He watched the guard turn the request over, the process laborious. It was clear thinking for himself was discouraged. His life would consist of long hours of boredom punctuated by moments of malice when he could make someone else's life a misery. Thomas's mention of the Sultan appeared to be a deciding factor in his eventual decision.

"Come with me, we'll go to the palace. I can't allow you through the gate without permission."

"Of course."

Thomas glanced at Helena as he followed the guard. He nodded, letting her know she was released. Despite the standard of her acting, she had done well.

Chapter 17

The last gate crashed open against a high stone wall, the third they had passed through on their way to the foot of the cliff. A narrow track cobbled with stones from the plain switched backward and forward. Houses rose precipitously on the town side, the land dropping steeply away on the other. The baths lay beyond the gate, abandoned now, the owner no doubt complaining about loss of business. Thomas wondered why he had not remained open. There was, after all, an entire army arrayed nearby, and soldiers would have availed themselves of the services on offer even if they had no wish to wash the stink from their bodies.

"You're on your own from here." The guard who had accompanied them this far carried a bunch of heavy keys he had used to unlock the barriers as they descended. "I'll wait until sunset. If you recover the body I can let you in. If not return before dark. Any later and you'll have to take your chances."

Thomas nodded to the two men accompanying him and led the way beyond the town wall. He had wanted to bring Jorge but had not been allowed to see him. Instead, Abraham al-Haquim had assigned two soldiers, a sign he didn't altogether trust Thomas. It had taken several hours to first find and then persuade the Governor of what he wanted. Thomas was aware of their vulnerability, weapons' belts empty. One man carried a long pole that once contained a battle banner, now it was replaced by a torn bed sheet which was more or less white. He held it down for the moment, a safeguard in case they were caught.

There was no sight of the Spanish army, which lay behind a low rise in the ground where wheat still grew, the heads beginning to fatten. Thomas led the way, following a narrow path that snaked along one side of the field past an abandoned farmhouse. He knew the Spanish would normally burn all crops for miles around, part of their policy of total destruction which left towns to starve after defeat. He was surprised they had not started to do so here yet.

As the path rose cannon appeared to their right, arrayed along the low ridge they were about to cross. The closest was no more than a hundred yards from the path, and one of the artillerymen called out a warning. It took a moment for Thomas to place the language before he identified it as French. He had heard they provided the best mercenaries for working with gunpowder and shot, but was surprised all the same. There was no love lost between France and Spain, and the northern borders were constantly encroached on. Still, mercenaries fought for whoever paid best.

The man beside Thomas raised his pole, the grey-white flag barely moving. It would have been better not to have to use it, but Thomas knew they were likely to be spotted and had planned for such.

The bombardier approached, calling his companions after him. The man was short, whip thin, his face dark on one side from the back-blow of gunpowder ejected from the cannon.

He called out in the French of the south that bore little resemblance to that used in court, wanting to know who they were and what they wanted. Thomas replied in the same dialect, having spent four years in that land, pleased to see surprise on the man's face.

"You are not a Moor?"

Thomas shook his head. "My companions, but I am not."

The man grinned, exposing three teeth, and those did not appear to be any too secure. "You are from Languedoc then, like me? What are you doing with these heathens?"

"I could ask the same," Thomas said, nodding at the arrayed Spanish army.

The man held a hand up and rubbed his fingers together, the grin plastered in place. "You want to talk with someone?"

"I do."

"Someone important?"

"Is that you?"

Thomas's response caused the man to laugh hard. "Yes, that is me, of course it is me."

"Is the King here?"

The man straightened, his face losing all humour. "Even a mercenary like me will not tell you that. You want to see someone I'll take you, but only you. The heathens stay here." He waved an arm to his companions. "Watch them. If they even look at you oddly gut them both. Slowly." He turned and walked away surprisingly fast on short legs. Thomas had to trot to catch up. When he glanced back it was to see his two companions seated on the ridge starting a game of dice. They had lowered the flag of parley.

The bombardier led the way along a series of paths

that wound through the massed soldiers. Tents were erected in places, but most of the men slept on the ground, blankets marking a few square feet of territory. Fires burned, the smell of roast meat strong in the air. An army this size would have spread far and wide, slaughtering all the livestock they came across to leave a swathe of hunger behind.

Soldiers sat up to watch Thomas pass. He knew they would note the way he was dressed as an Arab nomad in dark blue robes and a tagelmust, and they would mark him as an enemy. Thomas had to trust in their sense of chivalry, something he had witnessed at first hand before. But the men around him were not knights and knew little of chivalry. They dealt in mayhem, in blood, pain and death; and they relished that role.

Two large tents lay ahead, the path through the throng more direct. The bombardier led Thomas to the entrance of the first and left him without a word to anyone. Two pikemen guarded the entrance, their gaze cold.

"I am here to talk," Thomas said, switching to Spanish.

"On what business?"

"A woman has fallen from the cliffs and I wish permission to recover her body."

The guard appeared to be taken aback. Perhaps he believed Thomas had come to surrender the town.

"I'll fetch someone." He ducked through the entrance.

Thomas waited, knowing any attempt at conversation with the other was pointless. The first guard appeared after a moment and motioned Thomas inside.

Thomas ducked as he passed through the entrance. He drew his tagelmust aside so it hung down his back to leave his head uncovered. The tent was divided by a thick canvas barrier, the side he had entered taking up barely a quarter of the interior. A man in a grey robe was bent over a table and he waved Thomas to approach. When he turned his head an expression of shock crossed his face – almost the same as the one on Thomas's. His hand fell to his waist, but there was no weapon there.

"Lawrence," Thomas said, fighting for calm. "You're meant to be dead."

"I'm surprised to see you too, old friend. Although I hear of your exploits now and again. I was told you had returned to Granada."

Friend? The last time Thomas had seen Lawrence the man had revealed himself as a companion to Abbot Mandana, the cleric who had been killing women in a perverse fashion while Thomas was in Qurtuba to heal Prince Juan. He had believed both men dead, attacked by wolves.

"Sit," said Lawrence. "You look like you've seen a ghost."

His voice was unchanged, as was his manner. Thomas had liked the man once, as much as he had liked anyone. Considered him a kindred spirit until he revealed his treachery.

Thomas remained on his feet, incapable of movement, so Lawrence stood. Thomas took a step back, his hand twitching to grasp something. Perhaps they were both lucky he had no weapon.

"It is me." Lawrence laughed and slapped his chest. "I'm alive and well. I serve the King now."

"Does he know of your treachery?" Thomas had never spoken of it to Fernando, only telling him the ex-priest had been killed in the wolf attack. There had been too many involved with Mandana, many who remained at large, to worry about the dead.

"There was never any treachery," said Lawrence.

"I saw you with my own eyes, heard you with my own ears. You and Mandana worked side by side."

"It was not as it appeared," said Lawrence. "I stayed close to *prevent* further death."

Thomas shook his head. "All the time I was trying to track him down you were helping him. You could have told me who the killer was at any time and you chose not to."

"Because he had to be exposed completely. You saw the power he possessed. Even after you uncovered his crimes he remained at court. It was only kidnapping Juan that placed him beyond the pale."

"Who knows any of this? Fernando? I doubt it."

"No-one knows, no-one at all. And I would prefer it remain that way."

"So you can claim whatever you wish? There is no-one to tell the lie of it. What, are you going to call the guards in and tell them I am an assassin, have them deal with me?"

Lawrence smiled. "I could, but I speak the truth. I mean you no harm, not now, not then."

"Prove it." Thomas's mood was unforgiving. To fight a man he knew as an enemy was one thing, to discover someone he had once considered a friend fought on the wrong side rankled.

Lawrence cocked his head to one side. He looked as if he was about to speak when a voice from beyond the partition called his name. He went past Thomas into the inner chamber, returning a moment later and calling Thomas through. Their argument, it seemed, would have to wait.

Inside was another man Thomas recognised, but

not the one he expected. Sitting at a table picking at a haunch of lamb was Martin de Alarcón. The man had acted as Muhammed's gaoler during his capture, and had returned the captured Sultan of Gharnatah to Thomas's door a year before because there was no longer a place for him in the palace of al-Hamra.

Martin rose, smiling. "Thomas!" He embraced him, slapping his back. "What in the name of all that's holy are you doing here? Still getting involved in matters you shouldn't, I expect. Come, sit, join me for dinner. Lawrence, fetch a chair for Thomas."

This time, when the chair was brought, Thomas sat.

"What is my friend doing with himself these days?" asked Martin, having no need to explain who he was talking of.

In turn Thomas felt no residual loyalty to the man who had once ruled Gharnatah, albeit badly. "There is a new Sultan on the hill, or rather an old one. Muhammed is living on the Albayzin, in the house of his mother."

Martin laughed. "Run home to Mamma, has he? That doesn't surprise me. He was never strong, not where it counted." He tapped his forehead. "So tell me, what brings you into the heart of the enemy camp? You are still loyal to your heathen masters, I take it?"

"I come to ask a favour," Thomas said, "but I need a moment to gather myself." He glanced at the canvas barrier, knowing Lawrence would be able to hear everything, but spoke anyway. "How long have you known Lawrence?"

"A few months. The King trusts him – they have a little history, I believe. Why, is he a friend of yours, too?"

"He is…" Thomas hesitated. He had liked Lawrence, trusted him once with his life. Yet he struggled to accept the explanation offered. It was too easy to claim innocence when the only man to disprove it was dead. Yet if he raised his suspicions now it could result in the man's execution. "Not a friend, but I knew him in Qurtuba. I believed him dead."

"No, as alive as you or I, but who knows what tomorrow brings for any of us. So, what is this favour you seek? If it is in my power to grant it I will, you know that." He smiled. "As long as you haven't come to ask for my surrender."

Thomas made an effort to pull himself back to the matter in hand. "A woman fell from the cliff two nights since – murdered, I believe. I wish to recover her body so I can find out who she is and what befell her. I need your men to allow me and two companions to enter the gorge so we can return her to the town."

"Still getting involved in matters that are none of your business, I see. Of course you can recover the body. I'll send Lawrence to pass word. Now eat, and tell me of how low Boabdil has fallen."

CHAPTER 18

"I think I know who she is," said Lubna. She stood beside Thomas as he began to examine the dead woman. Jorge remained in one corner, as far from the body as he could get without leaving the room. His eyes sought something fascinating on the ceiling. The place that had been provided for them to work in lay outside the walls of the palace, some kind of vestibule to the barracks, but it possessed a stout wooden door which was now closed. From beyond, the occasional voices of soldiers passed to and fro.

Thomas asked for more light as he cut away the woman's clothing to reveal her dark-skinned body. It showed few clues beyond the damage done to her by the fall. Her left eye remained undamaged and Thomas bent close to study it, finding no blood vessels burst. He was sure something had been knotted at her throat in the moments before she was thrown, but if so it had left no sign, no marks on her ebony skin. He considered the fragility of existence, ended in the moment between two heartbeats.

"So who is she?"

"Her name is Katarina Morales. Married to a Rodrigo Morales, a wealthy trader. He came to Ronda five or six years ago, already rich, and set himself up as a provider of African servants. She became his wife a year later. She had been considered for the harem but rejected."

Thomas glanced at her. "You've found out a great deal. African servants? I assume you mean Morales deals in slaves."

Lubna nodded.

"Have you finished?" Jorge asked without looking at the body.

"Not yet. Wait outside if you want, you're no use to me here."

"I am offering comfort to the deceased. Does the husband know yet, Lubna?"

"I don't think so. He has been going around town telling anyone who will listen his wife is missing. I managed to ask someone who knew her well what she looked like. This is her, I'm sure."

"I would like to be the first to tell him," Thomas said.

"You want to see his face when he hears the news," said Jorge to the wall.

"What do you know of the husband?" Thomas checked the entire body but learned nothing new. She had been tossed over the cliff alive. It had been the fall that killed her, the man at the top its cause. "I think we're done here. Let's go find this Don Morales. You will prepare her, Lubna?"

"Of course. The name sounds Spanish so I assume she is Christian."

"I'll ask. They may have converted if they've been in al-Andalus for some time, but best not to assume anything. Tidy her up as best you can in case he wants to see her."

* * *

Rodrigo Morales lived in a tall house whose rear walls rose directly from the top of the cliff face. There was no shop on the ground floor. If he was a slaver he would conduct trade well away from where he lived.

Thomas knocked on the door and waited until a servant opened it. The man was tall, as dark as the dead woman, dressed in some kind of uniform that looked both uncomfortable and out of place. His Arabic was perfect, coloured only by a slight accent from the far south beyond the great desert.

"I'd like to speak with your master," Thomas said.

The man looked from him to Jorge, appearing to find more to like there.

"To what purpose? He does no business here. If you wish to discuss a purchase you will need to wait until the end of the week and visit the marketplace like everyone else."

"This is in regard to his wife. I understand she is missing."

The Nubian's mouth tightened and he stepped back, but only so he could close the door in their faces.

"I like him," said Jorge.

"You like everyone."

"That is true. But he has a presence, don't you think?"

"I must have been looking the other way."

"There's a lot to—" But Jorge was interrupted as the door opened again and the servant waved them inside, his face less welcoming than the gesture.

The hallway was double height with a gallery that ran along three sides. They were shown into a room at the rear where a man waited. If he was Don Morales he was considerably older than his wife. He rose from a stuffed chair to face them.

"You have news of Katarina?"

"Can you describe her to me?" Thomas said.

"If you know something," said Morales, his voice curt, "tell me now."

"We should sit and discuss this in a civilised manner, sir."

Morales took a step forward, obviously used to getting his own way. "Tell me now or I will have you thrown out!"

"There is no need, we are perfectly capable of leaving on our own." Thomas turned, annoyed when a hand fell on his shoulder. He was tempted to grab the man's wrist and inflict some hurt. Instead he allowed himself to be turned.

"My wife is dear to me," said Morales, his voice softening a little. "She has never stayed out all night before, let alone two. If you know something then tell me, please."

"Was she originally a slave you brought to Spain?" Thomas asked, watching Morales's face.

"What business is that of yours? She came to me of her own free will. There was no coercion on my part, none at all."

"But she is of Africa?" Thomas said.

"She is. Tell me, sir, tell me what you know."

"Sit." Thomas walked past Morales and sank into another overstuffed chair across from where the man had been when they entered. He waited until Morales took his place. Jorge remained standing behind Thomas's chair. "I have some difficult news for you, Don Morales. A woman was killed two nights since, but her body only found today. I believe she may be your wife."

Morales shook his head. "You are wrong, that cannot

be. Nobody would kill my Katerina. She is loved by all who know her."

"You must have enemies in your trade," Thomas said. "Can you think of anyone who might wish you harm?"

"All men of trade have rivals, but who would harm an innocent woman?" Morales half rose. "I want to see her."

"As you wish. But I should tell you she fell a great distance."

"Is her face…" Morales slumped into his chair and put his head in his hands. "She was here, breathing, alive not three days ago. She went to meet with friends. She kissed my cheek and said she would see me on her return."

"Can you provide the name of the friends?"

The man stared into an empty fireplace for a moment before shaking his head. "Katarina has many friends. Perhaps one of the servants will know. I never pressed her on where she went or who she met with. She valued her independence. You can understand that, surely."

Thomas wondered how long the woman had been a slave before Morales took her as a wife. And why he would do such a thing instead of simply using her.

"Do you share a bed?" Thomas asked. It was an impertinent question, but one he thought he might get away with while the man was distracted.

"We have our own rooms. I am a heavy sleeper and Katarina is not. When we slept together she would often rise to come downstairs. It was my suggestion we have our own rooms so she would not disturb me. But she was…" He stopped, his breath coming in gasps, face paling. "I don't believe this is happening. It cannot be. Katarina is a loving wife. Attentive to my needs. This woman you speak of must be someone else. I have to see her, I must be sure." This time Morales made it all the way to his feet and Thomas rose too.

"We will take you, sir, but you must prepare yourself. Or perhaps the servant who let us in could identify if this woman is your wife."

"Simon? Yes, he knows her. But, but—" Morales shook his head. "It is my duty."

"Your duty is to act correctly if it is her, and to do the same if it is not. If Simon can identify her I would recommend he does so. I will send him back immediately with the news."

"Yes." Morales moved backward until the edge of the chair caught his legs and he sat heavily. "Yes, a sound suggestion, we should do that. Take him, but send him here as soon as possible. I would know the truth."

Thomas almost believed Morales cared for his wife. He allowed Jorge to leave the room, waiting a moment.

"If it is her you will want to know how she met her fate."

Morales looked up from where he had been examining the floor, a frown on his face. "Yes, yes, of course. Send me a bill and I will pay it."

"I need no payment," Thomas said, "but my companion would like to talk with your household. There may be clues as to what occurred."

Morales nodded. Thomas saw his mind was elsewhere, but took it as permission all the same. He turned and left the man to his thoughts.

Jorge was waiting in the well-appointed hallway with the Nubian servant. Thomas nodded, letting him know the plan had been agreed, before leading the dark-skinned man to where his mistress lay.

Lubna had washed the body, repaired the clothes as best she could and dressed her. A muslin cloth covered the damaged side of her face but the other was almost unmarked. She might have been asleep, other than for the stillness of her chest.

Thomas watched the servant's face carefully as he entered the room. They had walked in silence, the man unwilling to be drawn into conversation, and Thomas lacked Jorge's skill in small talk.

He waited to one side, observing as the servant approached the table. The man stared down at the body for a long time, then a shudder ran through him and he gasped.

"It is her?"

The man nodded.

"You knew her well?"

"The master does not know it but she is – she was – my sister. We were captured together, taken from our village and brought to this savage land. When Kisera was raised up by marriage she made sure the master found a place for me as well. She saved my life."

"Why would you keep the fact you are brother and sister from your master?"

The servant looked up, his face showing anger rather than grief. "Why? Only a man who has never been a slave would need to ask such a question."

Thomas felt a flare of his own anger. It was not the right time to confront the man, but he would remember his reaction. "Kisera – is that her true name?"

The servant turned. "It was until the master gave her a new one. As my name is Simki. Do you know who killed her?"

"That is what I am trying to discover. My companion is questioning Don Morales's household to see if they know anything that might help."

"I can tell you whatever you need to know. Kisera is a woman of many needs, few of which the master was able to satisfy. But she has always been discreet. He more than likely knew why she left the house but forgave her because of her beauty, and because of what she could offer him on those few occasions he asked her to share his bed."

"She was extremely beautiful."

Simki patted his chest. "Inside as well as on the surface. Inside where it counts for more." His dark eyes met Thomas's, the anger gone now, replaced with a look of cold determination. "When you discover who did this you will tell me who he is so I can kill him with my own hands."

"He will be captured and put to trial," Thomas said.

Simki's face twisted into a scowl. "And if he is a man of importance? He will be admonished and released, you know this as well as I do."

"If I tell you who it is and you kill him you know what will happen to you."

"As a mere servant, you mean? Yes, I know. But I will run. I will run fast and far, and in this land of chaos I may find a place. Or I will cross the sea and return to my homeland."

Thomas was touched by the man's loyalty, his sense of justice. He also saw in him a kindred spirit, a stranger cast adrift in a foreign land, much as he had once been himself. Except Thomas knew this man had had no choice over what became of him,

"I can make no promise."

Simki offered a soft nod, and Thomas knew a bargain had been struck between them, but whether one he would be able to deliver on he didn't know.

CHAPTER 19

"They tell me you went to the Spanish camp." Al-Zagal once more stared over the plain, a lowering sun casting long shadows. This time only he and Thomas occupied the room, which felt too large without an array of servants and concubines. "That you went without my permission, without speaking to me first."

"I consulted with your Governor, Malik, who gave permission. A body had been found."

"So I understand. What business is that of yours or mine? Even less what business of the Spanish?"

"I required access to recover the body."

"And they gave it?"

"They did, Malik."

Al-Zagal shook his head. "You are a strange man, Thomas Berrington." He turned from the view. "Are they preparing for an attack? Could you tell?" He shook his head again. "No, I doubt it, you are no soldier."

"The camp appeared peaceful," Thomas said.

"Peaceful?"

"I believe the woman was another victim of the killer you have tasked me to find, Malik."

Al-Zagal's dark eyes rose to meet Thomas's, who saw a sharp intelligence behind them, sharper than that of his brother. He knew he could not trust the man. "Does it lead you any closer to a solution?"

"Not as yet."

"So you risked yourself, you went among my enemies, and it has done you no good at all? I am beginning to wonder if what I've been told about you is true. I always considered my brother a keen judge of men, but perhaps he is not the man he used to be."

"They look lazy, the Spanish," Thomas said. "They do not appear as men who are preparing for war."

Al-Zagal waved a hand. "So why are they here? Is this some visit they are making to view the cliffs of Ronda? No – people do not care for sightseeing. And they have cannon. Cannon!"

"Which have not been prepared."

Al-Zagal scowled. "So now you know of cannon too, do you? Is there anything you do not know of?"

"A great deal, Malik, but it is true I have seen cannon used in combat, and they take a great deal of preparation. The instruments we see here are a show of force, nothing more."

"So how long does it take to prepare them?" al-Zagal asked, and Thomas realised the Sultan may never have seen artillery in action.

"Half a day, if they are skilled. The bombardiers I saw were French, so I expect them to be skilled."

Al-Zagal sighed. "What good will it do them? They cannot breach our walls nor climb the cliffs."

"Can I return to the task you set me, Malik, and pursue this killer?"

"Was the woman who died important?"

"Does it matter?"

Again the scowl. "Don't be stupid, of course it matters."

"She was the wife of a man called Morales," Thomas said.

"Rodrigo Morales? The woman's name is Katarina?"

Thomas nodded.

"I know them. Her in particular. She was considered for the harem a number of years ago but I dismissed her as–" A dismissive wave of the hand, "inappropriate to my needs."

Thomas wondered if it was the darkness of Katarina's skin that al-Zagal objected to. He had seen it before, as if the invaders with their own dark skins yearned for something belonging to this land. Helena's restoration to her position in the harem was testament to the power of northern blood. Al-Zagal's brother, Abu al-Hasan Ali, had grown besotted with a fair skinned, fair haired Greek woman. So much so it led to his own downfall and the raising up of his son, Muhammed. Who had since discovered how difficult the retention of power could be.

"It is a thread I will need to follow," Thomas said, "her presence close to the harem, even on the periphery, might be of significance."

"I forbid you entry," said al-Zagal. He turned once more to gaze through the arch, perhaps hoping the Spanish would be leaving the next time he set eyes on them.

After a moment Thomas decided he had been dismissed.

The last of the light was leaching from the sky as Thomas walked away from the palace. He followed the now familiar roadway south to his accommodation close to the town walls. He could barely believe they had arrived only three days before. Even less that he and

Lubna had been secure in their expanded house on the Albayzin only two weeks earlier. It seemed to Thomas his life was no longer his own to control, and sometimes he wondered how much worse it would get before things got better. If they ever got better.

The house was poorly maintained, lime plaster flaking from the outer surface, damp staining the walls. At least with the sun gone the room in the eaves might be a little cooler. But it seemed he would not find out yet.

As he approached the doorway a voice hailed him from up high and he saw Jorge's face at the small window.

"Stay there. We're going to eat."

Thomas waited in the street until Jorge and Lubna joined him. He hadn't thought of food, but the mention of it made him aware of how hungry he was. He tried to remember the last full meal he had eaten and couldn't. Snatched scraps, no more, for days, and he knew he should have taken up Martin de Alarcón's offer to eat with him.

"Where are we going?" Thomas asked as he fell into step beside Jorge. On his other side Lubna reached out and took his hand, a tentative gesture here in public but one she couldn't stop herself doing.

"Where everyone else is going," said Jorge, but explained no further.

"Did you get anything from the servants?" Thomas asked.

"A little. I'll tell you while we eat. What did al-Zagal want with you?"

"He heard I'd gone outside the town walls and visited the Spanish."

"Ah. Mistake?"

"Almost certainly. But it turns out he knows Morales

and his wife. He said she was unsuitable for the harem."

They turned west, the alleys narrowing until they came out into a small square. Orange trees grew, fruit beginning to form on their branches. Palms soared into the sky, birds nesting noisily in their tops. A small pool sat in the centre of the square, people resting on the stone walls around it. Buildings rose on three sides, but the fourth gave way to empty space. The last of the light clung to the western hills, and a crowd of people had gathered along the top of the cliff.

"They're watching the Spanish," said Lubna. "It's as if they are drawn here."

"They won't see much now it's growing dark," Thomas said.

"The fires," said Lubna. "They are hypnotic, and they stretch far across the land. People are afraid. They want to know when the attack is coming." She glanced at Thomas, her face shadowed.

"I know no more than they do. Al-Zagal asked me the same thing, but the Spanish are just sitting there. I got an impression they are planning no attack, but quite why I thought so I couldn't really say. Oh, and I met an old friend. One I thought dead."

"Who?" asked Lubna. "Someone I know?"

"You've never met him," Thomas said. "He's from Qurtuba."

"So someone I know?" said Jorge.

Thomas pulled a face. "Lawrence."

"Lawrence is dead. You told me you saw him die."

"Apparently I was mistaken. I didn't actually see wolves attack him, I assumed they did because he was nowhere to be found. Are we going to eat here?" They had reached a stall where braziers burned, scented smoke rising into the air, sizzling cuts of meat dripping fat which sparked into flames, only adding to the smoke.

"I heard this place was good," said Jorge, "from Morales's servants."

Tables had been set in the square, arranged in Moorish fashion so they were expected to sit on the ground. Thomas crossed his legs uncomfortably, Lubna lowered herself without effort. Jorge remained on his feet.

"I'll tell them we want to eat, shall I?"

"Do we have any choice?" Thomas said.

"None at all, but that only makes life simpler, doesn't it?"

When he returned Jorge sat on the other side of the small table and poured himself a cup of water. More people entered the square and walked to the edge of the cliff to stare at the Spanish. Thomas recognised a face among them as the man passed beneath a torch.

"Giovanni is here," he said. "Perhaps I should go and question him."

Jorge turned, but the figure was lost amongst the others. "I don't see him. Is he on your famous list?" There was amusement in his voice.

"I'm sure it was him, but I don't see him now either." Thomas drank some water, thirsty as well as hungry. "So what did you learn?"

"The woman—"

"Katarina, although she is Kisera to her brother."

"Her brother?" said Jorge. "Who is her brother, and what's he got to do with this?"

"Simon, although his true name is Simki, which I like better," Thomas said. "Morales is clever, he has changed their names to sound Spanish, but they are similar enough not to cause confusion. They are brother and sister, captured together and brought here. Simki claims no-one in the house knows of their relationship. Why they want it kept a secret he didn't say."

"It explains something," said Jorge.

"What?"

A serving girl brought a stack of meat and put it in the middle of the table, together with a plate of flatbread. The smoky richness of the meat filled the air and Thomas reached out, starving.

"The other servants are afraid of him. Simki, that is. They were reluctant to say anything about the wife. He is a big man, isn't he, and strong, I'd say."

"He was protective of her?" Thomas said through a mouthful of food. He wiped grease from his beard, ignoring the look Lubna gave him.

Jorge nodded. "Though none mentioned they were related. I think they believed them lovers."

"I still don't see why it was kept a secret, unless Simki thinks whoever killed his sister is after him as well." Thomas shook his head. "So what did you find out about Kisera?"

Jorge wiped his fingers on a piece of bread before popping it into his mouth, then selected another piece of meat. "She's been part of the household for almost two years. Before that she had been sent to the harem, but rejected."

"Al-Zagal said she wasn't suitable."

"It happens, however skilled they might be. I suspect she knew how to please a man well enough. A month after she came to the house she began to share her master's bed. Three months later and they were married. A Christian wedding at the church beyond the town walls."

"If Morales brought her here as a slave why would he marry her?" Thomas said.

"She was beautiful. That was obvious even in the state we saw her."

"Morales must have access to many beautiful women."

"Perhaps they loved each other," said Lubna, who had listened in silence. "Sometimes it is the reason people marry." She glanced at Thomas, her face expressionless.

"More often for money or status," Thomas said.

"Is that why you asked me to marry you?"

"Of course not. I asked because—" Thomas stopped when he saw the expression on Jorge's face.

"You asked Lubna to marry you?"

Thomas nodded. Lubna offered a shy smile.

"Will it be a proper wedding?" said Jorge. "With guests and music and dancing? Will you have your hands and arms painted, Lubna? I know the perfect person to do it for you. She hennas the women of the harem, she is the best there is. Does Olaf know about this? Does he approve? Of course he does."

"It was a—" Thomas stopped again. He had been about to say it was a casual suggestion, nothing more, but even he realised saying such would hurt Lubna. "I wasn't thinking that far ahead. I would have thought something simpler might suit us both. That is, if you agree, Lubna. If you wish for an ornate ceremony then you can have one, I don't mind."

"It will be simple, yes," said Lubna.

"It will not," said Jorge. "The daughter of Olaf Torvaldsson marrying the great Thomas Berrington cannot be some quiet little ceremony." He held up a hand. "Don't worry, I will take care of everything."

"That's what I'm afraid of," Thomas said. "We should

talk of this another time. Finish telling me about Kisera. Did the servants have any idea who might have killed her?"

"Oh, they know who killed her," said Jorge. "Her lover killed her."

"Her lover?"

"She's had several, but there was a new one, fairly recently. They say she was besotted. They also say she was obsessed with sex."

"If she wanted to join the harem that is an asset, I would have thought," Thomas said.

"Oh, you think you know so much and yet you know so little," said Jorge. "To be a concubine is to be expert in the sensual arts, of course, but that does not mean the same thing as enjoying them. And they are so much else as well. So, so much else. One day you may understand."

"I doubt it," Thomas said.

"Perhaps you are right. Her obsession is no doubt another reason why she was rejected by the harem. But it's how she worked her way into Morales's bed, and the reason they slept in separate rooms after a time. I believe she may have worked her way through the entire count of male servants and half the women besides."

"Apart from her brother," Thomas said.

Jorge gave him a glance.

"So who is this lover?"

"Ah, now that is where things fall in shadow. The servants don't know a name or even what he looks like. She never met him at the house, not even when Morales was away on business, which was often, and she never mentioned a name."

Thomas cursed. "So we're no further forward."

"We have eliminated the husband as a suspect, and I

would vouch for the servants." Jorge reached for another slice of meat.

"And Simki?"

"He loved his sister," said Lubna. "You were there when he saw the body. You heard what he said."

"We need to question the neighbours," Thomas said. "Someone will have seen something. Ronda isn't like Gharnatah, it's a small town, and the couple will have had to meet somewhere for their liaisons."

"Would they?" said Lubna. "What if they always met outdoors? Before the Spanish surrounded the town they could have gone anywhere, even out onto the plain."

"She enjoyed danger," said Jorge, and Thomas leaned forward. Jorge would know of such matters far better than him. "Some people cannot separate between the two, love and danger."

"Agreed," Thomas said. "But they would have had a place, I'm sure. And not far from that walkway above the cliff. An inn, a house, they will have had somewhere. We need to find it."

"Who was the other woman?" said Jorge. "Is she significant or not?"

"Until we find her we won't know." Thomas studied the remnants of meat on the plate, the grease solidified as it cooled, and decided he had eaten enough. He wondered where they might be able to buy wine. In Gharnatah he would know, here he did not. "We need to look at the earlier killings. The woman I found in the gorge, Najma, what was her position, her duties? I allowed myself to be distracted by this latest death, but the answer might lie at the start. The letter talked of other deaths." He looked at Jorge. "She came from the harem. You will have to do the asking, al-Zagal has refused me access."

"What will you be doing?"

"Talking to Morales again. I want to discover what he knew about his wife's affairs, if anything."

CHAPTER 20

Thomas was roused from the depths of sleep to find Lubna leaning over him. He reached for her, his hands resting a moment on her narrow waist before she slapped them aside.

"Get up, there's something happening."

He shook his head, the last traces of sleep reluctant to depart as he put his feet on the floor and reached for his clothes.

"What is it, are the Spanish attacking?" He heard no explosions, no shouting.

"The opposite. They are leaving."

"Leaving?" It made no sense. Thomas could understand if they hadn't come at all, for Ronda was known to be impregnable. But why come only to sit on the plain for three days before leaving? He needed to see for himself.

"What hour is it?" he asked as he drew a shirt over his head and began to search for boots. He found them, glancing through the window as he pulled them on. The light was grey, all colour leached from the view across jumbled rooftops.

"A little before dawn."

Lubna was fully dressed. The last memory he recalled before sleep took him was of her naked, curled against his side with the bedclothes loose to allow a little air to cool their bodies. Thomas had been unable to find wine, but life had other compensations. Sometimes he barely remembered a time before Lubna slept at his side, those days shaded with unreality.

When they reached the square a significant crowd had gathered despite the hour. Thomas shouldered his way through, Lubna's fist gripping his belt to stay in touch. There were a few grumbles, but a glance from Thomas stilled them.

He reached the front rank which stood sensibly back a yard from the low stone wall marking the edge of the cliff. Thomas wondered how many slipped or tumbled over that edge in a year, for there must surely be some.

The far side of the plain was in sunlight, but shadow covered the land closer to Ronda where the cliff face cloaked the rising sun. All over the land men were moving. The cannon had been rolled back from their positions and tied to enormous carts, the biggest Thomas had ever seen. These guns were far larger than any he had come across in France.

"When did they start?" he asked the man standing next to him.

"They were already moving when I arrived an hour ago." The man half turned and raised his voice. "Who was first here?"

A youth raised an arm. "I have been here all night." He pushed his way toward Thomas, pleased his opinion was wanted. "I was woken by a noise when it was still dark. I crawled to the edge to see what was happening and saw they were breaking down the cannon. Fires were winking out across the plain, and as the light grew tents started to be taken down and horses brought in."

"It takes a lot of work to break a camp of so many," said the man next to Thomas, who studied him a moment, finding someone who looked as if he had seen fighting. Many in al-Andalus had, its days of peaceful co-existence long in the past.

"Why did they come?" Thomas said, more to himself than anyone else, but his new friend answered anyway.

"They wanted to see if he would ride out amongst them."

"Al-Zagal?"

"Who else?"

Thomas thought about it, but it made no sense. Al-Zagal was known for being headstrong, for being relentless in battle, but he hadn't reached the age he had by being hasty.

Shouts rose to them, the sound masked by distance, filtered through a wind that plucked the words apart to remove all sense. Men mounted horses and rode directly south without looking back. Carts began to move, those holding the cannon bringing up the rear. They would fall far behind and need to be driven several hours to catch the main party at the end of the day. Other carts carried field kitchens, tents, weaponry and anyone who could cling to them to save their legs. An army on the move. It was an impressive sight. Even more impressive for going away instead of coming toward them.

Thomas pushed his way out through the crowd, larger now, a party atmosphere spreading as people realised the enemy were retreating. He heard someone say the Spanish were afraid of al-Zagal, did not want to meet him in battle. Except, Thomas knew, there would have been no battle. Ronda did not lend itself to riding out to fight directly. It protected itself behind cliffs and walls, self-satisfied in its position.

People were still streaming into the square and three

of the stallholders had opened early. Thomas bought bread and fruit for them and they ate it as they walked into town.

"I need to talk with Jorge," Thomas said, "to see if he's managed to find anything out from his women."

"They're not his women—"

"Al-Zagal's women, then."

"That's not what I meant," said Lubna, "if you would let me finish for once." She walked on several paces. Thomas waited for her to speak again, knowing she was right. His own thoughts moved too fast and there were times he jumped ahead, often leaping to the wrong conclusion.

"Jorge was brought here to put discipline into the harem," said Lubna. "While you were with al-Zagal he told me the women have grown insolent while their master was away, starting to believe they could act as they wished. So it might take more than a few sweet words, and more than a few days, before he finds anything out."

"The more time passes the harder it gets."

"Go to Morales then," said Lubna. "I won't come with you, he won't talk with a woman present."

"What will you do?"

"I have my own life," said Lubna.

Thomas glanced at her, wondering what was wrong. Wondering what he had done. Then he dismissed it. He could come back to it again when he had time.

"I'll see you in the room this evening," he said, and turned down a side street, leaving her behind. Morales was almost certainly still asleep, but his staff would be awake, preparing the day for their master, and Thomas was in no mood to be as gentle as Jorge clearly had been. He would get answers to his questions.

CHAPTER 21

"I need names," Thomas said. He sat at a scrubbed oak table in the large kitchen which occupied the rear of Morales's house. The cook, a thin woman who obviously didn't partake of the rich food she prepared for her master, sat across from him.

"I know only two," she said, her eyes on her hands, refusing to meet Thomas's.

"How many lovers did she have?"

"Two dozen I know of, and those only the ones she formed an attachment to. There were others, an hour here, two hours there, a night at most. She was a woman driven by desire."

Thomas heard the note of disapproval in the cook's voice. Personally he had no opinion either way. If Kisera wanted – or more likely from what he had heard, *needed* – lovers, then he saw nothing wrong in her taking them. After all, she had been stolen from her homeland and brought here to be sold to the highest bidder before gaining a position in this household. Thomas had experience of women who possessed more desire than could be accommodated by a single man. In his case it had been Helena. Briefly he wondered if that was what was wrong with Lubna. Was he not attentive enough to her needs? They did not make love every night, not even most nights, but she wasn't like her sister. Or was she?

Was it a matter of blood, of family?

"Did the master know of these liaisons?"

"I don't see how he could not."

The cook was the seventh person Thomas had spoken with. He had avoided Morales for now, also Simki, but he wanted to talk to both before he finished. The first six interviews had been unhelpful. He found out why when he spoke with the cook. He already knew Kisera had worked her way through most of the staff in an effort to satisfy her desires, and it became clear those he had spoken to had succumbed. The cook, it seemed, had not. Her face was pinched, gaze turned inward. Perhaps she was bitter not to have been chosen, hence her willingness to tell all.

"And names? He would know who?"

"Likely more names than me. Ronda isn't a big town, it's not like Gharnatah. Everyone knows everyone else here. Her trysts were common knowledge, and word spreads."

"Can you write?" Thomas asked.

"Of course I can write."

"Then put down the names you know, and where they live. Ask the others if they know of anyone and add those names too. Someone she knew killed her."

"It might have been a stranger," said the cook. "Come back when you have finished your questions, I'll have a list for you."

Thomas thanked her and rose. He knew he had put off too long the interviews that would prove most useful, but a reluctance still clung to him. Simki made him uneasy. After what Jorge had implied Thomas didn't know how to even begin the conversation. He wished Jorge was with him, doing what he did best.

Thomas followed a narrow corridor to the front of the house. He knew Simki had a small room near the entrance, set apart from the other servants. The cook had been Spanish, but most of the others were African like Kisera and her brother, but without the beauty they possessed. Thomas shook his head. He must have been too long in Jorge's company, because he could see that Simki was beautiful. His sister, alive and unblemished, would have been a thing of wonder. He took a deep breath, steeling himself to confront the man and get some answers.

Simki came out of his room when he heard Thomas's footsteps on the marble floor. "Have you finished with the others?"

"I would speak with Don Morales, and then you."

"My master is out on business," said Simki.

"You then."

Simki offered a nod. "Of course. We can do so in my room." He stood to one side to allow Thomas to pass. Within was a narrow bed pushed against the wall, neatly made. A small table stood beneath the only window which looked onto the street to afford a view of anyone coming to the front door. A journal lay on the desk, a pen resting on the open page. A small jar of fresh ink sat to one side. Thomas glanced at the words, unsurprised to see they were Arabic.

Simki caught his glance and said, "I thought you might find that interesting." As though he had expected Thomas, or someone, to want to read what he had written.

Thomas looked more closely, saw a pattern. A name followed by a paragraph.

"What is it?"

"My sister's lovers," said Simki. His voice showed no emotion.

Thomas turned back a page, his finger smearing the ink of the last entry as he did so and he saw Simki wince.

"All of these were her lovers?"

Simki nodded. "Those I know the names of."

So much for the cook's two dozen. "Why did you record them in such detail?" Thomas looked Simki full in the face. The man was an inch taller, broader across the shoulders, but he sensed no danger. Almost the opposite – there was a gentleness to him that was appealing.

"I worry – no, worried – about her. There were times she made a poor choice of companion, so I watched, and I judged."

"And discouraged?"

Simki nodded. "In some cases, yes." He spread his arms. "I can be intimidating if I wish."

Thomas was sure he could. He was also aware the figure at the top of the cliff had been too distant to tell the colour of their skin.

"How intimidating? Do you ever resort to violence?"

"The threat of violence, but never the act."

"And your sister – did she object to your interest in her lovers?"

"At times, but I believe in her heart she knew I only did it because I loved her."

Which raised the other question. Thomas wished for Jorge's presence, but it seemed Simki had seen the expression on his face and was ready to help out.

"I loved her as a sister, nothing more. I have heard the rumours but they are false. People saw Kisera and could not believe any man capable of resisting her. It is also true that in our village it was not unusual for brother to

157

marry sister, for mother to marry son when a father died. But we are not in my village anymore, and here we live by the laws of this land."

Some land, Thomas thought, where the King and Queen of Spain were close cousins, their marriage only allowed after being sanctioned by the Pope. It had always been thus, one law for the rulers, another for those they ruled.

"Can I study the list?" Thomas asked.

Simki nodded. "Let me help you. Some have moved away, others died—" He glanced at Thomas. "No, not that way, old age or accident, nothing more. If you tell me what you are looking for perhaps I can speed up your search. Please, take a seat, let's talk." Simki pulled a second chair across and set it beside his own.

It occurred to Thomas he hadn't yet thought about what he was looking for. Events were moving too fast. Now Simki had pulled him up short, and he knew he needed to consider what had happened and what they knew as fact so far. He pulled the seat out and lowered himself, pleased to see the African preferred real chairs, as did he.

"I don't yet know what I'm looking for, except the man I seek has killed others. There have been deaths in the town. You even have a name for him, I hear. I am sure he was in the company of a woman taking a message to the Sultan, for which she was killed."

"Where is this letter now?" Simki took his own seat, turning it so he faced Thomas, their knees almost touching. He leaned forward, gaze intent, and Thomas knew the man was even more focussed on finding the killer than he was. "And who was the woman?"

"I have the letter," Thomas said. "And the woman's

name was Najma. Did you know her?"

"The name is not familiar. Of course, it is possible Kisera would have known her. She had friends in the palace."

"Was one of those friends the librarian, Khalil?"

Simki shook his head. "I think her friends were all women."

"Najma was taking a message to the Sultan regarding events in the harem," Thomas said. "It claims there have been other deaths, both there and in the town."

Simki gave a nod. "I suspected as much. Women have gone missing, men too, for some time now. You spoke true when you said there is a name for him. They call him the Incubus, because he comes in the night and takes the lives of the beautiful, and because he is never seen. A wraith. A ghost. A supernatural being."

"You believe that?"

Simki laughed. "Of course not. It is a man. A man who will make a mistake."

"Why has nothing been done?" Thomas said.

"You have to understand what Ronda has become," said Simki. "Al-Zagal has been gone a year. The man he left in his place lacks authority, but even worse he lacks curiosity."

"Do you agree with Najma's estimate of numbers?" Thomas said.

"At least a dozen, perhaps as many as a score."

"Over what time frame?"

"Ten or eleven months. The first death I heard of was a woman in the harem, another friend of Kisera's."

"You are precise about the time," Thomas said. "Ten or eleven months, but not a year?"

"It was the month of *Rajab*," said Simki. "Al-Zagal

left during *Jumādá al-ākhirah*, several weeks earlier" He waited, his eyes on Thomas. It was obvious he did not consider the timing a coincidence.

"So we are looking for someone who came here after al-Zagal left, or someone triggered to take action after he left?"

"I believe the latter," said Simki.

"Explain." The small chamber had grown warm. Sweat trickled along Thomas's back. Simki's skin remained unblemished by perspiration.

"As I said, Ronda is a small town. New faces stand out, and there were none that stood out at that time, none that could have done the deed."

Thomas made note of Simki's explanation, judging it brief, but he could come back to it later if need be.

"Was an investigation launched?"

"None."

"Why not?"

"The death was considered natural. I believe it still is. It was only after the others, when a pattern emerged, that I came to believe they were connected."

"How did she die?"

"You would be a better judge of that than me. I never saw the body, and it was burned before the sun set."

"So how do you think she died?"

Instead of answering Simki rose and crossed the room to his bed. It took no more than three strides. He reached beneath the pillow and drew out a length of cloth. He took the three paces back, sat and handed a slip of soft linen to Thomas. "Kisera came to me some time ago. She was not herself, reluctant to talk, but I knew she had something on her mind."

"She told you what?"

Simki nodded, the cloth moving between his fingers. "She showed me this and asked did I know of the practice, where a man would wrap it around a woman's throat at the height of their pleasure so as to increase the ecstasy."

"What did you say?"

Simki's gaze turned from the cloth to Thomas's, held it for a moment. "I told her I knew of the practice, but not how. I did not want to burden her with it."

"What burden?"

"I will not burden you either. You only need to know I have experienced the practice myself. I didn't tell Kisera that. I told her it was unusual, but not unknown. I think she was unsure of her lover's intention, afraid he would go too far."

He lifted the cloth, wrapped it twice around his neck and pulled. The linen hissed as it slid across itself. Veins stood out in Simki's neck and his already dark face took on a darker hue.

"At this tension I can still talk, still think. But if I do this—" He drew the cloth tighter still. His eyes bulged and the prominent veins became rigid. He held the tension for a while, seconds ticking past until Thomas was obliged to reach out to draw the cloth from the man's throat.

"You have done this before?" he said.

"As an experiment," said Simki, his gaze darting away, and Thomas wondered if he felt shame.

"How far have you taken it?"

"To unconsciousness."

"That was dangerous."

Simki nodded. "I thought it necessary. I had to know how it felt, and I considered it a reasonable risk. The material is soft enough. Once I passed out my grip relaxed and the pressure was relieved." He gazed at Thomas. "You should try it. It has certain side effects that are… interesting."

"I have heard of them." Thomas leaned close. "It explains why the deaths were considered accidental. Done the right way the cloth would show no mark. Do you think the other deaths were caused by this? An experiment gone too far? That cannot be, not so many. The first I could understand. An act of passion gone wrong. The man heightens his partner's sexual pleasure by restricting the flow of blood to the brain. And then he discovers a different kind of pleasure – in killing. Does he inflict the same practice on himself? Do you think it was accidental, the first death?"

"Was it the first?" Simki sat up, as though their closeness had grown too intimate. "The first here in Ronda, perhaps, but has he been inflicting his perversions elsewhere? And for how long?"

Thomas glanced at the open journal. "How many?" he asked.

"Seven," said Simki, knowing exactly what he meant. How many were young enough, strong enough, to inflict death in such a way. Though little strength was required unless the subject fought, and Thomas suspected they did not. Whoever was doing the killing, the victims were willing participants until the final moment.

Simki tore an empty page from the back of the journal. He wrote the seven names down and handed them to Thomas. He tore another sheet and headed it *Victims*. He filled the page with names, which took longer than the first page. His sister's was the last.

"This might be useful as well. It's all I know of, but there could be others. It's a start."

Outside on the street Thomas read the list of suspects – most were Arabic, with one Spaniard. There were locations too, each dwelling identified. Simki's theory was plausible, but Thomas hadn't examined the earlier bodies, only Najma's and Kisera's, and they had both been killed by falls. It was likely there was no connection between them.

He moved along the street, starting to study the longer list of victims when a cry halted him. A door opened in the side of the house and the cook emerged. She too carried a scrap of paper.

"I thought you were going to return for this," she said.

Thomas had forgotten his request for her to also make a list. "I was about to come and see you."

The cook looked at him with doubt on her face. All the same she held the paper out. It was a corner torn from a larger sheet. Thomas glanced down quickly – four names, three already familiar, the third not, and female. A name familiar to him, though not the surname, which came as a surprise. Francesca della Caccia. She had to be related to Giovanni, it was too much a coincidence otherwise. And if so, what was its significance?

"This last one?"

"She was a friend to Katarina. She works in the palace. It was she who put the idea in her head she might join the harem." Her eyes skittered away.

"And afterward?" Thomas suspected why she was reluctant to say more. He had, after all, asked for the names of Kisera's lovers.

"They stayed friends," said the cook. Her eyes continued to find something interesting in the gutter that ran down the middle of the street. "Good friends. And she is a strange one."

Thomas thought back to his introduction to the woman. There had been a strangeness about her, but nothing more than shyness might explain. He nodded and tucked the scrap of paper next to the other in his pocket. "My thanks."

"Just find this Incubus," said the cook. "Nobody knows who will be chosen next. It might be me."

As he walked away Thomas doubted the cook was in much danger – so far the man, and man he was convinced it was, had chosen beautiful women. All the same he was intrigued at the additional name she had written. Thomas knew he had to find Jorge and, if possible, speak with Francesca again to find out what she knew.

Thomas made a note to add another name to the list Simki had given him – the man himself. He was good looking, charming, and attractive to women. The same characteristics the one they called the Incubus would need. Everything Simki had shown Thomas might be no more than a diversion.

Chapter 22

As Thomas approached the palace he was forced to one side by armed soldiers streaming along the roadway from the barracks. Entering the walled square he saw others emerging through two gates, as well as men coming from the palace itself. He moved to one side, away from the melee, and took in the situation, wondering what had happened. Had the Spanish returned, their leaving no more than a ploy?

He saw a face he recognised and pushed through the crowd toward Giovanni del Caccia. The Italian looked up as he approached and offered a smile, his features showing the same familiar welcome Thomas always saw on it.

"Have you been visiting your sister?" It was a guess, but a logical one. The pair of them shared an unnatural beauty.

Giovanni frowned. "My sisters live in Naples, if they still live at all. It is not the safest of cities."

"I have heard another of the same family name as you lives within the palace," Thomas said. "Her name is Francesca."

"Ah. Not sister but cousin. She is the daughter of my father's brother. And no, I have not been visiting. She lives within the harem, and as a man I am not granted access to such a place."

Thomas knew he would come back to the matter, but the courtyard was getting busier, louder with the clash of weapons and shields. He would seek Giovanni out later and question him harder. "What's going on here?"

"A rider came this morning with news. The Spanish are moving toward Malaka. Al-Zagal is taking his men through the mountains to reinforce the town. If they move fast they'll get there before the Spanish."

"Are you riding with them?"

"Me?" Giovanni laughed, shaking his head. "You know I'm no fighter. I was looking for Jorge but couldn't find him. Who knew so many men could gather so quickly? It looks like chaos, but I believe there is order to it."

Thomas glanced around. Giovanni spoke the truth. Foot soldiers drew into ranks. Horsemen were being corralled into groups of twenty, each with a senior man to lead them. There would be no artillery here, no muskets or cannon. Al-Zagal believed in the old skills, the ones that had served the Moors well over many centuries – fast horses, bowmen and, above all else, skill with a sword. It was one more reason they were losing the war.

Thomas looked across the throng.

"I need to find Jorge myself. Come with me if you wish to see him."

"I'll leave it for now, it was nothing important. I doubt you'll have any more luck than me." Giovanni waved a languid hand at the soldiers. "Though looking at this lot it may be chaos inside the palace as well."

Thomas moved away, knowing Giovanni had been lying about wanting to see Jorge. Why would he want to? No doubt the man had been planning to visit another of his myriad women. He possessed the same attributes as Simki, Thomas knew, even more so. Except there was some weakness in him that Thomas sensed. A weakness that made him dismiss the man, even as he knew he would have to add him to the list of suspects.

After a moment he slowed, stopped and looked back, but Giovanni had melted into the crowd. It was an aspect of him Thomas had noted before, his ability to melt away. Yes, he should be on the list. Except when the woman had been thrown from the cliff, Giovanni had been outside with the others because Thomas had seen him as they came through the tunnel.

At the palace gate all movement flowed outward, and Thomas was aware pressing against the tide made him stand out. He conjured a story that might suffice if he was challenged – he had been summoned to attend a member of the harem who was taken ill – but knew it would not stand up to scrutiny if anyone checked.

He made it as far as the outer bailey when two figures appeared in the far doorway. It was too late to turn away, so Thomas kept going, trying to look as though he belonged.

"Berrington!" Al-Zagal's voice was sharp, brooking no dissent, and Thomas stopped four yards away. The Sultan was in heated discussion with the town Governor, Abraham al-Haquim, the man who had led them to the tunnel entrance on the night they arrived.

Al-Zagal ignored Thomas but held up a hand to hold him in place until he was finished. The conversation went on for an age but Thomas knew he could not move away. Eventually the business was concluded and al-Haquim bustled – as much as his girth and age allowed – back into the palace.

Al-Zagal dropped his hand, a signal for Thomas to approach.

167

"You are to ride with me to Malaka," he said. "I have doctors, but none as skilled as you are claimed to be. Let's see if those claims are true."

"Malik." Thomas nodded, a sense of defeat settling through him. Just as he was started to make a little progress on the killings he was being dragged away. He knew it was useless to try and argue, but there remained one chance.

"I will need to fetch my instruments, Malik," Thomas said. "And sutures. I will need many sutures."

"Whatever you must. If we are gone ride hard to catch us. Report to me before dusk. We ride to the valley of the Wadi al-Conrocalejo. The Spanish will take the easy route south to the coast before turning east. If we ride hard we can arrive two days ahead of them."

"You expect them to attack Malaka?"

Al-Zagal scowled. No doubt the logic was so clear in his own mind he expected everyone to understand without explanation. "Where else would they be going?"

Thomas turned away, knowing it was impossible to enter the palace now. Once the soldiers had left he would return. He had no intention of obeying al-Zagal's orders. It would take the assembled troops several hours before they were ready to depart, and he needed to make himself scarce until they had gone. He would use the time to track down the names on the other list Simki had provided. First he needed to return to his lodging and fetch Lubna, she would be useful to him. They could split the list between them and halve the time. He had grown to trust her quickness and ability to read people, and she had proven herself tough when necessary.

CHAPTER 23

It was late before Thomas returned to the palace, the courtyard empty now, stinking of dung left by the horses. He was hungry, tired and frustrated. He had given Simki's list of victims to Lubna, keeping the suspects for himself. He didn't want her talking to those suspected of killing, but his enquiries had done no more than rule out the names he had been given. All but two. Simki himself and the woman Francesca. He hoped Lubna would have better luck and find some common thread linking the dead.

The last call to prayer, *Salat al-'isha*, had rung out over the town hours since and now the streets were empty. Thomas was not ready to return to their lodgings, even though he knew Lubna would be there. The prospect of her arms was enticing, but he had more questions to ask if only he could get them straight in his head.

As he approached the main entrance he saw at least one guard remained. He slowed, expecting to be challenged, conjuring a story that would allow him entry, but the man merely nodded him through. As he entered the inner hallway Thomas considered the person he sought must also be known, as was he, one who is nodded entrance to the inner sanctum. How else could he gain access to the private chambers of those who lived here?

"What do you want?" Jorge said when Thomas

found him in the kitchens, the words were curt but his expression benign.

"I'm looking for Francesca. I'd like to question her if a private place can be found."

Jorge laughed. "There are many private places within a harem." He clapped Thomas on the shoulder and led him out.

As they approached the inner sanctum the air grew scented with perfume and seemed both warmer and softer as a result. Thomas had visited the harem in Gharnatah often, and although this was his first time here, he was only mildly curious; his mind already seeking ahead, thinking of the questions he would ask.

There were a dozen women in the main room. At least five were asleep, supple bodies curled around cushions, loosened hair covering their faces. Two others showed heavily lidded eyes.

Jorge pointed, "She's over there."

Francesca had not noticed them and Thomas took a moment to study her. She stood at a narrow table working on something her body obscured. More relaxed now than when he had seen her with Khalil, her face even more beautiful, dark hair falling across one eye.

"I understand she's not a member of the harem," Thomas said. "What does she do here?"

"She cares for the women. She is good with kohl and henna, even better with oils and herbs. It is said if a woman is reluctant Francesca has a potion to turn them into a wild thing."

Thomas smiled. Perhaps he would benefit from some of that potion himself. Between interviews he had continued to wonder what he had done to annoy Lubna. His lack of attention to her as a woman kept coming back to him.

"What is she like?"

Jorge raised a shoulder. "I don't know her well. She does her job, and the other women like her well enough. What is your interest?"

"She knew Morales's wife, and she was mentioned by some of the others I spoke with today. She was also a friend of Khalil's. I want to find out anything she knows that might be relevant. Do you have somewhere we can go?"

Jorge smiled. "Of course, I'll show you. Francesca." Jorge called her name, not loud, but she turned toward them. The beauty of her face made the breath catch in Thomas's throat. Yes, he could believe she was Giovanni's cousin.

Jorge beckoned and Francesca rose in a single lithe movement, came toward them on bare feet. Her toes appeared at each step, painted, henna patterns marking the skin.

"This man is Thomas Berrington. He wishes to speak with you."

Francesca's eyes studied Thomas and he saw recognition there, but when she spoke she made no mention they had met before. "Only speak? Is he a eunuch like you? He does not look like one. Not pretty enough."

Jorge ignored the teasing, used to it. "Take Thomas to the garden room and answer honestly. He will report to me afterward, and I will know if you are not truthful."

Francesca lowered her gaze, a picture of innocent obedience. Thomas believed none of it, but followed her through the room. One or two of the courtesans looked up, incurious. If this was the harem in Gharnatah he would know them all, would have treated most for ailments minor and major. Here only one or two were familiar and even then only vaguely. When al-Zagal had arrived in Gharnatah to support his brother he had brought his own harem, setting up a court separate from the one in the palace.

Francesca led them to a walled garden, the night air warm, fragrant. Water ran along a rill in the centre, entering through a grill and disappearing into another. Palm trees and yew grew, roses and other well-tended flowers and shrubs. Light came from enclosed windows behind which burned torches, their illumination reflecting on the almost motionless water. One of the walls rose only to waist height and from the darkness that lay beyond Thomas knew it must look across the plain. It was to this wall that Francesca walked. She jumped on top and span around, the silk of her clothing whispering. Thomas moved to stand close, afraid for her. When he glanced over the wall he saw the cliff descending into infinite darkness. He held a hand out, afraid if he tried to grab her she might tumble over.

Francesca laughed, almost stumbled, and this time Thomas had no choice. He grabbed her wrist. Instead of allowing him to draw her to safety she stepped the other way into empty space.

"No!" Thomas gripped the wall with his left hand, tightening his right as Francesca swung into nothing. It was fortunate she weighed little, and after a moment of panic he drew her back and pulled her across the lip of the wall, deposited her on the solid tiles of the floor.

"What do you think you're doing?"

"I wanted to see if you would save me." She cocked her head to one side. "I was sure you would, but it was an interesting test, wasn't it?"

"And if I had not?"

She gave a brittle laugh, something not quite right in the sound. "Then I would still be flying."

"No, you would be dead." Thomas stared at her face, the beauty almost unnatural, and he wondered why she was a servant of the harem rather than a member.

She lay her hand against his chest. He felt a tremble in the touch. "What is it you want of me?"

"Can we sit? Away from the wall."

Francesca pulled a face, her bottom lip jutting like a spoiled child. "I suppose so, if you are afraid." She tripped away to a stone bench barely a foot off the ground. When Thomas joined her he heard the soft sound of water as it flowed through the grill into the garden.

"I want to ask you about Katarina," he said, sitting at a distance along the bench.

"Kisera. She did not like the name they gave her. She was always Kisera to me." A tear gathered in her left eye, grew and spilled across her cheek. She raised a hand and touched it. "She was too beautiful to die as she did. Is that why you are here?"

"I seek the man who killed her. The man who has killed others, too."

"You mean Najma? I heard someone found her discarded in the mountains."

"It was me who found her," Thomas said.

Francesca closed her eyes. Her chest rose and fell. Insects batted against the illuminated glass windows. Orange blossom perfumed the night air.

"Did she suffer?"

"I don't know." As always unable to be anything but honest. "If she did it was not for long."

"And you seek her killer here, in Ronda? Do you suspect someone in the palace?" Francesca leaned close, her scent enfolding Thomas, but he was used to such ploys having lived with Helena.

"I seek her killer, but have drawn no conclusions yet. Which is why I want to speak with you. Who might want to harm both Kisera and Najma? And there were others before. Najma carried a letter saying such and I have my own list now." He thought briefly of the names. He had assumed all the victims were female, but on Simki's list almost half the names were men.

"Women die in the harem," Francesca said. "Women die every day in many places. Men too. But I am not aware of anyone murdered here."

Thomas shook his head, knowing he had distracted himself. "These deaths, the first ones, I believe they may not have been murder. Perhaps no more than a game gone wrong."

"A game? What kind of game ends in death?"

The kind where you stand atop a wall over a three hundred foot drop, Thomas thought, but did not say it.

"A game of arousal."

"The ladies of the harem have many of those, as I am sure you know. What game do you speak of? Tell me, for you cannot shock me."

"Kisera had a linen tie at her throat."

Francesca nodded, a tightness showing on her lips. "Yes, I know of what you mean. But what you speak of does not lead to death unless you are stupid."

"Or mean to kill," Thomas said.

"Yes. That too. Is that how Najma died? She was not young, but I suppose to some men she would still be attractive."

174

"I don't believe attraction has anything to do with the killer's motives."

"His? You know it is a man?"

"I saw him," Thomas said. "When we arrived in Ronda we witnessed Kisera's death. I watched her—" Thomas stopped abruptly. There was no need for this woman to know the details of what he had seen.

"If you know who he is why are you asking questions of me?" Francesca paced away, but stopped short of the wall.

"It was dark. He was at the top of the cliff and we were at the bottom. All we saw were shapes, nothing more."

"What were you doing there?" Francesca returned and laid a hand on Thomas's shoulder, standing over him. He wanted to stand, to dominate her with his height but didn't want to make it obvious.

"Why we were there doesn't matter, only that we were."

"Was he taller than her?" Francesca asked.

Thomas thought about it. The elevation made judging height difficult, but thought the man was. "I believe so."

"Because Kisera was tall for a woman. She told me all her tribe are tall."

"Did she also tell you of her lovers?" Thomas could hold himself in check no longer and stood. Francesca's hand slid from his shoulder to hang at her side.

"We shared everything. There were no secrets between us, none at all."

"So it's likely she told you the name of her killer," Thomas said. "You may not know who it is but you will know his name."

Francesca shivered, lifting a hand to touch her lips. "There were many names. She would come and tell me of each new conquest. And conquests they were. I do not believe Kisera loved, nor even liked the men she seduced. A fire burned inside her, one that only making men want her and then abandoning them could put out. And the quenching never lasted long."

"Is that why she was not suitable for the harem?" Thomas asked. "Was there bad feeling over that?"

Francesca smiled, her hand sought his wrist as if she could not be in his company without touching him. This time her fingers curled around it. "Her skin was the wrong colour. Too dark. She had all other attributes necessary. Kisera would have made a fine concubine."

"Why are you a servant and not one yourself?"

Francesca laughed, the sound like shattered glass. "Not all women wish to be used as playthings. I have the privilege of working in the harem without the obligations."

"Why did Kisera marry Morales? A man who deals in slaves when she came here as one herself? Wasn't that strange?"

"It was not him who brought her here, she told me. He merely purchased her. He is rich, he is old, he is undemanding. And he understands. He knows what she is and accepts it for the glory she brings him. A man like that married to someone as exotic, as beautiful as Kisera? He wanted her and she needed a place of safety. When he demanded it she went to him. But he did not kill her."

"No, he didn't."

"So who did?" asked Francesca, although she turned away as if uninterested in his reply.

"Why – will you punish him?"

"Me? No, I am a woman and weak. But if I ask my cousin he will kill him for me."

"Giovanni," he said, wishing Francesca would turn so he could see her face. He walked to the low wall and sat, facing back toward her, but she was looking down at her hands clasped in front of her.

"You know him?" she said.

"He travelled here in our company."

Francesca nodded. "He is a good man. But weak, like all men are weak." Now she did look up, her eyes meeting his fully. "Is that not true, Thomas Berrington?"

CHAPTER 24

Thomas returned Francesca to the harem and asked where he could find Jorge. One of the younger eunuchs, a lad of little more than fifteen, led him a short distance to a suite of rooms set hard against the bathing chambers. Jorge sat on a wide, well-appointed bed, his head nodding.

"Did you know they were related?" Thomas asked.

Jorge snuffled, his eyes opening slowly. It was obvious he had not heard the question so Thomas repeated it.

"Who related?"

"Giovanni is Francesca's cousin. Did you know?"

Jorge stared at the far wall, and for a moment Thomas thought he might not answer. Then he shook his head.

"No, I didn't. But we've only been here a few days. I'm sure I would have found out eventually. Does it matter?"

"Had he not entered Ronda alongside us he would be on my list." Thomas urged Jorge to make a space before sitting at the foot of the bed. Beneath him the mattress was soft, its surface covered in fine cotton. He thought of the bed he and Lubna shared and wondered why they couldn't have been offered accommodation in the palace.

"What list is this?"

"You know what list. The suspects." Thomas reached inside his robe and withdrew the page Simki had torn loose.

Jorge took the paper from Thomas and pretended to

read it. "There are eight names here." Able to count, at least.

"Plus one here." Thomas tapped his brow.

"You said you wanted to add Giovanni. Was it because you do not like him?"

"I don't dislike him, but he was nearby when Najma died, and he left the camp early before we entered Ronda. I thought he could have made his way into the town ahead of us. It might have been him we watched at the top of the cliff."

"But you said he entered alongside us."

"Which is why he is no longer on the list."

Jorge laughed and looked at the sheet of paper again. "His name is here?"

"No. I told you, it was in my head."

"With one other. Who is that?"

"Simki." Thomas remembered something that was not said. "Francesca doesn't know he is Kisera's brother. I'm not sure anyone does."

"Is that significant? Is it secret enough to kill for?"

"I don't know, but secrets can be dangerous. I could do with knowing who the others who were killed in the palace are."

"Ah, that I do know," said Jorge. "There were two – three if you count Najma. The others were not of the harem. One was a cook, the other a seamstress."

"What do you know of them?" Thomas asked. "Were they beautiful?"

"I knew you would have questions, so I tried to ask them for you. They were not as beautiful as my charges, but pretty enough, I am told."

"When did they die?"

"The cook eight months ago. The seamstress six

months since. And Najma, as we know, two weeks ago. Is that a pattern or not?"

"Najma died because she carried a letter. We need to find out why the others were chosen. Do you know what they did before working here?"

Jorge shook his head. "I can try to find out, but it's more than likely nobody knows. If they were skilled there would have been no need of questions. Is it pertinent? I know you, you like to ask questions for the sake of it."

"I don't know until I have the answers," Thomas said. "I never know which question, which answer will prove crucial until it occurs."

"You know there may be no rational reason. You have pursued enough killers these last years to have learned that. Sometimes death is reason enough. Besides, nobody knew these were murders until we started to ask questions."

"Exactly," Thomas said. He pushed himself up from the bed. His body ached and his head pulsed with fatigue. "I'm going back to Lubna, unless there is somewhere I can rest here? I have yet more questions to ask in the morning, if doing so doesn't offend your sensibilities."

"Tiredness makes you grumpy, doesn't it? Go find the boy who brought you here and he will show you somewhere. Tell him I said you can stay. And close the door when you leave."

Woken from a dream of being pursued by wolves Thomas flung am arm out and yelped when it crashed against stone. He struggled through layers of consciousness, sleep trying to draw him back into its embrace. Lawrence had been in the dream, standing off to one side, laughing as the wolves drew close, as if it was he who controlled them.

When Thomas opened his eyes it was to find light flooding the narrow chamber. His fist ached, but not as badly as his back. What mattress there was on the palette owed more to straw than feather, but it had been welcome enough in the small hours.

Thomas swung his legs out and sat up. The toes of his boots touched the far wall. There was a single high window but no door. The room was little more than an alcove in a corridor. It looked far worse in the light of day than when the boy had brought him here, and Thomas wondered if this place was some kind of a joke being played on him. His skin was waxy and he knew he stank of his own sweat. He needed to find a place to bathe, and then a place to sleep for a week, but knew both would have to wait.

He stood and moved into the corridor if only to ease the sense of imprisonment. In the distance he heard voices, but there was nobody in sight. He made his way in what he thought was the right direction for the kitchen. It was the library he wanted, but didn't know how to find it. As he approached the smell of baking and roasted meats came to him and his stomach rumbled. Another hundred paces and he found himself surrounded by activity.

A woman turned to him, approached.

"Are you lost?" She looked him up and down and Thomas knew she was judging. He suspected he failed whatever test she applied.

"I'm looking for the library."

The woman frowned and half turned aside. He wondered if she was searching for a guard.

"I am friend to Jorge," he said, the words that usually worked amongst all women, young or old, tall or short, fat or thin. Except in this case they failed.

"Who is Jorge? A Spaniard?"

Thomas supposed the few days they had been in the palace was not long enough for Jorge to spread his charm. "He is a eunuch in the harem."

"A Spanish eunuch?"

"It's a long story, but a true one."

Still the woman remained unconvinced, but she did call out, her voice loud to rise above the clatter of pans and trays. "Does anyone know a Spanish eunuch named Jorge?"

Thomas surveyed the dozen or more women, relieved when one raised a hand.

"He came from Gharnatah with the Sultan's party." The girl was young, little more than fifteen. Flour dusted her face but failed to hide the blush that spread across her cheeks, and Thomas suppressed a smile.

"This man claims to be a friend of his."

The girl nodded. "He told me he has come with people, but I know the name of only one. A man named Berrington."

"That is me," Thomas said. He saw the girl study him and offer a brief nod. He wondered how Jorge had described him. "The library?" he said again. "And, if possible, a little bread?"

The senior cook turned away, already dismissing him, but she called out to the girl, "You know him, you sort him out."

The girl came across, shy, even a little afraid. She held out a hand containing a sweet roll. Thomas took it and smiled, unsurprised when the unease in her eyes grew.

"Do you know where the library is?" he asked, trying to put a softness into his voice as he had heard Jorge do when calming young women.

"I never visit there, it is not for the likes of one such as me, but I can tell you where it is." She began to reel off directions. Thomas held up a hand.

"Show me."

She glanced over her shoulder, but the cook was at the far end of the room. The girl nodded once and hurried past him.

After two corridors Thomas gave up all attempt at conversation. Her longest response had been 'Yes' in answer to one question, but most were met with silence. Other servants began to appear. At one point the distant perfume of the harem reached him before fading once more. The library, when they reached it, was set against the outer palace wall, but Thomas was not convinced he would be able to find it again on his own. The girl left, hurrying back to her work, feet slapping on the stone floor.

Thomas had come to talk with Khalil, the librarian, again. Francesca had interrupted them before, and now he'd had time to think about the man there were other questions, other matters he might be able to help with.

Thomas pushed at the door, finding it unlocked. He stepped inside and called out, only to be greeted by silence. He allowed the door to close and stood for a moment, breathing deep of the scent of paper, ink and vellum. It was both comforting and exciting.

He walked deeper in search of the librarian to where the corner turned and the space opened out.

"Is anyone here?"

The books and papers swallowed Thomas's words as

though hungry for more. At the far end of the room the low table was scattered with papers, exactly as it had been on his first visit. He wondered were they the same ones. Beyond something lay on the floor, partly concealed. Thomas made his way forward, speeding up as the object resolved into the body of Khalil. He lay on his back, arms outstretched, legs straight. Even before Thomas knelt to check for a pulse he knew he was dead.

Thomas sat on the edge of the table and let his head drop. Another death, another dead end. Frustration ran as a tremble through Thomas's body. He looked around at the papers scattered across the table, but they were only random pages, nothing more.

He glanced at Khalil. What had the man known of this? Did he draw this before or after writing the letter? Thomas knelt and searched through the pages and books on the table. The maps were still there and he pushed them to one side. A large book lay open a quarter the way through and Thomas pulled it close, bent to examine it. Lists of names. Against some were drawn coats of arms and family crests.

Had he been reading the book when someone interrupted him? The same person who killed him? Almost certainly.

Thomas flipped through some pages but saw nothing that might lead to murder. He closed the book and slid it into a gap on a shelf, memorising its position. If Khalil had thought the answer lay in the pages it deserved closer study.

Thomas turned away. He would find Francesca, question her harder this time, not allow her to distract him. She had been a friend to Khalil, perhaps more. At least that was the impression the pair had given. If anyone knew who his killer was she might.

As he made his way toward the doorway, steeling himself for the confrontation, he glanced through the window and stopped in his tracks.

The broad plain below Ronda had been transformed overnight.

Thomas cursed, knowing his investigation was about to be interrupted again. The Spanish army had returned.

CHAPTER 25

This time as Thomas entered the Spanish camp it was astride a horse, a fine white Arabian. It was meant to reflect his status, the effect marred by the roughness of his dress. He looked more like a Berber come direct from the African desert than a civilised man. At least they had allowed him the luxury of bathing first. Not that it would impress the Spanish. They were more likely to consider his lack of body odour ungodly. His companions would attract respect. Three well-dressed soldiers, and Faris al-Rashid who rode at Thomas's side.

Smoke from half a thousand fires streaked trails across the plain. Thomas pulled his tagelmust across his nose and mouth to keep the worst at bay. Smells assaulted him. Burning meat. Filthy bodies. Sweat stained leather and, above it all, gunpowder. The largest cannon were drawn up with their wheels in the ruts left from their previous visit, except this time the bustle of activity around them showed real purpose and not a pretence. Behind stood smaller artillery ranged at lower elevation. As far as Thomas could see soldiers covered the plain to the horizon.

Four Spanish escorts accompanied them, two in front, two behind. They had not drawn weapons, but their hands rested on the pommels of their swords. Thomas was unarmed but unafraid. As he passed men stopped what they were doing and turned to watch the strange figure who stared only ahead, back straight. Thomas didn't want to be here. He should be pursuing the death of the librarian. After the Governor had sent for him and given instructions, Thomas was forced to wait for the others to gather and had managed to discover Khalil had worked in the library for twenty-four of his thirty-five years. Nobody could think who might have wanted to kill him. The man was quiet, studious, a nobody. Thomas had asked Lubna to go examine the body to see if she could find anything he had missed.

He shook his head in an attempt to scatter the thoughts. The other matters would have to wait. He had a negotiation to undertake.

A large tent stood at the heart of the army. Pennants flying above hinted the King was in attendance. Thomas had not seen Fernando since they met in al-Khala over a year before. He hoped the King retained a fondness for him, though he knew the circumstances were vastly different. Once they had fought side by side. Now they were enemies.

He watched as a group of men cast rough dice fashioned of bone, a small pile of coin beside each, a larger pile between them. Thomas had seen the same at every battle he had ever witnessed, had done so himself many years ago. If a man was lucky at dice it was taken as a good omen – he would be lucky on the field of battle too. On the other hand, if he lost then he had used up all his bad luck on the game and tomorrow would be a better day. Soldiers needed little excuse to persuade themselves they would live through whatever the fates planned for them.

A hundred feet from the tent a group of guards blocked

the path. Thomas dismounted, knowing the horses would be considered potential weapons. As he shouldered past the men he admitted grudging admiration for the professionalism of the Spanish army.

The three Moorish soldiers remained where they were, but Faris accompanied him, drawing back a little to allow Thomas to lead.

At the entrance of the tent a figure appeared. Fernando, King of Aragon and Castile. A tall man with dark hair worn long and a trimmed beard, short on his cheeks, drawn to a point at the chin. He wasn't handsome but he was impressive. He was dressed for war with a fine vest of chainmail. A helmet hung loose in his left hand.

He nodded at Thomas. "I heard you were around somewhere."

"Your Grace."

Fernando glanced at Faris. Offered a second nod. "Yes, formality is best in company." His gaze returned. "I take it you have come to negotiate? We will do so, of course, but first the Queen wishes you to dine with us." Again he looked at Faris. "I apologise, the invitation does not extend to yourself, sir. Someone will come for you."

"She is with you?" Thomas was unable to mask his surprise.

"Her presence raises the morale of the troops. They respect me well enough as a general, but they love her unconditionally as their Queen. I wish I could foster the same devotion."

"Men respect strength, Your Grace."

"Yes, you are right. But not so much as they worship God and their Queen." Fernando shook his head as if the thoughts of men were a mystery to him, which Thomas knew was untrue. The man was sharp, with a native cunning. "Come inside and we can put aside the formalities for a little while." He stepped close and clapped Thomas on the shoulder. "It's good to see you again, old friend. There's someone other than Isabel who wants to meet you, too."

As Fernando led him toward the tent Thomas glanced back to see Martin de Alarcón appear. He stopped beside Faris and spoke to him in Arabic. Faris replied in Spanish, his eyes locked on Thomas, a scowl on his face. There would be questions later, but for now he didn't care.

Beyond the entrance lay an outer chamber. A table held a map of Ronda and surrounds, stones laid across its surface. Fernando caught Thomas looking and laughed.

"Forget those. I had the pieces moved when I heard someone was coming. Martin told me you were here, so I hoped it would be you, unless your master had taken you to Malaga." He laughed. "Was that not a grand subterfuge?"

Thomas said nothing, and Fernando walked on. An inner chamber contained another, larger table, this time laid for a meal. On the far side of the canvassed area a short figure turned at the sound of their entry.

If he had not seen Fernando in a year, it had been more like two since he had stood in the presence of Isabel, the Queen of Castile. She was not beautiful, but she was pretty, and it was her intelligence and humanity Thomas admired more than her looks. He knew the respect was reciprocated. Even so all she could do was nod at him and smile.

"I had hoped you would come, Thomas. Welcome." As if they were indulging in a social meeting rather than war. She indicated the table. "Come, sit with us. We have much news to share. I hear you have taken a new wife, a Moor." She said it without judgement, and Thomas wondered how much they knew of him, and why they had bothered to find out.

"I have a son, too," Thomas said. He waited while Isabel moved to the table and sat at its head. Fernando took the chair to her left. Thomas pulled out the one on the right. More places were set around the table, but he sensed there would be only the three of them. For now, at least. Later commanders would be summoned, Faris allowed to join them, and the atmosphere would grow tense.

"A son?" said Isabel. "That I had not heard." She smiled. "I will have to chastise my spies."

Thomas returned the smile. "Tell me who they are, Your Grace, and I will do it for you."

Isabel made a moue of distaste. "We are not in company now, Thomas, you may call me by name. My husband too. Are we not friends?"

"Are we? Once, perhaps, now I am less sure."

"The offer we made before you left Córdoba still stands. All you need do is say the word and a place will be found for you. A fine house. Wealth. You deserve better than to have to dress as a nomad." There was no judgement in her voice. "And yes, we remain friends, I hope. You have done more for us than we can ever repay."

Thomas saw her fingers twitch and for a moment he thought she was about to reach to touch his hand, but of course she could not.

"What is the name of your son?" asked Fernando. "And what age?"

"William, and he has fifteen months."

"He walks?" said Isabel, leaning forward, a mother's

curiosity in her eyes.

Thomas smiled. "The last time I saw him his grandfather was training him in the sword. He has a few words, too."

"He is bright then, like his father. Did you not bring him with you? And I assume his grandfather is the Sultan's General, the northman?"

Thomas nodded, choosing not to explain that although Olaf Torvaldsson was William's grandfather, the woman he now lived with was not the mother.

"Intelligent and a good swordsman," said Fernando. "You are a lucky man, Thomas. It is good he will be safe."

Isabel clapped her palms together and a woman entered through a flap in the canvas wall Thomas had not noticed before.

"We are ready to eat. And you can send him in now."

The woman withdrew. A moment later there was a commotion at the entrance and a young figure slipped through, looking around. His gaze fell on Thomas and a wide grin spread across his face before he made an attempt to stifle it. A Prince was meant to act correctly, but Juan was not yet eight years old, and his excitement got the better of him. He ran to Thomas and threw his arms around him, burying his face against his chest.

Thomas looked over his head toward Isabel, embarrassed at the show of affection, but she smiled and offered a nod of the head.

Thomas untangled himself and stood Juan away from him. He could feel a tremble in the boy's shoulders, saw his attempts to regain an appropriate demeanour.

"You have grown, my Prince."

"Use my name, Thomas."

Thomas suppressed a smile. "I hear a lack of formality

191

carries severe punishment."

"So does defying the heir to the throne of Castile."

"In that case, Juan, come tell me what adventures you have had. What books you have read and what learning you have acquired."

Juan pulled a face at the mention of lessons. He tried to climb onto Thomas's lap, all skinny arms and legs, and once more he glanced at Isabel, but she was distracted as two servants brought a tray of food and bottles of dark red wine. There was plump capon stuffed with herbs, an array of songbirds steeped in oil, even a dish of spiced lamb that would not have been out of place in al-Hamra.

"I can't enjoy this good food with you on my knee," Thomas said, easing Juan off. "But pull your chair up close so we can talk without your parents hearing." Thomas turned to Isabel. "Is it only Juan you brought with you?" He thought of the others, all female, Isabella the eldest, a serious girl who favoured her mother, excitable Juana and the baby Maria, though the baby would be three years of age now.

It was Fernando who answered. "A male child is never too young to learn of war. One day Juan will rule this land. He needs to know how battles are fought."

Thomas glanced at Isabel. Her face was set, offering nothing, but he believed the subject might be a bone of contention between the pair. Fernando was a strong general and no doubt made little allowance for Juan's tender years.

"It will be a long time before he needs such skills, I hope," Thomas said.

"Which is why I ask you again to join our court," said Isabel. "There is no better physician in Spain, which means no better in the world. War is dangerous, but pestilence worse."

"Even I cannot defeat disease," Thomas said. "I wish it were so, but there are some things a physician will never be able to heal."

"Indeed, some things are the province of God, not man," said Isabel.

Thomas drank a single glass of the wine – finer than any he had ever tasted – while Fernando finished the rest of the bottle. The conversation remained light, with both Juan and Isabel prompting Thomas for tales of the exotic Moorish kingdom. He already knew from his time in Qurtuba the Queen held a fascination for the strange customs of the world which existed so close alongside her own. A hatred too, but a love of its knowledge, culture and ways. Fernando was less enamoured, because it was he who conducted the war. The Moors were feared warriors, but now the end was becoming increasingly clear. There would be only one victor in this battle, and the script on the palace would be proven wrong.

Eventually when Juan turned sleepy he was ushered away and the table cleared. Isabel remained, but now there was a clear transfer of power to her husband.

"I don't suppose you have come to offer a surrender?" said Fernando.

Thomas shook his head.

"It was worth the asking. And I don't suppose you are willing to help us?"

"You know my answer," Thomas said. "Do we need to bring my companion in?"

"Will he have anything to add you cannot?"

"I doubt it."

"Then leave him with Martin. He will pretend to negotiate, but it is you and I make the decisions here.

I offer you a word of advice. Tomorrow we unleash the guns. If you can, take those you love and flee as fast and as far as you can, because soon there will be nothing of your town left standing."

It was a threat Thomas ignored. No doubt he was meant to return and try to persuade Ronda's Governor to surrender without resistance. Fernando saw it on his face, his own grim.

"Many will die needlessly."

"It will be what it is," Thomas said.

"You have no intention of fleeing, do you," said Isabel. Thomas shook his head.

"So have you come with an offer?" asked Fernando.

Thomas raised a shoulder. "I am willing to accept your surrender, Your Grace. Or you can return to Qurtuba and my masters will spare your men." He deliberately used the Moorish pronunciation for the city.

Fernando smiled, but there was little of humour in it. "So why are you here? To count our number? Well, I will tell you now to save you the trouble, we are forty cannon, two thousand mounted knights and eight thousand foot soldiers. Plus the women and water carriers and hangers on.

"How many reside within the walls of Ronda? Sixteen thousand, now your leader has left? How many of those are fighting men? I am fully aware your Sultan has scuttled back to his stronghold in Malaga, leaving you at my mercy. There is no need for unnecessary death. Take that as my message to whoever now rules in the eagle's nest. You have until sunset tomorrow to send a reply, and then the guns will spit destruction."

Fernando accompanied Thomas outside, the formality between them restored. While they had been in the tent the day had drained away and shadows now fell long across the trampled ground.

"Last time I was here I saw Lawrence," Thomas said, and then, in case Fernando had forgotten who he spoke of, "The man who rode with us to rescue Juan. It is good to see no ill effects. He is a fine lad."

Fernando nodded. "That he is. I am a lucky man in both my wife and children. My only wish is more of them might live longer. Isabel struggles to carry some to term." It was a strange statement to make, far too personal, but Thomas supposed Fernando felt able to say such to him, who had lived in their palace for over half a year and had cured Juan's leg when no-one else could. "And yes, I know about Lawrence. He is around here somewhere, talking no doubt. He came to me and explained his deception of Mandana."

"And you trust him, after what he did?"

Fernando glanced at Thomas. "What did he do? He rode beside you and I, fought with us."

Thomas had forgotten he hadn't told Fernando of Lawrence's treachery. He should mention it now, for the man wasn't to be trusted. Instead he said, "I thought him dead. As I thought Mandana dead." A memory of the men on the ridge came to Thomas, accompanied by a shiver of dread.

"Ah," said Fernando. "I take it Lawrence said nothing of the Abbot to you."

"Should he have? The man is dead, isn't he?"

Fernando stared across the ranks of soldiers, their noise a constant buzz in the air. "There are times a King must deal with people he would prefer not to, Thomas."

It was no answer, and yet it was. Thomas waited but Fernando offered no further clarification. There was no need.

"I wondered what became of his body," Thomas said, when the silence had stretched to uncomfortable levels. Fernando continued to examine his troops, perhaps something more on his mind yet. "If it is true then a dangerous man walks the earth. A man who stole your son away, who would have killed him."

Another minute passed before Fernando shrugged a shoulder as if he had made a decision. He turned to Thomas. "Mandana claims Juan was always safe. And dangerous men can prove useful – they do work others will not."

This time it was Thomas who was silent. He replayed the King's words in his head. Abbot Mandana, the twisted murderer Thomas had unmasked during his stay in Qurtuba, was now working for Fernando. Thomas thought once more of the men he had observed on the mountain peaks when he lay beside Yusuf. The grey cloaks, the hoods, the familiarity of their leader. He wondered what task Fernando had set Mandana to take him to such a desolate spot.

"Does the Queen know he is alive, that he works for you?" Thomas asked.

"Of course not. And she never will." Fernando's eyes bored into Thomas's. "Will she, my friend?"

"Feral animals bite their masters, Your Grace."

"Only if the master is weak and shows fear. Do not be concerned for me or my family. The man has been brought into the fold, but he knows his place, and is useful to me."

* * *

It was full dark by the time Thomas and Faris al-Rashid made their way up the steep cobbled street that led to the top of the cliff, winding up through sheer-walled houses on one side, gardens clinging to the slope on the other. The presence of an army on its doorstep had subdued the mood of the town and there were few people on the streets. Faris had said little, only enough to make it clear he believed he had been instrumental in the negotiations. Martin de Alarcón would have seen to that. Thomas passed on what he knew, knowing the Governor would listen to Faris sooner than him.

He returned the fine horse to the stables and made his way into the palace, thinking to see the Governor in any case. He wanted to ensure Faris passed on everything he should. But Abraham al-Haquim had already gone to bed with orders not to be disturbed.

Shaking his head at the stupidity of the man, Thomas wound through corridors that were growing more familiar. Al-Haquim had made a suite of rooms available to him and Lubna, a distinct improvement on their previous lodgings. Thomas found her there, poring over a medical text.

She glanced up, smiled. "I liberated this from the library after taking care of that man."

"Did you examine him carefully first?"

"Of course." Lubna slipped a piece of thread between the pages to mark her place and closed the book. "Like the others it was made to look accidental. The method is subtle. Most would miss the signs unless they knew what to look for. It is near impossible to tell the cause of death, it is nothing like a violent strangulation. Oh, and he'd had sex recently before he died."

"You could tell?"

"Of course I could tell. Men leave more obvious sign than a woman."

Thomas sat and offered a distracted kiss to her cheek, his mind already following skeins of logic. "So are we seeking two individuals – a woman as well as a man? Or do they work in concert? We saw a woman at the top of the cliff. I thought her presence a coincidence, but perhaps she is part of it."

"How long have you known Jorge?" asked Lubna, causing Thomas to frown.

"What has he to do with anything? You know how long, it's been…" He hesitated, working it out in his head, subtracting to come up with an answer that surprised him. "Twenty years. I operated on him when he was twelve."

"And still you think because the librarian had sex it must have been with a woman?"

"Well, no, but…" Thomas stopped, knowing Lubna had caught him out. "Jorge has sex with women, he tells me all the time."

"Only women?"

"Is there any way to tell if Khalil had been with another man or a woman?" He began to warm to the subject. "A man would make sense, of course. So a man then."

"It was a suggestion," said Lubna, "nothing more."

"A good one, though." Thomas unwound his tagelmust and scratched at his head, convinced he had picked up fleas as he passed through the Spanish camp. "I should find Jorge and ask if he knows of a way to tell."

Lubna laughed and Thomas frowned at her, only making her laugh harder.

"Sometimes, Thomas Berrington, you are beyond price, and it is then I remember why I love you so much."

"You do?"

"Love you, or remember I do?"

"Either." He worked to keep a smile from his lips. "Would someone know they were being murdered, or are the effects so subtle they would not fight their assailant?"

"If they were indulging in what I think they were he would not even consider them an assailant, would he?" said Lubna. "Now forget about Spain, forget about murder, and come to bed."

CHAPTER 26

Had Ronda not been surrounded by ten thousand Spanish soldiers it would have been a perfect morning. Wisps of pale cloud streaked the sky, promising rain before the day ended, but for the moment the breeze carried a welcome freshness, clearing the air of dust. Distant peaks sparkled as if newly washed, and it appeared they had uprooted themselves overnight and marched closer. Or, Thomas thought, this might all be caused by his state of mind. Lubna had been demanding the night before, taking command, keeping him awake long after exhaustion tried to claim him.

Thomas knew he should be reporting to the Governor but felt the need to clear his head first, so had come to the square above the cliffs to look at the army spread over the plain. It too was sprinkled with the fairy dust of the day, each figure etched in clarity. Men moved slowly as if they had all the time in the world. At the heart of the gathering Thomas saw two figures emerge from the large white tent. A woman and a boy. Isabel and Juan, come to taste the clarity of the air. He wondered if they looked up and saw him watching, but if they did he could not tell.

Duty dug insidious fingers into his shoulders, making them tense. He bought a handful of roasted almonds from a stall and chewed on them one at a time as he returned to the palace. He stopped at one of the many water spouts that dotted the town and drank. As he was about to turn away he hesitated, staring at the flow emerging from a stone pipe. He cocked his head to one side. Did the water flow less strongly than it had? It appeared to. He tried to recall how it had emerged before and failed. He knew the water was carried from the mountain snows through a series of stone troughs and pipes, over forty miles directly into the town, exactly as it was in Gharnatah. Thomas had always taken its bounty for granted, and he did so again, turning away to his task.

In the square fronting the palace soldiers were gathered, horses being saddled, pikes stacked in one corner. Men strapped leather jerkins on, tightened belts hung with weapons.

When Thomas found him the Governor stood with another man in the throne room. He looked uncomfortable in a place steeped in so much power, but no doubt willing to use it to bolster his own.

"I expected you last night," he said. "You are too late now. Faris has already told me everything."

"I came," Thomas said, "but was told you had already retired and were not to be disturbed."

"You should have overridden them, as Faris did. Well, tell me what you know, in case you have some other information. How many are there?"

"Ten thousand," Thomas said. "Rested and well-armed."

"Ten thousand?" It was the other man who spoke. Obviously a soldier in a senior position. He wore clothing of good quality, a fine sword hanging from his waist that reflected shards of sunlight against the walls. The man turned to al-Haquim. "We cannot fight ten thousand, Malik." The honorific was not due a governor, but these were not normal times.

"You do not have to fight them all, only those manning the cannon and those closest to our walls. The Spanish are cowards. A strong show of force and they will flee." Al-Haquim glanced at Thomas. "The King's flag flies over the large tent, does it not? Is he in command?"

"The King is there, yes." Thomas made no mention of Isabel or Juan, feeling no loyalty to this man or his town. He was thinking about how much damage a small force might inflict. He had seen enough battles to know the ferocity of the Moors and the skill they displayed, but the Spanish outnumbered them many times over.

"Good. Perhaps we can take him prisoner. A fine catch that would make. We could end the war today. Go with Tarik and tell him all you know before he rides to victory."

The soldier said nothing as they walked fast along the corridors, populated now but nobody looked their way, and all made sure they left room for the two men.

"You don't think he truly believes you can win, do you?" Thomas said.

"Don't underestimate my warriors," said Tarik. "How are the Spanish armed, other than the bombards?"

Thomas saw no reason to hold anything back. "They have crossbow, musket, swords and pikemen, obviously. Their men are well armed."

"No archers other than that pretence for a weapon?" Meaning crossbows, a weapon spurned by the Moors as too slow to reload, even if they were effective over a longer range than their own short bows.

"None I saw, but that doesn't mean there aren't any. I

wasn't given a grand tour."

"A Moorish archer can fire a dozen arrows while one of their bows is being drawn. And a Moorish swordsman is worth ten of the Spanish." Tarik laughed. "I feel sorry for them. Few we may be, but victory is ours to take. Tell me everything you know."

There was little information to pass on other than numbers, and the man could see those himself from standing on the clifftop.

Thomas stopped at the main gate as Tarik strode across the courtyard, greeting favoured soldiers, slapping backs and punching shoulders. Watching him Thomas saw he was a good general, liked by the men. A hard man who would reward those who fought well and give respect to those who fell.

Thomas turned away, thinking of the hospital tents on the edge of the Spanish camp, a sight he had not expected. Isabel had spoken proudly of them, an idea Thomas had set in her mind which she had improved on. He knew he needed to find Lubna and tell her to prepare an infirmary here. There must be an empty house somewhere, or if not one would need to be requisitioned. Tables could serve as beds. He had to find out what other medical men lived within the town walls. There must be some, and he would want them on hand when the battle started. If the general had been Olaf Torvaldsson, Thomas knew he would have demanded his presence at the rear of the attack to take care of the injured. But Tarik was not Olaf, who would have judged the odds better and not planned such a futile attack in the first place, one that would serve only to get men killed.

It took an hour to brief Lubna, half that to persuade Abraham al-Haquim to instruct for a place to be requisitioned, preferably close to the palace. When Thomas found himself alone, knowing he could trust Lubna to do her part, less sure of al-Haquim, he made his way to the library. Too much was going on to give his full attention to Khalil's death, but it nagged at him. It was the most recent, thus the most likely to yield a clue to identify who stole the man's life.

The library door was closed but unlocked – everyone knew what had happened and few wanted to visit. Thomas needed time alone to think. Throwing the bolt on the door was like a wash of cool water on a hot day, locking out the chaos his life had become. His mind stilled.

He walked the aisles, fingers trailing across binders and shelves, not seeing what he touched. The scent of knowledge filled the air, a scent more seductive to him than any of the perfumes that sweetened the harem.

The table where Khalil had lain remained as it had been when he discovered the body. Thomas sat on one corner, staring at the floor. There was no sign death had occurred here, none of the detritus of murder he had witnessed so often before. No blood, no fluids, no discarded weapon. Nothing missing ... or was there? He knew, with a sense of despair, he wouldn't be able to recognise if there was. None of the material here was recent. Even if something incriminating remained Thomas was aware he had no chance of finding it, not amongst the thousands of documents. He wondered if a new librarian would be appointed, then smiled. Ten thousand Spaniards sat on the plain below Ronda – there would be no need of a new librarian.

He went to where he had placed the book of crests Khalil had been studying before he died. It was no longer where Thomas had placed it. He searched the other shelves nearby in case he was mistaken, but the spine of the book was ornate and couldn't be missed. Someone had come and taken it.

Thomas sat at the table, legs drawn beneath him. Had whoever took the book known it would identify the killer? Or had they done no more than he had and hidden the volume in plain sight? What had Khalil claimed, ten thousand books? Too many to search every one. Thomas wondered how many people had access to the library and knew the answer. Almost anyone could have taken it. Not just residents of the palace, but townspeople too. With chaos reigning normal process had broken down. He had seen people wandering in and out who would not have been admitted a week before.

He picked up a map he had examined before, examining it even as his mind moved in other directions. It was printed on vellum rather than paper, which meant it was unlikely to be Arabic. He turned it around, unable to tell which way it was meant to be viewed. There were tiny marks indicating waves so at least he could tell which was land and sea. The coast was indented with two deep river estuaries. To the north – or south – of one of them was a settlement. Beside it other marks might have represented a name, but Thomas was unable to read them. He peered more closely, something about the letters sparking a memory. He stopped chasing it and let his mind still as he stared at the map. Yes, he thought, the settlement was north of the river, which meant the coast faced east.

Was it perhaps the far side of Africa, an almost completely unknown land? Or the Indies? Thomas shook his head. It could be anywhere. And then it came to him, the scratching on the vellum. They were runes, the scribblings made by northmen. Ancient symbols that were no longer used, so even if Olaf had been there he would have been unable to read them. An excitement sparked inside. Was this another clue? Is it why Khalil had brought it to the table, because it offered another link? Was the killer a northman, like Olaf Torvaldsson? There were many in al-Andalus, mercenaries come in search of riches. He wondered how many northmen were in Ronda, and if they could be identified. Some would be soldiers and have left with al-Zagal, but others must remain. It was another tangled trail to unravel.

Thomas put the map to one side and picked up another. Was everything on the table a pointer? Khalil would have placed them here for a reason. The second map Thomas recognised immediately. The coast of North Africa, circles showing familiar towns and cities. Fine lines linked some to the coast of Spain and Portugal. Malaka, Cadiz, Lisboa. Slave routes, he was sure, others leading inland to where all towns, all features faded. The northern and western coast of Africa, the known world, and in the centre nothing, a blankness that hid a million wonders.

Was Khalil's killer with him when he studied these documents? Was it a woman who'd had sex with him first? Would a woman be strong enough to overpower a man, even one as cosseted as Khalil? Thomas knew it was not a matter of strength. Lubna had explained how. A woman would be more than strong enough.

Thomas let the map drop and closed his eyes. He considered who a slavers' map would interest. Kisera had come to Ronda as a slave, but was already dead when someone stole Khalil's life. Her brother was not, so was Simki the killer? Thomas shook his head. If Simki murdered Khalil did that mean he killed his own sister too?

Thomas stood, pushing hair back from his face. He went to the window and stared out, but nothing had changed. An attack would take time to plan, and evening would be a better time, when the enemy was eating, lulled into security, bored from the waiting.

As he leaned closer to find the front ranks he saw the bombardiers working on their weapons, and recalled Fernando's promise. Noon tomorrow.

Had Khalil left the maps and papers on the table on purpose, hoping he would find the them? If so he hadn't known how little it meant to Thomas. Worse than nothing, because it only brought more confusion.

When Thomas found him Jorge didn't know where Francesca was. He hadn't seen her all day. It wasn't unusual, he said. There were many women who served the harem, all of them busy.

"In Gharnatah, perhaps," Thomas said. "How many here?"

"You're right. There are no more than a dozen concubines," said Jorge. "I have barely anything to do, even less now the Sultan has gone."

They had met as Thomas made his way back to his rooms and instead of returning he had fallen in step beside his friend. His unease remained, a mix of excitement and bafflement. Their footsteps had taken them toward the harem itself. There were no guards posted at the entrance, nothing more than an invisible barrier, and Thomas realised they had been called away to prepare for the coming raid. He wondered if they would return to this, the most coveted of assignments.

"Does Abraham leave you in peace?" Thomas asked.

"I wish he would. Nothing to do with my work here, the man doesn't understand protocol. My responsibility is the harem, nothing more. But he expects me to undertake administration." Jorge glanced at Thomas. "Me."

"Have you told him you don't read or write?"

"Tried. I don't think he heard."

"So what do you do?"

"Nothing. What can he do to me? When al-Zagal returns all will return to normal."

Thomas opened his mouth then closed it. He had been about to point out it was unlikely the Sultan would return. Unlikely Ronda would exist come the end of the summer, but it seemed cruel to do so. Here inside the palace life continued, barely changed, as though an army was not camped beyond the town walls.

Thomas caught sight of Helena. She was talking with a short, dark haired woman and at first Thomas thought it was Lubna until he noted the clothing she wore, or barely wore. The colour and smoothness of her skin matched Lubna's, but she would never go uncovered in public.

Helena looked up and saw him. For once a grimace did not twist her features. Instead she smiled, touched the other woman on the shoulder and walked toward them. As she came near her scent reached them and her gaze switched to Jorge.

"Have arrangements been made for us to assist if needed?" she asked.

"Assist in what?" Thomas said.

"In the infirmary. We might be unskilled but we can

help."

The shock of her statement stilled his tongue. The offer was so unlike Helena it took him a moment to respond.

"Are you sure? It will not be pleasant."

"We must all make sacrifices. I have already spoken with the others. One or two refused, but the rest are willing. Lubna can tell us what we need to do."

"What about Francesca?" Thomas judged her too fragile to agree to tend the wounded.

"She has made herself scarce," Helena said. "Perhaps she heard what I was asking the others."

"Do you know her well?"

"Barely. She is strange and does not welcome attention."

"What do you know of her? There must be something. I know you see more than you pretend."

Helena smiled. "Be careful, Thomas, or I may start to believe you are softening toward me." She laid a hand against his chest. "You should talk with the others, they know her better than me."

"Then that's what I'll do." Thomas turned away, needing to escape her touch. He half expected Helena to follow and was not disappointed. He moved to a window and stared out. The view was toward the north, the land unstained by soldiers. One or two men on horseback crossed the rolling countryside, dust hanging in the air behind them. Scouts looking for a weakness, perhaps, or no more than knights stretching their legs. He narrowed his eyes, trying to make out faces, wondering if it might be Fernando. But despite the clarity of the air the distance was too great.

Helena stopped at his side, her shoulder touching his

arm. He knew he could not move away without giving offence and, for some reason, he did not wish to do so.

"Could she kill a man?" Thomas said, feeling Helena tense. He was sure his question reminded her of events a year and a half before, when the concubine Eva had been Helena's lover while she carried his son. Before anyone knew of the corruption buried within her new friend. Since saving her life Thomas had sensed a change in Helena, a lessening of the self-preoccupation that had always defined her.

"I told you I don't know her well. How am I supposed to answer a question like that? Do you suspect her of murder? Of killing the librarian?" She turned, her eyes scanning the room. "Are we safe here?"

"Safer than out there," Thomas said. He didn't know if he suspected Francesca or not, only that she knew Khalil and had been present in the library a day before he died. For all he knew she was a frequent visitor. No, he didn't suspect her, but believed she might know who killed Khalil even if she wasn't aware of the knowledge. She had been a friend to Kisera. Was she also friend to Simki? Did she invite him into the palace where he discovered something in those maps and books? Simki was literate, able to read the contents of the library.

"I know you will look after me, Thomas – like you did before." Helena came on tiptoe and brushed Thomas's cheek with her lips. "I am grateful you care." And then she was gone, a shimmer of silk, a trail of fingers, her smell lingering long after she swept from the room.

Thomas looked around, afraid someone might have witnessed what had happened. Wondering why he was concerned if they had. He was still remembering Helena's touch when Lubna found him.

"I've been looking for you everywhere. It never occurred to me you might be here."

"Have you found somewhere for the infirmary?"

"Yes, there is a place, but that's not why I'm here. You have to come. There's been another death."

Chapter 27

The house of Bartolomo Giminez lay within two hundred feet of Rodrigo Morales's, not that Thomas paid the fact much heed. Ronda was small, and being perched atop its eyrie meant houses were of necessity built close together.

A gathering of the curious blocked the entrance but Jorge shouldered his way through. Thomas and Lubna trailed close behind. The entrance door was closed. Jorge entered without knocking, to be greeted by an old man, tall and exceedingly thin, who demanded what business they were on.

"There has been a death, has there not?" said Jorge. "My companion and his wife are physicians."

"Physicians are of no use to my mistress," said the man.

Thomas pushed past Jorge, a sense of impatience running through his body. "I have been tasked by the Governor to investigate all deaths in the town. Take me to the body."

"She is being prepared—"

"Take me now and have them stop their work. I would see her as she was found."

"That is not possible." The man made no move, still half blocking the hallway. Thomas made a signal to Lubna who, being smaller, slid past him in search of someone more amenable. Jorge pushed through on the other side and climbed the stairs two at a time.

"Stop!" called the man, but he was too frail to catch Jorge, and as his back was turned Thomas followed, another cry coming. From the gallery it was obvious where the death had occurred. Two female servants, both cooks from the stains on their clothing, stood beyond an open door trying to peer inside. Jorge was already within the room, and as Thomas followed he saw him pulling a woman away from a body sprawled on a wide bed.

"You cannot be here." The servant from below arrived, his chest heaving as he tried to catch a breath. "My mistress must not be seen by—"

"What is her name?" Thomas overrode him, and when he made no reply raised his voice. "I want her name, now."

"Valentina. Valentina Giminez. But you cannot be here, she is being prepared."

Thomas turned away. "Jorge, get rid of them. All of them."

Jorge drew the female servant away, pushing her toward the door. As the man tried to pass he placed a hand on his chest and turned him around, steering them both from the room.

"Lock the door," Thomas said. He turned to the body, relieved to see that little had been done to it. "On second thought, go find the woman you ejected and bring her back."

"Are you sure?" Jorge stared at him.

"I want to know what has been done to her."

Jorge nodded, unlocked the door and stepped outside. Thomas knelt on the edge of the bed, his eyes scanning the figure. Another beauty, and he wondered were there any ugly women in Ronda. Possibly not. He had noticed how some towns contained predominantly handsome

213

men and women, whilst others seemed populated by those ejected from the gates of hell.

The woman lay on her back, arms at her sides, legs straight. She would not have been found this way, he was sure. He bent to examine her throat, thinking of what Simki had told him. This woman had died in bed, not at the foot of a cliff, but if a length of cloth had been used to steal her breath it had left no sign.

He looked up as the door opened. Jorge led the woman in, a hand on her arm to prevent her escaping. After being expelled she now showed a reluctance to return.

"Show me how she was when you found her. Was it you who found her, or someone else?"

"Elsa – her chambermaid. She always brings tea first thing."

"At what hour?"

"Dawn. Always at dawn, but no specific hour."

"Fetch her," Thomas said, and the woman fled, glad to be dismissed.

"I can't find it," Thomas said.

"Can't find what?" said Jorge.

"A length of cloth, linen most likely. It was used to kill her."

"What cloth?"

Thomas looked toward Jorge. "What do you know of this household? Go see if anything was taken from this room."

"I'm a eunuch, not a scribe," said Jorge. "But I will go and find out, if you wish. Rather that than remain here while you work."

"There will be nothing gruesome," Thomas said.

"Not for you," said Jorge, and left once more, holding the door open as he passed to admit a small woman barely older than a girl.

"You are Elsa?" Thomas said, and she nodded, curtseying, dark hair caught beneath a cap. Her pale blue robe was fashioned of rough cotton, the front marked with a stain.

Thomas motioned to her. "Come here. I want to know exactly how your mistress lay when you found her." He looked around. "Where is her tea?"

"I don't understand, sir."

"The other servant said you always brought her tea. How did you carry it? In a cup or on a tray?"

"On a tray, sir. I dropped it when I saw her." She put a hand against herself. "It went all over my skirts. I will have to wash them before I bring…" Thomas watched realisation spread across her face. There would be no tea tomorrow. Perhaps no job.

"She wasn't lying this way when you found her, was she?" Thomas said.

Elsa shook her head, biting her bottom lip.

"Then how? Tell me."

"She was…" Tears filled her eyes, rolled along her cheeks. "What will become of me now? I have been in service less than a year. The master knows my father."

"If that is true you will be found another position, now tell me exactly how she was when you came in." Thomas fought impatience, knowing losing his temper would only serve to frighten the girl even more than she already was. "She was naked, wasn't she?"

The girl nodded.

"And was there anything at her throat?"

A shake of the head. "Nothing sir. She was as you see her now."

"Except she is not, is she. How was she lying?"

Elsa approached a little closer. "Half turned away..." She took another step and Thomas moved aside. He saw Lubna stand closer to the girl, pleased with her empathy. He watched as she turned the woman, exposing a pale back and slim buttocks. The girl glanced in his direction as if ashamed of her mistress's exposure.

"We are both physicians," Thomas said, as if that made everything all right. And it seemed, to some extent, it did.

"Her arm was stretched out... no, the other one, the one beneath her."

Lubna lifted the body, tendons standing out in her slim arms. She pulled the woman's arm out, looking toward Elsa until she nodded.

"Her legs?"

"One knee bent... yes, like that. The other was more this way."

"And she was as we see her now?" asked Lubna.

Elsa nodded, a flush pinking her cheeks.

"Did she usually sleep naked?"

Elsa nodded.

"So it was not unusual to come in and find her this way?"

"She slept beneath a sheet," said Elsa, "even in the hottest weather."

"She slept alone?"

A nod. "When master wanted her she went to his room." No shame here, only the normal operation of a household.

Thomas stepped closer. "Are there secrets in this house?" he asked.

"I don't understand, sir." But her eyes would not meet his.

"I think you do. The master is an older man, is he not?"

"He is, sir."

"And your mistress is, what, not yet twenty?"

"Twenty-three, sir. She takes care of herself for the master."

"Only for the master?"

Once more Elsa's eyes skittered away, lips pursed to contain the secrets she knew.

"Someone was here last night, wasn't he?" he said. "Who was it?"

"I do not know."

"Your mistress had lovers, did she not?"

"I do not know," said Elsa again, and Thomas knew he would get nothing more from her.

"Thank you for your help. You may return to your duties."

Elsa turned to him, firming her narrow shoulders. "My duties lie there on the bed." She looked him up and down, unimpressed. "Sir." She pushed past him and left the room.

Thomas went to the body. He slid the linen strip around the throat, wrapped it twice and drew it tight. Then he turned to Lubna, who nodded.

"Like this?" he asked, half kneeling on the bed so he almost covered the body without touching it. He understood why the strips of linen were as long as they were. Twice around a neck left plenty free to get a firm grip on.

"Most likely," said Lubna.

Thomas straightened, examining the bed before shaking his head. "Too much disturbance." He touched a spot. "This might be where a knee rested, but it

217

could have been made when they turned her." He slid his hand along the cold thigh, drew it back to show Lubna a glistening on his fingers before wiping it on the bedclothes. "Whoever did this took his own pleasure first."

"Or after," said Lubna.

"I prefer not to think on that."

"You may have to."

"Not until I must. So how is this different to Khalil? Other than he was male?"

"He was not naked, or had been re-dressed," said Lubna, and Thomas nodded in approval.

"Is it significant?"

"You know men," said Lubna. "They have no need to remove all their clothing to achieve their ends."

Thomas frowned as her words sparked a thought. "So whoever did this may not have undressed either."

"Undressed enough," said Lubna.

"Obviously." He leaned across the body once more, reached for the right arm that lay stretched out and examined the nails. They were long, well-cared for. Nothing lay beneath them, nor under those of the left hand.

"I don't think she fought him," said Lubna.

"Neither do I, but sometimes you get lucky. Not this time." He felt the arms, thighs and neck. "She died sometime in the depth of the night. After midnight but before dawn."

"She took tea at dawn," said Lubna. "So whoever did this would be long gone by then."

Thomas sat on the bed, ignoring the body that lay beside him. "Do you get any feeling about this?" he asked. "Is this the culmination of an affair or a single act?"

Lubna smiled. "I'll get Jorge, shall I?"

Thomas stared at her, then laughed. "Yes, fetch him, tell him we have finished our inhuman deeds."

When Lubna brought Jorge she said, "If you don't need me anymore I'll go and talk with the servants. I don't think that girl knew anything more, but somebody will."

Thomas nodded agreement.

"What do you see here?" he asked Jorge when they were alone.

Jorge cast a brief glance at the body, as brief as he could make it.

"Look harder, man," Thomas said. "This is important. A woman is dead and we are no closer to catching the killer. How many more will there be if we don't find him?"

Jorge seemed as if he was going to object, then shook his head and turned to face the bed.

"She has a good figure. Her legs in particular. Is this how it was?"

Thomas nodded. "As far as I can tell. I believe them all linked, even if two died in other circumstances. It's too much of a coincidence for there to be so many deaths in such a short space of time." He raised his gaze to meet Jorge's. "There is a theory I heard, that some of the deaths might have been accidental."

"How can you kill someone by accident?" said Jorge.

"Do you know of a practice where a cloth or rope is tightened at the throat to increase sexual pleasure?"

Jorge offered a withering look. "I have lived in the harem over half my life, of course I know the practice."

Thomas wanted to ask a question but swallowed it back, searched for another. "Do all rich men feel the need to own a beautiful wife?"

Jorge raised a shoulder. "You know as well as I they do. What is the point of money if it cannot buy you whatever you want? Houses, clothes, horses, people."

"So why do they sleep in separate rooms? Would a man not want this woman in his bed?"

"It's not about sex, it's about power and the prestige a beautiful wife brings. And when he wants sex all he has to do is ask. She is his chattel, to do with as he wishes. As good as a slave. No, better than a slave, because here there is a pretence of willingness." Jorge stared at Thomas. "You know it is so, my friend. It is why Helena was sent to you all those years ago, as a gift to raise your importance. The Sultan preferred to deal with a man of substance, not some ragamuffin."

It was a long speech for Jorge. Too long, Thomas thought.

"We need to talk with the husband," he said.

"Already done. I don't waste my time hanging around hallways." Jorge glanced at Thomas, at the woman lying beside him. "Doesn't it bother you, having her lying there that way?"

Thomas glanced down. "She's not going to attack me. What did you discover?"

"He had no expectation she would be exclusively his, only that she appeared to be so, and was discreet."

"The servants knew?"

"How could they not? This room is on the upper floor, and in a house such as this there is always someone on duty."

"Even in the small hours of the morning?"

"Is that when it was done?"

Thomas nodded.

"Even then. It is like the palace. A house this rich doesn't exist without a great deal of work, and there are no more than eight staff in all. That stick man who met us when we arrived has a room beside the front door, just like Simki. It is the way things are done, so they are always available for whoever knocks on the door, at whatever time of day or night. Do you believe someone could sneak past that one?"

"No," Thomas said. "So you asked him who the lover is?"

Jorge gave him a look that was answer enough.

"Does he have a name?"

"He claims he saw no-one," said Jorge.

"You believe him?"

"I see no reason why he would lie."

Thomas looked at the body. "Somebody killed her."

Jorge walked to the single window. It was small but large enough to admit a man if he was not fat, and was flexible enough. He pushed one of the small mottled panes with his finger. The window swung open.

"I thought you were the clever one," said Jorge.

"I'd have gotten around to it." Thomas rose, pushed Jorge aside and peered through the window. There was a twenty foot drop to the street, but only a few feet away on the other side of the narrow lane sat a single-story building.

Jorge pushed against him as he too tried to peer out.

"Could you do it?" he asked.

Thomas judged the distance. "Once, but not now."

"I'm younger than you and I wouldn't risk it."

"You might if you had killed a woman and this was your only means of escape."

"And entry," said Jorge.

"It explains why nobody saw anything. But getting in would be a lot harder than getting out."

"It often is," said Jorge, and Thomas threw him an impatient glance, not entirely understanding him. "But we both saw the man on the cliff top. This is someone who revels in risk. The more danger the better."

"At least we know we are looking for someone young and fit enough to leap the distance and climb through the window." He poked his head out for a moment, testing its limits with his shoulders. He could fit through, Jorge too if he wanted. Which meant Simki could. "If he missed the window he'd likely break a leg, if not two."

"Our man would not miss," said Jorge. "You can almost admire him."

"Apart from the killing," Thomas said.

"Yes… apart from that."

Thomas began to pull the window shut, intending to lock it, when he heard the commotion of many horses' hooves on stone. He leaned out and looked along the street in time to see a stream of soldiers filing past.

"It begins," he said. He pulled back inside. "We need to go and prepare the infirmary. This will have to wait until tomorrow."

Jorge peered briefly through the window. "You don't need me, leave me here. I will ask questions of the staff."

CHAPTER 28

A huge cheer rose from the top of the cliff where the inhabitants of Ronda had gathered to watch a magnificent victory. The entire town were convinced they would see the Spanish repulsed. Ronda had always been considered invulnerable.

Thomas and Lubna rushed through almost empty streets toward the palace. An infirmary had been set up in one of the barrack blocks housing the soldiers, and they would be needed there soon whatever the outcome of the raid. Despite knowing what that outcome was likely to be Thomas wanted to watch, so he led the way to the library and the wide windows that looked over the plain. It was, if anything, a better viewing platform than the square – and considerably safer. He feared at least one watcher would be jostled over the edge of the cliff there.

There was no hesitation. The gates at the foot of the cliff were thrown wide and the Moors streamed out, riding hard and fast for the opening ranks of Spanish. Archers lined the base of the cliff, releasing arrows which arced high before falling in a rain of death. Each archer was able to release six or eight arrows a minute. Watching, Thomas saw their range was less than English archers would achieve, but it forced the front ranks of the opposing army into a stumbling retreat.

Mounted men rode hard at the confused ranks. Scimitars flashed and blood flowed. Thomas felt a sense of unreality, as if the scene wasn't really happening, events playing out silently, distance and the barrier of glass masking all sound.

A small group of riders struck off along the front of the Spanish force, their swords sheathed as they drew short Moorish bows and began to fire into the ranks. They headed directly to where the large cannon were fixed into position. More Spaniards fell before their own archers could make their way to the front. Crossbows were slow in comparison to a bow, and although a few mounted Moors fell, the majority continued to take a toll on the enemy. Then a group of a dozen Spaniards came to the fore. Thomas narrowed his eyes, trying to make sense of what he saw. Each of them carried a crossbow, but it was like none he had ever seen before. The extended section was far deeper than normal, with a stacked rank of platforms. The men placed the head of their weapons on the ground and began to attach some form of pulley which they proceeded to wind hard.

"Do you see that?" Thomas said.

Lubna leaned close against his side. "Crossbows," she said, familiar with weapons. Being the daughter of a general made her more knowledgeable than most men in the art of war.

"A different kind of crossbow," Thomas said. "I don't have a good feeling about this. Our archers need to target them, but they're concentrating on the bombardiers."

"Crossbows are slow, they're doing what they've been told. The cannon are the biggest threat to the town."

Thomas saw one of the Spaniards raise the weapon to his shoulder, sighting, seeking targets. He ignored single men until he found a knot of riders galloping parallel to the cannon. Without hesitation he released, but instead of a single bolt six flew, one after another. The first took a Moorish soldier in the arm. Only one other found a target before the man began once more to load his weapon. By then others had loaded their bows and were firing, staggering their release so that a solid stream of bolts brought mayhem. Moors fell from their mounts to be trampled underfoot.

The Spanish were responding now. Muskets appeared, even slower to reload than the crossbows, but the sound of their firing finally penetrated into the silent library, and beside him Thomas felt Lubna flinch and move away.

"I cannot watch," she said, sitting beside the wide table.

Thomas saw smoke explode from the barrels of the muskets, the sound coming long seconds later. Ragged scraps of cloth fluttered out, the metal ball moving too fast to see. The flash and sound scared the attacking force as much as the threat of being hit. Muskets were notoriously inaccurate and if badly loaded could be as dangerous to the wielder as those aimed at.

The main force of Moors had speared their way deep into Spanish ranks, using bow and sword to inflict damage on those not yet prepared. But the Spanish didn't take long to gather themselves. Mounted commanders rode through the ranks, shouting orders. Lines were formed, pikes creating a solid barrier the Moors could not penetrate.

Slowly the Spanish began to advance, a yard at a time, each line holding firm. The area the Moors had managed to clear began to shrink. Their general, who had been in the forefront of the attack, now saw their escape route being blocked and waved for his men to retreat, but already it was too late. The Spanish closed the circle, a solid wall of pikemen preventing flight. Arrows flew in both directions. Slowly the number of Moorish soldiers mounted or on foot dwindled until no more than two hundred remained.

The Spanish paused their attack. A mounted man rode into the space before the Moorish general, still astride his stallion. Words were exchanged, both sides tense. Then the general threw down his sword. He turned in the saddle and shouted something, and one by one his men followed suit. Spaniards moved in, cautious, and took the general's reins. They pulled him from the saddle, a knot of men forming around him. A fist flew and the general went to his knees. For a moment it looked as if he would be killed until the Spanish commander rode close and got between him and his men.

Slowly the Moors were rounded up and led deep into the Spanish camp as prisoners.

Thomas turned away from the window.

"There won't be much for us to do," he said.

"What?" Lubna rose and came to the window, a piece of paper in her hand.

"You didn't expect them to return victorious, did you?"

"I expected them to return bloodied."

"One or two, but most are taken prisoner." Thomas watched the small force that had attacked the artillery riding hard toward the gates. A small opening had been left and they had to form a single file to enter. Others, injured and slower, were hunted down and despatched or, if an officer was present, tied and led away.

"We should go to the infirmary anyway, there will

be injured arriving soon. But you should see this first." Lubna held out the paper she was holding.

Thomas glanced at it. "A slaver's map," he said. "Yes, I've seen it."

"And this, on the back?" Lubna turned the page over. Written in a tiny hand were two numbers separated by a dot.

"What is it, a date?"

"It's a reference to another document. I looked, and almost all the maps have one. I think they refer to supporting documents. So I checked the bookcases and they all have numbers burned into them. It's quite logical, really. The numbers start nearest to the door and go up as you come this way. The second number indicates a shelf counted from bottom to top."

Thomas looked at the map again. "So this is case thirty-eight, shelf seven." He checked the nearest one.

"I found it earlier," said Lubna. She walked to a shelf and pulled down a slim volume. She returned, holding the book out.

Thomas took the journal. The cover was smooth leather, dark, and for a moment he experienced a horrified suspicion it was made from the skin of one of the slaves. He tried to push the thought aside and opened it. Within lay pages of writing, less well formed than that on the back of the map. Some of the names listed were smudged, others almost obscured from water damage.

Each page contained between twenty and thirty names. Beside each were cryptic notations that meant nothing, but which Thomas suspected gave the origin of each individual. He was also sure the names shown were those assigned the slave and not their owners. A third column showed a number. These ranged from low single digits up to the high forties, but nothing beyond. Age, he suspected, as far as it could be determined. As he leafed through the pages he noticed that some of the names had been scored through with a line. Slaves who died in transit, he wondered?

"You believe the map and journal linked?" Thomas said.

"If that is what the number means. We should go, the injured will be arriving by now."

"There are others who can deal with them for now." Thomas turned to the final page of the journal, curious to see if there was another number on the back linking it to something else, but it was blank. He looked through the pages once more, noting that they were arranged in blocks with a bold name at the head of a new page. After a moment he concluded it was the name of a vessel, the list of names after its cargo. He wondered which of these pages related to Simki and Kisera, then knew how. He flipped pages quickly until he found the first entry scored through, then turned back to find the name of the craft. *Cadiz.* The list of names beneath were unmarked. Thomas turned the page. Still nothing. On the next he found what he was looking for.

He continued to flick through until he saw the name of the next vessel. There were no more names scored through.

"Yes," he said, "we should go." He picked up the map, slipped it inside the journal and started out.

"You're going to take it?" said Lubna.

Thomas stopped, looked back at her standing beside the table. "Do you see anyone here who cares? I want to study this more, it might offer some clue as to what's going on."

Lubna started toward him. "Do you think the deaths have something to do with slaving?"

Thomas patted his robe where the journal lay. "I have the proof here. The dead are all from the same ship. For some reason this Incubus is working his way through them one by one. He's looking for something. Once we know what it will lead us to him."

But he was sure he already knew who. Simki had been held prisoner on the *Cadiz*. All Thomas needed to discover was what had happened onboard to trigger his madness.

CHAPTER 29

The courtyard was a scene of chaos and carnage. Handcarts were being used to carry the injured to the top of the cliff and through the streets. Women wailed and cried as they wandered between the carts in search of husbands, brothers, sons.

At the entrance to the infirmary one of the local physicians stood beside four grim-faced guards who were preventing entry. The man allowed individuals from a single cart through at a time, calling to his compatriots within, only allowing a new cart to approach when the earlier injured soldiers had been treated or died.

Thomas strode to the guards and confronted the physician. "You need to have people go through the carts and decide who to treat and who not," he said.

"We don't know who to treat until we get them inside."

"Don't be stupid. You only have to look at some of these men to know they're going to die. You're wasting time on them when you could be saving others."

"Only Allah decides who lives and dies," said the physician.

"Indeed he does. But sometimes he needs a little help. If you won't do it I will." Thomas turned to Lubna. "Go inside and help."

As Lubna started forward her way was blocked.

"She is a woman."

"Well done for noticing," Thomas said. "And she's a better physician than anyone in there, I wager. Let her pass."

"I'll work out here," said Lubna. "I can judge them as well as you."

Thomas thought about it a moment before shaking his head. "True, you can, but I will help them pass beyond pain when there is no alternative. Can you do that?"

"I never have, but I believe I could if need be."

Thomas stared at her, once again surprised at her strength. He drew a narrow dagger with a long blade from his waist and held it toward her.

Lubna stared at it for a long time before eventually shaking her head. "I'll help inside."

"First thing, find poppy and hashish and make up beads. I'll use them to ease suffering, but I won't use the knife unless I have to. And water – have men bring buckets from the trough so we have enough."

He stared into her eyes until she nodded.

When the physician made a second attempt to block her way Thomas pushed him aside. Once Lubna had ducked around the guards Thomas caught the physician's robe and drew him close.

"Follow her. You're no use to anyone out here. I'll send only those who can be saved. Make sure you do so."

Thomas strode toward the nearest cart. He saw, as he had once before, that only one man would live. Thomas pulled him free and carried him to the infirmary. He held his bundle out to the closest guard.

"There is no need to protect this place. Come with me and I'll give you men to carry back."

The four guards stared at him.

"Who placed you here?"

"The Governor."

"Why?"

The men exchanged glances until one spoke. "He is afraid of civil unrest."

"He told you that?"

"He had no need. Why else send us?"

"Do you have friends who rode outside?" Thomas asked, and each of the men nodded. "Of course you do. Then you likely know some of the men brought here. If you want them to die continue with the duty assigned you. If you prefer to save their lives come with me."

After a moment one of the guards reached out and took the man from his arms. Thomas turned away without waiting to see if the others followed him.

Thomas began issuing orders, the authority in his voice unquestioned. Uninjured soldiers milled around, their faces streaked with sweat and blood. They didn't know what to do now their leaders were captured or dead. Thomas had them form a human chain, sent others to find a suitable place to keep the dead and to lay the men out with respect. Wives and mothers, daughters and sons would want to claim the bodies. Anyone not claimed by sunset would be prepared for burial before dawn, as their religion demanded.

As Thomas turned to start on the injured he glimpsed two familiar figures on the far side of the courtyard, the first time he had seen them together. The family resemblance was clear. Giovanni caught his eye and gestured. Thomas glanced around, then started across.

"I didn't expect to see you here." He looked at Francesca. Her face was set, a grim determination that she appeared to have to hold in place for fear it might shatter.

"What can we do to help?" said Giovanni.

"The infirmary is brutal," Thomas said. "Could you bear it?"

"I, but not my cousin. There must be someplace you can use us."

Thomas only needed a moment's thought. "Go through to the square beyond the gate." He pointed. "They are laying out the dead. I know you are good with people, and they will need much help. Take what names you can so we have a record, in case anyone cares."

Giovanni glanced at Francesca, who offered a tight nod. He reached out and gripped Thomas's hand in thanks, took Francesca's arm and led the way from the courtyard. Thomas watched them go, pleased he had struck Giovanni from his lists of suspects. The man might be odd, might take himself off at a moment's notice, but when he was needed he was always there. There were many who would not have been.

Thomas turned back to his own work, steeling himself. He had to use the knife on only a handful of men, the most seriously injured where the poppy beads failed to alleviate their pain. He delivered the endings as cleanly as he could, knowing none of them would have lived until morning, every second an agony. Others, where the poppy worked, he set to one side. Most would die of their injuries before long, but if pain woke them again he would administer a stronger dose to help them pass. He had the beads in the pocket of his robe, his fingers stained by them.

At least two-thirds were capable of treatment. Some had little more than flesh wounds and Thomas sent those away with instructions to clean and bind the wounds themselves. Some he treated outside, stitching

233

cuts shallow enough to warrant it, sending others inside. The injuries were the result of a range of weapons. Sword thrusts and slashes, crossbow bolts which had to be worked free or pushed through, musket balls, deep injuries where a pike had crushed flesh and bone.

As he worked Thomas lost track of time, forgot completely about the deaths he was meant to be pursuing. He ignored the morning's promised rain when it came. He worked fast, his mind cold, knowing most of the men feared what they saw when he approached, but he had grown used to their opinion of him over the years and gave it no heed. They might like him more if he was gentle, but not for long, for death would claim them in his absence.

As Thomas took a moment to find a jug of water to quench his thirst he turned to find the Governor, Abraham al-Haquim, blocking his way.

"I heard you are killing the few men I have left."

"I offer them the mercy of a swift end," Thomas said.

"I should have you arrested and thrown into a dungeon."

Thomas spread his arms. "Then do it, if you can find any of these soldiers willing to help." He took another swallow of water. His beard dripped the excess onto his chest. "You need to bring more water from the river. A lot has been used here, and the Spanish will know how vulnerable we are."

"I have men guarding the entrance to the tunnel," said al-Haquim. "The access is difficult at best, they will be unable to bring enough men to cause us any problem."

"Have you ever been down there?" Thomas said.

"To the river? Why would I need to? I have others who report to me."

"They have bowmen," Thomas said. "Today I saw the Spanish use a fearsome weapon. A crossbow that fires six bolts in a matter of seconds."

Al-Haquim's mouth drew into a sneer of contempt. "I don't know what you thought you saw, but such a device does not exist."

"Ask your men," Thomas said.

"I don't need to. If there is something I need to know the information will be brought to me."

"At least gather large stones at the head of the cliff. There is a walkway directly above the tunnel. If the Spanish reach the entrance the stones might discourage them from coming farther."

"I suggest you return to what healing you can do and leave matters of war to those of us who understand them." Al-Haquim turned away, two ornately dressed soldiers following their master as he strode away. Thomas dismissed the man from his mind. He had more important matters to attend to.

He looked around and saw Jorge standing outside the palace gate. Jorge nodded, and Thomas knew he had observed the conversation with the Governor. He raised a hand to call him over, but Jorge remained where he was, perhaps wishing to remain dry. Thomas knew he couldn't go to him, not yet. Not until he was finished.

He made a sign which to him meant later, but Jorge only continued to stare. Thomas turned away, a spark of annoyance flaring. Only a few carts remained and he went to the first. All three could be patched up to return to the battle within a week. He had the man pushing the cart take them directly to the infirmary. By contrast the next cart contained only those from whom life had already fled. Thomas directed this cart to where the dead were being laid out. He stretched, easing an ache at the base of his spine, and started toward the infirmary. He might yet do some good inside. When he glanced across Jorge had disappeared, returned to his scented charges. Thomas could hardly blame him. Beautiful women or mutilated soldiers – he knew which he would prefer if allowed a choice. Which of course he was not.

With his own work done in the courtyard Thomas knew he should go to the infirmary to offer help there, but first he wanted to see how the management of the dead was progressing.

In the square beyond the palace ranks of bodies lay with arms folded across their chests, except the few that had lost an arm in the battle. He stood for a moment, watching Francesca as she moved between them. Something fragile remained wrapped about her, but she did the work well enough, kneeling beside each, staring at their faces as if to memorise the features. Giovanni stood to one side, a small booklet in his hand. He spoke with people as they arrived, questioning, directing them to one area or another.

Women wailed, children cried, while others wandered the ranks with faces downturned. Thomas had witnessed the aftermath of battle before, but rarely had he been so moved as he now was. These deaths had been pointless, inflicted to satisfy the pride of a vain man.

When Giovanni looked up Thomas raised a hand and went to him.

"I have to thank you for this," he said. "There is no-one better for it than yourself." He glanced at Francesca, still working despite her obvious unease.

"Jorge is good with people, too," said Giovanni.

"But not with the dead. He claims too great a

sensitivity."

Giovanni laughed, causing a few to glance in his direction, but his smile eased any concern they might have. "He forgets I saw him fight in that valley."

"True," Thomas said. "He forgets when he has a sword in his hand." He looked around. "How many remain unclaimed?"

"A little less than a quarter. We'll stay on until people stop coming, but I am meeting with Faris and Yusuf later."

"You are friends?"

Giovanni raised a shoulder. "Of sorts. They have both taken a liking to Francesca and she, I think, to them. One of them, anyway. I like to escort her as protector." He smiled. "Though she is a woman who cannot be swayed if she sets her mind on a thing."

Thomas nodded, turning to watch Francesca rise and move to another body. "How is she bearing up? Her appearance surprised me. And I would talk with her when you are finished."

"She manages," said Giovanni. "I know it is hard for her, but she feels an obligation to the dead. Is it anything I can help with?"

Thomas reached beneath his robe. The journal remained where he had tucked it away. "Perhaps. Even more than your cousin." He drew the book out. "You were a mariner, weren't you?"

"Not were, am. I intend to return to the sea as soon as I can. It has its dangers, certainly, but they are ones I know. Why do you ask?"

Thomas opened the pages. "I believe this contains the names of slaves carried across the sea. I also believe here," he pointed, then turned over several pages, "and here are the names of ships carrying them."

"What is your interest?" Giovanni leaned close. He reached out a hand, "May I?"

Thomas handed the journal across, watched as the man leafed through it. He stopped when he came to the list of names where some were scored through and glanced up, but Thomas offered no explanation.

"Yes, they are the names of ships," said Giovanni. "I recognise most, have even sailed in some. But whether they carried slaves I wouldn't know. Unless you say this proves they have?"

"I believe it does."

Giovanni peered more closely at a page. "This name, here," he placed a fingertip on one of the entries that was scored through, and Thomas knew which it was. The entry read Chisara. Giovanni looked up at him. "This is Don Morales's wife, if I am not mistaken. The spelling is different, but the men who write the names down record what they hear."

"You know of her original name?"

"I must have heard it somewhere, but cannot recall where exactly. It is her, is it not?"

Thomas nodded, and pointed to another entry on the opposite page. "And this is her brother." He placed his finger over an entry so far unmarred. Samchi. "I believe he is the Incubus I seek."

"Brother and sister?" said Giovanni. Something in his voice made Thomas look up from the page.

"It's not so unusual when slaves are captured, is it?"

Giovanni raised a shoulder, his usual laconic nature restored. "I expect not. But what leads you to such a conclusion, that he is the killer?" A smile played at the corners of Giovanni's mouth, as if such a wild assertion amused him.

"I have my reasons," Thomas said. "But it is too soon to offer any explanation, not until I question the man further. And to do that I have to find him." He glanced around at the bodies. "If, that is, he still lives."

CHAPTER 30

Thomas was reluctant to go in search of Jorge, but knew he was the best person to give them access to a bathhouse. Thomas had washed his hands as best he could, but the stink of death clung to him. His clothes might as well be discarded, he had others.

No guards blocked the entrance to the harem quarters so Thomas and Lubna walked straight in.

"I will find Helena and ask her permission to bathe," said Lubna. She smiled. "I would ask you to join me but I expect there will be other women."

"I wouldn't mind," Thomas said, and Lubna slapped his chest with the back of her hand.

"I'll see you back in the room." Her eyes sparked a promise, one Thomas knew well. He also knew she was experiencing the same arousal as him. It came often after dealing with death, a need to celebrate life in its most basic form. He watched as she moved away, short, lithe, hair uncovered here inside the palace where she would only encounter women, and Thomas was stunned at the emotion that welled inside him. Her beauty, her intelligence, had combined to sneak up on him until the depth of his love for Lubna stole the breath from his lungs.

He turned away and went in search of Jorge, so he could sooner return to their room.

Thomas found him after a quarter hour. He was playing a game of chess against two women of the harem. Others sat reading, but Thomas did not see Francesca among their number. He was half-relieved she wasn't there. He didn't believe he had strength left to question her. Later, when he had slept.

Jorge looked up and raised a finger. "Indulge me, I am about to win."

"You are not," one of the women said, a dark-skinned Nubian.

"We'll see," said Jorge. He patted a pile of cushions beside him and Thomas sat. He watched the game progress, his impatience subdued by lethargy. His mind drifted as he observed the moves. He knew how to play the game but preferred the simpler and more fiendish challenge of mancala.

The women put their heads together, talking soft strategy. Jorge's response to each move was instantaneous, and Thomas wondered how often he must play this game. It was popular in the palace, the best chess sets fashioned of richly inlaid boards and ivory pieces carved far to the east, each worth more than an average man's annual income. Around the room pieces lay scattered on abandoned boards and across the floor.

The women pressed close together, convinced victory was only one move, two at most, away. Thomas studied the positions of the pieces for the first time and saw their mistake. He tried to make no show of the knowledge.

The Nubian moved, placing Jorge's king in danger.

Jorge's fingers gripped the head of an ornate dragon and moved it diagonally. He sat back, stretching his arms.

"Thank you both for an interesting challenge. Next time you will have to play Thomas here, you might have more luck." He seemed to notice Thomas's disarray for the first time and an expression of distaste crossed his face. "You need to get clean. Come, I'll take you to the baths."

"We can help," said the Nubian, her expression almost comically innocent.

"Thomas is a strange one," said Jorge, "he continues to believe in fidelity, against all evidence to the contrary." He led the way from the room, continued along a narrow corridor whose walls were unadorned by the religious carvings to be seen elsewhere.

"What did you find out at the house?" Thomas said.

"I will tell you while we bathe."

"You don't need to bathe."

"A man can always benefit from bathing," said Jorge. "Besides, it would be impolite to leave you to bathe alone."

They came to a point where four corridors met. Jorge turned left and shortly led the way into a small bathing area.

"This is where the eunuchs come," he said, "but I'm sure we can make an allowance for you. Do you need your clothes..." He glanced down at Thomas, "throwing away?"

"I think so, yes. Can someone fetch clean ones from my room?"

"I'll ask. Undress and cleanse yourself, I'll be back in a moment."

Thomas removed the stained garments. He drew the journal Lubna had found and placed it in an alcove which might hold a lamp after sunset. Now, in the late afternoon, light spilled through openings built into the ceiling, cut into the shape of stars and the moon. The rain had stopped and brightness spilled through, making patterns on the walls and floor.

There were two spigots jutting from the wall. A small square bath set into the floor was already filled, the water steaming, entering through a pipe at one end and draining from another, constantly circulating. Thomas turned a handle on the spigot and stepped beneath a cascade of warm water. He scrubbed himself to remove the worst of the grime, then applied soaps and oils, working them into his hair and beard. When he turned he saw Jorge had returned, a female servant accompanying him. She ignored Thomas's nakedness and partial arousal. She knelt and picked up his clothes after removing the weapons belt and leaving it at the base of the wall. When she had gone Jorge undressed and slipped into the bath, his arms along the side, legs stretched out. His hairless body floated, the puckered scar between his thighs testament to what had been done to him. *What I did to him*, Thomas thought, knowing Jorge was lucky it had been him and not someone else. At least he had left his manhood, a fact Jorge occasionally thanked him for.

"Do you like what you see?" asked Jorge, smiling. "Because you know if you do you only have to—"

"One day you will go too far," Thomas said.

Jorge grinned. "Oh, I think I have already done that, my friend, and no doubt enjoyed myself immensely."

Thomas allowed the falling water to wash the last of the soap from him, turned it off and padded across to slip into the pool on the opposite side to Jorge. Fortunately enough space separated them so there was little chance of their legs entangling.

"Tell me what you found out, if anything."

"I discovered a great deal," said Jorge, "but how much

is any use is another matter. Servants love to gossip, and their mistress was, like Morales's wife, not averse to taking men into her bed on a frequent basis."

"Did her husband know?"

"That was the strange thing, the servants couldn't decide if he did or not."

"And you?"

Jorge shook his head. "Neither could I. Some men truly do not see what is held in front of their faces, others do not wish to see and choose to avoid unpleasantness, while a few, such as you, see everything whether that is to the good or not."

"It is always better to know," Thomas said.

"Is it? If your wife is taking lovers, if what she did could even be called that, might it not be better to continue in ignorance? What could he have done about it?"

"Confronted her."

Jorge lifted a hand and allowed water to spill across his scalp and face. "Whether he knew or not is beside the point. She was bringing both men and women into the house, and the servants knew."

"Do they know who?"

"That's what is strange. She was discrete. Her seductions remained a secret, including the latest, who I suppose is the one who killed her."

"All the deaths are too similar for it to be someone else," Thomas said. "You spoke with the husband?"

"At length. And there is a connection to Morales."

"Tell me." Thomas sat straighter.

"Morales is a slaver. This man supplied him, and others, with clothing for them. Cheap clothing and expensive clothing. Cheap for the slaves who were worth little, expensive for those such as Kisera who would command a high price. And he purchased slaves himself. As well as a seller of clothes he makes pots in an establishment on the other side of the river. Most of the workers there and in his house were brought from Africa, or are Christian captives forced into slavery."

"Could one of them have killed his wife, to get back at him?"

"One might have killed him, certainly, but not her. Everyone in the household and the pot works worshipped her."

"Why?"

"Because she was kind and treated them as people, not chattels."

"Is that enough for them to love her?"

"No, of course not. But she did things for them. She encouraged them to learn, she helped them if they fell ill, and would not allow them to be dismissed, even if their illness was terminal. She did many kindnesses both large and small. That is why they loved her."

"If she was so perfect why did someone kill her?"

"As a punishment?" said Jorge.

Thomas splashed his hand into the water, frustration building inside. "For what? What had she done?"

"Not her, the husband. I believe it was the same for Morales. The killings were done to punish the husbands, not the wives."

Thomas stared into space, trying to work out how that would lead back to Simki. He needed to think harder about how everything was related. He wasn't yet ready to disclose his suspicions to anyone else, not until he pulled all the threads together. "Is that punishment? These husbands do not seem the kind to miss a wife when there are others so easily available. There is a surfeit of women in this land with so many men killed or captive."

"That is true," said Jorge. "But what if it was a threat to them – to demonstrate they could be killed just as easily – that they might be next?"

"What man would subject himself to such treatment? I can understand it from a lover, but not one man to another."

Jorge laughed, shaking his head. "You know better than that, Thomas, even you know better than that. Besides, this was not a matter of love, was it?"

"Of course I know, but we are not talking about mere sodomy here, we are talking of one man allowing another to kill him without fighting back. Why would he allow such a thing?"

"How do we know the men are killed in the same way?"

"Khalil was," Thomas said.

Jorge nodded agreement. "And he had enjoyed sex, too, but we don't know who with, man or woman."

"You suspect a woman now? No, even you can't believe a woman is doing the killing."

"Eva did," said Jorge, reminding Thomas of the events of a year before.

"Eva was mad."

"And this woman isn't? Is murder not an irrational act?"

"Not always," Thomas said. "Possibly not even the majority of times. There are a thousand petty reasons to kill, from an argument over a game of dice to someone failing to step out of your way in the street. A thousand ways to kill and be killed. But most killings are done by someone people know, for trivial reasons that make you wonder at humanity. Then there are those who kill more than once, and for a purpose."

Jorge inclined his head. "It appears to be so."

"In that case—"Thomas pulled himself from the pool, water cascading from his body. The servant had brought cotton cloths to dry themselves with and he began to use one. He heard Jorge leave the pool but did not turn to watch him. "We need to know the purpose of the deaths, and that will lead us to the man."

"Or woman," said Jorge.

"The man," Thomas repeated, convinced he knew who that man was.

"There is an auction of slaves in the morning," Jorge said, distaste colouring his voice. "We are at war with the Spanish, soldiers are dead, but trade must go on. Morales will be there, so too I suspect will Giminez. I think it would be wise for us to attend as well." He offered a grim smile. "Perhaps we should use some of the gold we stole last year to buy all the slaves and set them free. That would be a fine joke, would it not?"

Thomas said nothing, distracted but unable to work out by what, then it came to him. The small bathing area always contained a background of running water. It fell heated from spigots, flowed cold around the sides. Now the constant babble of its falling was stilled. Thomas walked to where a line of water normally ran around the edge of the room and stared into an empty channel.

"Has someone blocked the water?" he asked, turning to Jorge.

"Who would do such a thing? It simply runs."

Thomas went outside, passed through the corridors and entered the courtyard where they had set up the infirmary. He went to one of the stone troughs. The spigot above was also dry, only a small remnant dripping.

"What is it?"

Thomas turned, unaware Jorge had followed.

"The water," he said. "The Spanish have blocked the water supply. Have someone tell the Governor, he needs to issue orders to ration what remains. The siege has begun in earnest."

CHAPTER 31

The pot works of Bartolomo Giminez was situated on the flat plateau beyond the ravine cut by the river. A single stone bridge, reputedly over a thousand years old, was the only access to and from the town. The slopes beyond were steep but nowhere near the barrier that protected other directions. Beyond the walls Thomas felt vulnerable, and he wondered why the Spanish had not sent men to take this ground, but believed he knew the answer. They had been working miles away to break the channels bringing water from the mountains. At least the town still had the river, and the Governor had set all the captives in the tunnels to carry up as much as they could and store it.

In the cool hours following dawn women came to the market in search of food, which was also growing scarce. The stalls contained less produce than they had a week before. Scraps of meat that would have been rejected were now in demand, even fought over.

Thomas and Jorge picked their way through the crowd, which thinned to stragglers beyond the square at the head of the bridge. As they crossed it men were laying charges of powder on either side, ready in case the enemy attacked from this direction. The pot works was set within a brick wall that rose to twice the height of a man. A solid wooden door blocked the way inside, but

Thomas heard the sound of industry from beyond.

He banged on the door while Jorge leaned against the wall, looking around. Badly maintained houses lined the far side of the street, a jagged line of shadow cast by the staggered rooflines. Smoke rose from holes in the tile roofs. A few children dressed in rags played a game known only to them, their high voices sharp in the morning air.

"There's someone inside, I can hear them working," said Jorge.

Thomas hammered again. This time there came a sound from the other side, a scraping of metal, and the door swung inward.

"We don't sell anything here. If you want a pot you must go to the market."

"We're not here to buy pots. I want to speak with your master." From the corner of his eye Thomas saw Jorge push away from the wall and come to stand beside him. The pair of them presented a threatening sight, and he saw uncertainty in the man's eyes.

"Don Giminez does not conduct trade here. You need to visit his house to make an appointment." The man began to close the heavy door, but Thomas pushed his foot out and stopped it.

"It's not trade we're here to discuss." Thomas pressed against the door. For a moment the man tried to resist, but he was malnourished and did not possess the strength. Jorge moved in close behind Thomas, taking the edge of the door and closing it. He shot the bolt.

Across the yard was an array of stacked pots, clay still wet, waiting to have glaze applied if they were intended for well-off customers, or fired unglazed for common purposes. Two brick kilns had been used overnight, and now ashes were being scraped from within. Sweating men dressed in no more than loincloths reached in with wooden paddles to pull out the pots. They were still too hot to work with so other men, their hands protected with thick cloth, lifted them from the paddles and stacked them on the opposite side to the unfired clay. A third kiln was being stacked with wet pots, the unglazed kind that required less control. It was a busy scene, men performing familiar tasks with a casual skill born of long practice. Most were of African origin, their dark bodies gleaming with sweat. Here and there paler-skinned workers laboured alongside. There seemed no hierarchy. Even the man who had opened the door turned away and began to load pots.

To one side sat a small wooden building, its roof formed of reeds, and it was to this that Thomas led the way. He didn't bother knocking on the door, not sure it was capable of withstanding the attention. Inside a short man sat at a table made of the same planks that formed the walls. He was writing in a journal. Thomas stepped close before he could close it, but the marks he saw were different to the book he had taken from the library. That had yielded nothing, which was disappointing – he had been sure some clue must reside in its pages, but if it did he was incapable of deciphering it. He had found both Kisera and Simki's names scrawled on separate pages. Kisera's, mispelled, had been scored through. It was information, certainly, but nothing he didn't already know.

The man looked up from his work, an initial expression of fear fading, and Thomas wondered who he had been expecting.

Gimiez rose to his full height, looking up at Thomas.

"I do not conduct trade here, sir."

"Your employee told me that already. It is not trade I am here to discuss." He stepped to one side so Jorge could move forward, saw the man's eyes widen in recognition.

"Do you have news?"

"No news," Thomas said, "only more questions."

"More questions? I answered this man's questions last night. Now leave, I am a busy man."

"Who does not appear to be upset at his wife's death."

"Not all men wear their heart on their sleeves. Trade must continue even through this chaos. People need to store goods and eat."

And others need to turn a profit, thought Thomas.

"It is not you we want to speak with, but your workers."

"Why? They know nothing."

"Your wife visited the works. I hear she was popular. She may have said something to offer a clue to her killer." Thomas hesitated, studying the self-important little man. "Unless you prefer her killer go unpunished?"

"Of course not. It is unlikely anyone here will know anything useful to you, but if you must at least try not to distract them too much from their work."

"Distract them from their work?" said Jorge as they stood outside. Giminez had returned to his ledger. "Truly he does not care about his wife, does he?"

"War breaks pots," Thomas said. "And he seems to be a man keen to benefit from the misfortune of others."

"Sometimes I despair of humanity."

"Only sometimes?" Thomas looked across the yard. "You take the left side, I will go to the right. We'll meet at the door as soon as we're done."

"The sooner the better," said Jorge. "I grow tired of your diligence, Thomas, and wish to return to my life of sensuality and luxury."

"The Spanish may have something to say on that." Thomas started across the yard, his gaze on a dark skinned man almost as tall as Simki. It was the Africans he wanted to question most. This matter was connected to the slave trade. There was a key someone possessed that would unlock the entire mystery, if only he could find it.

"Whoever is doing this killed the wrong person in that household," said Jorge as they made their way into the town outside a town, moving away from the dubious safety of Ronda's walls.

Thomas nodded. "You heard the same stories I did, then. Anything useful to us?"

"The same tale over and over. He beats the men, abuses the women, sells on the children and keeps them all prisoner. They are little better than the water carriers locked in that tunnel." Jorge slowed and looked around. "Why are we going this way? The bridge is the other direction."

"There is a slave sale today, you said. One of the workers told me Giminez always goes. And you know who is running the sale. I want to see if they know each other."

"They are both bastards, so it wouldn't surprise me," said Jorge. "Can we get something to eat and drink first? I missed breakfast."

Thomas glanced at the sky. "The sale doesn't start until noon. I want to get there early to see how Morales treats them and observe who else comes to bid. But we have time, as long as you don't expect a banquet."

Jorge pulled a face. "One of the women told me something interesting. Not about Giminez but his wife. Even then not really about his wife."

"You do need food, you're not making sense. Will here do?" They had reached a small square. Across from them an inn had set tables outside in the shade where the air was a little cooler. Locals were eating even though it was only halfway through the morning. The scent of roast meat and spices drifted to them. Flagons of ale and bottles of wine sat on some of the tables, showing this was not a Moorish establishment but one of the new kind that fell through the gap between religious practices. Moorish food with Spanish alcohol, a perfect combination. Far better than the other way around.

They took a table and ordered whatever was good that day. Jorge stopped the owner and asked for a bottle of wine.

"I need a clear head," Thomas said. "So do you."

"Only one bottle then. I have missed it. Besides, it was you who corrupted me when we were in Qurtuba."

Thomas knew it wasn't true but didn't argue. He had drunk alcohol often enough, both with Jorge and alone in Gharnatah. But that was a city of half a million, home to citizens from a score of lands, each bringing their own customs. There it was possible to indulge in almost any pleasure. In Ronda the influence of Islam was stronger, and within the town walls alcohol was officially banned.

"So what did this woman tell you? You're aware they're all slaves."

"Of course. She told me Valentina Giminez visited often. Two or three times a week."

"We already knew that."

"Indeed," said Jorge. "But sometimes she would bring

a visitor. Another woman who had much in common with the dwellers in that works."

"Kisera?" Thomas said, and Jorge nodded.

"Not all of the time, but it seems she knew some of the people who worked – or rather, were imprisoned – there."

"What else?" Thomas knew there would be more. What he had heard could be deduced from what he already knew.

"We got to talking," said Jorge.

"You surprise me."

Jorge stuck out his tongue, pulling it back in quickly as the innkeeper brought their wine and food, clattering it down on the table. There were cups, not glasses, but unfortunately the wine would no doubt taste the same whatever it was served in.

"The woman I spoke with was of an age with Simki and his sister. She claimed she arrived here at the same time, though on a different boat."

"She has fallen on far harder times, then," Thomas said.

"Except she is still alive." Jorge drained the wine from his cup and topped it from the jug.

"What's it like?" Thomas asked. His own remained untouched, but the food was good.

"I've had worse."

"That's little recommendation. So tell me this tale."

"It is short and brutal, as they often are. She heard this from someone who knew someone who claims they were on the same boat as Simki and Kisera. They told her there was some kind of argument as they crossed the ocean, serious enough to come to blows. There was a particular man, another slave, and he and Simki had a falling out. Simki killed him. Strangled him and threw the body overboard."

Thomas looked up from his food. "Strangled?"

Jorge nodded.

"As the others have been strangled?"

"That the woman didn't know. How could she?"

"It sounds far-fetched," Thomas said. "Aren't slaves chained together? How could Simki kill a man then have him lie next to him? It would be impossible to escape punishment."

"Not if you broke his ankle and separated the foot from the leg."

"She told you that's what happened?"

"Whoever told the tale claimed it as truth. Remember this story is second or third hand at best."

"So it may mean nothing."

"It may not. Are you going to drink your wine?"

Thomas reached out and lifted his cup. "I'm not as thirsty as you obviously are, but I intend to drink it when I am ready. It is an interesting tale, all the same. Do you think Simki will be at the auction with his master?"

"He has gained his trust, I believe. And he is clever. Morales is rich, but I wouldn't say he is a clever man. He needs Simki."

"Enough to condone murder?"

"You suspect Simki of killing his sister? For what purpose?"

"Pride. Envy. Greed. Jealousy. I could go on, but we need to leave soon. There are many reasons for a man to kill. I am constantly surprised we are not all in our graves."

"It will be so dull to be dead," said Jorge, "but I suppose it comes to us all in the end. Even you and I."

256

"Later rather than sooner, let us hope."

Jorge raised his cup. "I can drink to that." And Thomas finally lifted his own cup and drank the wine, much better than he had feared it would be.

CHAPTER 32

The auction of slaves was to take place in a clearing close to the last of the houses. Beyond it scrubland stretched to the base of mountains which rose to the north. Despite it being the hottest part of the day the turn-out was larger than Thomas expected. The slaves were corralled into a fenced off area to one side. Bidders wandered behind the stakes, judging the goods for sale. There was nothing to prevent any of the slaves from slipping through the open fence and making a run for it. Nothing but the thought of capture, being beaten and returned to the pen.

"I see Simki," said Jorge.

"So do I. He obviously works alongside his master in this endeavour."

"Did you expect him not to?" said Jorge. "He has little choice in the matter. He might have advanced himself since he was like these poor devils, but that only makes it more likely he will do as asked. I'm no free man, but I would draw the line at selling my own people."

Thomas glanced at him. "You are more free man than anyone I know."

Jorge shook his head. "Do not delude yourself. We are none of us free, we are all beholden to someone. For some of us there is a delusion of self-will, but do not mistake that for freedom."

Thomas had rarely heard Jorge so philosophical. He

might be right, but now was not the time to discuss it.

"I want to talk with him. You stay here and keep an eye on proceedings."

"I may bid," said Jorge.

Thomas kept walking, ignoring what he considered a joke.

Simki sat at a small table, journals lying open before him. He didn't notice Thomas approach until he was almost there, allowing him to lean over his shoulder to check the writing. It was different to the journal. Thomas had not expected it to be the same but was disappointed all the same.

"How many for sale today?" he asked, feigning an interest.

"What is it you really want?" said Simki. "If my master sees you he will have men beat you and drag you away."

"He can try. I want to talk to you about a story I was told."

"About me?"

"That is what I heard."

"Does it involve a death at sea?" asked Simki. "If so it is an old tale."

"Old and true, or old and false?" Thomas said.

"Come find me after the sale. I have no time to tell it now. And I mean what I said, if Don Morales sees us it won't be only you who finds himself bloodied."

"How much are you expecting to make today? I would have thought it a bad time for selling slaves with the Spanish on our doorstep."

"It is never a bad time to sell slaves. Go now. I will talk to you no more here."

Thomas waited a moment, but Simki had returned to his ledgers and refused to acknowledge him. No matter, he knew where the man lived, and would take him up on his offer to hear the tale as soon as he could.

He wandered through the small crowd that had gathered in front of a low platform, ready to bid on the first lot. A group of six men were led out, each dressed in nothing more than a cloth wrapped at their waist. They were thin. Four showed the signs of a beating. One man had a right eye swollen tight shut. From the severity of the wound Thomas believed he might lose the vision on that side.

Desultory bids were made, barely enough money passed to make it viable to bring the men across the sea, though it was obvious little had been spent on feeding them.

As Thomas turned away, bored by the pace of proceedings, he caught sight of a familiar face, then three. Faris al-Rashid stood next to Yusuf, well back in the crowd. The quality of their clothing set them apart so that a small space had cleared around them. Leaning against Yusuf, her arm linked through his, was Francesca. Thomas still wanted to talk to her but knew here was not the place. He would follow them when the auction was complete and try to catch her alone.

More groups of male slaves appeared, each a little more impressive than the last, and Thomas saw the logic of the auction. The best was kept for last, scarcity causing the bidders to raise their offers.

Voices called, strident, and one or two small fights broke out, quickly stifled by four tall, black-skinned guards.

An hour passed before the females appeared. The first offering consisted of the very young and very old. The youngsters attracted heavy bidding, and Thomas tried not to consider the reason why, but he wasn't stupid.

By the time the beauties appeared the price had risen a hundred-fold. Thomas scanned the crowd, searching again for Faris and finding him. This was more likely to be of interest to him.

He and Yusuf stood to one side as if not wishing to be associated with the common bidders. Francesca remained close. Yusuf occasionally leaned toward Faris and whispered, and Faris raised an arm to bid.

A final group of five walked onto the platform rather than being dragged. Women from fourteen to less than thirty. This time all clothing had been dispensed with and the women stood naked. Thomas saw them standing stiff, trying not to cover themselves. They had obviously been told to display everything that was for sale.

Yusuf put his head together with Faris again, his hands moving rapidly as he pointed at the women. They walked closer to the arena to study them, leaving Francesca behind, and Yusuf nodded in satisfaction. Faris made a bid in excess of anything anyone else would be able to match.

Morales tried to suppress a smile. The auction might have been slow so far, but this last offer would pay for ten ships to cross the sea. Morales was dipping toward Simki to get him to write the details in the ledger when a new voice called out, doubling the bid.

The crowd turned as one, wanting to know who the lunatic was.

And of course the lunatic was Jorge. Thomas stared at him, knowing his mouth hung open.

Jorge grinned as Thomas started toward him. As he walked he turned his head to look toward Yusuf and Faris. An argument was going on, decided when Faris shook his head and turned away. Yusuf reached out and grabbed his arm, more words spoken.

Thomas was startled at Yusuf's boldness. He might be a prince of the Nasrid dynasty, his father might be the Sultan in Gharnatah, but Faris was not someone to be manhandled, nor spoken to in the way Yusuf was doing.

Beyond them Morales waited, looking between the arguing pair and Jorge.

"If you're not careful he'll take your bid," Thomas said, reaching Jorge. "What will you do then?"

"I have enough to pay a surety, and I can send for additional funds from Gharnatah." Jorge glanced at Thomas. "We are rich men, remember?"

We are thieves, Thomas thought, recalling the three trunks of gold and jewels they had liberated from a dead man's cellar. A small part of the man's fortune, to be sure, the remainder of it spirited into the palace. But it had still been theft.

"Why are you doing this?" Thomas said. "What do you plan to do with them? And could you not bid on those who are cheaper?"

"It's my own money, I can do with it as I wish. Besides, I might want to start my own harem," Jorge said, then smiled. "There is little point choosing ugly women, is there? But I expect I will find some way to free them. Not here, perhaps, that would appear strange, but when we return to Gharnatah."

On the far side of the clearing the argument ended and Yusuf appeared to have won. Faris raised a hand to increase his bid. Yusuf moved away to join Francesca and she wound her arm around him once more, pressing tight against his side.

As Jorge began to raise his own hand Thomas grasped

it, holding it down.

"No!"

Jorge tried to pull away, but despite his size Thomas held him firm. He turned to see what Morales intended, and saw him pass a swift instruction to Simki. He was a greedy man, but knew where power lay in the town.

Faris smiled and turned to Yusuf, but the young prince was distracted for the moment. Then Yusuf broke Francesca's embrace and glanced across. He saw Thomas watching and grinned, and Thomas realised the youth had been aware of his scrutiny all along. He feared it might even have been what persuaded him to continue bidding, but he forced a smile on his face as the young prince approached, Francesca in tow.

"Faris is displeased with Jorge," said Yusuf. "He has cost him a great deal of money."

"Cost Faris, or you?"

"I offered to pay, but he insists they are a gift. He will want something in return, no doubt."

"No doubt," Thomas said. "What do you want them for?"

"I have a mind to start a harem of my own. I am of an age to consider such things now." He glanced at Jorge, who had moved away, but not so far he could not overhear the conversation. "You can help me train them, Jorge, if you wish, though Francesca says she knows all there is to know in the training of concubines. Is that not so, my sweet?"

"I already have duties," said Jorge, showing his back. "They should have been mine."

"The highest bidder won," said Yusuf. "And what would a eunuch want with five Nubians? It would be a waste."

It was a different prince who returned to Faris's side, and Thomas wondered if Yusuf had changed in other ways too. If he had been too swift to dismiss him as a suspect, still considering him as the sweet youth of earlier days when the entire world seemed more innocent. Helena claimed Yusuf was too gentle – but with his own women, women he had bought, would that remain so? As the small group moved away, six guards falling in around them, Thomas realised he had lost his chance to question Francesca.

As he and Jorge returned through the streets, houses clustering ever closer as they neared the old bridge, Thomas was silent, trying to work out why he was angry. Finally words spilled from him, not what he had meant to say, coming from somewhere primitive.

"Would you have fucked them all, or only the best looking?"

"Oh, all, I expect," said Jorge. "But only if they came to me. Not that they can now." He shook his head at the unfairness of life.

"If you owned them they would have come to you, as they will to their new master. They know the reason why they were chosen to be displayed last."

"Perhaps I should have bid on everyone," said Jorge, "but I was unsure how much money I had brought, and how much surety would be required."

"Can you imagine a world where no slaves existed?" Thomas said. "Who would do the work others don't want to? You can't free everyone."

"Why not?"

Thomas laughed. "You're insane. The Spanish are camped outside the town and you want to start some kind of revolution?"

Jorge scowled. Thomas could see him preparing an answer, no doubt a sharp one, when there came a sound, a deep rumble. Thomas glanced at the sky, searching for thunder clouds. Above them lay an unbroken blue. A fine day.

The sound came again, two of three times in a row, and Thomas broke into a run as he realised its source. He heard Jorge follow, not yet knowing what the meaning was but trusting him.

Beyond the town walls smoke rose into the air, and then the tower of a building exploded in a shower of stone and tile.

The Moorish attack had goaded the Spanish and they were not waiting for sunset. The long awaited Spanish bombardment had begun.

CHAPTER 33

It took the Spanish a while to find their range. It also took them time to work out a system before the explosion of each cannon fell into a regular pattern. The bombardier's were obviously expecting a long siege because one in four of the projectiles were rocks gathered from the plain, where they lay in abundance, allowing them to save ammunition. These stones did minor damage, shattering on contact with the solid town walls, but occasionally one found a roof to crash through. The iron balls were a different matter. They did not break. Instead, whatever they hit exploded in a cascade of stone and mortar. And it would only get worse.

Thomas ducked as a stone shattered above, shards falling around him, one piece cutting the back of his hand. Men and women ran in panic through the streets but there was no safety to be found. One or two made their way into the tunnels used to bring water from the river, which was a sensible idea. Underground was the safest place, despite being where the prisoners were held captive.

As he ran Thomas barged into people rushing in no particular direction. One family headed north toward where they had just come from, others south, east and west. The few soldiers that were on the streets panicked as much as the general population. As Thomas and Jorge progressed through the streets the worst of the bombardment fell behind. Here people remained indoors, afraid to venture out. Thomas had seen such bombardments before, but always from the other side. He was trying to recall the sequence of events. How long would the cannon continue to fire? Would they change their aim to target areas of the town so far spared? He didn't know, he had never been part of such decisions, and his experience was long ago. The Moors used artillery rarely, and only as a last resort, considering it inhuman.

At the palace, despite the continued thump of explosions, the sound of destruction was muted. Three score of soldiers, some of those who had returned uninjured, stood around awaiting orders. Thomas went directly inside, grabbing the first servant who passed.

"Where is the Governor?"

"Throne room," the man said, shrugging Thomas off and continuing on.

"I'm going to the harem," Jorge said, turning away and breaking into a run.

"If you see Francesca try to keep hold of her," Thomas said. "I still have questions for her. And see if you can find out what she's doing with Yusuf."

Jorge laughed as he moved off. A fresh sense of urgency had taken hold, people moving with a new purpose. Thomas followed the corridors to the throne room, only taking a wrong turning once. Within he found Abraham al-Haquim with four other men, one of them Faris al-Rashid who must have made a swifter return. He was surprised the man had remained in Ronda after the failed raid. His instinct for self-preservation usually meant he was far distant from any action.

The group were arguing, al-Haquim turning to

Thomas as if he might have arrived in support of his argument, his expression turning to a scowl when he saw who it was.

"There are soldiers outside doing nothing," Thomas said, talking over the conversation. "Send them into the town, they have to tell people to get into a cellar if they have one, a neighbour's cellar if not, or the strongest part of the house."

"We need soldiers to protect the palace," said al-Haquim. "And I don't take advice from a bone-mender."

"Thomas is more than that," said Faris, his support surprising Thomas. "He has likely witnessed more battles than the rest of us combined. What advice do you have?"

"His advice is not needed here," said al-Haquim. He looked around, eyes wild, but there were no guards present and already one of his companions had disagreed with him.

"If what Faris says is true we should hear him out," said one of the others, the tide turning against the Governor, but he was not finished yet.

"I heard all about this man from the Sultan before he left to save Malaka. He is a troublemaker, the same as his pet the eunuch."

Thomas looked between the men and shrugged. He was unwilling to remain and argue when action was required. He turned away, leaving them to their planning. Had he stayed he might have persuaded at least some, but it would have taken time, and that was a luxury the population did not possess.

He returned to his rooms but Lubna was gone, so he went to the courtyard where the soldiers continued to mill about.

"Who is in charge here?" Thomas demanded.

"Our commander is dead, we are awaiting the Governor's orders."

It only took Thomas a moment to make the decision. "He has sent me out with them, he is too busy to come himself. He says you must go through the town and tell people to stay indoors, to find the safest place they can. And to preserve water and food supplies. Nobody knows how long the bombardment will go on." He ducked as a rock took the corner from one of the towers behind, but the rubble fell away down the cliff face. With luck some might land on the Spanish.

"Who are you to give us orders?"

"I know him," one of the soldiers said. "He is close to the Sultan, his word is good."

Thomas expected more objections, but he saw the men were hungry for the certainty of orders and they began to move away, automatically organising themselves into small groups, making plans. As the soldiers passed through the gate to the street townsfolk entered, carrying the first of the wounded. Thomas directed them to the infirmary. When he followed he discovered Lubna already there, but only two other physicians. Lubna was directing the work, so he began to assess the extent of people's injuries. Most were minor, too minor to take up his time and he sent them away with a scolding. Others were more serious; broken bones, flesh torn by flying stone. One man had lost an eye. There was nothing could be done, but he would need treating. The remains of the eye had to be removed and pain relief mixed. Thomas handed him over to Lubna because she knew about eyes. Lubna was the second best physician present, and he took a moment's pleasure watching her work. Her swiftness mixed with gentleness was something he envied. Thomas knew most patients saw him as uncaring, but he didn't know how to be any other way.

Beyond the walls artillery fire continued to sound and a taint began to fill the air. The stink of sulphur, the grit of unburned powder. It settled on clothes, flavoured the tongue and filled the nose. Thomas wiped an arm across eyes which watered from irritation. He could see it in others, both those who worked and those they worked on.

The day passed without notice, and his concerns over the killings faded to a pin-prick at the back of his mind. Thomas lost himself in work, in helping people, in relieving their pain. Easing of fears he left to others.

Only when the stream of injured slowed did he look up to discover light had leached from the sky and lamps now burned. He hadn't noticed them being lit. He straightened, easing kinks in his spine, and looked around for Lubna. She was finishing up the treatment of a young girl who had crushed a hand when something had fallen on it. Lubna had splinted the injury and eased the girl's pain with poppy and willow liquor. The hand would recover given time. The memory of the pain would fade.

Thomas stared at Lubna, her face streaked with grime, hair falling loose from her hijab, and knew he had never seen anything more beautiful in his life. This woman had changed him, had broken loose something calcified within he had not been aware of until she entered his life. There had been one other, long ago, he had loved, but he had barely been a man then. The memory was so distant now he could no longer tell if the emotions he had felt were real or not. But he did know how he felt about Lubna. There were times they felt as one person, their thoughts moving together. And of course he knew there were other times he annoyed her intensely and she let him know so. Thomas smiled. Even here, under bombardment, there was nowhere he would rather be, because this is where she was.

She looked up and caught him staring, a frown touching her brow at the intensity of his study. Thomas tried to smile to put her at ease but only succeeded in deepening the frown.

He crossed the room. "You need to rest." He touched her arm, wanting to touch her. Wanting to hold her.

She looked around to discover no new patients. Narrow cots held those too sick to return home, or who had no home to return to. Thomas made a mental note to ask for a refuge to be set up, somewhere in the middle of town where it might be safer.

"We all need to rest," said Lubna, "but after our work is done."

"We are done," Thomas said. "Go and get some sleep, or pray. You have missed prayers today." He knew she continued to believe in some greater power, though he suspected she was starting to doubt its benevolence.

Lubna smiled. "Allah will forgive me under the circumstances." She cupped his face in her palm. "I will only sleep if you lie beside me. You are more tired than I am."

"I have work to do yet, but I will join you as soon as I can."

Lubna shook her head. "If you have work then I have work. We are a team, are we not?"

"This is something else," Thomas said.

"I know what it is, but we are still a team. The three of us. Each flawed, yet together invincible."

271

Thomas laughed, then saw her scowl because she had meant what she said. After the day he had experienced he hardly felt invincible, and was convinced more than ever that Jorge was a fool. Despite which he had need of him so went in search of the man, Lubna following beside him because it was where she belonged.

The bombardment continued into the night, but at a lower level. Perhaps the Spanish grew tired as well. Making their way through the streets was a more difficult affair than the day before, every roadway damaged in some way. Rubble lay everywhere underfoot. Larger stones sat in the way, forcing them to go around. They came to one street that was entirely blocked where a whole house had come down. People worked under lamps trying to clear the way. Thomas stopped in the process of turning away, returned to those working.

"Are there carts nearby?"

A heavy-set man with twisted dark hair stopped trying to lift a stone too large for him on his own and straightened. "Who is asking, and why?"

"These stones still have a use, if you can find carts. Take them to the top of the cliff where water is brought up." Thomas bent on the far side of the stone and nodded at the man.

The two of them heaved, but still the rock remained where it was. Jorge joined them on Thomas's side and the man moved around to give him space. This time the stone shifted. Little by little, heave by heave they worked it to the edge of the street.

"Don't bother trying to bring this one," said Thomas, and the man grinned and held his hand out. They gripped forearms in a gesture familiar to all soldiers.

"There are carts close by. Why do you want the stone taken there?"

"A precaution, in case the Spanish try to force a way through."

"There is a stout door and an iron gate" said the man.

"I know. Impossible for a man, even a dozen men, to break through. But the Spanish have gunpowder, and if they know of that way it will let them send soldiers directly into town."

The man nodded. The idea made sense. "It would be a hard battle through the tunnel."

"Even harder if rocks are falling on them before they get that far."

"Let us clear the way then you shall have your stones, sir."

As the man returned to his task Thomas, Lubna and Jorge moved away. There would be other streets tumbled down before the siege was over, but Thomas's spirits were lifted by the man's attitude. He wished there were more like him.

The side of Morales's house that faced the street showed no damage, but something was wrong. The front door lay open and a fog of dust billowed out. Inside Thomas stopped short. The entire back wall had once offered a panoramic view across the wide plain. Now it no longer existed. The view was all that remained, darkness pricked by a thousand campfires. Thomas picked his way across rubble and broken beams, getting as close as he dared to where the wall had once stood. He discovered it was not just the wall that had gone. Six feet of double thickness stone marked where a cellar had been. Here the smell of dust was touched with the sharpness of spilled wine.

"They've all gone," said Jorge, who came to stand at his side. Thomas was relieved to see Lubna remained at the door.

"There may be someone buried under this."

"In that case they will be dead. It's not our business to find bodies." Above them a beam holding the remains of the roof creaked. "And we will join them if we stay." Jorge tugged at Thomas's sleeve. "Come away."

He turned, a sense of hopelessness filling him. He had been sure Simki was the killer. He had been misled by the man, liked him too much, and had not thought rationally. But now he had heard the tales of him killing another man before he had even arrived in this land. Slaves were a thread running through the deaths. Khalil's book of names, the maps, even Simki's own sister. Thomas was sure Francesca knew of this and it was why she made herself scarce, why she had placed herself close to Yusuf for protection.

Above, the beam creaked again and tiles fell to shatter against rubble. Jorge darted toward the door, grabbed Lubna and pulled her outside. Thomas glanced up, not yet concerned, though why he could not say. Stars showed through gaps in the roof, puncturing the darkness as if this was simply another early summer night in Ronda. Then the far wall began to bow, loosening more tile and stone, and Thomas ran.

A piece of wood jutting up caught his foot and sent him sprawling. Shards of rock bit into his chin and his head banged hard on a stone. He lifted himself up, hearing the groan of collapsing masonry, convinced his time had come, angry at his own stupidity, angry for all the things he had left undone. Then hands grabbed him and he was dragged across the ground like a sack of grain, more cuts opening on his hands and legs.

They fell through the door, the three of them, as the wall finally gave up its battle with gravity and fell with a crash, the ground shaking beneath them and an explosion of dust rushing after.

Lubna slapped him hard across the face.

"Don't you *ever* do anything that idiotic again," she said, her face set, eyes ablaze. "I thought I had lost you."

"He's harder to kill than that," said Jorge, sitting with his back against the outer wall that somehow still stood, but for how much longer was a mystery.

Thomas pulled himself upright. He offered a hand to Lubna who knocked it aside, so instead he offered it to Jorge, who smiled and took it.

"That is the end, then," Thomas said. "Simki is gone, and with him our main suspect."

Jorge gave Thomas a look. "Simki? You kept that to yourself, didn't you?"

"I needed time to think everything through."

Jorge shook his head. "Without our input? I'm not so sure he's the killer."

"I am," Thomas said. "We need to know everything about him, how he came to Ronda, who he knew." Thomas looked at the remains of the house. The lower portion of the front wall still stood, the doorway an incongruity against the destruction beyond. "Wait here," he said. As Lubna reached out to grab him he avoided her grasp and ran back inside.

Chapter 34

Simki's room was to the right and Thomas entered through a door blown off its hinges. Within there was little sign of the destruction that had destroyed the rest of the house other than a thick layer of dust which coated every surface. Thomas glanced over his shoulder, relieved to see neither of the others had followed.

He went to the shelf and scanned books until he found the journal he had seen Simki place there. Then he examined the desk, opening each drawer. There was nothing of interest, household accounts and a supply of paper and ink. He pulled at the last drawer to discover it locked. He tugged harder but it remained ungiving.

Thomas looked over the room, seeing nothing to help. He returned to the chaos beyond the room and picked up a rock, almost too large to lift. He brought it down on one side of the desk, splintering wood. When he brought it down a second time the desk broke in two. Thomas pulled at the drawer, nothing left to stop it opening.

Within lay more journals. Five of them. Thomas added them to the other and made his way out to discover Jorge grasping Lubna while she kicked at his shins.

Jorge raised an eyebrow. "She was all for following you." He released Lubna, who stepped away, angry at them both. "What have you got there?"

"Simki's journals. He showed me one when I was here

before. Innocent enough, but I found others locked in a drawer."

"If he's the killer why would he write of it?"

"You know why. That man last year, Alvarez, relished in recording his perversions. I think it is a compulsion in some men, as if placing the words on paper deepens the experience."

"Then we should return to the palace and study them before dawn, for the Spanish will resume their attack as soon as they can."

Lubna had walked away, stood with shoulders hunched, deliberately staring away from them. Thomas walked toward her, an urge for reconciliation. There was enough hate in the world without them falling out too.

Before he reached her a sound came, a cry from Jorge, and Thomas spun around.

Simki ran at him at full tilt. Before Thomas could step aside, before he could prepare himself, the man ran hard into him, knocking him to his back. The journals flew from his grasp.

Simki landed on Thomas's belly with both knees, driving the air from him, making it hard to draw any back in. Lubna came from the side, a dervish, fists pummelling. Simki simply stood, lifted her and tossed her aside. She came back at once. This time Simki punched her on the side of the head and she went to her knees, a hand searching blindly for Thomas. Jorge darted close, but only to pull Lubna from harm's way.

Simki bent, retrieved the journals and stood over Thomas. Lubna squirmed in Jorge's grasp, but he was too strong for her to escape.

"These are mine," said Simki. "I thought I could trust you, but I was wrong."

Thomas discovered he could finally breathe, but before he could move, let alone rise, Simki fled into the night.

They tried to find him but the man was gone, faded into the darkness like a wraith. Like the Incubus he was. Except Simki was no supernatural lover but a man fashioned of flesh and bone, a man of terrible urges.

"Why did he do this?" asked Lubna. They walked through the streets, quieter now, none of them spared damage, and Thomas tried not to think what another day would bring.

"The woman in the pot works told us he strangled a man on the boat from Africa. I wonder had he done the same before? Is it something he has always done? Is it why his own sister had to die, because she knew?"

"Why now?" said Lubna. "If she has always known why wait until now? He could have killed her at any time, but he risked her passing on her knowledge."

Thomas walked on a moment, thinking. He slowed and turned to Jorge as Lubna continued to the end of the street. "Tell me, for you are more knowledgeable than me in such matters. Can a man both love someone and also kill them? Is such a thing possible?"

"All things are possible, but it is unusual. Both are strong emotions, and killing is not normally linked with love. They are at opposite ends of the scale, but in some individuals that might only serve to bring them closer. We're not dealing with someone who thinks like the rest of us."

"True. And love and hate are the strongest of emotions."

"What we have may be some kind of twisted love,"

said Jorge.

"When did the story of the Incubus start?" Thomas asked.

"I don't know," said Jorge. "They talk of it in the harem, but I never thought to ask when the tale began. They have little else but gossip to amuse them, so they ration it like a sweet delicacy."

"And what are the stories?" Thomas started to walk again, looking for Lubna, but she had turned the corner out of sight. "Did the first death occur in the harem?"

"The first I know of. There may have been others, but if so they were not regarded as suspicious. People die, you know that better than most."

"Usually it's clear why."

"But not always. You have seen how these deaths are inflicted. They leave no ordinary sign."

"Tell me what you have heard of the first death," Thomas said.

"What I believe to be the first," said Jorge. "Another African. Beautiful by all accounts, and extremely skilled. But wicked too. She had to be disciplined on more than one occasion."

"Could she have come here with Simki?"

"I don't know," said Jorge, "but I'll ask. There should be a record somewhere, there always is. Most likely stored in the library."

Thomas slowed, stopped. "Of course. Khalil would be privy to all the records, he would know where they're stored, which bookcase, which shelf." He shook his head. "Something must have made him look for them."

"Or someone," said Jorge. "Is it why he was killed, do you think? Because of what he found?"

Thomas started up again, reached the corner and

found himself looking at an empty street. "Where is Lubna?" He stopped and turned a circle but she was nowhere to be seen.

"She must be this way," said Jorge, starting down the cross street in the other direction. He ran to the corner, came back. "The other way then."

There was no reason to fear for her safety, but they were living in a town under siege, and an invisible killer was stalking women. Not so invisible now, for they knew Simki's face.

"Come on." Thomas began to run hard. Simki had been with them only minutes before, and he had struck Lubna. Did he carry a hatred of all women, was that what this was about? Had he hated his own sister enough to kill her?

At the end of the street Thomas skidded to a halt because the roadway crumbled away into nothing. Houses that once stood here had disappeared entirely. He realised they were close to the walkway where Kisera had been thrown from.

Thomas eased along the side of one of the remaining buildings, the ground falling away in pattering flurries beneath his feet. He feared it would collapse altogether but didn't want to waste time looking for a safer passage. He only hoped Jorge's extra weight would not send him over the edge. At the far side, stepping onto solid ground, he turned back and offered an arm. Jorge reached out, too far away. He took another step and a block of soil tumbled into darkness, the sound of its falling loud in the night. Jorge reached again and this time Thomas grasped his hand, pulling him forward.

"Slow," said Jorge. "If I go I'll pull you with me."

Thomas laughed, an edge of panic rippling through

him. "If you fall I promise to let go." He pulled harder, hurrying Jorge, and it worked. The ground crumbled away behind him, but with one last heave he was on solid ground beside Thomas.

"And I thought you loved me," Jorge said.

"Think again." Thomas began to run once more.

He almost missed the narrow entrance that gave access to the precipitous walkway, caught himself and darted into it. A thick wall rose at his back, the walkway barely six feet wide, falling away vertically from the unprotected edge. The wall curved so they could see no more than twenty feet ahead and he moved quickly, beginning to think Lubna would not have come this way.

The walkway unspooled ahead, always the same distance, then the wall straightened and he saw the end of it. A hundred feet away a set of steps led to the head of the water tunnel. Two figures were on the steps, obscured by shadow. One tall, the other tiny. A first glance might take them to be locked in a lovers' embrace, except one figure was definitely Lubna. The other, almost certainly Simki, held her from behind, one arm around her waist, another at her throat where something light showed in the darkness. Lubna's fists stuck her attacker on the shoulders and face to no effect.

Thomas sprinted, closing the gap in seconds. The man looked up, features hidden in the gloom, white teeth showing, but not in amusement. Thomas could hear him breathing hard, meeting more resistance than he had bargained for.

Lubna kicked out and the man yelled, pushing her away. She stumbled on the edge of the drop, hesitated a moment, then slipped over.

Thomas cried out, caught between attacking the man

and going after Lubna. Except he knew what lay beyond the edge of the path. Nothing for three hundred feet.

Jorge came barrelling past, almost knocking him over the edge as well. Thomas teetered before regaining balance, giving the man time to turn and flee, Jorge in hot pursuit. Thomas ran to where Lubna had disappeared and flung himself flat, dreading what he would find. Instead of what he feared, a small face looked up at him, and fingers white with strain gripped a narrow ledge six feet below.

Thomas eased himself farther out, reached down, but the distance was too great. He looked left and right, saw the ledge ran only a short distance in either direction. It wasn't wide, no more than four inches. He suppressed impatience, trying to examine the situation with a calm mind, then swung himself over the edge, taking his weight on his forearms as his legs dangled. He had made an estimate of the distance and thought his plan should work. When he was fully extended and his toes still touched nothing he moved, transferring his entire weight to his hands as he lowered himself further. Still not enough. Slowly he straightened his arms.

A toe caught, a stone rattled away, and Thomas flailed for a moment before he found the ledge and jammed his foot against it.

He twisted to glance down. Lubna still gripped the edge, but he could see she was tiring.

"Grab my leg," he said, trying to keep calm in his voice.

"If I let go I'll fall," she said. "And if I grab you we both fall. Climb up and fetch help, a rope, other people."

Thomas knew she wouldn't be able to hold on long enough.

"Do it," he said, voice harsh. "For God's sake, just do

it. I'm tired of you always arguing."

He saw Lubna's face tighten. She released her left hand and reached out, caught his ankle. Her grip slipped, scrabbling wildly for the ledge again.

"You'll have to come lower," she hissed.

"I can't. One good swing and you'll be safe."

"That's easy for you to say up there."

"I'm not going to lose you," Thomas said. He saw something change in Lubna's expression, a slackening of fear, and for a moment he thought it was acceptance of her fate. Then she swung on both hands before releasing once more.

This time there was only one chance. Her left hand caught his robe and clutched it tight as her right lost its grip on the ledge. She hung away from the cliff, her slight body pulling the robe tight at his throat, cutting off the supply of air.

"Now the other hand," Thomas said, his voice strained.

Lubna twisted as she swung back, her right hand wrapping into the folds of his cloak, drawing it even tighter.

"Climb," Thomas gasped. "Climb along me to the path. Climb fast."

He pressed his face to the cliff, trying to ease the pressure around his throat. He felt each effort as Lubna reached up to pull herself along him. Her knees gripped his waist and then she was scrabbling over his shoulders. But it was too late. Her weight had cut off the supply of blood to his brain and darkness span around him. Thomas barely felt himself grip the cliff face. An ecstasy flowed through him, as it must through the victims of the Incubus. It brought him hard, images spilling through his mind of all the women he had ever known. And then the cold presence of the cliff fell away.

CHAPTER 35

Thomas woke at the third slap, reached up to grab a wrist before a fourth landed. He opened his eyes to find Lubna leaning over him. Tears spilled against his face, salt on his tongue.

"I am dead," he said.

"Sometimes I wish," said Lubna, before gripping his face and kissing him.

From a distance a cough sounded and Thomas broke the embrace to find Jorge standing over them.

"Should I stand guard or something?" he said.

"What happened?"

"Lubna was trying to haul you up by your cloak but you were too heavy. She managed to stop you falling, but you were hanging yourself. I joined her and between us we pulled you over the edge. For a while there I thought we'd killed you, but I should have known better."

"Simki?" Thomas sat up, washing a hand across his face. His head felt distant, but slowly the world coalesced around him, the ground no longer like a sponge beneath his hand. "It was Simki had you, wasn't it?" He directed the question at Lubna.

"He was behind me, I couldn't tell."

"You must have been able to," Thomas said. "Didn't you see his hands?"

"Whoever it was is gone," said Jorge.

"We need to find out where he's hiding. Al-Haquim will have a dungeon for him while we find out what's been going on."

"There's something you need to see first." Jorge said, turning. "This way."

Thomas tried to stand, staggered, and Lubna placed herself under his arm. He tried not to lean on her, but she was stronger than she looked, taking his weight without complaint. They made their way up stone steps, emerging at the side of the same small square their party had been led to when they arrived in Ronda.

The stone building that protected the head of the tunnel remained undamaged, but the door giving access stood open. From within came the sound of voices crying out, others raised in anger.

"Why do I need to see this?" Thomas's head felt strange and he wanted nothing more than to find a bed and sleep. Everything else could wait until morning.

"Because of this." Jorge took hold of Thomas's robe and led him to the edge of the cliff, gripping tight in case he was still unbalanced. "Look."

Thomas leaned on the corner of the building and peered over. In the darkness of the gorge torches lit the base of the cliff where the tunnel emerged. The ground beyond was muddy and disturbed where prisoners had filled their buckets. In guttering torchlight men worked.

"What are they doing?" he said.

"Don't look to me for explanations. What do I know of war?"

"Are they trying to break in? That's foolish, four men with swords could block the tunnel." Thomas reached out a hand and when Jorge gripped it he leaned farther over the drop, trusting him to take his weight.

Far below in the moonlit gorge men moved, a score of them. Barrels were being carried from a cart which had been brought as close as possible. As Thomas watched it occurred to him that they would have been equally visible when they had been in the same position, and he wondered had Simki seen them when he threw Kisera over the edge. Had he gained extra pleasure from the knowledge he was being witnessed by those unable to identify him? Or had he been too wrapped up in the moment?

The men below carried the barrels into the mouth of the tunnel. The door was open but should not have been. There was no sign of destruction, which meant someone inside must have gone down and allowed them entry. It didn't surprise Thomas that enemies had infiltrated Ronda, as they had in every town and city in al-Andalus. The same as there were Moorish spies in every Spanish town.

"What are they doing?" asked Jorge.

"I think they mean to use powder to make the entrance bigger," Thomas said.

"Why? They'll still have to climb through the tunnel."

Thomas pulled back, stepped away from the edge. "Or they're going to block it. They know it's our only source of water now. We have to go down there."

Jorge shook his head.

"If they spark the powder it could bring the entire cliff face down," Thomas said. "They're using too many barrels."

"And if they spark it when we're down there?" said Jorge.

"What – do you want to live forever?"

"I had been planning on such a thing, yes."

"Stay here then." Thomas moved away, his head beginning to clear. A knot of soldiers stood at the head of the tunnel, brought here by the noise of the prisoners within who continued to shout and scream. Thomas went to the man who appeared to be in charge.

"The Spanish are planning to explode the tunnel. We need to stop them."

He expected resistance, as he had earlier in the evening, but now as then these troops were hungry for someone to command. It made Thomas think al-Haquim was an even worse leader than he already believed, and he had considered him useless to begin with.

He directed the men, setting three to guard the upper entrance. He told them to use some of the rocks that had been brought here to keep the Spanish occupied. He took the other five with him, running down damp steps cut through the interior of the cliff. As he descended Thomas tried not to think of how much rock pressed above, how far they were from the open cliff face.

As Thomas's group moved past the cages with their complement of Spanish and Christian prisoners they rattled the bars and cried out, but their cries went unacknowledged.

The steps seemed endless, almost longer than they had on the way up. Torches burned in sconces at intervals, light growing brighter as they neared the bottom.

Thomas raised an arm and the men behind halted. The last flight of steps descended ahead, the Spanish hidden from them only by the slope.

The men looked at him, expecting orders, but he had none. He had descended with no plan, only a need to do something, and now he was on the point of action he had no idea what.

The men shuffled, anxious.

"There cannot be many of them, sir," said the man Thomas had identified as the leader before he had taken command. "If we rush them three of us can hold them at bay while the others push the barrels out."

It was a plan. Not a good plan, but better than anything Thomas had. He knew he had acted on instinct, not logic, and was regretting it.

He nodded. "Me, you and... who is your next best with a sword?"

"I am." A soldier stepped forward. He was short, wiry, and Thomas had seen his like before, recognised the coiled energy within and the scars on his arms.

"We attack fast. Drive them back to give the others time to roll the barrels out. Once they're clear close the entrance and bar it." He looked around. "Is everyone ready?"

All answered with tight nods. It felt good to command men as he once had, and Thomas recognised the strength of this small group. If the Moors possessed ten thousand such as these they might have a chance of winning the war, but he knew they did not. Moors did not fight, they paid others to do the fighting for them. Only one of these men was of Moorish descent, the others a diaspora from the northern lands attracted by the prospect of gold and killing.

Thomas counted off on his fingers. With loud yells they ran down the last set of steps.

Spanish soldiers jerked upright in surprise from where they were laying trails of powder. Thomas lunged at the nearest on his right, pulling his sword at the last moment so he struck an arm rather than the chest. The men beside him had no such reservations and five fell to the floor. Seeing the savagery of the attack the remainder fled, Thomas's band in pursuit.

Once outside the Spanish regrouped, forming a line now only a dozen strong. Twelve men against three, not the kind of odds Thomas liked, and he realised it had been a mistake to follow the men outside where there was space for them to turn their flight into attack.

But they were still forming a line, so Thomas screamed and ran at them, hoping his companions would follow. He broke through the line, inflicting flesh wounds on two, then he was past and turned before anyone could respond. He saw the others attack fiercely, taking down three more before the Spanish surrounded one of them. A sword thrust took him through the belly and he fell. The last man, seeing the odds change, turned and ran back to the tunnel entrance, but was taken down by a figure who emerged in his path. The two tangled on the ground, the new figure first to regain his feet.

It was Simki, who stood in confusion to find himself confronted by Spaniards. Before anyone could react he turned to one side and ran toward the waterfall. Without hesitation he dove into its maelstrom and disappeared. The soldier he had knocked down gained his feet and ran into the tunnel. Thomas wasn't even sure the Spanish had seen either of them, for they had all turned to confront him. Nine men, eight if he excluded the one he had wounded. Too many.

He placed his sword on the ground and held his arms out to his sides.

"Pax. My name is Thomas Berrington, and I am friend to the King of Spain. Take me to him."

One of the soldiers laughed. "If you are friend to the King then my arse is married to your Queen."

Thomas didn't think it the right time to point out the Moors did not have queens.

"If you kill me and they discover what you have done you will die a slow and painful death."

"If you are friend to the King tell me who is in his party," said another, who appeared to be in charge.

"The Queen and Prince Juan," Thomas said. "And there is a man, an ex-priest, by the name of Lawrence. An Englishman like me."

He waited.

The leader nodded. "He sounds plausible."

"He has killed seven of us, he has to die. If you won't do it I will." A soldier advanced, sword raised.

"Stop!" It was not the leader, but the man Thomas had wounded. "He could have killed me but did not. It was his companions who did the killing, this man stayed his hand."

"I am a physician," Thomas said. "I can tend your wounds."

"The Queen has set up infirmaries, we have our own surgeons. I have no need of help from a Moor."

"We'll take him back," said the leader. "If he tells the truth we have captured a valuable prisoner. If he lies we will take our time killing him. His screams will rise to the town above. But first we have work to finish."

Thomas could do nothing as the majority of the men moved into the tunnels. Only a few barrels had been pushed outside and they jammed them back into the entrance while a trail of powder was laid. His captors jostled him as they moved away, the powder trail growing. Finally it was considered long enough and a man came forward with a flint. He struck several times until a scrap of oiled wool started to smoke. He cupped it in his palms until fire flared then dropped it onto the powder. Instantly smoke rose and trailed fast toward the tunnel entrance. The men holding Thomas loosed their grip and ran, and he followed.

The blast came sooner than he expected, with tremendous force, knocking Thomas off his feet and tumbling him down the slope. A deep thunder sounded, far more than the explosion could account for alone. Thomas came to his knees and looked back, dreading what he might find, but what he saw was nothing. A roiling black cloud rose from the base of the cliff.

The wind gusted along the defile, pushing the smoke upstream toward the waterfall, and Thomas was greeted by a towering wall of stone. The explosion had brought down part of the rock face on both sides, blocking the river entirely. Already the river bed showed, and when he turned to look downstream he saw water draining away as if poured from a bucket to leave bare rock. With luck, Thomas thought, Simki lay buried beneath those tons of rock.

One of the Spanish soldiers lay on his front, the side of his head missing. Another nursed a broken arm. Thomas looked around, judging it possible he could escape while they gathered their wits. He came to his feet, turning down the slope. The tunnel was no longer an option. His only chance of regaining entry to Ronda was at the gate next to the bathhouse on the northern side. He walked slowly, not wanting to draw attention, expecting at any moment to hear a cry or the pain of a thrown knife, but nothing came.

He reached a rock spur and used it to hide, gathering himself. He pressed as far into the crevice as he could and waited.

Raised voices sounded. Rocks continued to fall from the cliff, dislodged from higher up. Thomas's ears rang from the explosion and he could smell burnt powder on his clothes.

A figure appeared and he waited, hoping darkness would hide him, but it wasn't a Spaniard. Instead Simki crept across the slope, crouched double, looking over his shoulder. His clothes dripped water. As he passed, unaware he was observed, an anger sparked in Thomas. He wanted to leap on the man, hold him to the ground and beat him until all life was extinguished, but knew he couldn't. The Spanish were too close, so he did nothing but watch as Simki continued along the base of the cliff and disappeared.

Thomas stayed where he was. The Spanish weren't looking for Simki, but Thomas had been their prisoner, one he knew they would want to re-capture.

Minutes passed before the first soldier appeared. He walked with a limp, using his sword as a crutch. Others followed, more sure-footed. None of them looked around, all staring ahead to the mass of their companions spread across the plain. Thomas let them pass, waited another impatient five minutes. When he finally slipped away he turned in pursuit of Simki.

He found him a mile farther on, sitting at the base of the cliff, staring out over the dark plain sparked by cooking fires. The sound of an army is never hushed, and so it was here. Conversations merged and floated through the air, words mixed, indecipherable. A cry here and there rose above the general murmur. Dogs barked. Men laughed. Others shouted. In a few short hours dawn would come and activity would start once more. Already Thomas could make out bombardiers preparing their cannon for the morning assault.

Simki heard him when he was ten yards away. He jerked around, coming half to his feet, then sitting again when he saw who it was.

"I thought you were those soldiers," he said.

Thomas crouched beside him, close enough to grasp if the need arose.

"Why did you do it?"

"Escape through the tunnel? Why do you think? He came for me as soon as he knew I was the one he sought. I managed to escape only because the house exploded around us. I told you too much, and you passed what I told on to the wrong man. I don't want to be the next to be found dead."

Thomas stared at him. It was not the answer he had expected.

"Why did you run when we came to the house? Why attack Lubna if you're not the killer?"

Simki laughed. He seemed almost relieved that Thomas had caught him. "I told you why at the house. I trusted you. I liked you, Thomas, I genuinely liked you. I thought you would catch the killer without my having to tell you who it was, but you're not as clever as I thought. So I ran, as I plan to continue running, as far and fast as I can."

"Tell me who," Thomas said.

Simki shook his head. "And put you and your friends in danger too?" He turned aside. "I will take my dangerous secrets with me. I leave now."

"No, you're not," Thomas said.

"You think you can stop me? You are fast with a sword, I give you that, I saw it from inside the tunnel. But I am bigger than you, and stronger. We can fight if you like, but there will be only one result, and I am tired of hurting people. Let me go. I will start a new life somewhere and hope he never finds me."

"You know who, don't you."

"Of course."

"So why didn't you stop him? You say you are strong. Why did you allow him to kill your sister?"

"Do you honestly think I wanted that? He was her lover. She believed the words he whispered as he lay with her, and I believed them too when she told me. Sometimes I think the tales are true and he is a demon that can never be caught, never be stopped."

"Why did he kill her if he was her lover?" Thomas said.

"Because she wouldn't tell him what he wanted, what he has always sought. She wouldn't tell him my name."

Thomas turned from the view to stare at Simki. "Your name?"

"He has sought me over many years, and this time he came close. It is why I had to flee. I should have stayed to revenge Kisera, but he has killed so many I feared even strong as I am he would kill me too, and then no-one would know."

"Tell me who," Thomas said.

"You know who."

"I thought it was you."

"And now?"

"I don't know."

"Think. If you do you will know who it is. A friend of yours. A man of fine words, a man of taste and wealth."

Thomas pushed his hands through his hair, gritty with dust. "Faris," he said. "I never liked him, but this?"

"Who is Faris?"

"Faris al-Rashid. Friend to Sultans and the richest man in al-Andalus. Perhaps the richest man in the whole of Spain. You sold him slaves. He outbid Jorge."

"Ah, him," said Simki. "I have a tale to tell you, and then you will know of whom I speak."

CHAPTER 36

West Africa: 1471

Three caravels were drawn up at the small dock at Uachaim, a village on the west coast of Africa. Once they sailed others would arrive within days. The village and its neighbours had grown tenfold over the last thirty years as the trade in slaves increased.

Simki and his sister stood on the hot ground, heads bowed to ensure they did not accidentally meet the eyes of their captors. Their lack of clothing other than a rag at their waists did not concern them, nor the heat, but the master's whip did.

A metal ring was fixed around their right ankle, the same with every other of the twelve hundred captives around them. The journey from their home village to Uachaim had taken many weeks, and scores had already died on route. Simki wondered how many more would follow before they reached their destination, and what that destination would be. It was not his place to know. His place was to keep his gaze down, his mouth shut, and to obey every order yelled at him.

Simki was hungry, but had grown used to the pangs. There would be food aboard ship, for it was poor business to kill slaves before they could be sold, but he knew it would be barely enough to keep them alive during the voyage. Simki wasn't stupid, he knew what would happen to them both. He also knew Kisera would fetch a far greater sum than him, and the reason why. He had not yet explained it to her. She would need to know before the time came, but he knew she wasn't stupid either.

Shouts sounded, their meaning masked, but the whips carried the message. They began to shuffle forward, each shackled to the one ahead and behind. A man with skin as dark as Simki's sat at a table, a leather bound journal open in front of him. As each captive passed they were stopped and he asked them a single question in their own tongue.

Name.

He wrote what he heard in the journal, one column for men, one for women as they shuffled past and along to the wooden ramp. Beside the name the man scratched a second column, an estimate of age.

Simki managed to keep them in the last batch to board. He had learned that the holds below deck would be filled first, with the final group to board chained on the upper deck. He did not like the look of the boats. They were poorly maintained, their sails ragged. Should they sink he would prefer to die last. There was no chance of swimming to save themselves, the chains would see to that.

A tall man stood on the wheel-deck, well-dressed, hair slickly oiled. As Simki watched a slight figure came from below decks to join him, a small fist twisting in the man's robe. A girl of no more than twelve years. Dark hair spilled in curls along her back, her pretty face as pale as milk. Simki had grown used to the pale-skinned ones, was beginning to understand a few words of their language and knew he would learn more. He listened and learned.

There were no benches, so once they were loaded Simki sat on the deck boards, considering how many other backsides had been here before to make them so smooth. A master came along the line, spooling a chain through the round loop welded to the side of each shackle. Simki tried to ensure he and Kisera sat next to each other, but at the last moment a giant of a man pushed between, grinning. His interest in Kisera was obvious, and Simki feared he would have to fight him. He had fought others along the way, killing two. Each time Kisera had been angry with him. She told him she already knew what her fate would be.

It was cooler as they moved into the ocean. The deck rose and fell alarmingly and at least half of them began to throw up, not that there was much to bring up. Simki was pleased he had managed to keep them in clean air.

A breeze blew from the south-east and the caravel made rapid progress. The shoreline faded to a hazed line, but the masters obviously did not want to lose sight of it. Sailors ran across decks and climbed rigging. The small group of caraveles changed direction.

As darkness fell stars came out brighter than Simki had ever seen. And then the ship's master came along the line, walking slowly, examining each of his charges. The girl, who must be his daughter, for who else could she be, trailed behind. Her head turned, scanning the captives as if she had never seen their like before.

While the master was still out of earshot Simki hissed a command to Kisera, told her to scowl and cover her breasts, to hunch over to make them appear smaller. Except as the man came along the deck Simki saw he was not looking at the women but the men. He tried to take his own advice. Simki had no false modesty. He knew how the women of his village looked at him. He was tall, handsome, and intelligent. Here only two of those traits were being judged.

The master examined each of the men then turned and started back. He stopped beside Simki, who tried to curl even smaller.

The man barked an order and a sailor came over and released the chain from one end, pulled it through until it ran over Simki's foot. A hand reached down, but it did not touch his shoulder. It fell on the giant next to him.

The man shook his head, resisting. A sailor rapped his skull with a club and while his senses were scrambled he was dragged away.

After he was gone and the chain threaded once more to hold them together, Kisera shifted closer, her darkness no more than a shadow against the night.

"Where have they taken him?"

"He is to be used," Simki said. He knew she would understand. Like him she wasn't stupid.

"I thought it was going to be me when he first came. Then I thought it was you."

"Quiet!" A sailor yelled, one of the words Simki had learned early on after capture. They rarely used two words when one would do, and never three. It only caused confusion.

Simki looked for the girl. He found her sat on a stack of spare sails, leaning on a rail to stare across the ocean. For some reason he was relieved to see her there. She was too young to know of what her father was doing.

He raised an arm and Kisera came beneath it. The air had cooled. The sound of the caravelle's passage whispered as it cut the water. Simki watched iridescence peel away from the bow. Had he not been a prisoner awaiting an unknown fate the night would have been beautiful.

"Simki?" Kisera spoke, her voice barely above a whisper. Her skin was warm against his and he hoped she benefited from the closeness as he did.

He said nothing, waiting for her to continue.

"If they sell me to someone cruel, someone who looks as if they will beat me, you are to strangle me."

He kissed the top of her head. "I could never do that."

"It is better to die than what they plan for me."

"You are beautiful and you are clever. You will be fine. It is me that will have to be strangled, for I have little to offer."

Kisera hugged him, falling silent. The subject was never mentioned again.

Later the giant returned and the chain unspooled once more. This time he was placed beyond Kisera. Simki watched him, the arrogance stripped away. The man sat with arms hanging between his knees, head bent. He avoided meeting anyone's gaze.

The next night the master came again. Simki expected him to choose someone new, expected to be chosen himself, but it was the giant again. This time he rose without complaint and walked on large feet behind the master.

On the third night he returned with head held high. The sailor with him set him three places along the deck but the man shook his head and pointed to Simki. The sailor, obviously under orders to accommodate the master's new lover, pushed them aside.

"Not had enough yet?" Simki whispered after the

chain was locked and the sailor had gone. He steeled himself to fight, knowing his death was imminent.

The man pushed him away, the power of him frightening. He turned to Kisera and jerked her close. He tried to push her head down to where an erection continued to jut between his thighs.

Simki grabbed the man's ears and pulled his head backward. For a moment the man released Kisera and turned. The punch, when it came, sent Simki spinning into darkness.

When he woke the man was on top of Kisera. She had turned her face to one side, no expression showing as she waited for him to finish.

Simki knelt, pulling lengths of chain toward him, hearing a soft rattle as it passed through ankle rings, afraid the sound would alert one of the sailors. But it was deep night, and other than a few men keeping watch at the front everyone else slept. When he had enough chain he moved fast, wrapping it around the giant's neck. He jammed his knees into his back and heaved.

The giant rose up, Simki clinging to him. He twisted and turned, but however hard he punched Simki he could not get his full power behind the blows.

The battle continued in silence, air hissing through Simki's teeth, the giant incapable of drawing breath. Slowly Simki felt him weaken. The man went to one knee before toppling onto his face. Still Simki kept pulling until he was sure all sign of life had fled. He loosed the chain, ready to grab it again if the man moved.

"What have you done?" Kisera whispered. "You should have let him do as he wished. It is not as if I have not had men before."

"If I had he would never leave you alone. Next time it

would be the two of you taken below deck."

"It is what will come to pass, is it not? Why not now?" Kisera wiped tears from her face. "You are a fool. Now I will lose you."

Simki looked at the dead man.

He tugged at him, pulling his leg so his ankle lay across the nearest cleat the chain ran through. He glanced around. The night was deep, dark. A wind had blown up and the caravelle lurched against the waves, slapping hard into each trough. The girl was not in her usual place curled on the sailcloth. Simki was afraid she might have witnessed what he had done. He waited, judging the moment, then as the next wave peaked he lifted the man's leg and smashed it against the cleat. Not hard enough. He waited, lifted again and brought it down once more. This time he was rewarded with a loud snap. He repeated the action again and again until the ankle was a mass of pulped flesh.

Simki twisted the foot until skin tore. He continued until he could jerk the foot away from the leg. He pulled the iron link free.

"Help me," he said to Kisera.

"I will help," said the man beyond her.

"So will I," said the one behind Simki.

Between them they lifted the giant and tipped him over the side. The splash he made was loud, but so was the sea. Simki thanked his helpers, picked up the detached foot and tossed it overboard. He examined the deck. There was blood, but less than expected.

When the master came around the following day everyone feigned ignorance. Simki risked rattling his chain and shaking his head, making out the giant had not been locked back in.

That night the master chose Simki in his stead.

CHAPTER 37

"What did you do?" Thomas said.

"What could I do? I did as he wanted. I had to stay alive to look after Kisera. And it was only sex."

Thomas stared across the plain. The sky was lightening to the east, dawn no more than an hour away. They would have to move soon or risk discovery by the Spanish.

"I assume there is a point to this tale," he said.

Simki smiled. "It is in the first journal." He pulled it from inside his shirt, wrapped in oilcloth. "But I won't make you read it. The master's name was Amadore del Caccia. His younger brother was captain of another of the ships making up our small fleet. His name was Giovanni." Simki held up a hand when he saw Thomas's expression. "Not the one you are thinking of. There is another behind everything."

Thomas waited, impatient. The sky lightened further. The sound of the Spanish army grew as men woke and began to prepare for the day. Simki rose and walked away along the base of the cliff as the light grew stronger, the grey world around sparking into colour. Thomas followed until they were out of sight of the forces arrayed across the plain.

"If you knew who the killer was why did you keep it to yourself? You should have told me."

Simki turned his head to look at him. "If I had known

who perhaps I would. But I didn't know, not until he came for me at the house and then I understood it all." Simki stopped, sat and put his back against the rock, rested his head against it and closed his eyes. For a moment Thomas thought he might have gone to sleep, but then he began to speak.

"When the master took me to his cabin I discovered what he had done with the other man. To how many others over the years it is better not to think of. I had no clothes to remove, but he made me remove his." Simki took a deep breath, let it out in a long sigh. "It was nothing, as I told you. Then he took a length of sailcloth, long and thin, and told me to wrap it at his throat. It was not me he wanted to penetrate but the other way around, and he wanted me to take his breath."

"And did you?"

Simki nodded, eyes still closed.

"You're aware this only makes you sound even more like the killer."

"I know, but let me finish. This went on each night we were at sea, and the voyage was long, almost two weeks. We had to put in to shore during storms, but that didn't stop him. Then, on our final night we saw the lights of Cadiz in the distance and I was taken again. He had an expectation now, a twisted pleasure in our coupling. Except this time when I tightened the cotton I did not let it loose. I took his breath for good. And when it was done I looked up and saw a pair of dark eyes watching me from behind a curtain. His daughter had witnessed everything."

"What did you do?"

"I rose, meaning to kill her too, the cloth in my hand, but two sailors came for me. They must have thought the master asleep. I was afraid the girl would cry out but she made no sound, no sound at all. She didn't even cry at the death of her father."

"How did you avoid punishment? They would have found the ship's master dead come morning."

"I broke free from the sailors and jumped overboard, swam to shore. It was no more than a mile, and I am a strong swimmer. I followed the others at a distance, rejoined them when they came to Ronda. Nobody counted, nobody noticed. I was one more head, but I was with Kisera again."

"Explain the link," Thomas said. "I'm not saying I don't believe you, but you're not telling me everything."

Simki smiled. "I'm sorry, but it's not a simple tale. Not simple at all."

"I'm a clever man."

"So I've heard. The girl is the key. I haven't told you her name. We heard it on board ship. The master's daughter was called Francesca."

Thomas sat back so hard he cracked his head against the cliff. "Francesca's the killer? I know she's strange, but how could she kill so many?"

"It's requires little strength to draw a slip of linen taut, particularly when your victim believes it an act of love." Simki shook his head. "I believe Francesca has killed some, but it is her cousin who is the Incubus. It is Giovanni."

"How?" Thomas said. "No – I mean why?"

"The other Giovanni, the captain, the master's brother, took her in. His son of the same name was a few years older than her. They grew up together in Naples and eventually became lovers. But Francesca never forgot what had happened to her father, even if he brought it on himself. Children are like that, aren't they? Children believe their parents are perfect even when the evidence is clear to the contrary. Once he was old enough Francesca sent Giovanni to sea in search of the man who killed her father. In search of me.

"They have searched ten years, more. Questioning other slavers, sellers of slaves like my new master. All the time getting closer until they reached Kisera. Neither of them knew she was my sister, nor did they know I lived in the same house, but it was too close to risk. I told Kisera we had to leave, but she didn't believe Giovanni was evil. She loved him."

"And love killed her," Thomas said.

"In the same way I killed the ship's master," said Simki. "That is why they do it. Francesca hid behind the sailcloth curtain and watched me take the breath from her father, the father she loved, for all his faults. That single act turned her mind, or her mind was already turned. I told you she was a strange little thing. Pretty, but strange. She would walk along the line of us, staring as if we were not of this earth. For her, perhaps, we were not. I have not seen it, but somewhere in the palace, beneath her bed, hidden in a crevice, there will be a strip of the cloth. It will be old, no doubt stained, but sailcloth lasts a long time. It is the length I dropped when the sailors' took me, the piece I intended to kill her with before they came. It has meaning for her. The cloth that killed her father. It will have meaning for Giovanni too, once she turned him into what he became."

Thomas stared at Simki, believing him now.

"Will you hunt them down?" Thomas asked.

"Me?" Simki laughed, the sound lacking any trace of humour. "No, I'll leave that to you. I hear you make a habit of such things."

"The pair have made themselves scarce."

"But you will find them, won't you? That is also what I hear. You are relentless." Simki slapped his chest. He hitched a breath and rose. "Do you believe me, Thomas Berrington?"

"I do."

"And do you plan to stop me walking away? I am done with Ronda, there is a whole other world I have yet to see."

Thomas stood, awkward for a moment, then stepped forward and embraced Simki. The man returned the hug before breaking away. He walked down the slope, heading somewhere, anywhere away from where he was. Thomas watched him go, hoping he could find a measure of peace, but doubting it.

CHAPTER 38

It might have taken hours for the gate to admit him had Jorge not been awaiting his return. Thomas found him sitting on a low stone wall edging a terraced garden, each terrace barely a foot wide.

"I thought you were dead," said Jorge. "But then I thought no, it is impossible to kill Thomas Berrington, so I came and told the guards to let you in when you came." Jorge put his head to one side. "You're not dead, are you?"

Thomas held his arms out. Look, here I am.

"Why not?" said Jorge.

Behind Thomas the guards closed the door within the gate, heavy metal bars dropping to reinforce it. Already with the sun only just risen the air was dry and tasted of dust and the remnants of powder.

"The Spanish captured me," Thomas said as they started up the steep slope. To the left cliffs rose in staggered tiers, any gaps filled with stone walls. To the right lay gardens and houses, each perched almost on top of the one below. The view opened up as they ascended, the plain coming into view. From this side of the town it gave the appearance of a peaceful place.

"And yet you got away, obviously."

"When the powder exploded it was chaos." He laughed. "I walked away. Nobody tried to stop me. And then I found Simki. He was there. He went into the pool under the fall and managed to escape."

Jorge looked around, making a show of seeking someone. "So where is he?"

"He told me who the real killers are."

"Other than him," said Jorge.

"I believe him," Thomas said. "He told me the one doing the killings is Giovanni del Caccia, but it is his cousin Francesca who pulls the strings. She has seduced and enslaved him."

"She's not that beautiful," said Jorge dismissively. "Giovanni doesn't strike me as one who would be enslaved by anyone. The opposite, in fact. Apart from that we both saw him climb through the tunnel. He couldn't have been at the top of the cliff and the bottom at the same time."

"We didn't see him climb the steps, only saw him at the top. In the confusion it would have been easy enough to slip past us and then pretend to emerge with the others."

Jorge still didn't seem convinced.

"How can we know what passes through a man's mind?" Thomas said. "The two of them lived together from an early age, and she had a plan even then. She would have worked on him, bringing him to the same belief as herself."

"So now we have two people to seek." Jorge's voice was soft, tired, and Thomas wondered if he had been waiting all night.

"Is Lubna safe?"

"She went back to the palace. The tunnels are blocked. Destroyed. There will be no more water carried from the river."

"It was only a matter of time. We were never going

to win this battle. Al-Haquim, if he has any sense, will surrender now and save as many as he can."

"We both know he has no sense."

They reached the top of the climb, both breathing harder. The low sun cast long shadows from houses and roofs across the streets so they moved from warmth to coolness as they walked.

"I will check the new dead to see if Giovanni or Francesca are among them," Thomas said. "Both have been scarce of late."

"Which they will be if they are trying to evade capture," said Jorge.

Thomas stopped on a corner. A woman passed carrying a basket of washing, though she would find no water today. "I told them Simki was Kisera's brother," he said. "It was me who put him in danger. He was the one they have sought all along, and I told them where to find him. It was Giovanni who attacked Lubna, not Simki." He shook his head. "And I liked the man!"

"He made you like him. Some men can do that. It comes to them as easily as breathing. I have a little of it, but Giovanni is a master."

"If they're not dead we have to find them," Thomas said. "We'll search the entire town if we have to. They can't have escaped, we saw them both after the raid. I'm worried about Yusuf, she was with him at the slave auction. I'll have to go to al-Haquim and ask for men."

"He'll refuse, you know he will. He has others whispering in his ear now."

"And murder is not enough reason?"

Jorge only offered a look, but it was enough.

Thomas opened his mouth to speak but whatever words there were disappeared in the thunder of cannon opening fire. A flaming ball arced over their heads to crash into the roof of a house not yet damaged.

Abraham al-Haquim was rigid with anger, so angry Thomas knew there was no point in pressing his case. He would do as he had done the night before and find men hungry for order out of chaos. He had started to turn away when al-Haquim called his name.

"Berrington, here. You know these infidels. What is it they want? Why do they bombard us without respite?"

Thomas glanced around the governor's companions. Only one of them possessed the intelligence to tell the man the reason, and Faris al-Rashid was too wily to be the bearer of such news.

"They want you to surrender, of course," Thomas said.

Al-Haquim turned away, turned back. It looked as if he had slept in his clothes, which he might well have. "I cannot surrender Ronda. It is not mine to give away."

"Then the Spanish will continue their bombardment."

"No, they will not. We have weapons as well."

Thomas frowned. There was no heavy artillery in Ronda that he knew of. They had swords and bows, little else, and the last attack should have been enough to dissuade the Governor from trying the same again.

Al-Haquim clapped his hands together and a guard came to him.

"Go to my soldiers and tell them to bring the prisoners to the square, the one next to the tunnel, the one facing the Spanish. Do it now." He turned to Thomas, an expression of sly triumph on his face. "Now they will see what punishment I can unleash for tormenting me."

As al-Haquim swept from the room Thomas moved

to intercept Faris al-Rashid. He placed a hand on his arm and the man looked down at it until Thomas withdrew it.

"I'm seeking Francesca or Giovanni," Thomas said, wondering if the friendship shown to him by Faris was all used up. "She was with Yusuf and you yesterday."

"And still with him when we parted," said Faris. He looked around at the gathering that now followed the governor and frowned. "I was sure he was here too, but perhaps not. What do you want her for?"

"Nothing important," Thomas said. "A question that came up. Curiosity, nothing more."

Faris smiled and shook his head. "If I see either I'll tell them to seek you out."

By the time Thomas found Lubna and Jorge, intending to start the search for the pair, they had left it too late and were caught in a stream of those who had survived the bombardment, all heading toward the square. They were forced from a side street like a pip from an orange to be confronted with a dozen prisoners lined along the top of the cliff. A mixture of Spanish and other nationalities, all they shared in common was to be captured by the Moors and enslaved. Each was painfully emaciated. Each dressed in nothing more than a loincloth, ribs showing, skin mottled with bruises. How long they had been imprisoned in the dank dungeons, how long they had hauled buckets of water from the river up three hundred feet of dripping steps to the top, was unknown. Now they awaited their fate as they had accepted their punishment, silent, heads bowed.

As Thomas and the others had made their way to the square the bombardment slowed then stopped as the Spanish below caught sight of their countrymen. When

Thomas saw what was happening he turned to Jorge.

"Take Lubna back to the palace."

"I'm not a child," said Lubna. "I don't need to be protected from unpleasant sights."

"There is no need for you to witness this," Thomas said, pushing her away. "Go to the palace and find out if anyone knows where Francesca and Giovanni are. But don't approach either until I return."

Still Lubna resisted. Thomas put his arms around her and lifted, intending to carry her away if need be, but he had not reckoned on the force of those still streaming into the square. Word had spread through the town. At last the Governor was fighting back.

Thomas pressed himself against the wall, afraid they would be swept away. Already a few souls were dangerously close to the edge, the only thing protecting more from a swift death were the ranks of soldiers forming a barrier, and even they were starting to look worried.

Al-Haquim strode to and fro, declaiming something in a loud voice which was almost instantly swallowed by the noise of the crowd. His words were meant for the Spanish but were wasted by distance and language. Only a few below would understand Arabic, but not enough to transmit his message even if they could hear it.

When he finally came to a halt he raised his arm, and twelve soldiers stepped from the ranks, one for each prisoner.

Al-Haquim's next words were not meant for the Spanish.

"They go over alive," he said, his voice loud so the entire square, now hushed, could hear. "One at a time, as I call out."

The soldiers took another pace forward. The prisoners didn't bother to look up. They knew their fate, perhaps welcomed an end to their suffering.

Al-Haquim raised an arm. When it dropped he cried out in praise of God. "Allahu Akbar!" *Allah is greater*, the war cry of the Moors as they rode into battle. Except this was not the action of a statesman or general, it was the action of an angry coward.

The first soldier grasped a prisoner and lifted. With a heave he propelled the man into emptiness. The man fell without a cry, the sound of him hitting the ground below muffled. There came the roar of ten thousand voices ranged beneath the cliff.

Al-Haquim raised his arm and cried out over and over until all twelve had been despatched. Not all went as silently as the first, or without a struggle, but in the end they all became examples of the Governor's madness.

"Fetch another dozen," he screamed, and men ran to obey, afraid if they did not they would be chosen instead.

"Come away," Thomas said. "We need watch no more of this savagery." He pushed hard through the crowds, brooking no resistance. Jorge followed close behind as a path opened, and Lubna tucked in behind them both. The streets leading to the square were packed with bodies, all trying to catch a glimpse of what was happening.

As they reached the rear ranks the fearsome sound of the cannon started up, together with the creak and crack of trebuchets. Thomas ducked as a missile sailed overhead to land harmlessly beyond the far town walls. All at once their passage was made easier as the crowd streamed away from the square. Something crashed against a wall and Thomas skidded to a halt, pressing backward as the broken body of a man fell at his feet.

It was a Moorish soldier, one of those involved in the pointless raid, captured and taken prisoner. The Spanish had started their own campaign of terror.

CHAPTER 39

Thomas, Jorge and Lubna sat in a cool room with a view of the mountains, as if war was not being conducted all around. Now and again an explosion sounded, a moment later accompanied by the crash of falling masonry. The Spanish had continued the bombardment after dark, but it had become desultory, their anger sated, and the residents of the town who remained alive considered themselves invulnerable for the moment.

All three had bathed and dressed in freshly laundered clothes. A low table was arrayed with fine foods from the palace kitchen and Jorge had smuggled in two bottles of fine wine he had liberated from Morales's cellars. Lubna would not partake, but Jorge was always more than willing to drink another's share.

"They're most likely dead," said Jorge as he reached out and filled a flatbread with meat and fruit. "So many have died today. Even if we haven't found the bodies it's likely they're with the others not yet recovered."

The scent of the food was rich in the small room. The sound of occasional explosions beyond the walls belonged to a different world.

Thomas drank the wine. He had lost what little appetite he possessed somewhere in the maelstrom of the past days. When he glanced at Lubna the shadows beneath her eyes were clear even against the tint of her skin. Her eyes were half lidded, and he was sure he looked worse. Thomas had told her everything he had deduced from Simki's tale and she now knew as much as he and Jorge did. Whether that knowledge was welcome hadn't yet been decided, it seemed.

"Let's assume they live," he said. "And they are together. Where would they go?"

"They will have a place somewhere," said Jorge. "A bolt hole we know nothing about. Francesca lived in the palace, but Giovanni is a mystery."

"Would they know anyone at Giminez's house who might offer them refuge? Giovanni has a way about him." Thomas thought of the plain cook. It would be a simple matter to seduce her and persuade her to hide them.

"That occurred to me so I went there. It's abandoned. One wall is missing. I even went across the bridge, or what's left of it, and checked the pot works without any luck."

"There are a hundred houses the same," said Lubna, not asleep after all. "I don't think I've seen one without damage. Even the palace has been struck."

She and Thomas had spent most of the day attending to the wounded. The ranks of dead had grown as the sun crossed the sky, increasing further as darkness fell. Thomas stared at the meal laid before them and wondered what the dispossessed outside the palace would be eating tonight. He knew the answer.

"Al-Haquim has to end this," he said, rising. "If he waits for al-Zagal to return he'll wait forever, for there will be nothing of the town left by then. I'm going to talk to him."

"You saw him today," said Jorge, grasping Thomas's wrist to prevent him leaving. "He's as likely to stand you on the top of the cliff and have you tossed over before he'll listen."

"Faris, then," Thomas said. "He's not stupid. He knows there's only one conclusion to this siege and it does no good to draw it out. If I can persuade him to overthrow the Governor we could end this tonight. He can make Yusuf the new Sultan – he has as much right as anyone here."

"Nothing will happen tonight," said Jorge. "Sit and eat, sleep. As they will be doing."

Thomas pulled away from Jorge's grip. "Tomorrow will be too late." He turned and left the room, half expecting to be followed, but he heard no footsteps behind. He headed deeper into the palace, trying to remember where Faris al-Rashid had set himself up. He found a guard outside a closed door, his way barred.

"He is not to be disturbed," the guard said, blocking Thomas's path.

"I am on urgent business."

"Do you not understand? He is not to be disturbed. Leave a message if you must, but you cannot see him tonight."

Thomas eyed the man. He could disarm him, he was sure, but was less sure what good that might do. He turned away, picturing the layout of the palace in his mind. There would be another way.

The harem was quiet, unguarded. Only the rulers of the town were afforded the luxury of a soldier's protection since the coming of the Spanish. One or two women lifted their heads as Thomas passed, but none tried to him. He glanced around, looking for Francesca, not surprised she wasn't there. As Jorge had said, the pair would be hiding somewhere. Would they be planning more murder, or was this the end of it? Had Simki's tale explained the root of Francesca's obsession or not? Thomas thought it might, but couldn't be sure. The obsession might have taken over from the original reason, no end to it unless the pair were stopped. Thomas had seen it before. Sometimes one killing was done for a reason: fear, justice, betrayal, revenge, but then the killer discovered the power the act offered. Taking another life can either disgust a man or enchant him.

Thomas followed two more corridors before passing the bathing chamber, the splash of water silent. Faris's rooms were set at the heart of the palace, close to those of al-Haquim. They had moved here when the bombardment began, vacating more luxurious accommodation which suffered from proximity to the outer walls, their windows an invitation for a bombardier to aim at. So far, for whatever reason, the palace remained relatively unscathed. The only conclusion Thomas could draw was the Spanish wanted it undamaged for when they marched in.

As expected the small door on this side of the suite of rooms was unguarded. It was only there so concubines could come and go unobserved. Thomas passed through into a darkened room. He stopped, listening. An arch showed candle light beyond, and as he waited he heard the sound of a man and woman in the throes of passion. He started forward, stopped. Faris would be more than angry if he was disturbed, unlikely to help even if such was likely. Thomas leaned against the wall, waiting. It seemed to take an inordinate length of time, but then the woman's cries grew in strength before stilling.

Thomas waited some more. He heard voices, then the pattering of bare feet. Helena appeared through the archway. Silk clothing clutched against her body barely covered her. She didn't see Thomas until she was almost on him, then she stopped dead, a hand to her mouth. Thomas saw her take a breath to scream and moved fast. An arm circled her waist, a hand covered her mouth.

Helena struggled against him, the sensation familiar from happier times.

"Don't," he whispered in her ear. "It's me, Thomas. You know I mean you no harm."

Helena stilled. Thomas waited a moment before releasing her.

"What are you doing here?" Her voice was as low as his, her hair bright in the dimness of the room.

"I need to talk to him. I take it you left him in a good mood?"

Helena scowled. "What do you think? You were always satisfied, weren't you?"

Thomas patted her naked backside. "Go."

Helena looked as if she intended to object, then it became obvious she saw no advantage to it so she turned and trotted away. Thomas watched her go for a moment, memories roiling through his mind.

Faris was sprawled on the bed, the cotton sheets tangled around his legs. His body was lean, hard, a line of hair running across his chest and down his belly to his manhood, thankfully no longer showing signs of his earlier arousal.

He smiled. "You're too late, she's already gone. That would have been fine sport, would it not, the pair of us coupling her?" Faris made no effort to cover himself.

Thomas pulled up a cushion and sat at a distance from the bed, knowing he could not state his purpose while standing over the man.

"I take it you have not come here to couple with Helena or me, then? A pity, she tells me you are not as innocent as you look."

"We have to end this," Thomas said.

"What, meeting this way?" Faris made a coquettish expression that faded as fast as it came. He sat up, finally pulling the sheet to cover himself. "Do you have a suggestion?"

"How far can I trust you?" Thomas said.

"You know the answer to that. Not at all. I have nothing against you, in fact I am beginning to warm to you, but you know how I am. If it benefits me to betray you I will do so."

"Everything is influence," Thomas said.

"Of course."

"In that case you know that drawing this battle out benefits only the Spanish. I saw you in conversation with Martin de Alarcón when we were in their camp. You trade with them too, don't you?"

"What I do is none of your business. If you have something to say do so or leave. I was in a good mood, but it is starting to fade."

"Al-Haquim couldn't find his balls with both hands tied in front of him," Thomas said. "He careens from disaster to disaster. You have to oust him and end this. Surrender the town, save what is left."

Faris sighed. He clapped his hands and a servant, unobserved until then, appeared from the darkness on the far side of the room. No doubt she had been there the whole time.

"Fetch coffee and wine." He glanced at Thomas. "Are you hungry?"

Thomas shook his head.

"Only what I asked, then. As fast as you can." When the servant was gone Faris rose and walked naked to the side of the room where shelving held clothes. He took his time choosing before starting to dress, making a point of facing Thomas as he did so. "Tell me how it can work. I have men loyal to me, but if it comes to a fight…" He raised a shoulder.

"Make him an offer," Thomas said. "You and I to negotiate the surrender. He is allowed to leave, go wherever he wishes, his wealth intact. The town falls to the Spanish. The population are protected, all of them."

Faris pulled at his oiled beard, dark eyes turned inward in thought. "And what advantage do I gain from this?"

Of course, Thomas thought, it always comes to that.

"You survive. We all survive. You are seen as the saviour of Ronda."

"I do not want to be the saviour of Ronda. If we do this my name will not be a part of it, nor yours. Abraham must be seen as the benevolent Governor, concerned for the fate of his citizens." Faris sat beside Thomas, leaning close. There was perfume on his skin, both his own and Helena's. "You are friends with the Spanish King and Queen, are you not? I believed it only rumour until I saw you in their camp. You have influence with them."

"Not as much as you might think."

"But some?"

Thomas considered before nodding. "A little, perhaps."

He knew what Faris hinted at was dangerous. This man more than any other held power in al-Andalus, for money was power, and Faris al-Rashid the richest man in the kingdom. Faris made people disappear. He could make Thomas disappear if he crossed him. It would not even require an order, merely a hint.

"What you say has merit, Berrington. But where is the advantage in it? I have to consider where the benefit lies."

"You will be saving ten thousand lives."

Faris waved a hand, dismissing such a stupid notion. He leaned close, spiced breath reaching Thomas.

"I will do it if you introduce me to your friends."

"My friends?"

Faris nodded. "Fernando and Isabel. That are their names, are they not? Is that what you call them? Fernando and Isabel? Is it true you have mounted her?" He laughed. "I cannot picture it myself, but the Spanish are a strange people. I want to meet them. I want you to introduce me as a friend. I want you to make them trust me. That is the advantage I seek. We both know this war has but one inevitable end, and it will be those with friends in Spain who profit when the time comes. What better friends than those two?"

"I cannot make them like you," Thomas said. "That will be up to you."

Faris smiled. "Oh, well then, it is done." The woman returned, drew a table across and set it beside them, placed a glass jar of coffee down, four ornate glasses, and a pitcher of dark red wine. She bowed and backed away, not turning until she passed the doorway.

"She is such a sweet one," said Faris, reaching for the wine.

Thomas poured coffee into his own glass.

"We have an agreement?" Thomas said.

Faris sipped at his wine. "I believe we do. You are aware this binds us, aren't you?"

Thomas nodded.

"Good. I believe I may have underestimated you for

too long. It is time I rectified that mistake." He drained his glass and stood, offered a hand to Thomas.

He stared at it, aware of hidden meanings in everything, then reached out and allowed Faris to pull him up.

"I will tell him," said Faris. "He does not need to know of your involvement. It will be easier that way, and it is best done soon. Meet me in the training yard in an hour."

As Thomas made his way through the palace the distant thump of cannon balls punctuated his progress. He had no doubt that Faris would be able to persuade al-Haquim. He still wanted to find Francesca and Giovanni, but saving the population of Ronda was more important tonight. Tomorrow he could take up the hunt once more.

Chapter 40

Thomas returned to Lubna, who had gone to their room beside the gatehouse. She was asleep, but as he entered she stirred and rolled over in bed.

"Are you finished for the night?"

"Not yet."

She turned onto her front again and fluttered a hand in dismissal. Thomas smiled as he gathered the few things he needed. His weapons, a vest of chain mail so finely wrought he barely knew he wore it, and boots he had taken from his dead father thirty years before; boots that had been far too big, but he had grown into them over the years.

Leaving as quietly as he could he stood beside the gate to the street waiting for Faris. An hour had not yet passed, but staying in the room would have meant disturbing Lubna, and he was uneasy at the urges that had risen in him as he listened to Faris's coupling. Those and the sight of Helena, still able to move him even after all she had done. The last few months she had treated him differently, no longer scowling in his presence, even talking in a civilised manner. It only made him wonder what she wanted of him.

A rising moon painted the courtyard in monochrome light.

"Hey, *qassab*."

Thomas turned his head, searching for the source of the whispered hiss. Some guard wanting to taunt him, catching him alone in the dead of night, a means to stave off boredom.

"Here, *qassab*." The same voice, coming from beyond the gate.

Thomas peered around the stone wall but saw nothing. "What do you want?"

"I hear you're looking for someone," said the voice.

"Do you have him?"

"Her."

Thomas stepped through the gateway, curious now. How many people knew he was looking for Francesca as well as Giovanni?

When the first blow came he was not expecting it and went to his knees, clutching his left arm. It felt as if a mace had been used against his shoulder. He heard the scrape of steel on stone and looked up. One man stood in front of him, a second to his right, another on his left. He glanced back, but there were only three of them.

"You obviously know who I am," Thomas said. His arm felt like it was on fire. "So you know the punishment for this attack. Walk away now and I will forget it happened."

The man in front grinned, displaying a ragged assortment of stained teeth set apart by gaps.

"Nothing's going to happen to us. We have orders, *qassab*. You don't remember me, but I remember you. A long time ago. I should have killed you then, but I will take just as much pleasure in it now."

Thomas shook his head, coming to his feet. "I don't know you."

"Of course you don't. I'm a soldier, far too lowly to be

noticed by one such as you, but I've seen you worm your way into power while good men die. Now it's your turn."

The man nodded and his companion to the left came at Thomas. Not a mace this time, but a scimitar and a blade too long for a knife, too short for a sword. Thomas stepped back, his own sword falling into his hand as if of its own accord. Even as he span to meet the attack he wondered who had sent these men. Had he been wrong to trust Faris? He had gone to the man and opened himself, and this was his reward?

As the man advanced Thomas heard another approach from behind, and knew wounding them was not going to be enough. These men had been sent to kill him. He would do what he could, but he was in no mood to show mercy.

He parried the blow from the front then stepped sharply to one side, his knife deflecting the blade that came from behind. The leader of the small group moved closer. Three against one, not odds that worried Thomas, so long as he did not have to soften his hand, but it would be good if someone came along and put a stop to this foolishness.

The next time all three came together, seasoned men who had survived many battles. They would not be such easy pickings as some of those he had killed, but he was still not concerned.

The man on the right was a little slower so Thomas left him, knocking his blade aside before spinning to take the other with a hard blow to the neck. The man staggered back, clutching at his throat. Blood poured between his fingers as he went to his knees. Thomas turned away, dismissing him as no longer a danger.

The remaining two drew back. They had not expected

resistance, certainly not expected someone who could fight. Thomas saw the least skilled glance at his felled companion, who now lay on his side, feet kicking at nothing.

"Come on, then," Thomas said. A cold fire burned within, rationality set aside. Now there was only the blood lust he had once embraced, welcoming it once more now it was needed. He feinted forward at the leader, who took another step back. "Not so brave now, are you?" Thomas waved the tip of his sword. "The *qassab's* blade is hungry for more butchery. So who will be next? You?" He lunged and the man moved so fast he stumbled and landed on his back. "Or you." The other man turned and fled.

As swiftly as it had come the fire died and Thomas turned away, sorry he had been forced to take a life. He had not expected the last man to attack again, so it came as a surprise when he felt a sharp blow and the man wrapped his arms around his shoulders.

Thomas stepped back fast, caught the man on his shin with the steel heel of his boot, then as his grip slackened he turned, still within his arms, and raised his dagger. He slipped it through the soft flesh below the soldier's ribs, angled upward to pierce the heart. The man's eyes widened, his face as close to Thomas's as a lover, so close he felt the exhalation of rank breath as his life fled.

Thomas turned away again, uncaring. The men had brought their own fate on themselves and he felt no guilt.

A clatter of hooves sounded and Faris entered the courtyard. He had six men with him, from their clothing all of them his. For a moment Thomas was sure he had come to finish what the soldiers could not. Then he saw Faris glance at the bodies and knew it was not him who had sent them. A spare mount was held by one of his companions. Thomas walked to it and pulled himself into the saddle.

As they passed through the gate Faris glanced again at the two fallen soldiers, but said nothing.

"Yours?" Thomas asked.

Faris looked again, glanced at his own men in the fine clothes only those with money could afford. "What do you think?"

"So who sent them?"

Faris studied Thomas. The tear in his robe. The stain of another man's blood. The slump of his shoulder.

"They tried to kill you. Why?"

"That's what I was asking you."

Faris shook his head. "They are nothing to do with me. If I wanted you dead you would know who was behind it, as would the whole town. There is no point in a punishment performed in secret." The sound of their horses' hooves echoed from what remained of house walls.

They reached the top of the roadway to the north of the town and descended to the gate, iron horse shoes slipping on the steep slope.

Outside they turned left, heading for the Spanish camp. Thomas dismissed the dead soldiers from his mind, sure they had been sent by Francesca and Giovanni. She lived in the palace, it would be a simple matter for her to seduce any number of soldiers for when their services were needed. The idea raised his spirits, because it meant his quarry was still in Ronda, aware now Thomas was on their trail. If they wanted Thomas dead it meant he was getting closer.

"Did you have any trouble with the Governor?" he asked as they turned the corner of the bluff and the

Spanish army came into sight. There was no point in trying to approach by stealth so they rode close to the front ranks, watching men rise to their feet from uneasy slumber. The stink of the army washed across them, rank and bitter.

"I had no trouble convincing Abraham this was the right course of action. I only needed to explain how he could keep his riches. And his life, of course." Faris turned and spat onto the ground. "Jews," he said. "We have too many Jews in positions of power in this land. Al-Zagal humours them, as does his brother. But a time is coming, Thomas, when they will be humoured no more."

"Al-Andalus could not function without them," Thomas said, holding back his anger, knowing not to antagonise this man.

"The Spanish have the right idea. Drive them out. Burn them. They cannot be converted."

Thomas had never heard Faris express such sentiment before, but then he had always tried to have as little to do with the man as possible.

"I take it you have not told al-Haquim how you feel."

Faris laughed. "He continues to believe I have his best interests at heart. And of course in this instance I do. We will negotiate an escape for him, he need not worry on that score. What he does not know is what lies in his future once this land is united."

"And you do?"

Faris glanced at Thomas, a hint of old enmity showing. "Don't tell me you believe we will triumph?"

"Of course not."

Faris smiled. "And you a friend to the most powerful man and woman in Spain. Cunning… I like that in a man. You will broker the introduction I asked for?"

Thomas nodded. He lifted his left arm, trying to ease the pain in his shoulder. The ache of that first blow remained, growing worse rather than easing. There would be a fine bruise to show when he removed his chainmail.

"I have been thinking about Yusuf," he said.

"What of him?"

"When Ronda falls he will be in danger. A prince of Gharnatah, a Sultan's son, would prove a valuable prize. He listens to you, doesn't he?"

"As much as any man. Other than you, perhaps." Faris smiled. "He talks about you all the time. If I didn't know he preferred women I might wonder about the two of you."

Thomas ignored the feigned insult. "Tell him to dress as a guard and accompany al-Haquim when he leaves the town. He will be allowed to leave, of that I am sure. Yusuf can make his way back to Gharnatah once they are clear of danger."

Faris stared ahead. Finally he nodded. "I will tell him, if you cannot." He glanced at Thomas. "It makes sense to have someone I can control in the palace. His father will not last long, I hear. And better Yusuf than Muhammed on the throne, who is even stupider than al-Haquim."

They turned and rode toward the front ranks, heading for a wide pathway between them. Soldiers in fine armour had already ridden down to meet them, the flag of truce clear even in the dark.

"We would speak with the King," Thomas said, raising his voice and deepening it.

"On what matter?"

"That is for the King's ears only. You know who I am."

The lead man nodded and turned away. Thomas urged

his horse forward. As they rode through the massed ranks Faris scowled as a cannon barked.

"Why do they still fire those damned things? Are we not here to negotiate."

"They are angry. You saw what al-Haquim did. These men want revenge, and I cannot blame them."

"Well I can. There are rules."

Except it appeared the rules had been set aside. As they progressed soldiers stood to line the pathway, edging closer so they were forced to ride in single file.

A second explosion sounded and Thomas turned in his saddle. It wasn't cannon firing. In the narrow defile where the river once ran light showed. The Spanish were trying to destroy the dam created by the rock fall. They had managed to cut off their own water supply as well as that of Ronda.

A murmur started up around them, a murmur that became a roar. Thomas flinched as a man spat at him. Fists punched against his thighs and he kicked out, knowing it was pointless even as he did so.

"You!" Faris shouted at the knights that rode ahead and behind. "Control your men." He spoke in perfect Spanish, but the only response was a coarse laugh. Seeing the escort also mocking them the soldiers pressed tighter still, their blows growing in ferocity. One jarred Thomas's arm and he cried out as a sharp pain shot from his shoulder across his chest. He wiped sweat from his brow, breathing hard, but there was nothing for it but to take the blows without complaint. Fight back and he knew they would be pulled from their saddles and torn apart. He was expecting that to happen anyway, until another voice called out, this one high, with great surety.

"These men come in peace. Stand back now. Stand

back at once!"

Queen Isabel stood alone, dressed in a suit of armour that showed white and orange in the reflection of the burning fires and torches.

"Stand back I say or I will have your heads! The next man to attack will answer to their Queen."

All at once the path ahead cleared. The roar of voices stilled and soldiers turned away, eyes downcast. Thomas shifted in his saddle, trying to ease a pain that now gripped his entire side. He was no fool, he had seen others suffer as he did now. He had pushed himself too hard in the fight and strained his heart. He cursed the fates. To have come so far for it to end this way. He gripped his horse tighter with his knees, not wanting these men to see him tumble from the saddle.

At the hundred yard mark the knights ahead halted. They had come as far as allowed on horseback. Isabel had walked from the tent, her husband now come to join her. Beyond them Thomas saw Lawrence and Martin de Alarcón. Juan would still be in bed asleep. Off to the side two more figures stood on the edge of the light cast from the torches that illuminated the royal abode and Thomas gasped. The face of Giovanni del Caccia was unmistakable, as was that of Francesca. No wonder they could not be found in Ronda. The pair had been the first to switch sides.

Beside them stood a well-dressed man. Already the pair had cast their net and caught the largest fish. Though no, not the largest, not yet, but was that only a matter of time? Had Thomas felt capable he would have pushed through the men surrounding him and attacked the couple.

As he dropped from the saddle Thomas stumbled and

he heard Isabel cry out.

"Bring him through, he is unwell. Thomas, come to me. Fetch a physician."

Hands grasped, drawing him forward. As they gripped his left arm the pain rose to a new crescendo and Thomas screamed, struggling to remain on his feet.

Isabel came to him, waving the knights to release him, her own hand touching him gently on the right side.

"What is it, Thomas? What ails you?"

He couldn't tell her, not here in front of the King and her army.

"It is nothing, Your Grace. It will pass. Perhaps if I could sit and have something to drink."

"Bring him inside," she commanded. "Make way, make way."

As they passed Thomas glanced at Lawrence, the man meeting his stare. Was that triumph in his eyes? Did he still harbour a loyalty to Mandana? Even through his pain Thomas started to raise a hand to call him over, a plan forming in his mind, a test of loyalty. But before he could do so Isabel drew him into the tent. A chair was brought, together with wine. Thomas sat heavily, trying to draw breath into his lungs, each inhalation an agony. This was not how it was meant to end. He had expected to die in bed, of old age, with Lubna and his children beside him, William and the others, for he was sure there would have been others.

"Thomas, you are bleeding." The Queen knelt beside him, her hand where it clutched his stained red. She turned aside. "Fetch that doctor now! How many times do I have to ask? Fernando, go see to it, bring him here now."

The King turned away, leaving the two of them alone.

Thomas stared at her small hand, at the blood coating it. He tried to lift his arm but the pain was too great. Not his heart, then, but possibly worse. It barely mattered, death was death however it came. He tried to squeeze Isabel's hand but hadn't the strength, and then men entered the room, lifting him, carrying him into the fire streaked night toward the long infirmary tents the Queen had set up for her men, Thomas one of them now.

Chapter 41

Thomas made a terrible patient. He questioned the man working on him constantly, irritating him with instructions when he considered the treatment wrong. Once his mail vest and shirt had been removed the wound, despite the pain of it, proved minor. It was made worse by the point of a dagger which had broken off and remained embedded. The Spanish physician opened the wound and dug within, finally drawing a surprisingly large piece of metal free. Thomas wished for a Moorish doctor and Moorish pain relief, but here they did not believe in such niceties. At least the stitching was well enough done. Workmanlike, it would leave a scar, but Thomas already carried a score of such; one more would make little difference.

Isabel remained nearby, moving between the wooden pallets where other injured men lay, a word for each of them. Once he could sit up Thomas watched, seeing the love the soldiers held for her. They would respect Fernando and obey him, but they would die without question for this slip of a woman. When she saw he was alert she turned and came to him at once, the eyes of injured soldiers following, perhaps wondering who this man was their Queen showed such concern for.

"My surgeon tells me you will live," she said, standing beside the bed, a tension in her evident in the way she clasped her hands together, the fingers white.

"He did well enough," Thomas said. He still could not move his left arm easily, but knew the wound would heal provided no infection developed, and if that happened Lubna had the herbs necessary to stem it.

"Why are you here, Thomas? Was it my men who did this to you?" Isabel's expression was stern.

"It was my own side, Your Grace. And your husband knows why we are here by now. I assume he is speaking with my companion."

"Is it to end?" she asked, her voice softening.

"If our terms are accepted."

"Are they just? What was done was beyond the pale. I know it was not of your choosing, but I advise you to consider which side you are on in this war."

Thomas knew he could say nothing on that matter so changed the subject. "When I arrived I saw a man and woman I have been seeking, a pair who have killed others. I also saw Lawrence nearby. I would ask you to send for him if you would."

"The same Thomas," said Isabel. "Still taking on the world and its problems."

"Someone has to, Your Grace. You will send for him?"

She nodded. Thomas saw she was reluctant to leave, but the duties of a queen were many and she was nothing if not bound by duty. She turned with an act of will and strode through the ranks of pallets. Once more the eyes of the men followed like she was an angel fallen to earth.

Thomas leaned back and closed his eyes. His shoulder throbbed, but the raw pain he had experienced was a memory and he smiled, thinking of all the other wounds he had suffered in his life, remembering each fight that led to them but not the pain that came afterward. When a hand shook his undamaged shoulder he came up through layers of dreams he had fallen into. Lawrence leaned over, his amusement plain to see.

"You were talking in your sleep." He perched on the edge of the pallet, almost tipping it over.

"I wasn't asleep." Thomas sat up, washing a hand across his face in an attempt to banish the weariness. Beyond the entrance of the tent shadows grew shorter as the sun rose higher. "Help me up, we have work to do."

"You are in no state to do anything. Tell me what it is and I will do it if I can. The Queen said you had some task for me, but she didn't know what."

Thomas hesitated. Now was the moment to test the man, unsure what he wanted the result to be. He had liked Lawrence once, might like him again if he proved his worth, his loyalty. And if not… would he have to kill another man?

"Take me outside," he said. "I promise I will not act rashly, but I make a poor patient and the air in here makes my head swim."

Lawrence considered the request for a moment, then stood, the pallet once more rocking. Thomas swung his feet to the dirt floor and put out a hand. Lawrence gripped it and pulled him up. For a moment Thomas swayed, afraid he might have to sit again, then the world solidified and all was well. He started forward, then turned back and drew on his shirt. He left the pile of chainmail where it was. It had not protected him in Ronda and he preferred to trust his own skill over armour.

"There is a man and woman here," he said once they were outside, the air clearing his head even more.

"I assume you mean someone specific?"

338

Thomas offered Lawrence a sour glance.

"A man and his cousin. Both handsome, captivating. I saw them when I arrived. They have escaped Ronda somehow and are now hiding amongst your horde. Their looks are deceiving. Both are killers and must be caught."

"Again?" said Lawrence, and Thomas knew he was not talking of Francesca and Giovanni but expressing the same opinion as the Queen.

"Their names are—"

"I know their names," said Lawrence. "There cannot be another two like them. They came here two nights since, claiming to be captives who had escaped in the confusion. They said their prison wall had been destroyed by an iron ball and they managed to climb through. A lie, obviously, for both dressed well and their skin is too unblemished for prisoners. They are both of Naples, which endears them to the King. They charmed both him and the Queen."

"Then both are in danger."

"Fernando will not allow anyone close to their presences, however charming they might be." Lawrence glanced at Thomas. "Other than you, it seems."

"And that no doubt because I am far from charming. Where are these two now?"

"Somewhere in the camp. They know a number of those here. The man is a mariner, and we have a few of those who have left the sea for the land. It's easy to see how they know so many people. The woman is very beautiful, and there is something of both darkness and sin in her eyes that is most enchanting. I believe Fernando was much taken with her."

"You have to send word. They are to be detained and brought to me before they can do any more harm."

"They would be mad to try anything here. There is no privacy to be had, everything is done in full view. But I will spread the word. We will have them in chains before noon. Now you must go to the Queen, she asked me to take you there once we had talked."

"I should walk the camp," Thomas said. "I am more likely to recognise them."

"For once in your life you will do as you are told." Lawrence took Thomas's elbow on the right side and drew him across ground packed smooth by a thousand feet. As they wound through the cluster of bored soldiers an explosion sounded and Thomas jerked around, looking toward the cannon.

"We are talking surrender," he said. "You cannot continue to fire on the town."

"It's not cannon," said Lawrence. "They're trying to break the dam, or we'll be without water too." He glanced at Thomas. "But I did not tell you that."

"It doesn't matter," Thomas said. "The deed is done, the pact struck."

They entered the royal tent unopposed. Inside Fernando and Faris al-Rashid sat at a table, their heads together as they talked.

Fernando rose and came to Thomas. "What are you doing here?" He turned and spoke to a servant standing in the shadows. "Fetch the Queen."

"There is nothing wrong with me time will not heal," Thomas said.

"That is not the tale I was told."

Lawrence touched Thomas's good arm. "I will go do as you ask."

Fernando watched him go. Thomas expected a question, instead the King turned back to the table, motioning Thomas to join them. There was wine but Thomas ignored it. Soon he would have confirmation whether Lawrence was on his side or not.

"I have told the King of our terms," said Faris.

"And what is your answer?" Thomas stared at Fernando.

"I am still thinking on it. Had your Governor not done as he did yesterday morning I would be more minded to say yes, but that was not the action of a civilised man."

"You cannot expect war to be civilised, Your Grace."

Fernando inclined his head toward Faris. "This man has been calling me *malik* all night."

"Not now I know the correct form, Your Grace," said Faris, emphasising the final words, and Fernando laughed.

"I like him, Thomas. If all Moors were as reasonable as this one we could negotiate a peace before the year is out."

"It is a shame they are not then, Your Grace."

"No, indeed. I need to speak with Isabel and consider the terms. I am minded to refuse and continue the barrage, but I know I am often too hasty."

After he had gone a servant brought more wine and a plate of meat, pigeon and capon. Thomas poured himself wine, then offered some to Faris, who nodded.

"You explained the terms fairly? Thomas asked.

"Do you doubt me? I know you have reason to, but I told him everything, exactly as you would have."

"What do you think?"

"Of him, or his reaction?" Faris waited, but when Thomas made no reply said, "It is as you saw. He is angry, like his men, and he has justification. Abraham should not have done what he did, but he too was angry. Anger makes poor generals." Faris took a swallow of his wine. "As for the man, I like him. He is no fool, and neither is she." He stared at Thomas while he emptied his beaker. Thomas reached out and refilled it. "It seems it is true," said Faris. "You are friend to both. They talk of you as a friend, a close friend, but I could barely believe it. You and the King and Queen of Spain. There have been rumours, but there are always rumours."

Thomas considered his response. Faris al-Rashid was not a man easily fooled, and Thomas was unsure he even wanted to try,

"Yes, I think perhaps we are friends. As much as people on opposite sides in a war can ever be."

"Except you are not on opposite sides, are you? You are no Moor, neither are you Spaniard. A true neutral. Perhaps that is what they see. Someone who has no iron in this fire. How long will they make us wait?"

"Isabel does not make hasty decisions," Thomas said.

"And who rules in this partnership, the Queen or the King?"

"I don't know."

"Or won't say?" said Rashid

"One of those." Thomas rose and walked to where the entrance of the grand tent was pulled aside, took a deep breath of cooler air. He was weary of politics, weary of those who talked around a subject rather than state it outright, himself included. He had always thought he was straight talking, but being around people such as these had changed him.

He stepped into the morning, turned at a sudden commotion among the soldiers. Someone cried out in fear, then Thomas saw Lawrence running through men who scattered out of his way. He stopped and knelt to peer into a tent of enough size to belong to an important man. When he rose his head turned, coming to a halt when his eyes fell on Thomas.

CHAPTER 42

Two figures lay curled together on the ground as if in sleep. A sleep they would never wake from. Coarse rope was pulled taut around their necks.

Thomas knelt beside the woman, his fingers working at the knot as if he might make a difference, though he knew it was too late. There was just enough room for him and Lawrence in the tent. The top of Lawrence's head pushed at the canvas where he stood.

"He is a knight now, but was a mariner once. He is one of those known to the man, Giovanni. He claimed they worked the same vessels. She is..." Lawrence cocked his head to one side. "I don't know who she is. A camp follower, more than likely. There are a hundred for every thousand men, we'll be lucky to discover her name."

A mariner, Thomas thought. Another one. He gave up on his efforts and stood, looking down at the pair, wondering at the escalation of violence. Had Giovanni come here to question them? It made no sense – they already knew Simki was the man they sought. Had they lost all rationality now and were targeting anyone connected to the sea?

"Did he ever mention what nature of cargo he carried?"

Lawrence laughed. "Oh, it was his sole topic of conversation. Of course he didn't, and if he had nobody would have cared. Is it significant?"

"Possibly, but more likely not." The woman was an unlucky coincidence, but the man had known something. It was why he lay dead in the dark. Francesca and Giovanni could not risk the truth about them coming out. "Who last saw the man alive?"

"I'll ask. But the men will have been drunk and I doubt they remember."

Thomas knelt and placed his hand on the man's chest. It was still warm. As a precaution he leaned close and put his ear to the man's mouth and waited, but no breath touched him. He felt for a pulse and found it absent. Lifted the eyes to find them still bright.

He looked toward Lawrence. "This was recent, within an hour. They may still be close."

"I doubt it. They'll have fled. They could be miles away by now."

"Not this pair, they are reckless. They have killed so many they believe they are beyond the wit of man to catch them. You have to send word through the camp with their descriptions. We could end this today."

"I can try, but it takes time to pass a message through the entire army, and by the time it reaches the outer limits it will have become corrupted."

For a moment Thomas wondered if Lawrence had been turned by the pair as well, but he couldn't mistrust everything the man said. "Do it anyway. I have to return to the King for a while, but I will return as soon as I can and then we seek them out." Thomas rose, his eyes on Lawrence, seeking a truth he wasn't sure existed. But a thrill ran through him at the thought of capturing Francesca and Giovanni, banishing the ache in his body.

Faris al-Rashid remained at the table when Thomas re-entered the tent.

"Any news?"

Faris shook his head. "Where did you go?"

"There have been two more killings, but we have them now. There is nowhere to hide in the camp."

"They are here?" said Faris. "Are we safe?"

"Safer here than anywhere."

"Are you sure?" Faris reached a hand up and ran a nail along the canvas above him.

Thomas stared, then rushed through to the inner chamber, beyond to where he assumed the sleeping quarters were. Isabel sat on a wide bed, sumptuously appointed. Fernando spun around at the interruption, his face angry.

Thomas bowed his head. "My apologies, Your Graces. There is a killer loose in the camp, and I feared you might be a target."

"As you can see, we are perfectly safe. I am more than capable of defending my wife. You have gone too far this time, Thomas."

He began to back out, but Isabel held a hand up.

"Wait. What killer?"

"A man and his cousin. Neapolitan, of extreme beauty the pair. I believe you may have met them."

"I did," said Fernando. "They came with a tale of being captives who had escaped. There was something not altogether right about the woman, but the man was likeable enough. They asked to meet Isabel and I did not allow it." He looked to his wife, back at Thomas. "Did we have a close escape?"

"The woman pursues a man she watched kill her father."

"Then she is in the right," said Fernando.

"If that is all it was, perhaps so. But between them

they have killed over a dozen I can be sure of, even more I suspect. The woman has lost her senses, and her cousin does her bidding. They killed a mariner among your party."

"Don Columb?" said Isabel, a hand rising to her face.

"I don't have a name. Short man, dark skinned, hair cut short and a beard?" Thomas knew the description might fit half the men in the army, but Fernando nodded.

"Estaban. He left the sea for a life of even greater danger, to fight alongside me as a knight. Was he killed because he was once a sailor?"

"And for what he knew. The pair seek one man. They question those who might lead them to him, but I think as they do so their own true natures are revealed and they have to kill even more."

"Is Columb in danger?" said Fernando. "He claims to have sailed every sea in the known world and some that are not. He could have come across this Giovanni, could he not?"

"It's possible," Thomas said. "Where do I find him?"

"I don't keep a record of everyone on the field of battle," said Fernando. "Go ask Lawrence, he knows that kind of thing. And tell your companion we have come to a decision."

"May I tell him what it is?"

"Do you intend to pursue your killers?"

Thomas nodded.

"In that case I will give you our decision when you return. Try not to get yourself killed. You are a strange man, but it seems my wife has grown fond of you."

Lawrence was still at Estaban's tent, arranging for the bodies to be taken away.

"It's done," he said, as Thomas approached. "Word is

out, they can't escape now. I sent men to tell the perimeter guards."

"There is another mariner amongst us I have been told, a man called Columb?"

"Cristof Columb, yes. A strange man with even stranger ideas. He arrived in Qurtuba a month or two ago seeking funds for some madcap idea of forging a new route to the Indies. He was unwilling to give up his quest and followed us here. He is a favourite amongst the men for the tales he tells."

"Do you know where I can find him?"

"He set himself up on the southern edge of the camp, as far from the fighting as he could get. Do you want to go there?"

Columb's tent was makeshift, no more than four poles with a single sheet of canvas stretched across them. Rocks from the surrounding plain held down the corners. As they came close the side billowed out and a cry reached them. Thomas broke into a run, cursing as pain lanced down his side. Lawrence overtook him, ducking into the tent. Thomas arrived seconds later to discover him wrestling with Giovanni. There was little room inside, and as Thomas tried to help he became tangled in the canvas and the entire tent came down over them all.

Thomas lashed out, afraid a blade would come slicing through to find him, but all he managed to grasp was an arm. He gripped it tight, working his way from beneath the canvas only to find once he got outside he had the arm of a stranger. A stranger who was pulling at a rope knotted at his throat, his face already turning blue. Thomas rolled him onto his front and pulled at the knots. Mariner's knots, intended to draw tighter, not loosen. Thomas drew his knife and slid it beneath the rope, jerked upward to slice through it.

He rose from astride the man who rolled over, retching.

"I thought Giovanni a friend," he said, gasping out the words.

Thomas pulled at the tangle of canvas, trying to reveal who lay beneath. When he finally had it clear there was only one figure on the ground. It was Lawrence, as still as a dead man. Then he coughed, clutching as his side, and tried to sit up.

"Did he stick you?" Thomas asked, going to one knee.

"The woman tried. They were both here, but they are no soldiers, unskilled in a close quarter fight." Lawrence stood and looked around. "Where did they go?"

"I was busy with Don Columb," Thomas said. "They must have escaped through the back and slipped away, but they can't have gone far." He turned to Columb who was massaging his throat. "What did they want?"

"Questions. Strange questions. Had I ever carried slaves from Africa. I told them no, never, but they became insistent. The woman's eyes burned with a fire so bright I doubted her sanity. She would not take my word and drew a knife, accused me of lying."

"Go tell the King and Queen what you know," Thomas said.

"Why would they care?" said Columb.

"Then don't go, because I'm starting not to care either." Thomas turned away, taking Lawrence by the elbow and leading him to the edge of the throng. Grassland ran away to low hills marked by slabs of rock. Thomas scanned the view but saw nothing to indicate the pair had fled this way. He needed someone with better eyes and greater skill.

CHAPTER 43

There were five by the time they passed out from the gathered multitude. Lawrence had detoured to select two men he knew as good trackers, and a third a perimeter guard who offered his services.

Now the tracker roamed a hundred yards ahead, ranging left and right as he searched for a sign. He led on a relatively direct line away from camp toward a low rise. Behind them the stain of the army grew more distant, its murmur soon lost. Thomas welcomed the clean sharpness of the air, the silence of the empty land.

One of the trackers jogged back while his companion continued to follow the faint trail.

"How far ahead are they?" Thomas asked.

"No more than a half hour. The land narrows. There is only one route they can take, and it leads to a dead-end unless they can swim."

"How can you be sure?"

"There's good game in these hills," the man said, grinning. "Plump hares."

Thomas saw he was enjoying the hunt. He couldn't blame him. This was a game, a respite from the boredom of waiting to fight. To the bombardiers in the front ranks there was plenty to do, but for the other soldiers the days would be long.

"Will they have to turn back?" Thomas asked.

"The valley narrows and comes out next to the river that runs from Ronda. It is wider and deeper at that point and almost forms a complete circle, running hard against a cliff face on one side."

"Then let's go catch them. Run ahead, you and your companion, take the other man with you, we will follow on." Thomas knew he was incapable of running. He fell into step beside Lawrence as the soldiers sprinted ahead, fading into the night. He knew if Lawrence wanted him dead now was the time to do it. Thomas was weakened and they were alone, only the waving grass to witness the deed.

"Do you remember the last time we tracked a killer?" Lawrence said.

"How could I forget? Though as I recall you were on the other side then." Thomas glanced at him. "Have you changed sides again, or are you still there?"

"I have already explained. It was a ruse to gain Mandana's trust, nothing more. You still doubt me?"

"Isabel and Fernando see fit to trust you. They are no fools, but they didn't see what I did."

"So why am I letting you live?" Lawrence's words so mirrored Thomas's own thoughts a chill passed through him and he closed his hand around the hilt of the dagger at his belt. Lawrence saw the movement and laughed. "Do you think you can fight me with that shoulder?"

"Don't underestimate me. Other have and no longer live."

"I am not others," said Lawrence. He shook his head. "When will you believe I mean you no harm? I wish us to be friends again, as we once were. I respect you, Thomas Berrington, but this constant doubting of me grows tiring." He paced ahead, leaving Thomas to follow as best he could.

They found the first soldier, the perimeter guard who had been seeking excitement, at the entrance to the valley, his throat cut from ear to ear. From the way he lay it was clear he had been running away. Thomas was no tracker, but even he could read the story in the flattened grass. A man pursued and caught. A fight. A blade. He turned a full circle, muttering to himself as he searched for sign of someone fleeing the scene. The grass was disturbed where the attacker had moved away.

"Whoever did this went along there," Thomas said, pointing to where the valley narrowed. As the soldier had said, the slopes here drew together, steep but still climbable. "We have to catch them before they get away again." He looked at the slopes. "I wonder is there a way out if they climb to the top?"

Lawrence shook his head. "This is not my country. If this man is dead then the others are more likely the same."

"Or still in pursuit," Thomas said.

"This one was a trained fighter, but he met his match here. How many more have they killed over the years?"

"Too many."

"We need to take care, then. If they killed this man they will kill us too given the chance."

"We will not give them the chance." Thomas knelt and searched the fallen soldier, but found nothing that would prove useful other than a dagger he took from his belt and slipped into his own. As he rose a sound of distant thunder came. So the river remained blocked. He wondered how much more damage the Spanish were doing. If they weren't careful they might bring the entire cliff face down on top of them, defeating themselves. And as the thought came to him so did a memory of something the tracker had said.

"The river won't block their path," he said. "There is no river. There is nothing to stop them escaping to kill again."

Lawrence nodded, his face grim.

They found the next man sitting against a rock. He was alive, but would not remain so much longer. Blood crusted the corner of his mouth, and his thighs were stained dark from a wound to his belly.

"I should've known better," he said, voice barely a whisper. He coughed, expelling more blood. "But she looked so beautiful, so innocent. If I had seen him sooner..." A final breath left his lungs and he went still. Thomas reached out and closed his eyes.

The third man, the hunter, was hunkered down at the side of the valley, which had grown even narrower, though ahead a splash of blue sky showed the promise of escape.

The hunter was alive because he was careful. Thomas saw him raise a sword at the sound of their approach, then lower it when he saw who it was. Lawrence offered his hand and the man took it, pulling himself to his feet.

"They're two hundred paces ahead. I thought I'd wait, see if either of you were still alive."

"You saw your fellows?"

The man nodded. To one such as him death was a constant companion. He would have learned not to form attachments he had no wish to lose.

"They consider themselves safe," he said. "They're not even bothering to keep quiet. Step out into the middle and you can hear them talking."

Thomas did so, and it was true, but the words were too faint to catch any words and he returned to the others.

"You know the land this far?" he asked the soldier, who nodded.

"There's a narrow opening between cliffs, and then the river. Except there'll be no water in it now, not with the rock fall damming it. It's not much of a barrier anyway, even a child could ford it."

"So we need to take them before they reach the plain," Thomas said.

"There's nowhere to run to. There are trees and some farm houses, but the land is flat. All we need do is follow." He looked at Thomas, at Lawrence, judging them. "We should send one of you back to bring others while I continue to track them."

"You don't think the three of us can take them?" said Lawrence.

"You saw what they did to trained soldiers."

"I am trained as a soldier too," said Lawrence, no resentment in his voice. "And Thomas is more able than he looks."

"I'm not so sure that's true at the moment," Thomas said. "But Giovanni is no fighter. He kills by stealth, not skill, and Francesca kills with her beauty. I say we take them as soon as we can."

The high sun warmed their backs as they passed along the enclosed valley. It cut them off from the outside world, some private arcadia that lulled the mind with its beauty. Wild flowers bloomed, stunted trees held wild almond and mulberry. A man could exist here, Thomas thought, could escape the world and all its problems. It was a tempting prospect, but one he knew he would never pursue. That sense of duty refused to lose its hold on him.

Stones rattled and Thomas halted, looked around at the walls towering on either side. He had not caught sight of the pair they followed for some time.

"Do you think they've tried to escape some other way? By climbing the cliff, perhaps?"

"Why would they do that?" said Lawrence. "They won't risk falling when they can see the way clear ahead."

"They know we're after them," Thomas said. Ahead the tracker continued on, his head turning as he scanned for a sign. He moved without seeming to disturb the long grass, leaving no indication he had passed.

"Which means they go straight on," said Lawrence. "Why complicate matters by twisting and turning. They need to travel as fast as they can if they want to escape, and they won't do that other than in a straight line."

"So we go on, too," Thomas said.

"Unless you have some great mystical plan I have no notion of."

Thomas shook his head. "No plan."

The ground fell gently. The steep sides came closer, and then the exit to the valley lay ahead. The tracker stood outlined against the sky, waving them forward.

"I see them," he called, a trace of excitement in his voice for the first time. "Quickly, before they cross the river bed."

Lawrence ran ahead, Thomas following as best he could. He knew he had left his infirmary bed too soon, but believed he had been left no choice in the matter. The other two had started to descend to the plain by the time he reached the gap. He stared beyond them and saw Giovanni and Francesca. They moved fast, breaking

355

into a run, then slowing before running once more. They dipped from sight as heavy tree growth hid them, but they always re-appeared.

On the far side of the river, a quarter mile away, lay an abandoned farmhouse, but it would do them no good. They would have to keep running, it was all that was left to them, and eventually they would fatigue. Thomas knew they could almost certainly keep going longer than him, but Lawrence and the tracker were a different matter. They would be relentless in their pursuit. Thomas sat, favouring his left side where the ache persisted, and allowed himself to catch his breath. As he watched the chase play out movement drew his attention. A new figure appeared from within the farmhouse. For a moment they stood in the moonlight like a shadow painted on the landscape, and only slowly did recognition come to Thomas. He rose and started after Lawrence and the tracker. They needed to know that Simki had come to confront his sister's killer.

CHAPTER 44

They should have been in pursuit of Francesca and Giovanni. Instead the Spanish tracker confronted them, his sword raised.

"You don't remember me, do you." The tracker stood loose, relaxed, the sword moving from side to side to cover them both.

Thomas examined the man's face. He shook his head. "Am I meant to?"

The man spat on the grass. "Of course you don't. You wouldn't be here if you did. You killed friends of mine, and now it's your turn to die."

"I don't have any idea what you're talking about. We don't have time for this, they're getting away."

The man looked left and right, nodded. "It was another valley," he said. "Not unlike this. A little narrower, maybe. You were lucky that day, but on this one your luck's run out." He cocked his head to one side, seeing Thomas still had no idea what he was talking about. He sighed. "Your Sultan had abandoned you and the women. I came after you along the valley, but like I said, you got lucky."

Thomas was aware of Lawrence moving slowly to one side. Running again, abandoning him.

Thomas took a step closer to the soldier, but he made no movement, didn't even bother to move his sword. Thomas drew his own, swung it through the air. The soldier laughed.

"Kill me later," Thomas said, "after we've captured those two."

Again a laugh. "Why would I want to do that? I'm going with them."

Thomas stared. He looked beyond the man. Giovanni and Francesca stood on the river bank, arguing. She was tugging at his clothing, urging him to attack Simki, who stood in clear view. Thomas saw it now, how it had come about, what had happened.

"It wasn't either of them who killed your companions, was it? It was you."

"Were you foolish enough to think them capable?"

"They have killed others," Thomas said.

"So you say."

"What has she promised you?"

A grin. "What do you think? I've lain between her legs already. She's a wildcat. The best I've ever had, and I've had plenty. They need a good man to help them, someone who's not afraid to kill."

The soldier stepped forward, sword flashing, and Thomas barely had time to raise his own. The clash of blades sent a fresh jolt of pain lancing through his body, and he staggered back.

Lawrence came from one side, moving fast, a good swordsman as Thomas knew, but not good enough. The soldier turned, fast too, and Lawrence's sword tumbled through the air. Thomas attacked again before the man could gut Lawrence, but his own blade only followed.

"I thought you said he was good." The soldier shook his head. He moved closer.

Thomas unsheathed a knife but knew it wasn't enough, not against this man. Then a cry sounded and the soldier hesitated. He trotted backwards, his eyes on Thomas and Lawrence until he had moved thirty paces. Only then did he turn.

Simki was making his way across the dry river bed toward Francesca and Giovanni.

"Help us!" This time the words reached them.

"Shit," the soldier said. He looked toward his new found lover, back to the two men confronting him, and cursed again. He ran at them, his sword swinging. It caught Lawrence high on the chest, opening his shirt, blood welling. Then the soldier turned to Thomas, who stepped to one side away from the descending blade and raised the knife which until that moment had not been enough but now was. He thrust it as hard as he could through the leather jerkin, twisted and thrust again.

"Fuck!" The soldier stepped back. Thomas's knife slid free, followed by a thick trail of blood. The soldier looked down at the injury, unbelieving. "You've done it again. How did you do that?" Then he fell backwards, eyes still open, staring at the sun as it reached its zenith.

Thomas turned to Lawrence, who had gone to one knee, clutching his side.

"Show me."

Lawrence shook his head. "I'll live. Go, finish it."

Thomas looked up to where Giovanni and Simki were locked together. Francesca danced around, urging Giovanni on. The sound of another explosion came, louder than the previous ones, clearer now they were in the open.

Thomas tried to rise and stumbled, more tired than he realised. He caught himself and looked ahead, his thoughts scattered. He started forward. Lawrence might die, but he might die whether Thomas stayed or not, and the end of this matter lay a hundred paces away. His legs were filled with lead but he moved first one then the other, pushing aside any thought of what he might do when he reached them.

A deep roar came, faint to begin with but growing louder fast. Giovanni doubled his attack on Simki, but the man was strong. Then Francesca darted close and struck out. She must have held a blade because Simki cried out and staggered.

"Finish him!" Thomas heard her scream. "Kill him now, he is the one!"

The rumbling grew and Thomas turned, seeking its source. When he found it he couldn't work out what it was he saw. Entire trees and rocks were being tossed into the air as a foaming wall raced along the course of the river. Then it came to him, the sound of explosions. The Spanish had finally managed to break the dam, and this maelstrom was the result. A hundred thousand tons of water released in a second. It scoured the surrounds of the river, not as powerful as it must have been when set loose, but still an unstoppable force.

Thomas began to run as best he could. He saw Giovanni stop and turn, the noise now a deep growl, watched as the man recognised what was coming toward them and urged Francesca forward, thinking more of her than himself.

Francesca pulled away, still more concerned with finishing Simki, who was staggering toward Thomas.

The wall of water, rock and timber reached a turn above the farmhouse and spread out, too strong to be contained, and for a moment it looked as if Giovanni and Francesca would escape. Then, as if drawing new breath, the water filled the dry river bed and leaped onward.

At the last moment Giovanni clutched Francesca in his arms and turned his back, but it was a futile resistance. They disappeared instantly, a roiling maelstrom covering where they had stood.

Simki was more fortunate. Thomas reached a solid boulder bedded into the plain and Simki ran toward him, thrust out his hand as the water reached them. Thomas heaved, ignoring the fresh pain, and pulled him into the meagre shelter. Water surrounded them, but the boulder offered enough protection to prevent them being tumbled away. Whole tree trunks barrelled past, a loud grinding noise surrounding the pair as they clung to each other.

The sound abated. The water receded to fill the river bed from bank to bank, and Thomas released his hold on Simki.

"I thought you were going to find somewhere quiet and safe," he said.

Simki smiled. "I would never know when they might come looking, so I thought it wiser to catch them first." He looked out over the churning water. "Are they gone?"

Thomas rose and walked to the edge of the river, mud and stones beneath his feet. "We need to find the bodies if we want to be sure," he said. He thought of Abbot Mandana, someone else he had pursued until believing him dead. He would not make the same mistake again.

"Nobody could live through that," said Simki, and Thomas was minded to believe him.

"So you'll feel safe in your bed at night, not being certain?"

Simki nodded. "All right, let's look. But they're half way to the sea by now."

Thomas laughed, the relief of still being alive flooding

361

him. "It's a long way to the sea." Instead of moving downstream he turned, walking back toward Lawrence to find out how bad his injuries were.

Bad enough, it turned out, but he would live. Thomas inspected the wound, long but shallow. He tore lengths of shirt into strips, hesitating when he held one up. It reminded him of the length of linen Francesca and Giovanni used. Then he shook himself and bound Lawrence.

"Can you make it back to camp? I'll come find you once I'm sure they're both dead."

Lawrence looked beyond Thomas. "Who's the big man?"

"He's the reason for all this," Thomas said.

"He is? Shouldn't we kill him, then?"

Thomas shook his head. "The reason, but it was never his fault. He was protecting his own, nothing more." Thomas helped Lawrence stand.

He swayed, steadied. "I think I can make it."

"Wait here if you're not sure. I'll come and help you after."

Lawrence stayed where he was, his gaze searching the banks. Simki turned away and walked toward the river.

"I have a question before I go," Thomas said.

"You always have questions. More than any man I ever knew."

"Then this is one more." Thomas waited for Lawrence to say something. When he didn't he said, "Abbot Mandana – what does Fernando use him for?"

Lawrence continued to stare at the river. "Better you don't ask."

"He would have killed me. Jorge too. I have unfinished business with the man."

Now Lawrence turned, his gaze meeting Thomas's. "Forget about him. The man is dangerous, wild, feral. He and his supposed band of brothers." He twirled a finger at his forehead. "All of them, mad as rabid dogs."

"So why does Fernando use them?"

"Sometimes a rabid dog is exactly the weapon needed. A rabid dog will do what others refuse."

As darkness approached Thomas was starting to think they would have to give up the search, convinced Francesca and Giovanni had perished. Then he saw something bright fluttering in the breeze. It lay on the far side of the river. The water had calmed now and he waded across.

"What is it?" Simki called over.

Thomas bent and pulled at it, easing the object from rocks and mud, but it was held fast by something hidden beneath. He knelt and pulled at the rubble until he found what stopped it coming free. The end of a stained strip of linen was gripped tightly inside a small fist.

Thomas continued to dig, and after a moment Simki waded across to join him. Between them they uncovered an arm, then a shoulder. Francesca appeared to be untouched, as though she was sleeping. It was as if the water had protected her from damage.

They dug further until they could pull her body free. There was no sign of Giovanni.

"Do you feel safer now?" Thomas said to Simki.

"Not yet. There's another of them. The more dangerous of the two. Although..." Simki sat on his heels, leaned forward and reached out. As he touched the stained cloth gripped inside Francesca's hand his eyes widened.

Thomas watched, coils of the past winding around the present.

"Is that what I think it is?"

Simki tugged at the cloth. It was gripped tight, a death grip, but he reached and prised the fingers apart until the cloth hung from his fingers. "She has kept it," he said. "All these years she kept it."

And Thomas knew it was the same length of linen Simki had strangled the ship's captain with. Francesca had taken it, kept it... then used it.

"Here!" Lawrence's cry startled both men. "The other one's here."

Thomas straightened and walked as fast as he could to where Lawrence was dragging a figure from the water. He laid him on the bank and straightened abruptly, as if in shock.

"He's still alive." His voice was soft, but it carried to Thomas, close now.

He went to his knees when he reached them, leaning close, not touching yet in case he inflicted more damage. There was enough already. Giovanni's right leg was snapped above the knee, barely hanging on by a remnant of muscle. A wrist was broken, his face bruised, one eye swollen shut. But his chest rose and fell, and when Thomas reached to feel for the pulse in his neck Giovanni's eyes opened.

"I want a priest," he said, his voice coarse from water and his coming death. "Fetch me a priest. I must make confession, for I have much to confess."

Thomas glanced up at Lawrence, who nodded and came to his knees beside him.

"I am a priest. What is it you wish to confess."

"My sins," said Giovanni. "My many sins." His eyes

cleared for a moment, tracking Lawrence's face. He frowned. "You are no priest. You're a soldier."

"Soldier and priest both. Have no fear, I can hear your confession before God."

Giovanni emitted a long sigh, his chest falling and Thomas leaned close, afraid he had breathed his last. But when he touched the neck there was a pulse, stronger than expected.

"Hurts," said Giovanni. "Everything hurts." His eyes, which had closed, remained so. It was for the best, Thomas thought, because Simki had joined them, standing over the man who had killed his sister, an expression of raw hatred on his face.

Thomas felt inside his robe, searching, found what he had not been sure would be there. He drew out a small packet, unwrapped a dark nugget soft to the touch. The last of the beads of poppy and hashish Lubna had made up for him. He placed it against Giovanni's lips.

"Swallow this, it will ease the pain."

One eye opened. "You mean to kill me with poison? I would not blame you, Thomas." Giovanni parted his lips and Thomas pressed the mixture of poppy and hashish against the man's tongue. Giovanni swallowed, swallowed again, grimacing. "My sister wanted me to kill you," he said, barely a whisper. "She feared you were dangerous. You have a reputation, did you know that? But I refused."

Beside him the kneeling Lawrence crossed himself and began to recite in Latin. Giovanni relaxed. The end was coming, but there was still time to confess. Except as he opened his eyes he saw Simki standing over him and he flinched before steeling himself.

"It is you."

"Why?" said Simki, towering over the prone figure.

"What I did was self-defence, not murder. Why did so many have to die?"

"You must understand Francesca." Tears filled his eyes and he closed them. "She is so beautiful, so wondrous – you, as a man, must appreciate that. Your sister was the same. A thing of majesty."

"You could have stopped her," said Simki. "You cannot ask forgiveness now, not after what you have done."

Giovanni moved his head, but whether in agreement or not was impossible to tell. His body was relaxing as the poppy started to work. It had been a large dose but Thomas knew it hardly mattered if it killed him, though he was curious to hear his tale. He glanced at Lawrence.

"Ask him. Ask him for his confession."

Lawrence nodded and began to recite. "Jesu Christ, master of all we survey, triumphant Lord, your loyal subject Giovanni del Caccia comes to you in sorrow for his sins, to confess before you his weakness and unbelief." Lawrence made the sign of the cross on Giovanni's brow. "Speak your sins now, that God and Jesu may forgive them."

For a moment it seemed as if Giovanni would remain silent. Then he took a breath, filling his lungs as deeply as the damage to his body would allow. "Forgive me, Father, for I have sinned. I have been a weak man and done acts for my love of a beautiful woman. I have killed without cause other than her asking." Giovanni stiffened, and Thomas thought his end had come, but he was only trying to sit up. "Where is she? Does Francesca still live?"

"She has gone to whatever fate awaits her," said Lawrence, pressing Giovanni back down.

"Why so many?" Thomas said, unable to stop himself, but if Giovanni noticed the question didn't come from

Lawrence he showed no sign. The poppy was singing in his blood now, offering a brief moment of bliss before the end.

"It was not meant to be," said Giovanni. "Francesca – my beautiful Francesca – had only one goal in mind, to find the man who killed her beloved father." His eyes opened briefly, barely able to focus. "That man... But it took so long, and there were so many to question. And when questioned, we could not allow them to live, for then they knew what we sought and what we were willing to do. Oh, we came so close. The librarian was the final clue, the journals he possessed and did not know the true meaning of. If we had discovered them earlier fewer would have died."

"But they did, didn't they," said Simki. He glanced from Giovanni to Thomas. "Let me kill him."

Thomas shook his head. "You can't pretend it was all her doing."

"No. Not all her, I admit, I confess to the sin of lust, and worse. What began as a promise to Francesca turned to something else. It's the power... You must understand that, Thomas, for you have killed. I have seen it with my own eyes. There is an exultation in the act, in the taking of another life."

"And you confess these sins?" said Lawrence.

"Confess?" Giovanni tried to laugh but it came out as a strangled cough. "Why would I confess? Confession may grant me admittance to heaven, but she will not be there. No, I don't confess. I relish my sins, every one of them, so long as I can be with her. We will burn together."

Simki made a strangled sound and went to his knees. His big hands came out and closed around Giovanni's neck.

"No!" Thomas grabbed his shoulders, but the man was too strong even when Lawrence joined him.

Giovanni smiled as Simki squeezed. His eyes bulged and, at the last, his good arm tried to rise, slapping uselessly against Simki's chest. And then it was done.

Simki stood, staring down at the man. "We can all go home now." He grunted. "Well, you can go home. I will have to find a new one."

"I have no home anymore," Thomas said, but the thought didn't trouble him. Neither did what Simki had done. He would not have done the same himself, for Giovanni was a dead man waiting for the dark to claim him. But he understood. "Come back to Ronda with me, I could make use of someone like you."

Simki met his eyes, his own dark, unreadable. He shook his head. "You have your family, your friends. I need to find the same, to make a new life for myself."

"If you ever find yourself in Gharnatah look me up. We can share a meal and drink fine wines and talk of the past. I want to hear of your homeland. I want you to tell me tales of your sister in her memory."

"You do not blame me then?"

Thomas shook his head. "But he might." He glanced at Lawrence, who made the sign of the cross once more on Giovanni's brow. Not that it would make any difference. Thomas did not believe in heaven or hell, only the here and now.

Simki nodded, stepped close and embraced Thomas. For the second time he turned and struck off in search of something. Thomas waited until he was out of sight, then turned to where Lawrence continued to kneel.

So, not a traitor after all.

CHAPTER 45

Thomas stood on the edge of the roadway, Lubna beside him with Jorge beyond. The gates of Ronda had been thrown wide, allowing men and women to stream out. Some pulled carts holding belongings, others brought only themselves. There was a commotion out of sight. People scattered out of the way as a group of mounted riders cantered down the steep roadway at too fast a pace.

Four soldiers led, their mounts brushed until the coats gleamed. Each man wore a polished leather jerkin, scimitars at their waist. Behind came Abraham al-Haquim, head high, back straight. He stared directly ahead, looking neither left nor right. Another dozen brought up the rear, less resplendent than the front group. Thomas searched their number, pleased when he found Yusuf amongst them, even more pleased when the youth caught his eye and turned away, maintaining the subterfuge. There was a chance he might find his way to Gharnatah, a chance he would avoid the Spanish and make his way to his mother. And then…? That was the big question, Thomas knew. Yusuf was of an age when taking power was not out of the question. If he had the temperament for it, which was not yet proven.

Waiting beside the roadway a little distance away Fernando sat astride his mount, stern-faced. Isabel had chosen not to make an appearance. As al-Haquim approached Fernando urged his horse into the roadway to block the path. He was a lone figure and the Moorish soldiers could have gone around, or pushed him aside, but behind and beyond lay ten thousand Spanish troops.

Al-Haquim came to a halt five yards short of Fernando.

Fernando made a gesture and another man joined him. Thomas smiled to see Lawrence, looking uncomfortable in the fine clothes of a knight, canter up and come to a halt beside him. He wondered what he was doing there until Fernando spoke in Spanish and Lawrence translated. Thomas had not been aware the man spoke Arabic, though listening to him he did not speak it well.

It was a short conversation, made to remind al-Haquim that Ronda was now in Spanish hands and anyone wishing to leave was free to do so, but once Fernando entered the city new laws would apply.

Al-Haquim listened without response, staring beyond Fernando's shoulder, refusing to meet his eyes. Thomas saw it angered the King, and once the short speech was done he spurred his horse forward to push against the ex-Governor.

He leaned over and whispered into his ear and al-Haquim's face paled. Then Fernando slapped the horse's rump to send it cantering away down the roadway, sparks flying from its feet.

Across the plain the majority of the Spanish army was disbanding. Tents were being taken down, including the one that had housed Isabel and Fernando. The great cannon were being broken into their constituent parts and loaded onto carts. A rump of soldiers would remain to ensure order in the town, but this battle was over, and another of al-Andalus's jewels had fallen.

Thomas glanced beyond the horde, searching out the

route he had taken in pursuit of Francesca and Giovanni. Three days had passed and the bodies would have drifted downstream, but Thomas knew he had spoken true; it was a long way to the sea. However beautiful, however skilled, the same end comes to us all, Thomas thought, and a shiver ran through him.

"Oh, cheer up," said Jorge. "This is peace, and you helped broker it. When are you setting out for home?"

"Home?" Thomas said. "I'm not sure where home is anymore." He glanced at Lubna, who was watching Fernando, still waiting on the side of the road as the refugees streamed past. "Though I intend to return for William. He has spent too long away from his father. Besides, if I don't Olaf will have turned him into a berserker."

"I may stay here a while," said Jorge.

Thomas looked at him.

Jorge raised a shoulder. "Yusuf couldn't take the women he bought, so I may seek them out and offer my protection."

Thomas smiled. A movement caused him to turn. Fernando crossed the roadway toward them, taking advantage of a gap in the stream of people. He drew up and dismounted, clapped Thomas on the shoulder, taking care to ensure it was on the right hand side.

"You will dine with us tonight in the palace. I have people there already organising things." He glanced at Jorge and nodded before his eyes settled on Lubna. "All of you, of course."

"It would be an honour, Your Grace," Thomas said, knowing refusal was not an option.

"When you come, remember what my name is, won't you?"

"I will try, Fernando."

The King smiled.

"I have some friends you might like to meet," said Jorge, and Thomas kicked his ankle, shaking his head.

"Is this your wife?" said Fernando, indicating Lubna.

As so many times before it was easier to simply nod, though Thomas knew he would have to do something about that state of affairs before long; once events allowed him to gather himself.

"Lubna," he said.

"A beautiful name for a beautiful lady," said Fernando. He took her hand and kissed it. "But when you visit tonight do not tell my wife I said so."

After, when he was gone, Lubna said, "What a charming man."

"Never trust charming men," Thomas said.

"He is no Giovanni, that is true. In fact he reminds me a little of you."

"Apart from the charm," said Jorge.

"Of course," said Lubna. "There is a certainty to him, a surety he is right. And a strength he does not have to display for others to know it exists."

"He is the King of Spain," Thomas said. "I think it is expected of him."

"What is the Queen like?"

"You will find out for yourself tonight. She has strength too, perhaps even greater than her husband."

"They are going to win, aren't they?" said Lubna.

"I see nothing that can stop them now. Al-Zagal was our last hope, and he's holed up in Malaka and won't come out. Muhammed is too weak, too prone to changing his mind. And Abu al-Hasan Ali is sick. Men of influence are changing sides, I've witnessed that. Power is leaking away from al-Andalus. Its end is clear now."

"What of me, Thomas?" asked Lubna. "I am a Moor, a follower of Islam. I will not be welcome in this new Spain."

"If you are at my side you will be," Thomas said.

She reached out and took his hand. "Then that is where I will stay."

Jorge made a retching sound and crossed the road to talk with Lawrence.

Thomas entered the library, wanting a moment of solitude before going to meet with Isabel and Fernando. The scent of books calmed him, as it always did.

He expected to be alone but as he walked past shelves he heard a sound. Had a new librarian been appointed already? Not possible, unless Isabel had brought one of her own – even less possible, for why would a Queen riding to war bring such a man with her? When Thomas turned the corner he smiled. Of course.

Cristof Columb glanced up sharply as if concerned he had been caught doing something he should not have. His shoulders loosened when he saw who it was.

"This is a fine library," he said. He had pulled up a stool to the low table, leaning over to study the maps Thomas had discarded, still where he had let them drop.

"Do you speak Arabic?"

Columb smiled. "The dialects of Genoa and Naples, Spanish of course, and Portuguese. Even a little of your own tongue, Thomas Berrington. But I have no Arabic."

"Most of these books are written in that language." Thomas found another stool and pulled it close. He did not dislike the mariner but did not trust him yet. Columb claimed not to have been involved in the slave trade, but words were cheap, promises cheaper still.

"These maps are clear to anyone who knows how to read them," said Columb.

Thomas picked up the slave map. "Do you know this coastline?" His eyes settled on Columb's, posing a question he had not stated.

"All mariners know Africa." Columb met the gaze, confidence in his own. "But you know not all of us deal in the lives of men and women as the owner of this map did." He in turn reached out to retrieve the one Thomas had not understood. "This on the other hand is interesting."

"I believe it to be made up, a fantasy," Thomas said. "And neither of us can read the runes."

"But we can read maps, can't we? Me likely better than you. I hear tales the northmen crossed the great ocean and found a land beyond. It is my belief they discovered a new route to the Indies. A route I intend to petition the King and Queen to fund me to rediscover."

"They have more pressing matters," Thomas said.

Columb inclined his head. "Of course. But the war will end, and when it does I will be there to ask again."

"And if they refuse you?"

"There are others. The King of Portugal has shown interest in my ideas, as has that of France. Even your own King in England has an open mind."

"He has a war of his own to fight," Thomas said.

"Someone will see the advantage of a new route to the East," said Columb. He dropped the Norse map on the table and stood. "I hear you dine with them tonight."

Thomas said nothing. It was not something he felt worthy to boast of.

"Perhaps you might drop my name into the conversation somewhere, but only if you find it appropriate, of course."

Thomas smiled. "If I can." He rose and left Columb to his maps. He had no intention of mentioning the man, or his lunatic ideas. There was far more needed fixing in the world before idiots sailed to their deaths across an unknown ocean.

HISTORICAL NOTE

As in all the Thomas Berrington books I have taken some small liberties with historical accuracy in *The Incubus*, but the major facts are respected. The governor of Ronda was an individual named El-Zegri, but I have replaced him with al-Zagal. This is partly because such similar names might cause confusion, but also because Abū 'Abd Allāh Muhammad az-Zaghal was a major player in the defence and defiance of al-Andalus and I did not wish to dilute his contribution by leaving him entirely out of the story. He will re-appear in book six, *The Fortunate Dead*, for the siege of Malaga.

The main events as related in *The Incubus* did in fact take place. The Spanish arrived in late April 1485 (year 890 in the Islamic calendar) on the plain below Ronda, camped for several days and then took their leave.

The Moors, believing the Spanish intended to attack Malaga, made a rapid move to cut them off, only for an even larger Spanish army to arrive on May 5th.

The main Moorish force made an attempt to return to Ronda (I make no mention of it in this text as it is outside the scope of what I wished to cover and would detract from the pace of the story) but when they saw the size of the Spanish force they chose to make no attack.

A set of steps cut through the rock indeed existed in Ronda, and during the siege the Spanish destroyed this, cutting off the town's access to water. As far as I know there was no rock fall and no damming of the river, but without this conceit my story would have been different. The presence of Spanish and Christian prisoners as water carriers is historically accurate, as are the use of prisoners as a means of shock and awe on both sides.

During the siege the Spanish cut off the main water supply to Ronda, which was channelled through a series of ducts directly into the town.

Although artillery had been used before by the Spanish, and even introduced in Moorish forces, Ronda was one of the first battles where it was used to such an extent. Metal, rock and fire rained down on the town for several days, destroying almost all of the buildings, until on May 13th, Abraham al-Haquim, the ineffective interim Governor, negotiated a surrender.

The throwing of prisoners from the cliffs is recorded in several sources, as is the nature of the retaliation by the Spanish.

Both King Fernando and Queen Isabel were claimed to be present at the siege, but I have inserted the presence of Prince Juan merely to re-introduce him into the story. The size of the Spanish force is as accurate as research allows, as is the description of the weapons used.

Christopher Columbus – he is referred to in historical records by a number of alternate spellings, of which I have chosen Cristof Columb – is introduced perhaps a little early, but his being a sailor was too good an opportunity to pass up in light of the plot device I have chosen. However, less than a year after the events of *The Incubus* he presented his case for a new route to the Indies to the Spanish court, and would be strung along for almost six years before finally being granted the funds for a journey of exploration. The man will appear at several points over the remaining six books.

I must thank the Viking Sisters, Gee and Trish, who I met at the Harrogate Crime Festival in July 2016 as I was writing this book. They in turn told me of Wendy the Archer and her re-creation of a multiple firing crossbow, a weapon I had never heard of. Its inclusion in this story is entirely down to this fortuitous meeting.

Thomas Berrington is, of course, a creation of my own imagination, although as the series progresses he takes on an increasing level of reality in my own mind, as do his companions. However, it is true that the best physicians in Europe were trained in Moorish universities, and many Englishmen travelled to al-Andalus and Spain to take advantage of this education.

In Book Five Thomas will return once more to the Spanish court. Isabel is pregnant with a daughter who will, one day, be involved in events that change England beyond recognition. That infant, of course, is Catherine of Aragon, who was born on December 16th 1486.

The fifth book in the Thomas Berrington series, *The Inquisitor*, will appear before the end of 2017.

REFERENCES

Thanks to Gee, Trish and Wendy I was introduced to *The Crossbow: Its Military and Sporting History, Construction and Use* by Sir Ralph Payne-Gallwey, which details both the development, operation and plans for how to build a repeating crossbow.

For details on the use of bombards I used *Artillery through the Ages* by Colonel HCB Rogers.

Historical details of events during 1485 in al-Andalus and Spain came from:

History of the Moorish Empire in Europe, S.P. Scott
Moorish Spain, Richard Fletcher
Islamic Spain, 1250-1500, L.P. Harvey

Made in the USA
Middletown, DE
21 September 2017